What Desta's Rea

"What a passion for details, simplicity and readability! . . . Ambau did all these without any exaggeration or distortion of the customs or the cultural facts. . . "The key to knowledge is curiosity. I greatly admired Ambau's choice of the mountain, the sun and clouds as his objects of curiosity in the novel. How original can one be! This is not just another book on Ethiopia. I truly enjoyed reading it. Thank you, Ato Getty Ambau for writing this book!"
—Dr. Alula Wasse, Social Historian

"I read DESTA in manuscript form a year ago, and this amazing, lovely book is still in my mind. Getty is a fabulous storyteller, and Desta and his family are wonderful, vivid, flawed, and ultimately uplifting characters. I cannot recommend this book highly enough. Like Harry Potter or The Book Thief, it is a book for both adults and younger readers. READ THIS BOOK! You will be glad you did. It is a true literary and cultural treasure!"
—Lori Schryer, author

"A very unique, creative and exciting plot . . . extremely impressive usage of language. All the pieces to the story are brought to life cleverly and beautifully! There is a hidden, effortless, unintentional spiritual quality to the writing. . . And there is a truly magical world within which the imagination and the spirit can soar. I loved it."
—P. Sanders, writer

"A marvelous work. . . . I enjoyed it immensely. What fascinated me the most was how the author was able to weave in the book our cultural nuances, blending it well without deviating from the storyline. . . . I am certain there are many Destas who went through similar life experiences who could cherish this work."
—Getachew Admassu, Writer

"The language is graceful, the story and writing nourishing to the spirit. . . It would be great for students!."
—Monika Rose, author, educator

Desta
and King Solomon's Coin of Magic and Fortune
is the winner of Moonbeam's Young Adult Book award and
Independent Publishers' Children Book award.

Desta

AND KING SOLOMON'S COIN OF MAGIC AND FORTUNE

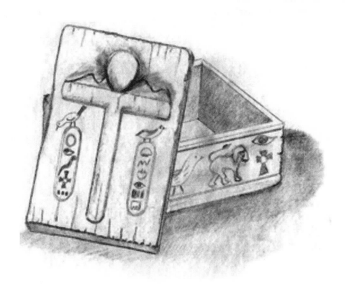

Getty Ambau

Book one of the epic adventure series of an Ethiopian shepherd boy
in search of his ancestral family's twin sister coin of magic and fortune

Published by Falcon Press International
P. O. Box 8671
San Jose, CA 95155

Printed and bound in the United States of America.
Cover Art and design by Philip Howe of Philip Howe Studios
Cover arrangement by Getty Ambau
Coin Illustration by Jin Chenault
Coin Design by Getty Ambau

Library of Congress Cat. Card No. 2010927259

Desta & King Solomon's Coin of Magic and Fortune: a novel/Getty Ambau—1st ed.

            p. cm.

      ISBN: 978-1-884459-01-6

      1. The setting—an actual place. 2. Wedding scenes—Fiction. 3. The coin and watch—Fiction. 4. The children's game and the robbery—Fiction. 5. Genealogy—Fiction. 6. The market events—Fiction. 7. The murder and funeral—Fiction. 8. Land ownership disputes—Fiction. 9. Child miscarriages—Fiction. 10. The boy's trip to the mountaintop—Fiction.

This is a work of fiction. Names, characters, places and incidents are either the products of the author's imagination or used fictitiously. The author's use of the names of actual persons, places and characters are incidental to the plot and are not intended to change the entire fictional nature of the work.

The cover illustration is solely a product of the artist's imagination. The reader may have a completely different perception of the boy after reading the story.

Manufactured in the United States of America

First Edition

To Sosiane — Enjoy Desta!
Betty T. Ambaw

Dedicated to:

the Desta-like boys and girls of the world.

Preface

A complete character list and cultural terms and their definitions are provided at the end of the book for your convenience. Please refer to these pages whenever the need arises, so you can understand and fully enjoy the story.

Although Ethiopia is located north of the equator, the seasons are the exact reverse of those found in most western countries. Hence, you may need to adjust your perceptions when you read passages that describe thunder clouds or lush green fields in July or a carpet of wild flowers adorning the mountainsides in September.

The Ethiopian calendar takes some getting used to as well. Firstly, there are twelve 30-day months and one mini-month of five or six days (depending on whether or not it's a leap year). Secondly, the Ethiopian New Year comes on September 11 in normal years and on the 12th of the month during a leap year. The calendar lags from Gregorian (western) calendar by eight years—from September to December and seven years—from January to September. This difference stems from the Ethiopian Orthodox Church and the Roman Catholic Church not agreeing on the date of Jesus' annunciation.

Being near the equator, most of Ethiopia receives nearly equal hours of sunlight and darkness. However, this fact may not always hold true for folks who live in isolated, mountainous valleys, such as where Desta's story takes place. In such locations, the sun often rises and sets half an hour later or early, respectively.

Although the story is fiction, the setting, natural features and events, and the culture and customs presented in this book are true to life.

This tale is probably unlike any you have read before. I hope you have a fun ride to Desta's far-off world!

GTA

ONE

January 1956

Abraham Beshaw had no intention of revisiting the painful memories of his childhood when he woke that glorious morning, January 6, 1956. Those memories, in compliance with his mother's wishes, had been stowed away in the far reaches of his mind for nearly forty years. His mother had been dead for some time, and he would have been free to talk about the events of his bygone days, but Abraham had no reason or opportunity to do so. That morning, however, the rite-of-passage ceremony he had planned to hold later that day for his youngest son, Desta, somehow brought those events of his childhood to the forefront of his mind.

These events were of things that deprived Abraham of a family treasure, paternal love and guidance and denied him his formal inauguration into manhood. These were the same things that caused his mother to gather up her belongings, cattle, and four children and abandon her seven hundred acre farmland estate to come to settle in a valley that the locals simply referred to as *Gedel*—The Hole. This place was two hundred and fifty miles northwest of Addis Ababa, the capital of Ethiopia.

All his life Abraham had been haunted by memories of his father and an ancient, precious family coin that went missing when he was barely seven years old. These incidents had made Abraham who he was as a man, a husband, a parent, and even a warfront fighter.

It was in Kuakura, a place one hundred miles north of where he currently lived, in the district of Agew Mider, on Wednesday—January 5, 1916, four days before his own seventh birthday—when the events that shaped his life began. That evening, Abraham was standing in the front courtyard, several yards away from the sycamore tree—now host to two vultures—waiting for his father to return from Dangila where he reportedly had gone to buy his son a birthday gift.

It was then that he saw, some fifty miles away, the sky above the western horizon awash in blood—poured, it seemed to him, by the setting sun. But where the sky met the earth Abraham noticed a larger-than-life man who lay prone, his mouth open, his knees bent, hands raised as if shielding his horror-stricken face. On either side of this giant figure, stood two grotesque men of the same size as the man. These men appeared to be horror-stricken as they watched the sun descend into the man's cavernous mouth. After a lingering look, Abraham determined that the blood that bathed the sky had actually flowed out of the man who had swallowed the sun.

Soon the sun vanished, leaving behind it a crescent amber afterglow at the horizon. The two vultures rose and flew west, making Abraham wonder if they were going to eat the dead man's body; the sun, a palate cleanser, capping the meal.

Past the sycamore tree and a row of thorn bushes, the Kilty River flowed silently beneath a horse-mane of verdant grass along its banks. Beyond the river, cattle and sheepherders drove their animals home across the vast fields and pedestrians scurried along footpaths before darkness fell. All were oblivious to the crime committed moments before on the horizon beneath the western sky.

To the boy, the scene was like a dream. After the evening haze had cleared and just before the filmy light from the mountaintop faded, Abraham realized that his eyes had deceived him. What he earlier saw as a vanquished man at the horizon turned out to be the profile of the mountain peaks, the hands and bent knees actually trees on the ridges, and the two standing men to be hanging dark clouds. Nonetheless the imagery made an indelible mark on Abraham's consciousness. As he turned to go inside, Abraham wondered when his father would return with his gift.

But Abraham's father did not come home that night.

Having given up waiting for the father's return, the family of five sat down for their dinner. It was at that moment, the too-familiar but unexpected call of an owl from the sycamore sent shivers down the mother's spine. "She died, so she got buried," the bird hooted repeatedly in its plaintive, human-like tone.

But there is nobody sick in the family the mother said to herself, knowing that the doomsayer usually makes that awful call when someone is about to die. To the children, the owl's call proved amusing. They mimicked the bird and giggled right up until they fell asleep. The mother went out twice and threw stones at it, and Kooli, their dog, barked insistently, but the bird was unrelenting. Feeling powerless as an infant, the mother contracted a sickening sensation in her stomach.

The father didn't come home on the second or the third day, which was the family's Coptic Christmas. In those two days, the mother was too preoccupied by the mystery of her husband's absence to do anything. Her hands moved mechanically, touching objects without feeling them. She ate her meals without tasting the flavor or smelling the aroma of the food. She walked through the house and outside into the grounds without feeling the floor or ground beneath her feet. Her eyes saw things yet didn't register them. Her mind took her to places she had never been. *Had her husband been tricked by a harlot and kept in her dominion?*

She reprimanded herself for her thoughts. Her husband was a God-fearing, Bible-reading man who wouldn't allow himself to fall into debauchery. The perverted thoughts came after she had ruled out more conventional possibilities: sickness, robbers, delays to help relatives in town. And then there was that damn bird's premonition that had chanted ceaselessly in her ears.

She spent much of Christmas day sitting misty-eyed on a bench in the courtyard, her three girls huddled around her. Abraham repeatedly ran to the gate to see if there could be a figure that resembled his father walking the twisted path to their home. The family's world had cracked but they couldn't know who or what had broken it.

By the fourth day, news had spread through word of mouth about the missing father and people came out in great numbers. Some were sent to search in Dangila; others combed the woods, fields, rivers and creeks nearby, but their searches turned up nothing.

On the morning of the fifth day, which was Abraham's seventh birthday, his mother was determined not to allow the misfortune that had befallen her family to interfere with the celebration of her son's birthday and rite of passage. On this important day, the mother also wanted to acknowledge Abraham as recipient of the family's ancient coin of magic and fortune, as his father had intended.

She prepared food and drinks for the family of five. Then she retrieved the ancient sandalwood box that housed the coin. When she opened the box, she discovered the coin that had been handed down through several hundred generations, the family's symbol of pride and identity, their emblem of fortune and prosperity—was gone! Her hands shook and terror gripped her brown face and eyes. She gasped, trying to cry out with stricken vocal cords, but no sound came. Abraham and the three girls watched their mother in stark horror. Her hands still clutching the ancient box, she staggered and came crashing down on her husband's bench in the living room. One hand anchored behind her on the edge of the bench, the other now cradling the box on her lap, she gazed at the fireplace and shook her head slowly, trying to fathom the mystery dealt to her family.

Several minutes later she recovered. Together with the children, they ransacked the house, but the coin was nowhere to be found. The family's world now felt as if it were shattering in a million pieces. It became clear to the mother: their missing coin was a poignant clue to her missing husband. Whoever had stolen the precious relic might have harmed the father. And it was not difficult to guess the culprits: her neighbors—those two, good-for-nothing, green-eyed brothers who had known that the family's wealth was linked to the coin.

The mother couldn't go forward with her son's birthday ceremonies. There was no gift, and now there was no coin. The shock of the lost treasure blotted out their appetites. To Abraham, the missing coin and uncelebrated birthday were the apex of the long and painful wait, and his mounting anxiety over the father who hadn't returned with a gift. He felt abandoned, unloved, and robbed of the excitement that he had looked forward to.

Noticing her son's distraught face, the mother was compelled to say something to ease his grief. "Only God knows what became of your father and the coin, son," said the mother, holding Abraham by the hand. "For now, all we can do is pray for his safe return. As soon as he comes home, we'll celebrate your birthday and hold your coming-of-age ceremony."

The boy was too disappointed to adequately register his mother's consoling words. He broke free from her hold and went outside, wishing to deal with his problems on his own.

In the following days and weeks, relatives and friends searched for the father but found nothing, not a murder weapon, body, skeleton, or witness. A theory took form: the father had probably been given medicine by the evil brothers that caused him to go mad and abandon his family. That was a consolation to the grieving family, because it meant that he could still be alive.

For Abraham, time had stopped moving. No longer did he stroll the springy, green Guendri fields with his father on sunny afternoons, with his dog Kooli trailing behind them. He no longer sat next to his father and listened as he read the Bible, or watched him paint trees, animals, and people. No longer could he look forward to his father's coming home with stories of the people he had met and the places he had visited. He would no longer have someone at home to call Baba.

Abraham would never accompany his mother, as he had been told he would do after he turned seven, to watch his father compete in the horse races at the yearly Ba'tha Mariam Church festival. There were so many ways he would miss his father. Abraham felt a deep void in his heart. To fill it, he vowed to avenge his missing father and coin once he got old enough and could afford a gun.

The mother, afraid more misfortune could befall them if they stayed, decided to abandon her estate and move to the valley where her beloved cousins, Adamu and Kindé, lived near her younger brother and an uncle. She thought that the mountains would serve as barriers to her past, and that she and her children would be with relatives who would protect them.

To this end, they walked the hundred miles, driving their animals and carrying their possessions on their backs and heads. And it was during this journey, when they rested under the seamless shadow of the gottem tree that the mother gathered the children around her and said, "You promise me that as long as I am alive, you will never share with strangers we meet in the new place what has happened to your father." She looked into the eyes of each child and waited until each answered with her or his verbal oath of "Yes, Mama." Only Abraham had to be cajoled and begged before he complied with his mother's request.

They settled in the hills of Avinevra, east of the Davola River, on a property owned by their relatives.

THE BRILLIANT RED AND GOLDEN yellow rays of the sun that greeted Abraham's eyes this morning were reminiscent of that childhood day so many years ago, when nothing was more important than the thoughts of what his birthday gift would be.

For a brief moment, Abraham even allowed himself a smile, as he reached for the bowl of face water his daughter, Hibist, had left him. He felt the cold, rough rim of the pottery and was uneasy about dipping his fingers into its contents. Abraham clenched his teeth and splashed the water on his face and dab-dried it with edge of his gabi. Afterwards, he gazed down at the leftover liquid, using it as a mirror. His father's eyes gazed back at him and the splendid joys of a short-lived childhood dripped down his face and fell into the folds of his gabi.

The cold fact that Abraham had lost his father before he was seven years old gripped at his heart yet again. The possibilities of his life were forever to be unknown. He would never be able to pass along to his own children the love and possessions he had never received from his father. Abraham buried his face in the soft white fabric of his gabi, making sure there was no trace of that which unmasked the burden of his soul.

He uncovered his face and thought. Just as his mother died without knowing what had exactly happened to her beloved husband, so Abraham feared that he, too, might pass away without discovering what had become of his father and the precious family heirloom. For Abraham, this was a greater shame than the gossip mill his mother had dreaded—*that their father had taken the coin and abandoned them! His own wife and children!*

As the now older Abraham grappled with these distant childhood memories, a tantalizing notion rushed into his mind. If he had had the good fortune to receive the coin, as his mother had promised, he would have passed it on to Desta, his son, the fragile, precocious boy who was treated as an outcast by his family, because of the circumstances of his birth. Abraham felt closer to Desta than his other children, because of experiences that linked them together. Giving Desta the precious coin for his birthday would have made him feel wonderful, and he would have been happy to give it to him.

Abraham was tempted to even give Desta the empty coin box, which he had placed next to him on the bench. In recent years, he used it to store a gold pocket watch he had collected from an Italian soldier he had killed in the war. Ironically, the watch, too, had been missing for two years. The box had been a symbol of his own fatherless childhood, and he had grown to treasure it over the years. He picked it up and studied the many mystic illustrations of birds, plants, serpents, people, and cryptic writings carved on its exterior and the magical cross on its lid.

It was from the birds he studied on this box as a boy that Abraham had developed an interest in their language. He had hoped that some day one of the birds would open its beak and tell him—either in dream or wakefulness—the story of the coin.

Abraham soon abandoned the idea of giving the empty box to Desta. Surely it would have no value, and would only evoke interminable questions from the boy and the rest of the family. None of the relatives had any knowledge of their grandfather's fate, or of the ancient coin.

All of these sentiments and contemplations were only fancies of his mind. What the family had lost so long ago would hardly turn up suddenly at their door, or fall from heaven in response to Abraham's longings. Abraham brought his thoughts back down to reality. He had to prepare Desta for the things he must do in the months and years ahead, and engage him with Deb'tera Tayé—the Sorcerer—to solve the family's present problem. They must find out why Saba, Abraham's daughter from his first marriage, had suffered a string of miscarriages.

TWO

On the eve of Desta's seventh birthday, which coincided with the day when his Coptic Christian family celebrated the birth of the Christ child, Abraham perched on a brown cowhide that his wife, Ayénat, had brought and placed outside their home. He waited for Desta to return from the creek, where the boy's sister, Hibist, had taken him to bathe. Abraham was planning to hold a rite-of-passage ceremony for Desta that evening.

Above his home, the tall and expansive mountain had eclipsed the setting sun and draped the foothills with its shadow. In the nearby bushes, finches, weavers, and sparrows chirped and twittered excitedly, welcoming dusk.

Fingers interlocked around his bent knees and his eyes on the mountain's shadow beneath his home, Abraham leaned back and thought about the things he would tell his son when he came to sit with him. In the front of his mind, though, were his daughter's problems with losing her babies, which Abraham hoped Desta would help solve.

For nearly two years, Abraham and Saba's husband, Yihoon, had taken Saba to some of the famous churches and had her drink blessed water, dabbed her belly with it, and passed the church's crosses and the Bible over her. She had applied the recommended herbs and roots to her belly and taken them internally. The family had pledged money to angels and saints of various churches if they would help solve Saba's problems. Finally, they had taken her on a two-day journey to a missionary clinic in Dangila. Unfortunately, the nurses there didn't have an answer to her problems, and shortly after they returned home, she lost another baby. After each failure, it was another heartache and more misery for Saba and her family, as well as a profound disappointment for Abraham.

Abraham shuddered at these thoughts. He unlocked his hands, folded and crossed his legs and let his arm and hands gather in the space between his legs. He looked out again to the shadow of the mountain which now had passed the lower fence of his property.

After all the known or proven methods of cure for such problems had failed, Abraham and Yihoon were poised to try something new; consulting with the spirits of the valley. Deb'tera Taye, the sorcerer, had convinced them that the spirits might be the causes of Saba's problems, including their dying animals and poorly growing crops.

Abraham knew that he would be turning his back on God and putting his own reputation on the line by engaging in witchcraft. Ayénat had vehemently opposed the idea, fearing Desta could end up being possessed by the spirits.

He had to give this last proposition a try. For Abraham, what his daughter and family were going through was akin to the mystery of his long lost father and the missing coin. He was determined to do anything to try to unravel this mystery.

A conversation from the side of the hill to his right took Abraham's eyes from the shadow and thoughts from his daughter's problems.

He turned and looked.

Desta and Hibist emerged, trailed by Kooli the dog. Desta wore his brand new white cotton gabi, which Ayénat had bought him for this important ceremony.

"There's Baba," said Hibist, pointing the moment she saw their father.

Desta looked up.

"You should go and sit with him," said Hibist. "There are important things he wants to share with you."

Desta's mind raced. This was the first time his Baba had invited him to sit together with him in such a formal setting—a privilege usually reserved for guests and older family members. Kooli, as if he were an extra appendage to the boy, limped behind Desta.

"Good, you are finally here, Desta," said Abraham the moment his son arrived.

Desta exuded the spring-fresh scent of *Lux* soap.

"You must feel wonderful after your bath. Sit here," said Abraham, pointing to the portion of the cowhide to his right.

Desta hesitated, then sat down. The soft, silky hair of the hide felt good on the soles of his feet.

Kooli, too, sat, but near Desta, on the grass just outside the skin. Desta studied the rich brown color of the hide. He thought if he went by the similarity of their color, he would be hard pressed not to think that the long dead cow was a blood relative of Kooli.

"The reason I invited you here this evening, son" Abraham said, looking at Desta, "is because you will turn seven tomorrow, and I want to share with you the things that will be expected of you. This meeting is your rite of passage to adulthood."

"What things am I expected to do, Baba?" asked Desta, looking up to his father.

"As a Christian boy, you should start to fast on Wednesday and Friday and before the major holidays like Christmas and Easter. Soon after your birthday you will be trained as a sheep and cow herder to replace your brother, Damtew, who will graduate into the farm work in May," said Abraham.

The idea of tending the animals excited Desta. This meant he would learn how to crack a whip, a device he would use to herd and drive the animals. This opportunity would also allow him to meet and play field hockey with the shepherds he had seen playing across the Davola River. But Desta didn't like the fasting idea. Not only it was hard for him to go past midmorning without food, but he did not want to feel guilty every time he didn't stay fasting until noon. He had seen the guilt and remorse on Hibist's face every time she cheated and ate before the prescribed time.

"In addition," said, Abraham, "You will be expected to bring firewood, take lunch to the farm workers, and protect the grain fields against baboons, vervet monkeys and birds."

Although Abraham's mentioning of the vervet monkeys pleased Desta, he didn't like the other things he had to do. Besides Kooli, the vervets were his only other animal friends. When he thought about all the other things he would need to do, Desta's brow knotted and his stomach lurched in fear. He began to caress the cowhide as if its soft and lustrous hair might ease his nerves.

When he noticed the frown on the boy's face, Abraham continued, "Furthermore, Desta," he said in a low, consoling voice, "During harvest time, you will help with the cutting of the grain stalks, and gathering and transporting of bundled sheaves to the threshing floor."

"How do you expect me to do all these things if I am going to be herding the animals?" Desta asked, disturbed by the list of things he must do once he left his childhood.

"We won't expect you to do all these things at the same time," said Abraham. "The extra things you will do only when we need additional hands."

Still, Desta couldn't believe his ears. The work his father itemized was overwhelming enough, but this was hardly what he had wanted, or what his mother had promised he would do after reaching his seventh birthday. He gazed into the shadow of the mountain, which had crossed the Davola River and was pushing the evening light up the flanks of the eastern hills, slowly measuring time and distance.

"This was not what mother said I would do after I turned seven," muttered the boy without turning.

"What did your mother say you would do after your seventh birthday?" asked Abraham, lifting his thoughtful gaze from Kooli to Desta.

"You know I have always wanted to climb the top of these mountains so that I can see the sky up close and touch it and feel the clouds with my hands," Desta replied.

"I know you have, son. It's admirable that you're still determined to go to the place of your dreams. But you need to wait until you are a little stronger before you go up there."

Desta had wanted to make the trip to the mountaintop since he was two. He remembered a summer evening when his mother, Ayénat, had held him in her arms and leaned against the fence while they watched the gargantuan moon rise over the eastern mountains. He had stretched out his little arms and waved his dainty fingers, warbling furiously, wanting to be taken to the mountaintop so that he could touch the moon. As he grew older, it was not merely the moon he wanted to touch, but the sky and the clouds.

"And there is one critical task we'll need your help with, Desta, once you become seven years old," Abraham said, pensively looking at his son. "But this would not be a part of your daily work."

"What would that be?" asked Desta, fixing his eyes on his father's big brown orbs.

"You know your sister, Saba, has had problems with her babies dying. I understand that you can possibly help us solve this mystery."

Desta knew Saba and Yihoon's problems and all the failed attempts to solve them. Now, the idea that somehow he could solve their problems sounded ridiculous to him.

"This is getting strange, Baba—Are you that desperate?"

"We believe that Saba and her family's problems may be caused by spirits who are angry with them for living on their roaming grounds," Abraham said. "We need to contact these spirits to find out why they are unhappy and if they will give us the solutions. These creatures reveal themselves only to young people with the help of the conjurer Deb'tera Tayé. We need you and your niece, Astair to contact these creatures and find out why. . . . We plan to hold a session with them next Saturday."

That spirits would solve human problems was a curious notion to Desta. He had thought spirits caused problems to humans by possessing them and causing them to do all kinds of crazy things. A year ago, he had seen a visiting woman engage in a wild act of eating fire while she coiled and uncoiled on the floor. Hibist told him that the woman was possessed by spirits. That he could be talking to the spirits directly both excited and frightened him.

"That was the day I had hoped you or ma could take me to the mountaintop."

"It cannot be on that day and I don't know when we could, either," the father said, caressing his goatee. After looking away for a few seconds, Abraham turned to Desta and said, "May I share with you a secret?"

Desta nodded.

"I also hope to travel to a distant place, but I cannot go just yet. We can make our separate journeys—you and I—when the time is right." Abraham had hoped sharing his own personal dreams of going to look for his father could lessen the boy's yearning.

When he looked up, Desta caught his father gazing at the dog once again. To Desta, Kooli always seemed more important to his father than he was. As usual, he felt like an outsider.

As Desta was about to ask Abraham where he planned to go, he saw his mother and Hibist coming toward them, wearing their long beautiful white gowns which they kept off the ground with multiple rounds of colorful cotton girdles, their tufts cascading down the fronts of the gowns.

Ayénat cradled a covered basket in one arm and swung the other as if it were a device she needed to move her body through space. She appeared pleased about something. Desta thought if there was still sunlight on their side of the valley, he would have seen the glint in his mother's patches of white hair to match her beneficent smile.

Hibist walked behind her mother carrying horn goblets, one in each hand and keeping an eye on one of them, as if worrying its contents might spill.

"I had a premonition last night as I prepared to make you something special for this meeting," said Ayénat, as she lowered the basket and placed it before Abraham and Desta.

Hibist gingerly placed the goblets in the grass near the edge of the cowhide and secured them with rocks.

"What do you have in here?" asked Abraham, pointing to the basket, as if he needed a verbal acknowledgement of what his nose had already noted.

Ayénat lifted the lid off the basket, revealing a steaming, redolent, circular loaf roughly seven inches in diameter.

Both Abraham and Desta peered into the basket.

Hibist sat down next to Desta and peered into the basket as well. She was as much trying to see her father's reaction to the loaf as to study the intricate relief on its surface.

Ayénat sat next to her husband and gazed at the faces of the onlookers, the way a magician would gaze at people whom he had put under his spell.

"This is an interesting *dabo*—loaf you have made. Thanks for bringing it," said Abraham, turning to his wife. "Why is its top so intricate? You had never made one like this before."

Desta's mouth watered, his stomach turned as the rich aroma of the freshly baked bread filled his nose and traveled to his brain.

"I know it's interesting-looking bread but does it remind you of anything?" Ayénat asked, studying her husband's face.

"No. Like I said, it's an interesting creation and I am glad you brought it to us because I was getting hungry."

Desta and Hibist's eyes shuttled from the loaf to their parents' faces.

"I know you have never seen the object this loaf represents, but I thought some of the details you see on it could remind you of it. . . . This bread is a recreation of your family's coin of magic and fortune!"

"*Era*—how . . . who showed you how to make this?" said Abraham, after it finally dawned on him. His heart leaped as if he were looking at the actual coin itself.

"Like I said, it all started with this strange premonition last night, but I must say it was from divine instruction how I actually created the design this afternoon. I don't know anything about the coin other than the pieces of information I remember from your mother's account. I started with the few details I recollected. With the rest of the work, a pair of invisible hands took over," bragged Ayénat.

Abraham looked at her in awe.

"Don't look surprised. The Good Lord, who knows about your wishes and listened to my prayers, made all this possible," said Ayénat, glowing. "This is what I have been trying to tell you with this thing you're fixed to do on behalf of Saba. We need to pray to God, not consult with the spirits," said Ayénat. "It disturbs me that you involve my boy. I fear for him."

There she goes, thought Abraham. When Ayénat was on the subject of *her* God, nothing of what he said mattered and he rarely challenged her. He needed to change the subject quickly.

"What do you have in those two cups?" he asked as if he wanted to hear in words, what his nose had already detected—*tej*—the sweet and pleasant-smelling honey wine.

"Those cups of tej, too, came by divine suggestion," said Ayénat. "Otherwise I would have brought the usual *tella*—homebrewed beer."

Abraham shook his head.

"Tell me, are we supposed to eat and drink these things?" asked Abraham, turning to the mother. The aroma of the loaf and the tej had triggered his desire for food and drink.

"Yes, of course," replied Ayénat. "Here, I have already cut the dabo, too." She pulled a slice out and gave it to him.

"Thank you! I have never dreamt our long-lost coin would appear in the form a loaf," said Abraham with a smile.

"Maybe this loaf will cure of your hankering for the real thing and of your father," said Ayénat with a smile. "You know, forty years is a long time to be thinking about an item and a person who have been lost." She looked at Abraham, like a father who was reprimanding his son.

"It's not a small matter to our family. It's something very old and very precious. I cannot die without finding what exactly had happened to both my father and the coin. Thank you for this bread. It's sweet and thoughtful. Its symbolism alone is great! I hope your premonition and whoever guided you to create it could help us solve the mystery of the lost treasure and of my father."

"I am glad I could do it on such a very important day. I know you have said you'd have liked Desta to be the inheritor of the coin. Talk about symbolism, why don't you take one of these slices and hand it to him first, as you had intended with the coin."

Ayénat picked up the basket and held it before Abraham. He put his own piece to the side, took another slice from the basket, and gave it to Desta. He handed a second slice to Hibist. He picked another slice and gave to Ayénat saying, "Thank you for making this meeting more meaningful."

Abraham's hand dove into the basket again and re-emerged with another slice. "This piece is for Kooli, the last but not the least member of our family," he said, placing the loaf near the dog. Kooli, who had been watching the activities of Abraham's hand, happily grabbed his share and began to eat.

Abraham then picked up his own piece and began to eat. The assembled family members ate quietly and thoughtfully. In the intervening moments, Abraham thought about the problems of his daughter and the impending meeting with the spirits.

The evening was getting on. The shadow of the mountain had climbed up the eastern mountains, having reached the crest of the ridges. The birds chirped and rustled in the bushes less and less, and the cicadas and the crickets which were barely audible earlier had begun to make their presence known more and more. The home-bound cattle from the field below had begun to moo.

"Don't forget the drinks," said, Ayénat, handing Abraham the full goblet.

He took the wine from his wife's hand after thanking her for reminding him. He swallowed his last bite of the coin-bread and cleared his throat. He then raised the goblet and said "Desta, may you become a reliable and responsible shepherd, and a good and obedient young man who brings no hardship or strife to your parents' hearts. And may you have the industry of the bee, the wisdom and foresight of your ancestors, and the courage and fortitude of all those in our family line who defended and protected our coin of magic and fortune.

"We have two cups containing honey wine. One full, the other half full. The full cup is what we all hope to achieve in life. The half represents what life is. The important thing is to remember that life is often half full and we strive to make it full. Our world used to be full when we had our coin of magic and fortune, but now it is half full." Abraham stopped and held his chest. He coughed, cleared his throat and continued.

"Always look at life as half full *not* half empty, no matter how difficult it may be. It's this belief that sustained my mother, sisters and me after we came and settled in this hole of a place. And that is why I am still hopeful that we can someday—in my lifetime—find that coin and discover what really happened to my father." Abraham's voice cracked.

Ayénat came to his rescue. "We need to go. The animals will start arriving soon."

Desta listened to his father attentively, but his eyes were on the half-filled goblet before him. He noticed that this cup was almost the exact shape as the gap in the mountain high up in the eastern ridges—the same pass through which the sun rises in the morning.

His father's association of the half cup to life and individual efforts made Desta wonder about the sun, which he watched just about every morning as it rose through the cup-like gap in the eastern peaks.

"Does this mean the sun's life is half full too?" asked Desta, turning to his father.

"What do you mean?" inquired Abraham.

"In December the sun comes out near the bottom of that gap in the mountain," said Desta pointing toward the peaks. "It rises at different places along the slope as the months advance. In June it comes out at the halfway point in the rising slope and then it reverses its course from June to December. It's almost as if it could not go to the full height of the cup."

"I don't know, Desta. I didn't know it was even trying?" said Abraham.

"Yes, I watched her for the whole year and was disappointed for her not to have made it to the top," said Desta. Suddenly his eyes filled; scared the same could happen to him when he finally went up there.

"I am sure someday it will clear the top so long as it keeps trying," said Abraham, smiling.

Ayénat tapped Abraham's arm. "We need to go."

"Let's share this wine first," said Abraham, taking a sip. Then he passed it to Ayénat. She took a sip and passed to Hibist, who in turn took a sip and passed to Desta. The strong, suffocating aroma was enough for the boy. After just a whiff of it, he passed it back to Abraham to finish the rest of the wine.

"The half cup of wine?" asked Desta.

"This wine, we will take and pour in the river tomorrow morning," replied Abraham.

That evening Abraham walked home happy and lightheaded, both by the effects of the honey wine and the vision of his family's ancient coin of magic and fortune on Ayénat's loaf. In some ways he felt he received his birthday gift forty years late. Abraham's birthday was on Monday, two days after his Orthodox Christians Christmas and Desta's birthday. But the last thing he thought as he crossed the doorsill of his home was the problem that had plagued his daughter and family, the one which he hoped Desta and the spirits would solve when they held the meeting in a week.

Ayénat didn't think about anything. She merely floated home buoyed by her preternatural association with God as she was creating the image of the family's treasure on her dabo.

Hibist was thinking about the number of cows she and Damtew would have to milk and animals they would have to put away before the evening was over.

The sparrows, the finches and the weavers retreated into their nests while the cicadas and crickets came in full force to reclaim the night.

As he walked home, Desta once more let his eyes climb the mountain. Now, only a thin ghost of light sputtered at the summit. He stood watching it, transfixed. As the last traces of light vanished, bidding him and his world farewell, Desta realized that he, too, had bidden farewell to his childhood.

THREE

In this nameless valley, Desta's paternal grandmother had come forty years earlier to hide from her shame and assuage her fears, here, where the air was thin and clear like a pane of glass, where the wind streamed out from the eye of a needle lodged between two boulders near the sky, where the sun rose late and set early and never got hot, where life came in colors of the rainbow, where people had so little materially yet were contented as if they had everything in the world, where God reigned supreme and his believers pretended to be his devout followers but still did ungodly things in their hearts—as in promising things to children they never mean to fulfill.

It was here in the pitch-black of the night the stars above gleamed like diamonds that would at any moment tumble down and blanket the mountainsides and valley floor, where life hummed and exuded scents that one could suck up all in one breath during the day to stow in one's lungs and nourish him while asleep. It was in this place that innocence was pure and abundant like the highland breeze, and all one could ask for to complement all this beauty and bounty was a little more love and kindness. This was Desta's world. With the mountains for walls and the sky for roof, it was his universe.

The east was separated from the west by the Davola River that sliced the valley floor as it snaked south to north, being fed along the way by rivulets of creeks that came down from the sides of the mountains. The west was wild, and at first, Desta's family was the only homestead. The rugged terrain was enveloped with a dense forest that ran for twenty-five miles along the mountain façade. In the north and in parts of the east, low-lying plateaus and rolling hills pegged against the mountains dominated the view. A hamlet of villages and a quilt of farmland adorned the flatter terrain, the sides of the mountains, and the sloping hills. Trees and bushes lined the meandering creeks and property boundaries. Two churches, one to the north, another to the south, were enveloped by their groves of *tsed*— juniper trees—that rose from the sides of the mountains like bumps on a tree trunk.

DESTA WAS A FOUR-FOOT, five-inch tall, dark olive-skinned boy. He lived with his parents, a brother and sister—the fourth and sixth youngest of his six siblings—along with three horses, three *mookit* goats, a dozen chickens, a dog and a cat, all in a single circular structure made of wood and earth and topped by a conical roof of bamboo and grass.

The living quarters were apportioned as follows: as one entered the home, the horses' stall was on the right, followed by the goats' cubicle and a larder that was used to store food and pots and pans, house three granaries and serve as a brewery. Continuing to circumnavigate the interior of the home, a closet containing two large wooden boxes and two round-bellied baskets was used to hold the family's spare clothes and jewelry. Next came a built-in bedding area approximately three feet high by seven feet long by twelve feet wide, partitioned in the middle by a four-foot wall. Each half of the bedding area could comfortably sleep three adults or four children. The last was the mill room, with two sets of grinding stones abutting the opposite walls.

The center of the house was divided by a two-foot by four-foot parapet on either side of a round, roof-bearing center post. The living room was on one side of the parapet, the kitchen on the other. There was a fireplace in each, with three tapering stones roughly six inches tall used to support cookware.

Above the animal stalls were two lofts. One was used to store firewood and as a roosting place for the chickens at night, the other as a sleeping quarter for Desta's brother Damtew.

The only pieces of furniture in the house were a two-foot by four-foot bench and a round, concave stool. The bench, made from a solid piece of wood, belonged to Abraham. The stool, often found in the kitchen, was used by Ayénat or any other woman who was cooking.

It was what he saw, heard and experienced in this home which molded and shaped Desta the boy and the adult he was to become.

LOOKING BACK, it would be exactly seven years earlier, on a frosty Friday morning, just after the first guttural calls of the colobus monkeys from the nearby forest, before the first fleeting rays of the sun landed on the peak above their home, that Desta pushed on his mother's uteral portal. It was as if he had timed his exit with the arrival of sunlight that was soon to come filtering through the cracks in the walls at the bottom of his parents' high earthen bed. At this time of the year, the sun rose near the lowest point but on the right slope of the cup-shaped gap in the eastern mountains.

Ayénat, who had been in labor since midnight, had expected the worst. So did Abraham and the rest of the family. The new baby's arrival had not been expected for another two months. Preparing for the worst but hoping for the best, Abraham had gone when dawn barely broke and returned with a root of a secret plant to promote the baby's fast delivery. The efficacy of the plant as a delivery aid was by association rather than by the direct contact with the patient. So Abraham had placed it in the exterior wall opening through which the horses' manure is removed from their stall, located to the right of the entrance. Abraham was now sitting next to his wife, not far from the fireplace in the center of their living quarters. Some of the family sat by the fire with their heads down, as if sad that their Christmas was about to be marred. Others hovered around the mother, encouraging her to push.

As fortune would have it, not long after their father placed the baby-delivering aid, there arrived a fist-sized squirming baby, much to the glee of the family.

The baby *wished* someone would quickly free him from the slippery cord that bound him to his mother. He had long waited for this moment, to be extricated from his mother and her problems. It had been a rough life inside the womb, and a tough journey to the exit. To everyone's surprise and fear, the boy didn't cry, as if wishing to preserve his tears for much-needed times down the road. He didn't open his eyes, as if afraid to see his brother, Damtew, who momentarily sat by their mother, quiet and gloomy, gazing at him.

Although the odds favored survival for a seven-month premature birth to a six or even an eight-month term, why the baby came so early without any attributable causes was a mystery to those who were now congregated around the mother and gazing down on the skinny baby who appeared to have shriveled by the morning chill. But there were causes. They just didn't know, except perhaps Ayénat.

IT WAS IN EARLY JUNE, at the time of the year when the sun rose nearly as high as it could go on the right slope of the cup-shaped gap in the eastern mountains, when Ayénat had conceived Desta. That was the beginning of the rainy season and a frantic time for farm workers. For Ayénat, besides the domestic exertion of grinding grains, preparing food, fetching water from the creek, washing clothes, part of her day; the other part—when she had respite from her domestic chores—she had to go help out on the farm for an hour or two. When her mind was so preoccupied in her work, she often forgot to feed herself and the baby inside her. When she did remember to eat, she nibbled on skimpy *injera*—flat, spongy bread—with pea sauce. Injera almost exclusively made from *teff*—a grain a quarter the size of a rice berry—which, along with pea or bean sauce, was the staple food of the family for breakfast, lunch and dinner.

The other grains, barley and rye, were used to make dabo or tella.

These foods, together with teff, were the only foods consumed daily in one form or another. There were no vegetables to speak of, except for the potatoes and *gomen*—collard green—that appeared on the family's meal platter during the rainy season. In those wet months, they had plenty of collard green that was chopped, cooked and served after being mixed with a spiced butter and sometimes ground flax seeds.

This was the only color in their meals, and the only food that kept its color after it went through their bodies. If one or two spoonfuls of cheese made a cameo appearance next to the subdued green and the muted brown injera and pea sauce, it was more for variety than its substantive benefit to the body.

Fruits never grew in The Hole. Nobody had ever heard of lemons, oranges, and bananas and people wouldn't have known what to do with them if they were given any. Berries and figs grew plentifully in the forest, but only during the dry season and even then, only used as snacks for children.

Although there were sufficient eggs and milk in the home, they were never part of the family's diet. "Milk is for babies," they'd say, "because babies don't have teeth yet to tear and chew the spongy injera." Eggs were to make chicks, which if they were spared from hawks by day and foxes by night, grew to become chickens that had one purpose—to produce more chicks and repeat the cycle. The family rarely killed a chicken to consume its meat as an everyday meal. They only did so when a very important guest came to visit, or sometimes as supplemental meat during the holidays. In the rainy season, no guests came, so Ayénat would forego killing a chicken for a meal. Lamb, goat and beef were consumed only during the holidays—Christmas, Easter, the New Year or at weddings and other major events.

Ayénat didn't eat until two or three in the afternoon on Wednesday and Friday—the two fast days of the week. For *Filseta*—the first two weeks of August—she fasted until four or five every day. Although as a pregnant woman she had the option not to fast, Ayénat would indeed fast. She would rather risk the life of the baby that was inside her than offend her God.

And then, too, with every emotional and physical stress Ayénat experienced, the baby became the recipient through the lifeline that linked the two. He *heard*, *felt*, *saw*, *tasted* and *experienced* what his mother heard, felt, saw, tasted and experienced.

Two of her assistants—a young man and a girl—vanished without a trace at the end of September. Abraham had brought the two people from a faraway land when they were just teenagers to help his wife before he went off to fight in the Italian war. They disappeared, possibly running off together, leaving Ayénat with not just part of the domestic work, but all of it.

Asse'ged, the second oldest son, was old enough to handle the farming. Teferra, the oldest son, worked for Abraham's mother across the Davola River, up on the plateau of Avinevera. Tamirat, the third oldest boy, studied at church school miles away. Damtew, the fourth male child, herded the animals.

Abraham was always gone on business trips, leaving the farm work to the family. As days added to weeks and weeks to months, miraculously, the baby continued to grow like an extra appendage Ayénat didn't need or want. She hated Abraham for impregnating her, especially since she had already given him six children and the two had so little love for one another. Not only was Abraham often gone, but when he managed to be home, he showed little affection for Ayénat.

Unloved, unwanted and malnourished by the mother and father, by the end of the harvest season, it seemed, the baby could no longer endure his hardships. He decided to exit two months earlier than planned that morning on January 7, 1949 and take his chances for a better life in the outside world. He no longer wished to stay in that dark, famished and trouble-filled world of his mother's womb.

LEAVING THE MOTHER and baby to rest, the family congregated around the fireplace. Enat, the baby's fifth youngest sibling had sprinkled the floors with *kettema*—long, pulpy grass—and had placed goat and antelope skins over them. These were sitting mats for the Christmas guests. That day Abraham killed a lamb in honor of the Christ child. The meat was made into a sauce and served to the guests.

Throughout the day, the new family member lay peacefully with just the company of his mother's breathing. He was cherishing the much-needed rest. The family got busy with the preparations for the celebration of the birth of Christ. Nobody came to check on the baby, other than Ayénat's hands and eyes that hovered over his chest and face to see that he was still breathing. Even with the rest of his family present, the baby *felt* unwelcomed and abandoned.

AFTER DINNER, the family discussed a name they should give to the new baby. Ayénat spoke up and said, "Let's call him Amanuel, to signify the day of the Christ child." Other family members proposed different names: Habtamu, Adissu and Mullat. Abraham quietly thought about an appropriate name, while the others were rattling off their choices for the baby's name. "Desta—happiness—would be a fitting name," he said with finality.

When Ayénat bridled at this, he said, "I think it would be appropriate because—" he began reciting his reasons and pulling up a finger for each as he did so—"One, this is a very happy time for our country. The Italians are long gone, and your father has won medals for warfront deeds against the invaders and our *Negus*, God bless him, is ruling the country peacefully."

He held up his second finger and continued. "Two, here at home everything is good with us. Our crops are growing abundantly, our animals are thriving, and we have all this land to prosper and flourish."

Abraham then pointed to the infant and added, "This boy is the first to be born here in this place. You know, after I returned from the Italian war I had an epiphany. I looked at you all—four boys and two girls—and I saw that some of you boys had grown to be strapping men since the last visit from the warfront. Then I studied the vast forested flanks of the western mountains. Knowing that I would soon need more land for my growing family, I crossed the Davola River and claimed a total of seven hundred acres of virgin land separated by deep running creeks.

"That is a wonderful story and those are wonderful reasons to call our son Desta, but I'm not so sure I like that name," said the mother.

"Ahh, but there is more." He held up a third finger. "The boy arrived on Christmas day, the day when we all are here happily gathered to celebrate the event. What is more, we had feared a miscarriage last night when Ayénat went into labor. Instead, we have a small, but healthy-looking, baby. So we all should be happy. So, Desta will be his name!"

Nobody would challenge Abraham once he spoke in that tone of voice. Ayénat whimpered a protest, but it was to no avail.

THE NEXT SEVEN YEARS of Desta's life were not an improvement over his life in his mother's womb, especially when it came to quality nourishment. But in this new world, which to Desta still felt like a womb, he had freedom. He no longer was the bearer of his mother's daily trials and tribulations, and he could move freely in the open space.

In Ayénat's mind, the question that had not been answered was why Desta turned out a boy instead of a girl.

To balance out the four boys that were born in a row, all Ayénat wanted was more girls. She already had two and hoped for two more if Providence was good to her. Was this what Damtew meant when he used to call him a mistake, that nature somehow mistakenly assigned a male organ to Desta instead of a female's? Neither the boy nor anyone else would have the answer to this question. He was happy, for better or worse, that he was a boy and not a girl.

DESTA WOKE on his seventh birthday, Saturday, January seventh, more confused and frustrated than when he had gone to bed the night before. In his dream, while standing in the middle of the cattle field below his home at high noon, when his own shadow circled his feet, mirroring the celestial orb above his head, a strange old man with cotton-white hands had appeared and given him a circular yellow metallic disk, one tenth the size of his own shadow. The man said that the disk was his birthday present. Desta was thrilled that somebody had loved him and thought of him as special—and not a mistake, and deserving of a gift unlike anything he had ever seen before.

He kept turning the yellow disk over and over, causing it to flash with each flip, as if the sun was taking a chunk away with each flicker. Desta curled his fingers over the item and held it tightly in his small fist. But then, the man said, "Keep it in a safe place. Guard it with your life," and vanished. When Desta woke and opened his fist, the object was gone, taking with it the excitement he was feeling in his heart. He kept running his hands again and again over his mat and folds of his gabi, hoping the disk was not a dream but real, and that the disk had simply slipped from his grasp and was caught up in the covers.

Sad and baffled, Desta sat up and surveyed his family's living quarters. He noticed there was more sunlight in the house than he could ever remember, causing him to wonder whether there were that many cracks in all the walls of his home. That morning Desta had awakened later than his usual time, which was half an hour before the morning light had come down from the mountaintop. His father was putting on his work clothes, just outside the closet to the left of Desta's room. Damtew was sitting by the fire, wolfing his breakfast before going off to tend the animals.

Desta waited until his brother had left because he didn't want to hear another snicker or mocking remark regarding Desta's planned trip to the mountaintop to touch the sky after his birthday.

Abraham brought out a pair of iron knives, each nearly the size of one of his hefty arms. He whipped the sharp edges against one another, sending terror into Desta's heart, and this caused the boy to cringe and place his fingers over his ears. For Desta knew what those pair of knives were about to do that day. His father picked up a round-bellied bamboo basket, dropped the knives into it, and left. He was going across the Davola River to kill a cow and bring a share of its meat for the Christmas dinner.

Ayénat was in the kitchen, baking injera for the holiday dinner. Hibist shuffled in and out of the house with rolled up goatskins and antelope skins, taking them outside and beating them with the stick to drive off the dust that might have accumulated on them since the last holiday, and hanging them on the fence to air.

Damtew also left soon after their father, giving Desta a much needed relief of his own from natural forces that threatened to come any moment from both ends. After wrapping himself with his gabi, he grabbed his penis and squeezed it tight, hoping to keep his piss in his bladder until he reached the bushes behind his home. He was doomed. Before he could even reach the door, his piss leaked and streaked his legs and wetted his gabi and the floor as he dashed to the door with his hand buried in his groin. His sister Hibist giggled heartily with her hand over mouth.

After Desta returned from his morning outing, he stood in the living room and tried to remember what was special about this Christmas day. Having been distracted by the beautiful object in his dream that vanished upon his waking, he had not thought about the significance of this particular holiday. The round basket near the parapet Ayénat used to serve the dabo to his right-of-passage ceremony the day before brought his memory back into focus.

This Christmas was Desta's seventh birthday—the day when he officially joined the adult's world! The one that was supposed to grant him the opportunity to travel to the place of his dreams—atop one of the mountains that circled his valley so he could see and touch the sky up close and run his fingers through the clouds.

Then he remembered something else. His father had told him the day before that Desta couldn't go to the mountain anytime soon because they planned to engage him with important and pressing family matters, including getting him to train as a sheep and cow herder. Desta's stomach lurched, his spirit flagged. The day he had longed to be the beginning of his adventure to the outer orbit of his realm was no longer to be. He needed to go out and think through the disheartening bombshell from his father.

The fallow land behind his parent's home was Desta's preferred place of comfort. The vervet and colobus monkeys and the rich verdure on either side of the creek at the bottom of the hill had always brought him happy feelings.

He liked to be with his sister Hibist whenever he felt down, but this time he had to go by himself. Hibist was busy helping her mother. He slipped out without his dog and dashed through the shade bushes and across the sloping earth. When he came to a clearing, he stopped and studied the view. The midmorning sun had made everything bright and pleasant to behold. He could see no monkeys in the trees near the property. The place was hushed as if all the animals of the forest were in observance of the holiday. Across the southern creek, up on the grade, Desta could see the rickety shed his father had built years ago in the middle of the forest, staking his claim to the land.

This broad and descending land—down to the valley floor—had been earmarked for Asse'ged and Damtew, Desta's older brothers. A fortnight ago he had heard his brothers discuss how they would divide it up. Desta could see now why Damtew wanted it split lengthwise because that way each would get fifty percent of both the flat and steep terrain. Asse'ged had insisted on splitting the land crosswise and drawing a lottery to see who would take which piece.

As Desta stared at the lush foliage, though, he wondered how much of the forest would remain once his brothers would cut the trees down and convert the land into farms like his father had done to his property on this side of the creek. While standing there contemplating his brothers' dreams, which he knew would be fulfilled some day, he thought of his own unfulfilled dreams—dreams which he had thought would be within his grasp after his seventh birthday, but which had now receded from him like a mirage.

Desta sighed. The years he had waited and the excitement he felt the last few days anticipating the arrival of this special day had all been for nothing. Then he remembered his fantasies. Desta used to imagine himself traveling up the mountains on a sunny day, walking along the ridges and letting the wind that came out of the eye of the needle flutter his gabi around his legs, filling his nose and lungs with fresh scents of the plants that grew on the peaks.

He brought his face and hands close to the sky and studied its texture and felt it with his fingers. And he envisioned himself sitting with his back against the sky and looking toward his home to see if it would be visible from where he sat. Now that he wouldn't be able to do these things any time soon, his eyes fluttered and he had a lump in his throat.

He snapped a twig from the nearby bush, stripped its leaves off and sat on his heels. He had seen his brother, Damtew scratch or dig a hole in the ground with a tip of a stick whenever something bothered him. Desta wanted to think about his own fate and what the future might hold.

He parted the grass and removed a flat rock and poked the dirt with the tip of his stick.

Besides his yet unfulfilled dreams, what saddened Desta the most was that none of his family members, save for Hibist and his mother, cared to listen or offered to take him up on the mountains. To them, going on such a trip just to see the sky up close was either frivolous or silly. Desta's eyes brimmed. His throat constricted and he felt sick in his heart.

And then there were those damning things his mother and Damtew used to say about him when he was little. Although Desta couldn't hear or talk for the first year of his life, he could hear and speak like a grown up after his second birthday. People flocked from far and wide to see and hear him talk. Visitors stood or sat and gazed at him, listening to him talk.

"Oh, he is just possessed by *Saytan*," Ayénat would say, dismissing the unusual nature of the boy.

"He is just a mistake—that's all," Damtew would sing, echoing *his* mother.

"No, he is just an unusual boy who has a remarkable gift for words. Who knows what else!" Abraham would say, smiling at *his* boy.

"What else could cause a baby to talk like this . . . ? Oh my . . . oh my," the women would say in unison, tapping their chests.

The men just gazed and shook their heads.

But after they all left, Desta remembered feeling empty and strange. The more he felt that way after each visit, the more withdrawn he became, until finally his father put a stop to the visitors.

A few years later Desta thought the reason Damtew enjoyed ridiculing him was probably because he didn't have nearly the same verbal skills that Desta possessed. Damtew must have felt inferior to his little brother. The only way he could preserve his own self-worth was by belittling and disparaging him. Desta felt better about himself by this revelation.

The hole he was digging had gotten deeper and longer, like a mini trench. He now began to stab and knock the soil from its side walls.

He refocused his thoughts. Over time, what these things did to Desta was make him feel less important than his siblings. Damtew always reminded Desta that he was not his equal because he didn't stay the full nine months in their mother's womb, almost saying that the boy was not a full human being.

Desta remembered asking his mother if she could put him back in her womb so he could stay in there two more months. When she told him she couldn't, he felt sad and miserable. Later his big brother even told Desta his desire to go the mountain was another example that he was not normal.

When Desta thought about all these things, his isolation and now his unfulfilled dream, his tears began to overflow. He tipped his head and they fell directly into the trench he was digging, soaking the soil.

He heard a noise, like someone walking across dry leaves or snapping a twig. He lifted his tear-streaked face to look. A white silhouette of a person flashed before him and vanished. Desta didn't know what to think. He was not even sure he had seen anything, but the transformation within him was remarkable. He felt cleansed, relieved of his burden and his mind felt clear. He wiped off his tears, sat back, folded and crossed his legs and looked around. Nothing about him was out of the ordinary.

He gazed toward the eastern mountains for a long time. His clear and happy state of mind allowed him to think of the good times he spent in his childhood.

IN THIS WORLD where beauty came in so many colors, shapes, features and sizes of people, of animals, of birds, of insects, of plants, of low land, of mountains, of clouds, of the sky, of the day, of night and of the seasons, alone in thought—but in the company of his dog—unbothered by anyone, Desta had lived mostly a life of dreams. So much of what he saw, imagined, and heard made him who he became as a boy then and as a man-to-be now.

As a little boy, during the rainy season of June to August, Desta loved to watch the clouds as they gathered above the eastern peaks. He perched on the threshold of his home and directed his eyes to the unfolding events with piqued interest. Their movements, changes of moods, and configurations fascinated him.

During those times above the eastern horizon he saw—or imagined—a multitude of creatures form and come alive. Braying donkeys charged at top speeds, teeth gleaming, eyes bulging, ears and hair brushed back by the ferocious wind. Trees became cows, horses took on ponderous human-like forms, wading water birds grew into tall devouring monsters. One cloud stretched its arms and touched the ridge on the mountain as if feeling for a grip or picking up a boulder, enthralling Desta. Another cloud rested its feet on the shoulder of the mountain and pushed itself forward into space like a snake might erect its head when seeking prey. Desta thought this event was incredible.

Not too long afterward, the clouds crossed the Davola River, driven by a powerful wind. They floated above his home, black and ominous and water-clogged, swallowing first the sun and then the entire sky—turning day to night. As the rain fell in sheets, he dashed inside to the warm comforts of his home.

Desta closed his eyes and shuddered, wondering what it would be like to be in the open field when such a storm occurred. That's exactly where he would be when put in charge of herding the animals, with just a skimpy *gessa* or tree for cover when a rain fell over him like that or when the day turned into night.

After he recovered from his imagined horror, Desta opened his eyes and thought of the spring season. September to November brought wildflowers. During this time, Desta and Hibist would go to the hillsides looking for the different flowers. They made garlands, festooning the flowers under the fillets of vine skins that went around a circlet of bunched grass and placed them on their heads. With their circlets around their heads, they went chasing the butterflies, laughing and giggling, and whenever one eluded their grasp, they tripped and fell.

It was during one of these escapades when Desta learned what it meant to be Christian and consequently became the inheritor of her treasured beads. Hibist noticed he didn't have a single cord around his neck, which she declared was a symbol of being *Islam*. "A Christian person," she had said, "should have something around his neck, even a simple cord. If the cord was broken or lost, they needed to quickly pick a long and flexible straw and put it around their neck until they got home and could replace it with something more substantial." She pulled a long supple green straw, put around his neck and had tied it. When they got home that day, she had retrieved her old beads and put them around Desta's neck, tying them tightly so they wouldn't come undone. She had wanted to save him from becoming Islam again. Desta never understood what Islam meant, except that when he had nothing on his neck, he was Islam and when he had a cord around his neck, he was Christian.

Desta pursed his lips and gazed down at his feet with a grin. He was sorry he would no longer share such experiences with Hibist once he became a sheep and cow herder.

Then he thought of his love affair with the sun. Every morning, he woke half an hour before the sunlight reached his home. He'd go outside and sit on the fence to wait for it to come down from the mountaintop. His dog Kooli curled beneath his dangling feet. Once the sunlight reached him and began to warm the air around him, Desta would stretch his arms and smile, but soon after the heat began to cloy, he would hop from his perch and go inside with Kooli in tow.

During the day Desta sometimes lay on his back with his hands over his face and stared at the sun through his fingers, defying his mother's advice not to do that because the direct rays might burn his eyes. At other times, he sat under a tree and thought about the sky and the mountains, and everything on them, places he hoped to travel to, other children he hoped to meet and befriend—all within his world, of course.

Desta puckered his lips again and grinned once more over the fun he used to have when he had all the free time in the world. Now all this would no longer be, because he was going to be very busy with his daily chores as the keeper of the cows and sheep.

He looked up and saw the sun was near at the midpoint in the sky. He felt exhausted, happy and hungry. He held his digging stick between his hands, fashioning them into a steeple. He brought the tips of his fingers to his nose, closed his eyes and thought of everything good and bad that happened to him once again. When done, he opened his eyes and hands and lay the stick in the trench he created. Shortly after, he pushed back the soil with the flat rock, covering and burying the stick completely. The stick represented everything that happened to him in his childhood. Then Desta rose and happily walked home.

FROM THE TIME Abraham had left home that morning, Hibist and Ayénat had worked feverishly, cleaning the house and preparing food. Hibist had swept the living room floor and sprinkled it with freshly cut kettema that Damtew had brought the day before from the banks of the river. Hibist covered the long, pulpy grass with a selection of goatskins and a cowhide, and then she washed the drinking horn and clay cups and arranged them on a woven straw tray.

In early afternoon, Abraham arrived with a basket of meat covered with dark green false banana leaves. He cut the meat into chunks with his knife and chopped the bones with an ax. He gave Ayénat enough for the dinner party and cut the rest into cubes that would be hung and dried to make beef jerky.

FOR THE CHRISTMAS DINNER, all Desta's brothers and sisters came, except for Saba, her husband, Yihoon and their daughters, Astair and Zen. Although they lived just across the northern creek from Desta's home, they were skipping the festivities that year. Desta had heard that Saba, who had lost her fourth unborn baby a month earlier, was depressed and didn't want to attend a dinner celebrating the birth of baby Jesus. They said she was bitter and angry with God for not listening to her prayers to stop her miscarriages.

Desta remembered when his sister had lost her last baby. It was a weekday, and he had gone to see a new calf born to a milk cow given to Saba and Yihoon by Saba's mother, Azal. This cow was a replacement for the one they had lost six months earlier and was intended to provide supplemental milk for the new baby.

When Desta had arrived on that sad day, Saba was lying by the fire under a pile of clothes, her face turned toward the fire, tears trailing across the bridge of her long nose, and nestling into the folds of the fabric. Her mother was sitting next to her, head bent, hands resting on her daughter's covered body, comforting her. Tears came from her eyes too, in slow periodic trickles that fell onto Saba's coverings. Yihoon didn't cry, but his soft, brown features were shadowed with sadness. Astair and Zena huddled near their grandmother until she instructed Yihoon to take the children outside. He went back into the house and came out again, carrying Saba's lost baby swathed in a cloth. He wrapped the bundled baby with two curled pieces of bark, tied the little casket with string, and took it to the cemetery by the Avinevra church.

Not wishing to see his nieces' sad faces anymore, Desta went home that day. The fun he had thought he would have playing with the newborn calf had turned to sorrow. He felt sorry for Saba and her lost baby.

So now at the Christmas dinner, Desta wouldn't be seeing Saba and Yihoon and Astair and Zena. His only young dinner companion would be his eleven-year-old sister, Hibist.

That night, Desta remembered his own birthday only in the context of Jesus' birthday. As in the past, no one in his family had made even a passing reference to it—even in this important milestone of his coming of age. He was not envious of Jesus or the boy whose family killed a cow in honor of his birthday, nor did he feel sorry for himself. He also knew that, as a rule, his family never celebrated birthdays.

But he was happy with the time he spent in the morning remembering many of the good times of his childhood. He might be a "mistake" in Damtew's eyes, or "the possessed one" in his mother's view, or "the unusual one" from his father's perspective, but Desta was happy with exactly who he was.

At night, as he clambered into bed, he felt sad for Saba and, once again, thought about the trip he hoped to make to the mountaintop someday. In the past, it was the years that were a barrier to the place of his dreams. Now it was his family. If they failed him again, he would be strong enough to journey on his own one day. This realization made him feel wonderful and free. As he closed his eyes, Desta now saw himself romping along the mountain peaks, running his hand over the deep blue surface, and letting the wind that streamed out of the eye of the needle whip his gabi around him.

AS FOR ABRAHAM, as he crawled into bed that night, it was not the usual Christmas festivities, the killing of the cow, the drinks, the food, and the happy dinner gathering with his children that he thought about, it was his unresolved past.

Ever since the previous morning, when the tender memories of his childhood came galloping back as he prepared for Desta's coming-of-age session, Abraham at one time or another had been ruminating over the events that snatched his father from his young life and the ownership and benefits of the family's coin of magic and fortune. So much he had been deprived of—the same events that forced his mother to desert her seven hundred acres of flat, loamy land and come to settle in this godforsaken hole—events that shaped Abraham's destiny, identity and role as a man, a husband, and a father. Incidents that altered the courses of not only his life and his sisters' lives but the lives of his and their progeny. But the last thing that crossed Abraham's mind before he fell asleep was his daughter's problems, which he hoped Desta and the spirits would solve.

FOUR

Desta should have been in a funk at best, or angry and mad at worst on this Saturday—the day he had long wanted to travel to the mountaintop. Once again any such plans must be postponed. Instead, here he was standing near his father, who, on the sunlit floor by the entrance of their home, was completely absorbed by what was before him. His father, face grave and thoughtful, was sitting on his heels on the floor and randomly arranging black horn and clay drinking cups, pint-size jars of honey, milk, and freshly brewed coffee and seven stacked miniature coffee cups. There was a basket of sliced pieces of dabo and injera, roasted coffee beans and a wooden tray. He also had put out two rolled goatskins, one inside the other.

From the conversation he overheard between his mother and father the night before, Desta figured the things set before Abraham were probably to be used in the spirit work they would be engaging in later that morning.

The boy's brain was brimming with questions, but not wanting to interrupt his father's concentration, he instead began to study Abraham's face, trying to understand why a woman recently referred to it as biblical. The baseline of his father's features, his chin, cut square angles at either side before joining with gently curving high facial bones that made union with a broad and arching structure at the summit. Beneath his brows, on opposite sides of his long and ever so slightly curving nose, nestled a pair of piercing brown eyes whose pupils were deep and spiritual, capable of shooting a volley of fire when at war, but also able to exude kindness and grace at peacetime. Abraham's sensitive, full lips were bound by a bushy mustache that curled around the corners of his mouth like a cat's whiskers. All these landmarks of Abraham's great physiognomy were bordered on the outskirts with a pair of perfectly spiraled ears and a pile of wooly hair. Desta still couldn't figure out why the woman likened his father's face to a book, but he wondered if he would look like his father when he grew up.

It was while both father and son were concentrated on what each was observing that Yihoon and Astair materialized out of thin air. Yihoon, a slight framed man of about five-foot-nine inches, his natural light brown complexion made darker by worries, barely acknowledged his father-in-law's greeting. Astair, nearly the same age as Desta, was a tomboyish girl with a fair complexion and attractive but not-so-dainty features. "Are you excited to meet the spirits?" she asked the moment she saw Desta.

"I am not sure. Are you?" asked Desta.

"I am not particularly excited to meet them, no. But I would even meet with the Saytan if he would have the answer to Mother's problems."

"I know what you mean," said Desta, remembering how his sister had cried when she lost her last baby.

Yihoon stared down at Abraham's collection, puzzled.

"Deb'tera Tayé ordered us to bring these things for the spirits," said Abraham, noticing his son-in-law's quizzical face.

"Hmmm . . . interesting," mumbled Yihoon, too preoccupied with the impending meeting to say anything else.

Deb'tera Tayé arrived next. Deb'tera was his title and Tayé was his first name. He was a short, stocky man with a dark complexion, stubby goatee and inquisitive brown eyes. Abraham and Yihoon greeted the guest with a handshake. The Deb'tera waved a hand at Desta and Astair, who were standing together a few feet away. They waved back but hesitantly.

"Is everything ready?" he asked, looking down at Abraham's neatly arrayed things.

"I think we have everything you wanted us to bring," replied the host, scanning the items as if to assure himself of what he had.

They gathered the provisions and set off on a path that went along the outside of a wattle fence down to the big cattle field. Deep in thought, Abraham and Yihoon walked with their heads down. The Deb'tera walked with his head up, but he seemed not to want to talk either. Desta and Astair, nervous and anxious, didn't dare speak lest they disturb their solemn fathers.

Desta saw his brother Damtew rise from his perch under the shade of an acacia tree, looking after the animals that were grazing in the field and nibbling in the bushes. Damtew started toward them, but Abraham discouraged him with a wave of his hand.

At the end of the field, the group crossed the creek that bordered Yihoon's property. They passed a patch of farmland on the other side of the creek and entered the wooded section of the Davola River. They crossed the river and arrived at a large, spreading warka tree.

About forty feet from the river, Yihoon and Abraham laid the goatskins next to each other and set out the food and drink.

"These things were brought as a reward for the spirits' goodwill," whispered the Deb'tera to the children when he noticed their curious expressions.

Deb'tera Tayé slipped two books out of the hangers that suspended them under his arms and placed them on one of the goatskins. From the pockets of his hunter-green jacket he produced a gleaming silver cross, a scroll, a five-inch square clear glass panel and a white handkerchief, all of which he placed on the goatskin. These things being done, he took a seat in the middle of one of the goatskins, leaving the other for his assistants, who would be sitting with him, one at a time, once the session started.

Immediately after he sat down, the Deb'tera ordered Abraham and Yihoon to go and stay out of sight and earshot until the sessions had been completed. The two men had come along to help carry the food and drink and to give support to the Deb'tera and the children. Thoughtful and anxious, they departed, leaving in their wake the sound of crushing leaves.

For fifteen minutes, Deb'tera Tayé described to Desta and Astair the two types of spirits they could expect to see. The Saytans, he told them, were dark, naked beings with strawberry eyes and grotesque features. The Zars were tall and spindly creatures clad in gauze-like fabric with frizzy golden hair and human-like features. Both species were known to be capricious, and worse, they could make one go mad and behave violently. In talking with these spirits, they needed to be polite but they should keep eye contact with them at all times. They should bow when the spirits arrived and when they departed. With this introduction, the sorcerer ordered Astair to be seated and told Desta to go away until he was called for his turn.

Desta sat under a canopying tree thirty feet away where he had a clear view of the Deb'tera and Astair's backs. Although he couldn't hear what they were saying, he wanted to see what they would do and he hoped to watch the spirits as they arrived. The idea that the whole place could soon be full of spirits frightened him, particularly those with grotesque features. As the session got going, he occasionally peered around, checking for lurking spirits.

After nearly twenty minutes of reading, chanting, turning and talking,

Astair's session was over. She was visibly confused and disappointed when she came to fetch Desta.

"What happened?" asked Desta.

"I didn't see anything," said the girl, nearly in tears. "I think these creatures just didn't want to be revealed to me. I was so looking forward to asking them about my ma's problems."

Desta didn't know what to say. He gazed at Astair, wondering if he would not see any spirits either.

She urged him to go with a slight push on his shoulder. "Maybe you will be lucky," she said, watching him shuffle across the dead leaves.

The Deb'tera also appeared disappointed to Desta as he took Astair's place on the goatskin. He noticed that the Bible and the silver cross were placed between the Deb'tera and himself. The scroll was partially unfurled and laid out to the right of the sorcerer. On his crossed hairy legs the sorcerer had propped open the second book.

The Deb'tera handed Desta the glass panel to hold up on its edges in the white handkerchief. He rested the hand that held the glass on his knee and gazed into it. He was eager and nervous.

With everything set, Deb'tera Tayé hunched his back and began to read from the book in his lap. Desta felt increasingly uneasy as he stared into the glass. He began to fidget. When he thought of the creatures the Deb'tera had described and what they were capable of doing, his fingers grew sweaty and his heart picked up its pace.

"Relax, Desta. Nothing will happen to you. We have these two weapons in front of us," said the Deb'tera, with a toss of his chin to the Bible and the silver cross.

Desta glanced at them to reassure himself.

By degree, the aroma of the decaying leaves, the herbal fragrance of the forest, and the fig-like fruits of the warka began to have a soothing effect on Desta's senses. The sibilant sound of the river, the Deb'tera's hushed, monotone reading, and his intermittent flipping of pages also helped ease the boy's nerves.

Turning inward, he thought about the trip to the mountaintop he hoped to make soon. He also considered his career as a shepherd and all the things his father had told him he must do as a young adult.

"Any movements?" asked the Deb'tera, glancing at Desta after he read for a few more minutes.

Desta shook his head, keeping his eyes fixed on the glass. The longer he looked through the glass and saw nothing, the more unlikely it seemed to him that any of the creatures the Deb'tera had described would actually reveal themselves. He began to wonder if they even existed.

After about twenty minutes, the Deb'tera finished reading the book. He turned to Desta once again and asked, "Anything at all?" He sounded exasperated and a little desperate.

"Nothing," said Desta, disappointed. As much as he had fears and mixed feelings about seeing the spirits, now that the creatures were not coming, he felt wistful.

The Deb'tera closed the book and put it aside. He presently read and chanted from the scroll.

Desta gazed into the glass now almost absentmindedly. Immediately after the Deb'tera started to chant from the scroll, however, he noticed something beginning to stir like swirling air. It jerked him back to alertness.

After a while, the whirling air was superseded by a gray mist. This was followed by a thicker, white fog, which gradually took on the appearance of a man in the form of a cloud. Desta's heart raced and his hand that held the glass shook.

"Something happening?" asked the Deb'tera excitedly.

"Yes, I see a strange . . . cloud-like man before me. But he is not anything like the kind of spirits you described," whispered Desta, leaning toward the Deb'tera while he kept an eye on the creature in the glass.

"Cloud-like?" asked the sorcerer, screwing up his face and dropping the scroll.

"Yes . . . and he has a yellow light around him. Also many brown dots all over his body," said Desta.

"We have never seen anything like this before, child! . . . No matter, let's just hope that he can answer our question." Deb'tera Tayé fumbled for his scroll and brought his face close to Desta's ear. "What is he doing now?"

"He's staring at me but not in a bad way. . . . He just sat down and turned himself into a cotton-like mass with just the head poking out from the center," said Desta, transfixed by the strange creature.

"Keep your eyes on him. When he is ready he may say something," said the Deb'tera, nervously.

"He just moved his head as if to say something," said Desta in a low voice.

"Good!" said the Deb'tera, pleased. "Ask him why Saba continues to lose her babies and why her animals have been dying."

Desta repeated the question.

"Well, young one," said the apparition, raising his neck a little like a hen. "The family and their animals inhabit a place where bad things happened to someone a long time ago. They need to move. Things will be normal again for them then, including the birth of a healthy boy within two years of their departure." The man gazed at Desta with his cone-shaped, spotted eyes as he said this.

After a string of additional questions, Desta and Deb'tera Taye learned that Saba and Yihoon's problems were caused by a missing family heirloom. Surprisingly, they were told that the same item was also responsible for Desta's many problems, including his premature birth and his early hearing and speaking difficulties.

Additionally, they learned that Abraham too had a problem, which the man also linked to the missing item.

Soon after these revelations, the man vanished. Desta dropped the glass on his lap, bit his lip and looked away, baffled and afraid.

Deb'tera Taye held the partially unfurled scroll in one hand while he stroked his bushy goatee with the other, mystified. "What problems do you have?" said the sorcerer finally, turning to Desta.

"I don't know what they all are," Desta said. "I can tell you the ones I know sometime if you will help me meet this man again. I've a lot of questions to ask him."

"You'll have to tell your father what the problems are first and then perhaps we can arrange another meeting together," said the Deb'tera, still caressing his goatee.

"But my father won't listen to me," said Desta.

"Please go and get your father and Yihoon for now," urged the sorcerer. "I'll see what we can do with your problems."

After the men and niece arrived and sat down, Deb'tera Tayé told them what the man had said.

Yihoon knotted his brow and cocked his ear, listening intently as the Deb'tera related the cloud man's revelations. That Saba could carry a baby to full term was great news, but the idea that they had to move made him frown.

His fingers twirled nervously with the fringe of his gabi. "What if we decide not to have a child?" said Yihoon, turning to the Deb'tera.

"He said you have to move, no matter what. The situation could get worse if you don't. He has given you many warning signals."

"Yes," added Desta. "The reason your animals have died and your crops have failed is because he doesn't want you to be there."

"Did he say anything else?" asked Abraham, craning his long neck toward Tayé. "The session seemed rather short."

"Well, the answer was very short and simple," said Deb'tera Tayé.

"Actually, he did say something else," Desta volunteered nervously.

"What else did he say?" asked his father.

"He said he knows all about you and me and our problems," said Desta. "He also said that all the problems have something to do with a missing item."

"Missing item?" said Abraham, puckering his brow.

"Yes!" said Deb'tera Taye, glancing at Abraham. "It appears you have a lot more problems on your hands than you thought. If you wish to find out the answers, we should arrange another meeting with the cloud man."

"No. Let's just focus on Yihoon and Saba's problems for now," replied Abraham. "How much do I owe you for your service?"

Abraham buried a hand underneath his gabi and dug around in his chest pocket for a few seconds. The hand re-emerged with a short, cylindrical object rolled in a piece of old cotton cloth. He carefully unwound the cloth with one hand while holding the object in the palm of the other.

"You don't have to pay me now," said the Deb'tera. "But if you insist, my fee is five shillings, as we discussed."

Yihoon's face crinkled. Desta, whose knowledge of monetary value was extremely limited, thought five shillings was a lot of money too.

To everyone's surprise, Abraham instead counted out seven silver shillings and handed them to the Deb'tera.

Deb'tera Tayé's knitted brow pulled and tightened and his big eyes grew puzzled. A bemused smile spread across his face. The sorcerer hesitated a little, and then extended a hand to collect the money.

"I think you misheard the Deb'tera," said Yihoon, glancing at his father-in-law.

"I heard him," said Abraham. "If this is going to work, we'll have to do it this way."

"Like I said, my fee is normally five but I thank you for your generosity," said Deb'tera Tayé, smiling. He quickly put the windfall in his pocket as if he didn't want to keep the coins in his hand too long, lest the father change his mind.

Desta's jaw hung. His father wouldn't give him two shillings to buy a shirt! Here he had just given away the same amount above what Tayé had charged.

Yihoon shook his head.

"It's getting dark," said Abraham. "Let's go home and break the news."

The three men and the two young people set off for home, leaving the food and drink behind for the spirits. Desta placed the rolled-up goatskin over his shoulder and walked behind the three men with Astair. His niece tried to listen to what the men were discussing but Desta was only half-listening to the conversation. The other half of his mind was busy with the being, the things he had heard, and the curious generosity of his father.

Why had his father given the Deb'tera seven coins? His mother always did things in threes because of her three confusing gods. Did his Baba have seven gods? He never prayed to them the way his mother did to hers. Desta had often seen his father do things in sevens, particularly when he counted his shillings and silver dollars.

He would count to seven, stop, and stack them on his bench next to him. His father seemed so much in love with that number. Desta wished his father liked him the way he liked his number seven.

FIVE

When Abraham rose the morning following the spirit work, he found himself thinking about the missing item the cloud man had linked to his daughter's problems. He had been surprised to learn there was an actual physical item responsible for the string of miscarriages and other problems that had been plaguing Saba and Yihoon and was curious what that item might be. He could think of two possibilities.

There was the ancient family coin that had vanished without a trace more than forty years before. Nobody knew what really happened to it or where it might be. The empty coin box left behind had been the only reminder of the missing treasure.

And then there was an Italian gold pocket watch that had been missing for two years. Since the cloud man had not been specific, either one of these two items could be the culprit—assuming Abraham could accept this strange claim. Complicating matters, the sorcerer had indicated that Saba and Yihoon could solve their problems by moving from the place they were currently living. Abraham shook his head, mystified. He needed private time to think through the riddle.

He washed his hands and face with water from a bowl Hibist brought to him. He put on his khaki breeches, a long cream-colored shirt and a gray wool jacket, over which he draped himself with his white cotton gabi. He collected his walking stick from the side of the mill room and prepared to leave for church.

He set out on the path that went around the wattled fence of the potato and collard green garden and down the north side of the cattle field. The sun was barely clear of the mountain peak. The air was cool, the sky cloudless.

With his eagle-beak nose pointing down and his big brown eyes on the path, Abraham kept his brain busy with the information that had been shared with him by Desta the day before. To make sense of the claim, he needed to examine the history of the two items.

There was the ancient family heirloom that had been lost when Abraham was just seven years old. Then there was the gold pocket watch. Abraham had collected it in 1937 from the first Italian soldier he had shot, ironically at a battle just twenty miles from his home, near Mount Wendegez. The recoil of the gun hit and chipped his right canine tooth, but the moment he saw the shiny timepiece, he forgot about his broken tooth. He fell in love with it because it reminded him of his family's long-lost treasure. Like the coin as his mother had described it, the watch had writings on the front and back. Because it looked old, Abraham believed it too must be an heirloom with special powers.

For nearly fifteen years, the watch helped him deal with the anger and resentment he had toward his parents' old neighbors and his yearning for the coin, but unfortunately, it too had been missing now for two years. Abraham had been grieving its loss when Saba and Yihoon had their second miscarriage and their animals began dying in greater numbers. For the following year, he had been busy trying to find a solution to their problems and so had not tried to search for the missing watch, but now the cloud man's mention of a missing item had brought back the memory of the watch and what it had meant to him.

He had left the trail that came down from his property and was walking on the main caravan route, going north along the Davola River. The birds chirped in the trees along the river. The water although low, still gurgled around stones and down granite slabs and was a comforting companion to him. The sun had cleared the mountains but was still a long way from reaching the bottom of the valley.

Being Sunday, the caravan route was quiet. And being early in the day, there were no cows, sheep or goats grazing in the fields. Abraham felt he had the world to himself. It was perfect for reflection and contemplation.

He resumed his thoughts. After a lengthy analysis, he concluded that the cause of Saba and Yihoon's problems, if he could believe the cloud man's claim, had to be the gold watch. The family coin couldn't be the answer. Not only had it disappeared over forty years ago and one hundred miles from where they now lived, his family had never had any problems like this the entire time it had been missing.

Although he was at a loss as to why Saba and Yihoon's move would solve their problems, he believed the cloud man himself could be the ghost of the Italian soldier he had killed, tormenting him by causing problems for his beloved daughter. *The timing couldn't be a coincidence*, he thought, recalling the severity of Saba and Yihoon's problems following the watch's disappearance.

Then there was the other issue. Where would he move the family?

Ten years ago, Abraham had moved his family to the west side of the valley and claimed three strips of property, totaling about seven hundred acres, separated by deep running creeks, hoping his growing family would have a comfortable place to live. He built his home on the middle property and earmarked the ones to the north and south for his four male children, two sons per piece of land. He knew that his daughters' needs would be met by their in-laws.

But five years after they moved, Abraham's mother, who lived on the east side, died, leaving all her land to her oldest grandson, Teferra, who at the time was living with her and farming for her. This allowed Abraham to invite Saba and her family, who lived fifty miles away, to come and settle on the property to south of him, which had initially been allotted to Teferra and Tamirat, his third oldest son, now studying to become a priest. The land to the north was put aside for Asse'ged and Damtew, his second and fourth sons, respectively.

Now to realize the cloud man's proposed solution for his daughter's problems, the only available property to which he could move Saba and her family was the one assigned to Asse'ged and Damtew. Asse'ged, who was older than Damtew and married, and who could, by seniority, share the property with Saba and her family, but Damtew would end up with no place to settle. Then there were other issues. Much of the northern property was covered with a dense forest full of birds and other wild animals. The forest had been a good source of firewood, furniture and building material as well as game animals. The governor had also been encouraging the farmers in his district to conserve natural resources by leaving forested land uncut.

Still, his daughter and her family's needs were urgent, both to bring a quick end to their long ordeal and because they had only five months before the rainy season would come in June. If they didn't move soon, they would have to wait a full year, because it would take that much time to do their farming and harvesting before they had leisure time again to clear the new land and build a home.

These reflections, instead of calming him, sent his brain onto an endless loop, his thoughts ricocheting from the missing items to the identity of the cloud man and his confusing message, to where he could relocate Saba's family, back to the lost items. In the end, he gave up trying to find a clear and logical answer. The man's suggestion that his daughter's problems would be solved once her family moved from their current domicile was good enough. Abraham would have to find them a new place to live and hope that the promise of better time would be fulfilled.

A side trail took him north toward the Avinevra church. After passing a cluster of houses, crossing a deep-running creek and climbing a hilly terrain, he arrived at the wooded church.

At the stone-walled gatehouse of the church, he crossed himself three times and repeated the act with his lips and forehead on the doorjamb. He retreated to a tree on the other side of the path, leaned against it and prayed that God had put him on a course that would one day unravel the mysteries that had long plagued his family.

SIX

The morning after the session with Deb'tera Tayé, Desta awoke with thoughts of the cloud man idling in his brain. He wondered why the man was not made of flesh and bones and why he didn't resemble the Saytans or Zars the Deb'tera had described. Stranger still, this spirit was revealed only to Desta and not to Astair. This in itself was another mystery.

And why did this cloud of a man come by himself? Deb'tera Tayé had said that the other spirits came in a group. The man Desta had seen had no wife, children or other relatives that accompanied him. Did that mean he had no family? Even Deb'tera Tayé had said he was surprised by the spirit's looks and also by his solitary appearance. Desta regretted not asking the being these questions. More importantly, why didn't he ask the being if he could help him find away to the mountaintop? Just then Desta realized he had not yet asked Ayénat if she was going to fulfill her promise of taking him to the place of his dreams.

He peeled off the heavier layer of gabi and climbed down the platform bed.

"Mama, can you take me to the mountaintop after you've returned from church?" asked Desta.

His mother was scurrying around in the back room, preparing *mekleft*—the bread churchgoers used to break their fast after the service. "No, son. I will be too tired to go climb a mountain after church. Some other time maybe," she said without looking up at him.

Although the first part of her answer was credible enough, the second part of her response disappointed Desta. After all those years of telling him she would take him when he turned seven years old, now she wouldn't even give him a definite promise. Her "some other time" felt hollow and uncaring.

"But you told me you'd take me once I turned seven," he protested, knotting his brow. "Yes, but these mountains are merciless," said Ayénat, finally fixing him with her small, stern eyes. "If you were to become exhausted halfway up there, I would not be strong enough to carry you back. We need to wait until you get a little bigger." She said this with a firm voice so Desta knew anything he said from that point on would be an upward battle.

Desta walked away feeling miserable like a wet chicken. Now he didn't have anything definite to look forward to. In the past, all he had dreamt about was turning seven years old so that his mother or another adult would fulfill the promise of taking him to the mountaintop.

Ayénat left for church. Desta's older brother, Damtew, had gone to the field with the animals. Only Hibist was at home.

"Hibist, do you think you and I can go to the top of the mountain so I can touch the sky?" Desta asked when his sister returned from putting away the milk she had collected from the cows. Desta stood by the fire pit in the living room.

"First of all, Mother is not here and I have many things to do," said Hibist. "Secondly, I think Mother said that you should wait for another year or two before you make the trip because it's hard to climb these mountains. She hopes after you become a full-time shepherd in another three months or so, you'll forget about your crazy idea of touching the sky because . . ." Hibist trailed off.

"Because . . . why?" demanded Desta, crinkling his brow.

"Because your trip to the mountaintop will be a lot more rewarding for you when you are better prepared to make it," said his sister. "Even if you were able to make it up there right now, you'd be so exhausted that you wouldn't really enjoy your time." Hibist caressed Desta's wooly hair with both hands as she spoke.

"Then why did Mama promise to take me to the mountaintop when I turned seven?" asked Desta, pursing his lips.

"I think it was probably her way of buying time," Hibist said as she massaged Desta's head. "So you wouldn't pester her every day with the same question! I think she also thought you might outgrow your dream by the time you became seven years old. Since you have not let up, I am sure she plans to take you up there when she has the time and feels you can manage the trek. What I want to know is why you are so obsessed with touching the sky?"

Desta felt good being caressed, spoken to, and loved like that by his sister. His parents never even listened properly to anything he said or asked.

"The sky just seems so much bigger than the earth. I want to know what it feels like to be near it," said Desta, twirling the fringes of Hibist's girdle. "That soft deep blue color is something I long to touch and see what it feels like."

He sighed. "I also want to see the holes through which the rain and clouds come out. It would be wonderful to see God's land through those openings. But most important of all, I wish to know what it is like to be in the most remote place on earth. As you know, I have never even been across the Davola River."

"Hmmm, you must have been thinking about this for a long time to have such a definite list of reasons," said Hibist, grinning.

"Of course I have. This is all I've dreamt of every day," said Desta, fixing Hibist with his big brown eyes. "And you know this would have been the greatest birthday gift I could have received from Ma. As it was, nobody even mentioned my birthday. It was all about Christmas. I guess it was my bad luck to have been born on Christmas day!" said Desta, choking up a little.

"I know . . . I just wish I had the power to take you up there myself," said Hibist as she continued to caress his head. "To Ma, going on such a long trip is a waste of time. And she would worry about our safety."

Desta turned his face away, focusing on the pool of sunlight by the entrance of their home. His thoughts of birthday gifts brought back a faded dream he had had the night of his seventh birthday. He struggled to reconstruct the details.

Hibist glanced at Desta's dreamy face. "What are you thinking?" she asked.

"You know what?" he said suddenly, pulling away from his sister.

Hibist screwed up her face, surprised by the abrupt change in Desta's mood.

"All this talk is making me depressed," said Desta, turning toward the door. "I need to go out."

"Where do you want to go?"

"I want to be with the monkeys for a while."

"They are your water, eh?" joked Hibist with a smile.

"What do you mean?"

"Well, Father always goes by the creek or the river and sits there listening to the water whenever he feels out of sorts. You like to be with the monkeys."

"After Kooli, they are my most soothing companions," said Desta, attempting to tease her.

"I don't count?" said Hibist, widening her big eyes and faking a frown.

"You are neither a dog nor a monkey—you are my sister and I love you," said Desta, showing his evenly set white teeth. He didn't want to hurt his beloved sister's feelings.

"You always have a clever way of mending things, don't you?" Hibist said, smiling. "I was just teasing you. But don't you want to eat something before you go?"

"I don't feel like eating. I'll see you in a little while," Desta called out as he parted from Hibist. On his way to the door, he filled his cloth pouch with grain from the mill room.

Hibist followed him out and stood on the threshold. Kooli, who had been napping under the fence a few yards from the door, raised his sleepy head. Kooli always slept in that spot until Desta came over and sat on his usual perch on the fence.

"You didn't have a birthday gift either, did you?" Desta said, bending over to pet Kooli when he came over and stood next to him.

Kooli was staring back at Hibist, who usually fed him breakfast.

"Talk to me, Kooli," pleaded Desta. He brushed off the bits of straw from Kooli's back.

"You know we were born at relatively the same time," Desta continued. "Baba brought you into my life to be my companion, Kooli. Now would you like to accompany me to the top of the mountain so we can touch the sky together?"

"Desta, you can be very strange sometimes," Hibist chuckled. "Do you think Kooli even understands what you are saying to him?"

"You don't understand," said Desta, looking up at his sister, who was still standing on the doorstep. "This is just my parting talk with Kooli. I know he would like to come with me, but I can't take him when I go visit the monkeys. They are not comfortable with him. Can you take him inside and give him some food, Hibist? I am sure he is hungry," Desta said as he stood up.

"If you don't return soon, I'll give your food to him too," said Hibist, winking at Desta.

"I don't mind. Kooli deserves to eat all he can get. He never breaks his promises. He is loyal and loves me," said Desta, fighting off tears.

"You better go then. . . . If you stay around here any longer, you're going to cry your eyes out," said Hibist with a light push on Desta's back.

She grabbed Kooli by the scruff of his neck and pulled him toward the door. The dog struggled to free himself, keeping a twisted eye on Desta as Hibist dragged him indoors.

Desta waved a hand at Kooli and his sister and left. He crossed the sloping, fallow land behind his home and stood at the edge of the forest. He looked for the vervet monkeys. On the trees along the creeks, he saw the luxuriant white, motionless tails of the colobus monkeys. *This is a good sign*, thought Desta.

When the colobus were around, their feisty neighbors, the vervets, were usually lurking nearby.

"Tottas! Tottas! Tottas!" he shouted, trying to make his presence known to them. It had taken Desta an entire year of diligent courting before he had become friends with the vervets. Now all he needed to do was just call them and they came hopping from tree to tree.

Desta knew that the aloof colobus rarely came down to the ground in his presence, no matter how much he tempted them with a fistful of grain. He also knew that both monkey species had long been persecuted by humans; the vervet for being pests because they raided crop fields, the colobus for being beautiful. Their luxuriant black and white skins were of great commercial value and hunters shot the prized colobus in staggering numbers. Their greatest threat was actually Desta's oldest brother, Teferra.

As Desta shouted and scanned the trees along the forest, he noticed some green foliage stir in the distant woods. He concentrated his focus on the direction of those trees until he saw the silver-gray tails of the vervets.

They must've heard me, Desta thought cheerfully. The vervets slowly made their way toward him as he kept calling. Once they reached him, they perched on the nearby branches and surveyed their surroundings.

Desta took pinches of grain and tossed them in the air.

"Come and get it!" he shouted in their direction. He saw them flicker their eyes and tilt their heads as they watched the grain fall to the ground. One or two yawned, then closed their mouths with loud snaps.

Desta knew it was only a matter of time. He settled himself on the nearest rock and intermittently tossed more grain. Eventually, some of the vervets descended from their branches. These were the bigger, fatter males. When the alpha males began to collect the grain and eat peacefully, the females and their babies took their cue and scurried to the remains. The females with babies eyed Desta warily while they picked up the scattered kernels. Once they had finished eating the grain, some sat where the grain had fallen, apparently waiting for more. Others paced the field, hunting for any missed kernels. This was a familiar routine.

Desta knew he was now in control. The monkeys were not as skittish as they sometimes could be.

"I know it's been over a month since all the grain was harvested from the field. You probably have not had any kernels of barley or wheat or rye for at least that long," Desta said to them as he scooped out some barley and scattered it around him.

All the monkeys—he counted twelve—came rushing over. The bright blue hair between the males' hind legs reminded him of the sky.

"Hey, have you ever gone to one of the mountaintops to touch the sky?" Desta asked one of the large male vervets near him. The monkey was busy eating. He didn't even turn his head.

Once again the monkeys sat and watched Desta after they had finished eating the second course. He gladly scooped out more barley and scattered it near him. Desta was enjoying himself as he watched the excited monkeys. He even held out his fist to encourage them to come pry it open and get the grain he held in it. He smiled and laughed outright as he watched some of the baby monkeys fight over a single kernel. The male monkeys rolled over rocks to get to the grains that fell in the cracks. Desta was completely at peace here with friends.

He dispensed the last batches of grain from his pouch. Watching the vervets eat so greedily had made him hungry.

"Now you go back to your trees," he commanded the monkeys. The animals still eyed him, silently pleading for food.

"I have no more," Desta laughed, gently shaking the pouch upside down in front of him to show his friends he wasn't lying.

Desta walked home happy. The monkeys always did this to him.

LATE IN THE AFTERNOON, Desta was reposing on the grass near his home thinking about the cloud man when he saw Astair and Zena running toward him.

"We have been meaning to come and talk to you, Desta, since that Saturday when we were by the river with the Deb'tera, but our parents wouldn't allow us to come across the creek," panted Astair, trying to catch her breath. "They think you might be a bad influence on us."

"If they think I'm a bad influence, how did you manage to come today?" inquired Desta.

"They've gone to visit friends across the river. Our grandmother, who is with us now, permitted us to go play. We came running straight over to ask you about that man you claimed to see in the glass."

"I wanted to talk about what happened with you and the Deb'tera too," Desta said in a low voice.

"First of all, did you really see anyone in that glass?" Astair asked, narrowing her eyes.

"Yes, I did."

"What did he look like?" Astair's eyes now were mere slits.

"He was cloud-like, with brown dots all over his body and he had a golden glow around him. He was very tall."

"You are lying!" cried Astair, stabbing the air with her index finger.

"No, I am not!" retorted Desta.

"My mother thinks you are lying because the Saytan caused her to not carry her babies to term. The Saytan is ugly, with long, sharp teeth and a pair of horns on its head," said Astair, staring intensely at the boy.

At a loss for words, Desta looked away at the grazing cattle.

Astair continued with her charges. "The other thing you said was that this Saytan—man, or whatever, came out of nowhere. Father and Grandpa chose that spot under the warka tree because it was close to where the river has carved a pool into the embankment. The Saytan lives in such waters. Right there is more proof that you made him up. And you said that man warned us to move from the place where we have lived for almost four years. You're cruel, do you know that?"

"Astair, the man I talked to didn't come out of the water. He came from the air, and I certainly didn't make him up or what he said about you having to move," Desta said calmly.

"I have an even stronger reason to believe you are lying," insisted his niece, shaking her head.

"And what is that?"

"My father said the reason we were chosen was because the Saytan is revealed to boys and girls that are virgins—and you are not one!" shouted the girl triumphantly.

Desta looked confused.

"What on earth are you talking about, Astair?" he cried, rising to face both girls squarely.

"Remember a year ago, when we were playing grown-ups over there by the woods near our home? We built houses, held weddings, made babies, then raised them. And as a mother of Zena, I married her off to you. You and her went away to your house and made babies."

"That's true," confirmed Zena, her cool eyes still on him.

"But we really didn't do anything like . . ." Desta began to say, trailing off as a memory of his parents' bed-time activities came to him. He closed his eyes and watched in his mind's eye as an old image of Abraham and Ayénat's intimate scenes played in his head.

Returning to the present moment, Desta opened his eyes and yelled, "It was not like that!"

"What was not like that?" demanded Astair.

With his left hand, Desta made a circle by touching his thumb and index finger together. Then he inserted his right index finger into the circle and pulled it in and out, slowly. "It was not like this."

Bringing his two index fingers together, Desta continued. "It was only like this. That was exactly what happened between your sister and me when you married us last year."

"It doesn't matter, it's all the same!" Astair shrieked.

Zena pursed her lips and moved her head up and down, concurring with her big sister's assertions.

"Let's go. Grandma will wonder where we have gone," said Zena, pulling on Astair's sleeve.

"Look," said Astair coolly, needling Desta's bare chest with her index finger "You and I both know that you saw no one in that glass, man or spirit. You imagined this man and made up whatever you claim he told you just to make life even more difficult for me, my sister, and our parents, as you have done to your parents, brothers and sisters. I hope somebody takes you away from this place so we can all live in peace." She finished her verbal assault with a shove of such force that Desta fell violently and gashed his bare thigh. The two girls took off, turning around once in awhile to see if Desta was going to rise and follow them.

But Desta didn't rise. He was in excruciating pain. Lying where he fell, he thought about what his nieces had said. Instead of being thanked for helping solve Saba's problem, he was being blamed for their orders to move.

What worried him even more was that the questions his nieces raised would now spread quickly among the rest of his family and he would be further disliked by everyone. The last thing he wanted was another obstacle that would further alienate him from his family.

Desta finally staggered to his feet. He wanted to go home and go to sleep and forget about his problems.

SEVEN

One February evening, Desta was sitting by the fire across from his mother when his father returned from a long meeting at church. Ayénat had told Desta that whenever his father arrived late on a Sunday afternoon, it usually meant he was settling disputes or solving problems for the parishioners.

Abraham went to the bedroom, removed his long white shirt, khaki breeches and a matching coat and re-emerged wrapped in his gabi. After this routine activity, he came and sat next to Desta on his long wooden bench. Having no undergarments, Abraham, had pulled one corner of the gabi between his legs, passed it over his front and tucked it in at his groin. Hibist brought a tumbler of tella and handed it to him as soon as he sat down.

Ayénat, sitting on a round wooden stool was baking injera on a circular clay pan, which measured roughly eighteen inches in diameter. The pan was supported by three small, stout stones that rose from the ashes like some ancient monuments. Hibist was preparing dinner sauces in the main kitchen behind the parapet from where Ayénat sat.

Shortly after Desta's father sat, Yihoon announced his presence at the door and entered the home. Both Abraham and Ayénat greeted him and invited him to sit down. Hibist brought him a goatskin to sit on and a tumbler of tella.

Yihoon drew a couple of sips from his tella, set it aside and wrapped his hands around his knees. "Saba and I have been seriously discussing our move but we don't really have a place to go to. I came to see if you would give us a suggestion," he said finally, turning to his father-in-law.

Abraham dropped his chin and glanced at Yihoon. "I have been thinking about it too. Unfortunately, we don't have any more land you can move to. My mother's death made it possible for you to settle on your current property because Teferra waived his interest in it when he inherited her property. As you know, the other piece of land has long been earmarked for Asse'ged and Damtew." Abraham stroked his goatee thoughtfully and stared into the fire.

"I know," said Yihoon. "But going back to our former property in Goota is not an option. My brothers settled their own families there after we moved here four years ago. We truly are in trouble now. We can't continue to live at our current place, not after what that spirit said to Desta."

"I understand. But where would you move to?" Abraham continued to stroke his goatee.

"That is why I came here, to seek your advice."

"I am not sure where you can go. It's a shame you have to leave your place, but then you have faced problems ever since you settled there. It may, indeed, be a good idea to move. But to where?"

"We were hoping you would give us permission to move across the other creek," Yihoon said quietly.

Abraham looked at him, surprised. "First of all, that land has been designated for Asse'ged and Damtew. Secondly, we cannot continue to destroy the forest or we'll run out of wood for building our homes and cooking our meals."

Yihoon stirred in his seat and pursed his lips as if searching his mind for the appropriate answer.

Before either of them spoke again, Desta's brother Damtew walked in behind three male goats. These were Abraham's mookits. Their testicles had been pounded into a pulp to stop them from chasing the females and wasting their energy. Damtew drove the goats to their stall in the back room and went out.

"Tell us, Desta," Abraham said. "Did you really see and talk to that man when you were with the Deb'tera by the river?"

"Yes, I did," said Desta in a meek voice.

Yihoon watched Desta keenly.

"He said Astair's mother and father and all the animals need to move. If they don't move, the animals will continue to die, things will get worse and she will keep losing her babies," said Desta, at a hurried pace as if he had memorized the words.

Abraham's eyes shuttled from Desta to Yihoon, then back to Desta.

His mother peered at him circumspectly. "Who did he say he was?" she asked.

"He didn't tell me. But he was cloud-like with brown dots and a golden glow all over him," said Desta.

"He must be a Saytan, but the Saytan is not cloud-like nor does he have brown spots," said Ayénat with a perplexed look.

Desta shrugged.

"It does not matter who he was," said Abraham. He turned to Desta. "Before it gets too dark, why don't you go and bring the horses in."

Desta had been watching his mother, hoping she would give him a piece of the freshly baked injera. He had not eaten all day except two wedges of bread and a tumbler of milk he'd had for breakfast.

"Go get the horses first. We'll have dinner as soon as all the animals are in," she said.

"Well, anyway," said Abraham, turning to Yihoon. "It doesn't matter who that man was or what he said. It would, indeed, be better to do something than do nothing."

"My wife and the children have been very unhappy about the idea of moving, but we have come to the conclusion that the alternative will be worse," said Yihoon in a halting voice.

After a long silence, Abraham said, "If we were to consider settling your family across this other creek, you could only cut just enough trees to build your home and raise your animals. You would need to do your farming elsewhere."

"At the moment, what we need is a place where we could resettle. I can always lease farmland," said Yihoon, relieved.

"We can talk about the details later. I still am not sure how all this would work out. At the same time, I certainly don't want to sacrifice my grandchildren or you and your wife and the animals to save the forest."

"You have been gracious to allow us to come and live here. Many thanks for being considerate of our needs and for giving us another opportunity to remain here."

Yihoon drew his last swig of tella and prepared to leave. Ayénat invited him to stay for dinner, but he declined. His family was waiting for him and he was anxious to share the good news with them. The two men shook hands. Yihoon bowed to Ayénat and turned to go.

"Wait, Yihoon. Let me get you a torch. You may need it in the moonless night," said Ayénat as she rose to get him the bunched twigs.

"Desta! Are you not going to go and get the horses?" Abraham turned to his son, glaring.

Desta, charged with anger for having to wait till dinner was served, left grumbling.

The night was nearly black. Desta found the horses a few yards away from the entrance, waiting for someone to come and bring them inside. He herded them back to the house.

Yihoon stopped when he saw the animals at the door, waiting for them to pass. But, to Desta's surprise, the lead horse stopped at the threshold with her ears standing straight and her eyes fixed on the stall. She snorted. The others too, stood unmoved. Desta tapped on their backs with his stick, but instead of going into the stall, the animals reared with their eyes still fixed on their stall.

"Go in. Go in. What is going on with you?" he said to them, tapping on their backs again. The animals didn't budge.

Ayénat came to the door to see what was going on. "Maybe they are afraid of you, Yihoon. Please come back," she said, pulling him toward the living room. The torch Yihoon held low to the floor was burning slowly.

The horses still stubbornly resisted, even after Yihoon retreated.

Despite Desta's pleading, the lead horse turned around and trotted away. The others followed.

He came close to the door and looked into the stall. "Oh my God," he cried, covering his mouth.

"What's wrong?" said his mother, coming to the door.

"I can't believe it. I saw that cloud man," Desta answered, terrified.

"What man?" asked his mother.

"The man we met by the river. He was just here and now he's gone."

"The Saytan you have been talking about?"

"Yes."

"God almighty," she shouted. "Please don't tell me you have brought the Saytan into my house!"

"I didn't bring him, besides he is not a Saytan, Ma," said Desta, trying to calm her. "Who else causes havoc in people's lives?" she replied as she grabbed her son and pulled him in.

"Wait a minute, wait a minute," said Desta pushing his mother's hand away. "I just saw him again. He said the new place they talked about will be al all right."

Ayénat began to recite, *Besmam*, besmam, besmam, calling after the trinity and pushing the air with her hands as if the specter were approaching her.

Yihoon heard what the boy said and walked to the door speechless.

Desta's father joined them too. "What do we have here? What happened?" he asked, looking from one to the other.

"I just saw the cloud man again," said Desta timidly, afraid his father might scold him.

"Did you really see something or is it one of your vivid imaginings taking hold of you again?" asked his father, lowering his gaze over the group.

"I saw him. I didn't imagine anything. The horses must have seen him too," said Desta excitedly.

"Calm down, calm down," said Abraham. "Tell me what happened exactly."

The boy repeated what he had seen. In the end he kept repeating, "The horses saw it too. The horses saw it, not only me." He wanted to make this fact clear in case they accused him of being a liar.

"This is very strange but . . . Yihoon, that place is yours," said Abraham, tapping the son-in-law's shoulder.

"Thank you sir, but I don't know what to think right now. It's too strange and worrisome. We've never experienced anything like this in our lives," replied Yihoon, shaking his head. "I think I will go for now, but thank you. My wife and daughters will be happy to hear what you said . . . and . . . and," he stuttered, losing his train of thought.

"You mean . . . and . . . what the man said?" piped in Desta.

"I don't know if they would like to hear that, Desta. They have been fearful of that man ever since they heard what he said," said Yihoon.

"This was exactly what I had feared—that Deb'tera would be bringing the Saytan into our lives," said Ayénat, turning to Abraham.

"Ma, it seems the cloud man had been around here before Deb'tera Taye brought him into your life. You just didn't know he existed," replied Desta.

This remark stunned his mother but impressed his father.

"Our little wise boy!" snapped Ayénat, fixing Desta with her small eyes.

"Thank you . . . Thank you very much for giving us another chance to settle in a new place," said Yihoon, bowing his head to his in-laws as he moved to the door.

"Let's just hope this will be the end of your problems," Abraham said. "Good night."

Desta gathered the horses once again, brought them back and attempted to put them in their stall. Ayénat and Abraham waited by the entrance to see what would happen. To their surprise, the horses went in without any hesitancy.

"I think Desta, too, may be possessed by the Saytan, don't you?" said Ayénat, her eyes darting about nervously.

"Nahh," said Abraham, dismissing the idea with a wave of his hand.

"I am going to the priest. . . . I need to consult with the priest," said Ayénat.

"I don't think it's necessary, but do what you please," said Abraham as he turned to go sit.

Desta, who was standing behind them, shouted, "I am fine. I am fine!" He strained as he swung the crookedly hung wooden door to shut it. The massive door creaked as the two pointed ends pivoted in the conical holes of the threshold and header. After it came to rest on the portal frame, he lifted a long pole and wedged it between two posts on either side of the door and the wall.

EIGHT

In late February, deep into the dry season, Desta began training as a shepherd with his brother Damtew, who in a few months would leave the occupation permanently to become a fulltime farmer. Until then, Desta had much to learn from his older brother about how to tend the cows, goats and sheep. He also needed to familiarize himself with plants and vines in the woods from which he would gather material for making ropes and whips.

They were sitting under a big sholla tree where the fire-red, succulent figs peered down on them. To Desta, Damtew appeared distant and thoughtful, his brother's hacked mole on the side of his nose, looking redder and bigger than when he saw it last. Desta was thinking about the amputated pimple and its rejuvenation when Damtew interrupted.

"I saw Saba and Yihoon last night," said Damtew, narrowing his small eyes.

"What did she tell you?" Desta asked casually, avoiding his brother's gaze.

"I am shocked!"

"What happened, Damtew? Tell me."

Hibist had once told Desta that Damtew was incapable of articulating his feelings and thoughts easily—it was worse when he was upset. Desta knew he needed to be patient with him.

"Wait till I tell our brothers," Damtew muttered, his eyes blazing.

Desta sighed. His eyes deep in their sockets, he gazed at his brother.

"Saba said Father has given them the land across the creek to live on. All this because of your ridiculous story. Father purposely designated that piece of land and the one they live on at present for us years ago, and now we are not going to have either of them!"

Desta blinked thinking about what he should say to appease Damtew.

"Do you realize that making up stories and telling lies is a dangerous thing? Do you know what a great problem this is, not only for them but for the rest of the family?"

No convincing ideas came to Desta. Giving up, he stared at the eastern mountains where the sky seemed deeply welded into the ridge. He wished he were there, instead, caressing the smooth deep blue surface with his bare hands, away from his barking brother.

"Talk to me!" Damtew demanded, pushing Desta's shoulders with surprising force. "I had no intention of doing all this. I just told the Deb'tera what the man told me," protested Desta.

"What man? The man you fabricated, gave face and form to in your mind to amuse yourself and fool the Deb'tera? This is not funny, Desta! You created an awful mess in our family and God knows where this problem will end!"

Desta sighed deeply once again and looked away. He was frightened by his brother's words.

"I didn't make the man up!" he insisted, tears gathering in his eyes. "The horses saw him that night when Yihoon came to see Baba. Go talk to him. He saw everything."

His brother's large frame and simmering rage was as imposing to Desta as if he were actually being smothered by him.

"Don't insult me!" Damtew cried. "I know all about it. You're trying to trick people by bringing dumb animals into the fray. Everybody knows that what you have said is a horrible lie!"

Overwhelmed by his brother's fury, Desta shrank further into himself.

"Talk to me," Damtew pushed him again, until Desta nearly collapsed on the ground.

"I have told you all I can tell you! I didn't lie and I didn't make the horses see what was not there!" blurted Desta, confident in the truth he told.

"You had better go and tell father and Yihoon that you have deceived them. You didn't see any man. He was just a figment of your imagination. And tell Father that Saba and Yihoon should not move from where they are."

"You can do whatever you want to me but I am not going to lie," Desta said evenly, picking himself up and preparing to run home.

"Do you know that once the property is settled by them, not only I but you too will lose your share? Do you know that you will not have a place for you and your future wife and children once this place is given to them? Do you know that?" Damtew grasped Desta's arm and bore down on him.

"I don't care! Let me go! I am not going to lie!" Desta said, tugging to free himself from his brother's hold.

"You don't care because you don't understand what you have done. You will not go until you promise to tell father and Yihoon that you made up that man," threatened Damtew.

"Will you let go?" Desta continued to pull as hard as he could.

"Do you promise to recant your story?"

"If that is what you wish to hear, I promise," said Desta, gazing into his brother's small red eyes. Deep down in his heart, Desta knew he could not change his mind.

"Just remember, things could get worse and you have the power to stop them—if you cooperate," Damtew snarled as he let go of Desta's arm with a hard push.

Staggering, Desta turned away from his brother and sprinted home at top speed. When he arrived sweaty and breathless, he found his mother bending over a large round wooden vat. She appeared to be mixing something.

"Desta, what happened? Why are you all sweaty?"

"Nothing, I just ran home because I was thirsty," he gasped, not wanting to tell her what happened with Damtew. She had already threatened to bring the priest to exorcise the Saytan out of him.

"Can I drink from this?" He pointed to the jar of water next to her.

"No, it's not clean. Go inside and get some," she said, reverting to her task.

"What are you doing?" asked Desta as he came out with a clay tumbler of water.

"I am soaking barley for wedding beer," she replied.

"Who is getting married?"

"Your brothers Tamirat and Damtew and sister Hibist will be married in May."

Desta stared at his mother, trying to make sense of this bombshell.

Ayénat saw the need for elaboration. "What it means, darling, is that our Hibist will go to live with her husband and in her place will arrive two beautiful girls who will be your sisters." With that she went inside the house, leaving the wet barley in the vat and a speechless Desta.

After the upcoming wedding, not only would he lose his sister, he would have to live with two complete strangers. Desta was choked with emotion by the time his mother re-emerged from the house carrying five bamboo baskets.

"Why do you look so sad, Desta?" She stared at him with the stacked baskets cradled in her arm.

"I was thinking about the wedding," he said, quickly looking away.

"My dear, weddings are something to be happy about, not sad."

"Not for me," sniffled Desta, shaking his head.

"Why not for you? Aren't you happy for your brothers and sister?" she asked, dropping the stacked baskets next to the vat.

"How can I be happy when the only friend I have is going to go away? And I'll be living with girls I don't even know," said Desta, biting his lip.

"With the arrival of your brothers' wives, everything will be better not worse, darling. It means you will have two sisters instead of one. You will be loved twice as much," said Ayénat as she separated the baskets and lined them around the vat. She covered their interior walls and bottoms with false banana leaves and filled them three-quarters of the way with the wet barley, pushing and cresting the barley around the basket to leave a shallow depression.

"We will get to see Hibist often," Ayénat continued. "She will be married to a young man whose family attends the same church as we do. When you get stronger you can come with us on Sundays and visit her."

"Not seeing her is not what's sad, it's just that trying to live here without her—my sister and the only trusted friend I ever had," said Desta, his voice breaking.

"Oh darling, no other person here cares for you? You are hurting my feelings," his mother said, knotting her forehead.

Desta sucked the air and compressed his lips, deciding not to pursue this conversation any further.

Ayénat flipped the false banana leaves and covered the top of the barley. She took additional shreds of the same leaves, wrapped the top and tucked them in. Desta noticed that although the crinkles on his mother's forehead were relaxed, they were not gone.

As he watched her shuttle in and out of the house, Desta's thoughts drifted back to what his brother had said. He couldn't believe all this had happened from just telling what he heard from that spirit man. The chain of events that had quickly unfolded was starting to terrify him. With his sister soon to be married and gone, he would have nobody to talk to anymore. His heart ached. He was also deeply troubled by his brother's words. "Just remember things could get worse. You have the power to stop them if you cooperate." The threat played again and again in his ears.

What could he do to reverse this chain of events? Should he lie and tell his father and Yihoon that he made a mistake? What would that cloud man think? How could he say he didn't talk to him when he did?

For the moment, Desta resolved not to say anything. He would take things as they came. *Maybe that man would notice all these problems and come to protect him. And tell him what to do with his problem involving Damtew,* Desta thought, rallying his mood.

His mother came back and crouched beside him. "I noticed you were shaking your head, twisting your lips and frowning. You must have been thinking about our conversation. I didn't want to disturb you. Are you through? Can I say something?"

"Sure," Desta shrugged.

"There are many benefits about the new girls, many of which concern you. With their availability you will no longer have to run errands for me, or take food to your brothers at farm sites and hold the calves when the cows are milked, or bring firewood. If you get sick, they might even look after the animals for you," counseled Ayénat.

"It's not just those things. It's everything else that is the problem," protested Desta, wiping away a tear that had involuntarily dropped down his cheek.

"I promise you, everything will be fine. Come inside. I will give you something to eat," she cajoled.

For Desta, there was nothing more to say. He could not make her understand the predicament he found himself in. Eyes downcast, he followed his mother into the house.

NINE

The morning Damtew came in the house to take Desta to the field for his first training as a shepherd and cowherd, Hibist was troubled by the fear she saw in her little brother's eyes. Desta was sitting near the fireplace eating breakfast his sister had just handed him.

"Are you ready?" asked Damtew towering over his little brother.

Desta lowered his eyes onto the tray on his lap and said nothing.

"Did you hear?" demanded Damtew.

"Something must be bothering him," said Hibist, glancing at Damtew. "Why don't you go by yourself; I'll send him after he finished eating."

"He can't be slacking off from the start. I've a lot to teach him. He should come as soon as he has eaten his food," said Damtew and left.

"Is something the matter with you, Desta?" asked Hibist, crouching near her brother.

"A dream—a horrible dream."

"What happened in your dream?"

"We need to go outside and I'll tell you."

Desta and Hibist left for the back of the house and sat in a clearing overlooking the creek below and across from the future home of Saba and her family.

"So tell me, what exactly happened last night," asked Hibist, resting her cool, big brown eyes on her brother's troubled face.

"I have never had a dream like it before. It was so scary that I could have died just from the terror. . . . It involved Damtew and Asse'ged," said Desta.

"What did they do to you?"

"It seemed that Saba and her family had moved to their new place over a year ago. She was with a baby again and was ready to deliver. It was late in the evening and she was lying by the fire. People were sitting around, and I was dragged there by Damtew and Asse'ged, held between them by my arms. Three of us were behind one or two people. Saba's mother was there by her side, holding her arm with one hand, and resting the other on her belly. There were other women, too, that hovered around but I never saw them before.

"So, what happened to Saba and the baby?" asked Hibist, anxiously.

"While she was in labor, the baby got stuck. Everyone, at least most of us who were close by the fire, could see the baby's head with his tussled dark hair peeping out of her. The women congregated around her and kept saying "Push, push, push." Saba pushed, but the baby still didn't come out. She shouted, "Kill me! Kill me! Kill me!" Still nothing happened.

"Damtew kept his eyes on me while Asse'ged just tightened his grip, constricting the blood flow in my arm and causing me severe pain. Once in a while, Damtew would bring his face close to me and say, 'Is this the normal baby that your man told you Saba would deliver, eh?'

"I said nothing. I looked down at the floor and prayed.

"Saba's shouting continued. Some people brought some roots and pounded them into a paste with mortar and pestle. They gave the paste to the mother to massage into Saba's belly. Others made her smell some herbs they brought. But it was all to no avail. The baby still wouldn't come out.

"Yihoon was pacing the room, eying me from time to time as if I should know the answer. Astair and Zena were also there, staring at me with hatred. The longer Saba's agony continued, the more I shrank and the tighter were our brothers' grips on my arms.

"I began to pray. 'God please don't kill this baby. God, please make it easy on Saba.' Then I was back to my own plight. 'Please don't let my brothers kill me . . .' I sobbed silently and continued to pray at the same time."

Desta breathed a deep sigh and blinked.

"Take a break," said Hibist putting her arm around him. "I am sorry to hear all this . . . It sounds horrific. Father is good at interpreting dreams. Tell him what happened and he'll give you the meaning of it."

Desta gazed into the distance for a bit, but he was also gazing inward. By degrees, tears gathered in his eyes. "You know what saddened me most during the whole time?"

"What?"

"To die without touching the sky," said Desta. The tears that had filled his eyes now gushed down his cheeks, as if they had waited for this moment before they could flow.

"My God, Desta! I know you have been talking about this for a long time . . .," said his sister, wiping her own tears and pulling him closer to her. "Look, maybe you and I can arrange a time when the adults are not around, like on a Saturday, to climb up the mountain so that you can touch it . . . but . . ."

Desta sighed again, feeling the warm air rush out through his nostrils. Having shared his greatest fear with his sister had given him a deep relief.

Hibist patted his shoulder and said, "Everything will be okay . . . So how did it end?"

Desta sighed. "When none of my prayers seemed to be answered, I started to say what father says whenever there is violent storm—you know which one?"

She nodded.

"I just kept saying, 'God of Israel, please help my sister have a healthy baby. God of Israel, please don't kill my sister. God of Israel, please don't make my brothers kill me.' I kept my eyes closed the whole time as I was saying these words.

"And then . . . you won't believe what happened," said Desta, glancing at his sister. The words got stuck in his throat, but there was serenity on his face and a sparkle in his eyes.

"Tell me, what happened?" asked Hibist.

"When I opened my eyes I saw that man."

"What man?"

"The man I saw by the river, the one the horses saw."

Hibist tightened her lips and knotted her forehead. "So what happened?" she asked nervously.

Desta closed his eyes. "It was really strange what happened. He came floating in the air, with the same features: tall, brown, with faded golden light around him, cloudlike but having human form. He glided over and hovered around Saba and finally stood beside her, directly opposite where her mother was sitting. The moment he landed, the whole place became quiet—hushed.

"I gasped. I wanted to say something but nobody would believe me. Instead, I said to myself, 'Now what? Now what? Are we going to see the baby? Is she going to be helped?'

"My brothers still had a tight hold on my arms, but I felt a great sense of peace descend on me. The man looked toward me just for a second, sort of winked at me and averted his eyes.

"When I couldn't hear Saba's voice or see her movements, I was blanketed with an enormous fear again. I thought maybe Saba had died. I thought nobody would forgive me. More than that, somebody, Yihoon or my brothers who had an iron clasp on my arms would kill me. Right there and then! As I was going through these feelings and thoughts, I felt the dread welling up from the depths of my throat. It choked me again. I began to groan as loud as I could.

"I woke up in a cold sweat . . ." Desta deeply sighed once more and opened his eyes. He didn't like what he saw on his sister's face.

For a moment Hibist said nothing, then she got up and said, "Let's go home." Desta hesitated, surprised by his sister's apparent indifference to his dream. He stared at the forest across the creek where Saba's family would soon be moving. Hibist started to head in the direction of their home.

Desta regretted telling his dreams to his sister.

"So all this is pretty weird stuff, huh?" said Desta, breaking the silence.

"I don't know, Desta. There is something very weird, indeed! To tell the truth, I think Mother may be right. You might be possessed by the Saytan. Or the Deb'tera has done something to you to make you see this man again and again. I am afraid for you."

Desta was quiet, disappointed by his sister. She sounded like everybody else. The two walked in silence for several minutes.

Desta was choking. He wanted to let out what was welling up in his throat.

"I hate you, Hibist! I hate you like I hate everybody else! Nobody believes in me!" Desta shouted.

Hibist stopped and wheeled on the ball of her heels and gazed at her little brother. "It's not that I don't believe you," said Hibist. "I just don't understand it! I have never seen anything like this. Nobody in our family has ever seen anything like this. Then again, it's only a dream . . . I'm sure everything will be all right . . . But for now you should go for your training with Damtew."

Hibist accompanied Desta to the edge of the field where his big brother was tending the animals, gave him a warm hug and returned home.

"WHAT'S THE PROBLEM? What took you so long?" asked Damtew the moment he saw his little brother.

"I had to finish my breakfast and was not feeling well. But I am better now," replied Desta.

"Good. There are a lot of things we'll be doing today and tomorrow," said Damtew bossily. "The first thing I want to teach you is the names of the key bulls and cows. Knowing their names will help you manage them better. From these animals we'll move on to the goats, the sheep and the horses."

As Desta trotted behind his brother, he was struck by Damtew's tall and broad physique, by his perfectly shaped calves and the high arches and by the way he walked. Damtew moved as if he had a set of springs beneath his heels: bouncy, rhythmical and graceful—just like their father. Also like their father, his heels clicked as if there were broken bones inside them.

There was something different about Damtew though. Unlike his father or any of his other brothers, he hardly spoke around the house, laughed or cracked a joke. He spoke only in one or two monosyllabic sentences and, even then, only when he was responding to a query or requesting something.

In the evening while everybody chattered away, Damtew quietly sat, wrapped in his gabi, with a portion of it slung between his legs, arms intertwined and rested on his bent knees. Desta thought Damtew always looked like a roosting hen—puffed up and guarded—a complete mystery. But here in the field he talked a lot and was relaxed and open. He was almost like a new person to Desta.

"Remember that goats are the hardest to keep in one place. They always seem to have a brain completely different from the other animals and also from each other. They climb rocks and sometimes get into tight places where it's hard to drive them out. They are the most independent and the hardest to manage."

Desta was mystified why the friendly goats he often fed grains and salt could be the hardest to manage but he didn't want to challenge his brother's comments.

"The sheep have their own problem," continued Damtew. "Easy to manage, yes, but they are hard to keep in a certain defined area. They are always bunched together and move in one direction so long as there is open space ahead of them. The horses are easy. They pretty much stay around the bigger animals, and they don't have the roaming and raiding instinct like the bulls or the cows."

Desta knew that the horses were, indeed, easy to manage, except when they saw a stranger like that cloud of a man in their stall.

"In all this information the most important thing," said Damtew, "is to make sure that the cattle stay in this field. If you have to take them across the Davola River to the fallow land on the opposite side of the river, you have to keep an eye on the bulls and some of the lead cows. They can easily sneak away and destroy the crops on either side of the field."

To Desta all that his brother was telling him seemed like a lot of work. After all, he had never done anything like this before.

"I will show you the animals that are hard to manage in a moment," said Damtew as he headed to where a knot of cows grazed on the south side of the field. "The next important thing—the first really, as far as I am concerned, because I have two goats with kids and I don't ever want to lose either of them to a wild animal—is to ensure that the goats don't go deep in the forest or stay too long in the woods. You have to be around them and sound the whip from time to time, or whistle or just talk to them. That way the preying animals won't dare to come and attack the kids. The same thing with the sheep and their lambs—just keep them out of the forest."

Damtew's coiled whip was hanging down his back while the shiny brown wooden rod that attached to it dangled in front on his broad chest. He absent-mindedly twirled the tip of the rod while he was talking to Desta, even as they were walking. His deep set eyes did not veer. His face didn't crack into a smile nor did his voice sound playful. He was all business.

Once they reached the cows, Damtew introduced Desta to each of the animals and emphasized their individual traits. Lomee the bull, the nastiest of all the animals who can travel for miles to do his day's raid of crop fields, Salle-Ayiset the cow, the most notorious crop raider who had gotten Damtew and their father into many problems with other farmers; and Begiziew, the young bull who was the rising star as a crop destroyer which, along with the other two, Desta must keep an eye on his whereabouts at all times during the crop season.

But Desta felt like an ant compared to these beasts. He couldn't believe that these mountains of animals would respond to any human commands, let alone his own.

Next Damtew and Desta walked off to the north end of the field where the goats were feeding, dispersed in a copse of acacia bushes. They strode gingerly through the thorns and dried twigs. Occasionally Damtew held up or pushed aside the branches so Desta could pass unharmed.

"This is how you will find these goats most of the time," said Damtew pointing to the scattered animals in the grove of thorn bushes. "What always worries me when I find these goats like this is that they could lose their kids

or a weak member to an Anir, an affin or a kebero. So you need to chase them
out of these bushes. Stand by here and make noises or crack the whip until they
come out on their own."

"What are anir, affin and kebero?" asked Desta, watching the busily feeding
goats.

"They are lazy beasts that prey on lambs, kids and sick adults of our sheep
and goats instead of hunting for antelopes or rabbits."

"Now let's go to the sheep side," said Damtew.

They crossed the field to the big sholla tree where the sheep were gathered
and busily nibbling on the wind-fallen figs. In the tree fire-red figs hung in
bundles.

"The sheep are a pain to handle and keep in one place," said Damtew. "They
move in a bunch as if their bodies were sewn together. If there are no rivers
to cross or steep mountains to climb, they'll just keep walking. Their home is
where their face is pointing—where the lead sheep is taking them."

Desta was only half listening.

"I see you keep eyeing the figs. Are you hungry?" asked Damtew.

"A little," said Desta.

"Let's stop for now. I am getting thirsty and maybe even a little hungry
myself. Why don't you go home and bring us water and bread. It's almost noon.
I can get us some sholla figs."

Desta loped home, relieved from his brother's lecture for now.

When he returned with the food and water, he found Damtew dozing under
the tree. And his brother had not picked any figs.

They sat on the grass under the shadow of the sholla tree and began to eat.

"Do you think you can handle everything I talked about?" asked Damtew,
eyeing his little brother and studying his slight frame.

"I guess so. This is what I must do before I become a farmer, right?" said
Desta.

Damtew nodded.

"As you said, I will have to get used to it then," said Desta. *Just like I've
gotten used to being an outcast in my family*, he added under his breath.

"Just remember that right now it is easy," warned Damtew. "It's harder when
the rainy season comes and when the farmlands are filled with growing wheat,
teff and barley."

Desta's spirit flagged.

"As I said, the bulls and that cow I pointed out are the worst. Just keep a close supervision of them—the lead animals. You also need to keep all the goats and sheep in one area, particularly when it rains. Speaking of the rain, we should get you a gessa that is proportionate to your height. Also a nice thickly furred sheepskin that can fit you well.

"The rain and the cold can be brutal at times, and no tree will keep you dry or warm. Also, you will have to be out here with the animals not under a tree or at home, particularly if the animals are scattered about the field and in the bushes. What I used to do was, the moment I saw rain clouds gather above the mountains, I would immediately collect them and drive them to this tree or other trees—away from the forest and bushes. *So* you need to do the same until the rain stops."

Desta gulped his water nervously with his eyes fixed on his brother's face. He was seized with fear. He knew how severe the rain could get. He wondered how he could possibly survive horrific storms like the ones that he had watched with his father standing at the threshold of their home. He remembered the horror in his father's face during those times before he closed his eyes and solicited God's intervention. "God of Israel, please abate this rainstorm, thunder and violent wind from our valley. God of Israel, please protect our cows, goats and sheep from this storm, violent wind and our farmed lots from flood."

He remembered that during these violent storms the rain came in sheets and sometimes like a billion zapping arrows. He had watched the earth beyond the cover of the eaves being punctured in a million places. And Damtew thinks he can protect himself against such a storm with a small double-ply papyrus that he will don over his head?

"What's wrong?" asked Damtew.

"Nothing."

"By the way, Desta," said Damtew, as if trying to take Desta's mind away from whatever might be bothering him.

"Did you tell Yihoon and Father what we talked about the last time?"

Desta thought for a moment. He gazed far away to the distant mountains.

"You mean about the move of Saba's family?"

"Yes," said Damtew in a guarded voice.

"I gave you my promise, didn't I?" shot back Desta without hesitating.

"Good! I suspected you had since there has not been any news regarding their move. As I told you before, it just can't happen. We'd have no place to go once Tamirat and I get married and when you get married in the future. Although Father wisely appropriated these three pieces of land for all of us, it seems our future is expendable when it comes to *his* daughter. Maybe it was because of our brothers' curse that she has had the problems with her babies."

Desta kept mum, afraid Damtew would ask for details of what was said when he supposedly recanted his story about the man to Yihoon and his father.

"You have told me a lot about my job," Desta said trying to change the subject. "I am not sure if I am going to remember it all. What should I make sure to remember to do every day?"

"The two most important things you should remember are that the animals don't steal away and destroy the crops and that they are kept safe from predators. If you do these things everything should be fine. If you don't, I will tell you that all hell will break loose with—father, crop owners and with me, particularly if something happens to one of my animals.

"I have three male goats and two kids that I have been nurturing along, hoping that some day father can help me maim their testicles and make mookit out of them. After they become fat and big, I plan to sell them for a lot of money, which should come in handy for my wife and me when we move into our own house," said Damtew excitedly.

"To come back to what I was saying," continued Damtew. "You know who else was very upset?" Damtew asked.

Desta shook his head.

"Asse'ged, Teferra and Tamirat. But frankly, I have the most to lose from this situation. Both Asse'ged and Teferra have their own homes. Tamirat will be a priest and won't need much land to farm. I want to make sure that my family will have a nice place to settle once I get married and begin to have children. What I have been dreaming about was that father would pass that land to me as soon as I get married. And of course I will give you a portion when you get married, too."

Desta didn't have any desire for the land his brother was afraid of losing, but the thought of living with two strange girls bothered him, particularly since his sister was also going to get married and leave home.

"Will you be happy living with a strange girl?"

"Yes, I'll be happy. I look forward to having my own house, children and farm. As I told you before, I look forward to moving onto that property across the creek after a couple of years. Asse'ged also told me that he would like to take a portion of that land. We are both happy Saba and Yihoon will not be moving there anymore. I am glad we stopped everything from the start."

Desta squirmed, knowing that he had not recanted his story about the cloud man's suggestion about Saba and Yihoon's move to their new place, as Damtew had wanted him to do.

"What's wrong?" asked Damtew. "I know, I told you that I can share some of it when you grow up and get married. It could still happen. My feeling is Asse'ged is probably not going to move. I'll talk to father about giving that property just to you and me."

Desta had his eyes on the shadow that slowly was forming at the bottom of the mountain across the river. He knew that soon it would get taller and taller, climbing up the mountain as the sun sets behind the peak above their home.

"The sun will be setting soon," said Damtew. "Why don't you take these food things home? I will bring the animals myself."

As Desta walked home, his mind drifted back to Damtew's consuming obsession with his dreams of the future: the wife he would marry, the children they would have together, the farm he would own and the home he would build on the property that Saba and Yihoon were poised to take. This fact gave Desta the chills. He wondered what Damtew would do to him once he realized he could no longer have the property.

THAT EVENING DESTA REMEMBERED his own dream from the night before and was anxious to ask his father for its meaning.

"Baba, Hibist said you are good at interpreting dreams. May I tell you the one I had two weeks ago and tell me its meaning?" asked Desta. He was sitting next to his father by the fire and across from his mother.

"What happened in your dream?" asked the father, glancing at his son. Abraham was perched on his bench, with a cup of tella in his hand.

Calmly but with heightened intensity, Desta told his father the dream.

The father listened to Desta thoughtfully. He kept pulling on his salt and pepper goatee, twirling the ends at times. Occasionally he pulled from his cup too.

"Well, let's see . . .," said Abraham caressing his goatee. "Firstly, I must say that I didn't like the involvement of your brothers and the way they treated you. But then again, sometimes there are dreams like this, nightmares, which are the re-enactment of things that we have thought or heard about. For example, in this dream you must have been thinking and worrying about your sister not carrying the baby to term or dying while delivering. And the dream manifested in your thoughts and worries. Am I wrong?" He turned to Desta.

"It's true. But I don't understand why my brothers treated me like they did," said Desta in a sad voice.

"I am not sure either. Are you in general afraid of your brothers?"

"Not Asse'ged, but Damtew yes because he is so much bigger and he is often rough with me."

"Well, there you go. Your mind acted upon the fear you have of Damtew, just like the fear you have about your sister not delivering a normal baby. The presence of Asse'ged in the dream was merely as an accomplice to Damtew."

"Why was the man there? Why didn't my sister deliver while I was there?" asked Desta, confused.

"Those are very interesting parts of the dream," said Abraham, sporting a grin. "I think it's terrible that poor Saba didn't deliver. And I certainly don't like that Saytan popping up in my son's life everywhere," said Ayénat indignantly.

"He is not a Saytan, Ma. He is a nice man. But I was disappointed with him when he didn't help Saba deliver her baby," said Desta, annoyed by his mother's comments.

"I've a rather positive feeling about that man too, particularly since he has been so unfailing in his recurrences in Desta's life and dreams," said the father.

"I am not afraid of him. He seems gentle and harmless, not like what mother thinks he is," said Desta.

"I just don't like him appearing in all these places, in real life as well as in your dreams. Although he doesn't have the appearance of the Saytan, he could be the Saytan in sheep's clothing as they say or just a bad spirit. That worries me."

"What really disturbs me is not that he appeared again but he didn't help Saba
deliver her baby," said Desta. "I woke up without knowing whether she had the baby or not or whether she had lived or died. Maybe you can explain the reason for this."

"It's that aspect of him that I have been intrigued with since you told the story. He showed up, hovered around, winked at you and then disappeared.

What do you think he was trying to do?"

"I have absolutely no idea," said Desta, gazing at his father.

"If he really was a helping spirit, he would have made you happy by seeing your sister deliver the baby. I really think he is playing the Saytan's advocate, torturing you. You said you woke up in cold sweat. What do you call that, fun?" barked the mother.

"Yes, that is right. This whole time I have been thinking that if these dreams had meaning, I should have known whether my sister gave a live birth or not. After all it was he who told them what they should do. I just didn't want him to let me down because ever since that meeting and what I said he had said, everybody has been blaming me for their proposed move," said Desta nearly choking.

"My feeling is, yes, if you had not made him up from the start, if you truly met and talked to him that time by the river, he probably wouldn't let you down," Abraham said. "I think what he was doing was testing your faith in him. It was his sudden disappearance after he made the effort of being in the room that I find fascinating."

"In the dream, you woke as soon as he left. Nothing happened with your sister and the baby was still inside Saba. Now it's up to you to believe whether or not he will fulfill his promise," said the father, glancing once again at Desta.

"I hope you are right," said Desta, relieved.

TEN

Like a fugitive, Desta was held by his arms between Damtew and Ayénat about to be taken out of his home and brought before a lean and tall priest named Aba Yacob. Hibist walked behind Ayénat and Damtew to give a hand if Desta became uncooperative.

"We're going to free you from the Saytan that seems to have possessed you, son. Be calm," his mother was saying as they tried to subdue him.

Desta was not interested in seeing a priest. These days he'd become touchy every time someone came near and grabbed him by his arms. To Desta such acts brought back the horrific dreams he'd had a few weeks earlier.

"I feared from the beginning that something like this would happen to him," said Ayénat to Damtew as they pushed Desta to the door. "I told your father about this possibility. That man Deb'tera Taye dragged into Desta's life not only appeared to Desta in life but also has begun to terrorize him in his dreams."

"I think it's a good idea to nip the problem before it gets worse," Damtew said as they passed the threshold.

"That is why I invited Aba Yacob, to exorcise it out of him," replied Ayénat.

Aba Yacob was sitting on a bench; his head drooped over an old cloth-clad book he was reading, holding it balanced on his folded knees. He had his silver cross by his side, its handle wrapped in a faded, multicolor handkerchief.

Aba Yacob raised his head and planted his sharp and inquisitive eyes on Desta. "Is this the boy you said was possessed by Saytan?" he asked Ayénat.

"This is he," replied the mother.

Desta turned and gazed at his mother scornfully. Her continued reference to the Saytan as the cause of all his problems had become tiresome to him.

"Give me a little time. Let me finish these two pages," said the hunched figure, re-affixing his face on the opened book.

About three feet from Aba Yacob was a round-bellied clay jar filled with about five gallons of water. A pitcher made from the same material stood to one side of the jar, while a silky kusha rope coiled into multiple loops lay on the other side. Desta noticed that they were the same items he had seen earlier under the eaves when he and Hibist went to milk the cows. Then, the pitcher had covered the jar opening.

"The jar contains water that mother brought from the creek before dawn, prior to any bird or animal touching the stream," Hibist had said when Desta asked her why the items were left outside. "It's for *medhaneet*—medicinal—purpose. The water has to be *nitsuh*—pure—and *dingle*—virgin. Before it can be used as a medhaneet, the jar with the water in it has to be left until a priest comes to bless it later," Hibist had said in response to her brother's additional query. But she had denied him any further details.

It dawned on Desta from the proximity of the reading priest to the open jar that the priest expected the passages he read to flow into the water, thereby transforming the liquid into something holy and curative.

The holds his mother and brother had on his arms were growing painful. He wished he could kick, punch and break free from his captors.

After Aba Yacob was done with his reading, he ordered the two adults to remove the gabi from Desta and fetter his legs with the rope that lay near the jar. His legs secured, limbs firmly grasped by his mother and brother, Desta was ready for the priest to exorcise the Saytan out of him. Desta slouched and closed his eyes.

Hibist poured the water from the jar into the pitcher and handed it to the priest, who momentarily held it above Desta's head and began to pour the water slowly as he recited, "*Besmam wold woamen fis kidus,* 'in the name of Jesus Christ, the Father, the Son and the Holy Ghost,' we ask you creatures of the unknown—the Saytan or you other spirits—to immediately depart from this boy's body."

The moment the first water hit Desta's head, he twitched, wriggled and stiffened his shoulders. But Damtew and his mother tightened their hold and pressed him down. Ayénat kept whispering, "Close your eyes, stay put . . . . Be strong . . . ." Desta bent his neck and turned his face one way and the other, trying to protect his eyes as the water was poured over him.

The priest repeated his mantra with the pouring of another batch of the water over Desta's head and body. "Besmam wold woamen fis kidus . . . we entreat you, creatures of the underworld, to leave this boy alone so he can lead a happy and normal life—free from bad dreams and nightmares. . . ."

With the third batch, he said, "It was not in the boy's power when he was engaged by Deb'tera Tayé to solicit your participation in solving the problems surrounding his sister's family. We ask your pardon for the unnecessary provocation and solicitation in bringing you to this boy's life. . . . We equally entreat any and all alien spirits that might have dwelt in this boy's body from the earlier years."

The priest handed the empty pitcher to Hibist, picked up his hand-sized silver cross from the bench, and passed it over Desta's face and body.

"Besmam wold woamen fis kidus . . . Additionally, we ask you to free his mind from the many tiresome questions he poses to his family and friends and wasteful imaginings he engages in daily."

When Desta thought the priest was about done, he heard him resort to reciting something in the ancient church language of *Ge'ez*. When he opened his eyes, he saw a cupped hand filled with water suspended in midair as if waiting till he finished his recitation. Immediately afterwards, he told Desta to close his eyes and he splashed the cold liquid onto his forehead.

Desta shook violently, again terrified. He gasped for air.

"The Saytan or alien spirits—are you leaving this boy?" demanded the priest, towering over Desta.

The man repeated the water treatment on Desta's face once again. Desta shuddered and attempted to get up and wriggle out of his brother and mother's grips. With each hit of the water, Desta's heart raced and pounded in his ribcage. He wanted to cry but didn't want to give his captors the satisfaction. He bit his lip, closed his eyes tightly and continued to take the onslaught of water on his face like a warrior.

The deluge of water on Desta's forehead went on for several more minutes. With each hit of the water, the priest commanded the Saytan or bad spirits that might be dwelling in Desta's body to depart immediately and to signal or vocalize their departure.

When Desta realized the man was not going to let up, he decided to pretend. "We'll . . . we'll . . . we'll," he said in terrified voice.

"Now?" The priest hit Desta's forehead with another batch of the water from his cupped hand.

"We'll depart immediately," said Desta.

The priest doused Desta's face once more.

"Never to return and inhabit this boy's body again?" demanded the priest.

"Never . . . we'll never come back . . . we will never, never, never come back," said Desta, wet and dripping.

"Good!" said the tall figure, pleased with the positive outcome of his efforts. He ordered Damtew and his mother to untie him, dry his body and give him dry clothes.

While Hibist ran to get Desta clothes, his mother turned toward the exorcist and said, "All those answers, do you know if it was Desta talking or the Saytan and alien spirits?"

"Those are both the Saytan and the alien spirits talking through Desta," said the priest, fixing his eyes on Ayénat.

In the meantime, the patient had crouched on the grass, embracing his knees, resting his chin on them, his eyes boring a pair of holes in the ground. His teeth chattered and his mouth whimpered barely audibly.

Hibist brought a large gabi, wiped and rubbed dry her brother's shoulders and body while the priest and mother were watching.

"Hopefully now you can sleep in peace, free from nightmares and bad dreams," Hibist said tenderly, putting her arm around him.

Desta, in turn, glared at her with a blazing rage.

She was confused and asked, "You don't believe me?"

Grim and mute, Desta just looked away.

Ayénat invited the priest to come to the house.

"Let him get dry and warmed by the sun but keep him company," Aba Yacob said to Hibist, before following his host inside.

"Bring him injera with leftover sauce from last night," said Ayénat. "He was denied his breakfast since he had to receive the treatment."

Hibist brought Desta a cup of warm milk and injera with a mound of thick, freshly-warmed pea sauce left over from the previous night's dinner. She put the tray of food next to him and handed him the milk.

Desta placed the tumbler in the grass beside him and looked away.

"Look, I know you are mad, but this is to free you from the bad spirits that have been dwelling in you and causing you problems all these years. When I told mother about that horrific dream, she was very certain your body had become a roosting nest for Saytans and all types of alien spirits. She was afraid that you would soon be taken over by them, that they would continue to torture you and play with your soul, the way a cat will torture and play with a captured mouse before killing it. We didn't want that to happen to you. We wanted to get rid of them before they could kill you.

"This problem with the alien spirits is not new, Desta. They have been with you since you were two years old, causing you to talk like an adult and to ask endless questions. Mother and I thought the Saytan or Zars would leave you as you got older. Now, the reverse appears to be happening."

Desta listened to Hibist with his eyes still on the distant mountains.

"So you mean you are now part of the adults that give me hell? I thought you were my friend," he said finally.

"I am . . . more than that, you're my best brother."

"You didn't act like one in this case. Do you realize how cold that water was and how terrified I became every time that horrible man flooded my face with it? How can you betray me like this, Hibist? I shared those dreams with you because I trusted you. I knew mother would threaten to take me to some church to get me baptized with holy water. That was why I wanted us to talk in an isolated place, away from mother."

Contrition had replaced Hibist's earlier relaxed and calm face. She had her hand on her mouth.

Desta tried to suppress the triumph that seeped through him. He continued with his indictment. "Do you know how hard it has been for me all these years? I cannot talk to anybody because the moment I open my mouth, they think I am going to ask questions they can't answer. You have been the only person I could really talk to, my confidant. Now I can no longer trust you either. Do you realize how lonely I've been, and how much more so I will be if I stop sharing my thoughts and feelings with you? Do you care?"

"I do . . . very much. Don't stop sharing your thoughts and feelings with me."

The more he thought about his ordeals and the loss of trust in his sister, the more embittered Desta became. He had long wanted to vent his anger and frustration at someone. For him, Hibist, at that moment, represented Damtew, Ayénat and the priest and all the others who had shunned him. He could see them all rolled into one—his sister!

He lifted the tumbler of milk, pretending he was going to drink from it. In a flash, he hurled it at Hibist, aiming at her forehead—the exact same area the priest had doused him repeatedly with the ice-cold water. She swayed a little and fell backward on the ground. The skin broke. Blood oozed out.

He watched as Hibist, wet and drenched with milk, moaned for help.

Her caterwauling reverberated through the house. The mother and the priest came running.

Ayénat was stunned to see Hibist gashed and bleeding. She crouched and planted her palm on her daughter's forehead to halt the bleeding. She lifted her and held her close to her chest. She looked up at Aba Yacob, baffled by Desta's vicious attack on his sister.

"Father, I don't think this boy is free from the Saytan," she said in a broken voice.

"Well . . . uhhh . . . ummm . . .," the priest said, face crinkled, eyes narrowed as he searched his brain for an explanation. "Well, these things take time, and I . . . I am sure he will be all right shortly."

Ayénat and the priest carried Hibist inside and put her to bed.

Desta sat expressionless.

He didn't eat the food Hibist had brought to him nor did he move an inch from the place where they left him. He stared into the distant mountains and watched the shadows of clouds race over the slopes and over the trees and fields as if they were flying saucers. He fixed his eyes along the eastern horizon and tried to remember what time of the year it was when the sun rose on which section of the cupped pass on the ridge. His mind was not clear. He wished he could run away from his problems. *But where can I go?* he asked himself.

ELEVEN

The morning sun was still up in the mountains above Desta's home, caressing the earth with its band of cool, golden light and chasing the shadows of the eastern mountains downhill.

Shortly after Desta and Damtew left with the animals to the field, Yihoon and three unfamiliar men arrived with axes thrown over their shoulders. Hibist was outside spreading hops on a large cowhide to dry all day in the sun. The hops would be used to brew tella for the upcoming wedding.

"We are here to see my father-in-law," Yihoon said to Hibist. "Is he home?"

"I think so. I'll look," she said, and dashed toward the door.

Abraham finally emerged from the house. He greeted Yihoon and those who had come to help cut trees.

"Wait here," said Abraham and he went back inside the house. After a short time he re-emerged wearing shorts and an old jacket beneath his gabi.

The four men followed Abraham down the gravel footpath that ran along the acclivity of the terrain behind the house. They crossed the northern creek and strode diagonally along the flank of the forested hill on the other side, finally reaching the clearing where Abraham had built a small shed, staking the land as his own, when he had first moved his family to this side of the valley ten years ago. The broad and long land, bounded by two sleepy, deep-running steams on either side, stretched from the River Davola below to the cultivated plateau above, spanning approximately 250 acres of mostly arable earth of thick forest.

Abraham led Yihoon and his men around the roughly 30 acres of semi-circular perimeters he had predefined a few days earlier by marking the trunks of one hundred five trees with an ax to delineate a semicircle whose diameter lay along the creek at the bottom of the canyon.

As the men hiked through the forest, several antelopes, dik-diks, quail and wrens fled into the distant woods. The vervet and colobus monkeys activated their guttural alarms and sped away, leaving behind them a wave of buffeting and whooshing trees. A surfeit of birds chattered wildly in the branches and on the ground, various creatures slithered and scuttled away as if, like the other animals, they sensed the impending destruction of their home. All these instinctual responses by the animals had disturbed the father-in-law.

After Abraham had walked them around the general perimeter within which they needed to cut, he suggested they leave a number of the large sholla trees intact as their figs would provide good snacks for children and the birds. The rest of the trees, they should cut methodically and as low to the ground as they could, staying carefully within the boundaries he had circumscribed. With these instructions, he wished Yihoon and his assistants well and departed.

As he walked home, his heart was heavy and his mind was crammed with agonizing thoughts. In the perfect world he had years ago imagined for himself and family, Abraham had planned to apportion this land and the one Saba and Yihoon currently live on to his male children. That way, he would surround himself with them and the grandchildren they would produce for him. At that time, many of the western mountains were shrouded with what appeared to him to be inexhaustible forest.

Now ten years later, much of wooded land on the property he had settled and those beyond his two other properties had been cleared by him and others who had crossed the river and staked their own shares.

His newly cleared farmlands had yielded great quantities of crops the first year but had rapidly declined thereafter, as their top, compost-rich soil was washed away to the creeks and the Davola River by flood. Having no access to fertilization to maintain production levels, they had to keep cutting more trees and clearing more land as the old farms became unproductive, consequently depleting the forest and the animals it contained. Additionally, the forest had been a good shelter for his animals during the dry season and a source of firewood, furniture and home construction materials, as well as a great repository of game animals.

Now he was concerned that what had happened elsewhere in the valley would eventually happen to this piece of property as well. He feared that within a short time they would have completely denuded the land, leaving it bare and barren. His children and grandchildren would have to struggle to eke out a meager existence in due time. He had not fully analyzed these things at the time he had offered Yihoon the portion of the land, when his daughter's predicament had superseded these newly realized concerns. His priority had been to provide a comfortable and problem-free homestead for his daughter and son-in-law and, hopefully one day, his first male grandchild.

To make matters worse, knowing that Abraham was a strong proponent of conservation, the district governor had chosen him as one of the local leaders who should advise and educate the rest of the farmers about the importance of conserving the forest and the animals within it.

How hypocritical it would be to enforce this mandate while I've allowed my own son-in-law to do exactly the same, he said to himself. He knew he had a compelling and life-and-death situation with his daughter. So did every other farmer who wished to acquire a productive land.

While ruminating on these thoughts, Abraham reached his home. He didn't remember any of his journey back, nor did he recall saying goodbye to Yihoon and his helpers or even what part of the forest they were going to start cutting first. He wondered if he was already losing his mind over the potential problems he had on his hands.

His decision to give Saba and Yihoon the new property could create issues beyond the risk of public and government scrutiny. He feared potential problems with his own family.

TWELVE

Desta couldn't believe his eyes. He was standing on the side of the hill behind his home in the predawn hour, gazing at the gutted trees across the creek. He had come here as much trying to distance himself from his angry brother, Damtew, as to find out what Yihoon and his men had done to the forest, home for the monkeys and countless other animals.

The night before, Damtew had been very upset after he learnt from Asse'ged what had happened to the property their father had earmarked for them. "I heard about what's going on with our land. It's all because of your stupid story," barked the big brother, glaring. "You think we'll forget this."

Desta was sitting next to Damtew by the fire, pensive and fearful. He couldn't wait till daybreak so he could find out for himself what really had happened to the forest.

Now standing here and staring at the felled trees, it hit him suddenly that it was not just Damtew and Asse'ged that would be impacted by the clearing of the forest. He, too, would stand to lose something personal and dear to his heart: his hard-won friends.

Desta wondered if the cloud man had not considered what would happen to the monkeys when he approved the move of Saba and her family to this place— particularly since the move was going to cause such problems for everybody. He wondered if his mother might, indeed, be correct in suggesting that the man could be a Saytan who had come to cause havoc for everybody, using Desta as a means for his dirty plans and games. Desta now was even more worried about what this chain of events could mean.

Aside from Kooli, the monkeys were the only animals Desta truly could call his friends. It had been only about a year since he had first befriended these animals, winning their trust and friendship through a complicated series of tricks, cajoling and bribery. He remembered how happy he had been the first time he had touched their bristly, silver hair. And how much happier he had been ever since.

Now, with the trees cleared and Saba and her family moving on the cleared land, his friendship with the monkeys would only be a memory. Desta was saddened and confused by this realization. Why was he in the middle of this mess? Damtew's earlier threat and prediction had also begun to ring true for him, "A mess you started, God knows where it will end."

Although Desta couldn't see the monkeys, he could imagine their horror as they had watched their shelters and source of food being savagely destroyed. As he stood there engrossed by thought and scanning the forest for any signs of his friends, Desta was seized with a new fear. *What if after all this destruction of the forest and loss of his friends, his sister still had miscarriages and Yihoon's cattle still became sick and died?* The consequences terrified him. He would be blamed. He would be hated not only by Damtew but by everybody in the family.

He sat down. With his arms embracing his knees, eyes fixed to a fist-sized round rock inches from his feet, Desta concentrated his thoughts on Saba and her problems. If his sister didn't have a healthy baby after all this, he would rather die than live with constant torture from his brothers.

But death was another matter for Desta.

He closed his eyes and thought about the meaning of death. "Once we die and are buried, we will never come back," Desta remembered Asse'ged once telling him. Since then every time he thought of death, he would close his eyes and think of its meaning.

If I die today, he thought, *I will not come back tomorrow, not next week, not next month, not next year, not five years from now, not ten . . . and . . . and not . . .* He opened his eyes and shivered. He looked around and touched his body to assure himself he was still alive.

Never again to see the sun, the mountains, the monkeys and birds seemed very sad and very wrong. The ultimate shame for him, however, would be to die without touching and feeling the sky. He didn't want to think about death and dying anymore.

He lifted his head and gazed at the felled trees, a tangled mess. The branches from the big trees stuck up from the pile, their leaves wilted by the strong March sun.

Those trees are now killed, Desta thought. *I can sit here and wait, and wait, and wait, and wait, and wait . . . for a long time, and they will never get up and become live trees again.*

This thought saddened, scared and depressed him. He needed to go home.

When Desta returned home, he found his mother crouched by the side of a large cowhide, crushing the dried and smoked barley with a round stone, the ingredient for the upcoming wedding tella. As she pounded, the barley crumbled to pieces, giving rise to a grayish green cloud. Next to this mat was another large old hide containing freshly picked hop leaves and finely chopped twigs of the same plant.

"Where did you disappear to, Desta?" asked Ayénat.

"Oh, I just wanted to see what Yihoon and his men did to the trees in the forest," said Desta trying to sound casual.

She looked at him sharply. "It's not just the trees in the forest that are being affected by the problem that just started," said Ayénat. "All our families are going to be affected as a result of it."

For Desta it was not only the problem that he was the cause that scared him, it was having to deal with the problem without his sister Hibist at home. His eyes filled with tears as he crossed the doorstep.

THIRTEEN

It was a brilliant morning in mid-March. Desta was sitting under a circular flat-topped acacia tree waving flies away with a horsetail whisker and staring at a large round clay jar which contained the whey he would be drinking all day. The gray liquid was meant to be a purgative to a horrific disease the family feared he would contract.

A week earlier Desta had been bitten by his dog. There was no provocation for the attack but Kooli snapped and sank his teeth to Desta's shin when he was about to enter the house, causing his leg to bleed profusely. Alarmed by the incident, Abraham immediately irrigated the bite with plenty of water, dabbed it dry and bandaged it with a clean, white cloth. Then he promptly quarantined the dog. Having seen him sad and listless for a few days, they were not sure what ailed him.

Kooli, however, not only continued to be melancholic and listless but he also began to drool and eat less. The only person he repeatedly displayed aggressive behavior toward was Desta. Every time Desta passed by the dog, he barked and snapped at him. This non-stop problem, together with his listlessness and drooling, had caused Abraham to suspect the worst and he had decided to put the dog down.

Damtew readily accepted the grim task, but there ensued a minor feud in the logistics of administering it. While Abraham wanted Kooli shot, Damtew thought it a waste and wished to club the animal to death. A hit on the spinal cord, near the head would instantly take him out, he said. The father overruled him and Kooli was killed with a bullet.

With the departure of his friend and companion, Desta, in turn, became sad and listless. The adults explained to him the severe complication that could arise if the dog had contracted rabies and transferred it to humans. It was better, they said, to put him down than to expose people to the potentially horrific disease, but no amount of explanation was sufficient to soothe Desta's grief.

Uncertain what exactly had ailed Kooli, Abraham and Ayénat had to assume the worst.

Two weeks later, they treated Desta with home remedies that could purge the disease if he had contracted it.

The effort involved finding cheese that had aged for at least seven years—twelve or thirteen-year-old cheeses were considered the best. Ayénat scoured the valley's homes looking for anybody who had cheeses of that longevity. To her delight she found a woman in the section of the valley called Avegira who claimed to have cheese that was thirteen years old—dried and covered with mold at the bottom of a clay pot. The woman had scraped the pot and produced a half a cup of the dried, bluish-green cheese and had given it to Ayénat at church.

A contact of Abraham gave him the dried leaves of a secret plant to be mixed and pounded with the horrid smelling cheese. This powdery mixture was added to water and stirred. Desta, holding his nose to avoid smelling the ghastly mixture, downed it with one steady swig.

The strong and nauseating aftertaste nearly made Desta vomit. Ayénat gave him a tumbler of water to drink and told him to walk around until the medicine settled in his stomach. "The dog disease manifests itself in miniature dogs and other animals that hatch in the stomach," said Ayénat. "This medicine should kill these animals or arrest their production in their tracks."

While Ayénat was helping Desta with the drink, Abraham and Hibist had identified a place with a good shading tree, away from human traffic. Desta was to spend the day alone drinking whey and purging the disease through his mouth or anus. They had brought five-gallons of the gray liquid in a clay pot and a black horn cup and placed both at the side of a goatskin, securing the pot with three fist-sized rocks. Desta was to sit there, pour the whey into the cup at regular intervals, drink and excrete it all day.

After Abraham and Hibist returned, Ayénat led Desta to the prearranged location, sat him down on the skin and informed him of his task for the day. Every time he went to the bathroom, she told him, he was to investigate his excrement with a piece of stick for any signs of living or dead things, which could be in a shape of tiny dogs, insects, worms or any other animals.

What he had drunk was already turning in his stomach, threatening to fly out with the mention of the creatures that would be coming out of him. His chest heaved and his throat gagged. Ayénat poured a half cup of the whey and urged him to drink and walk around some more.

After pacing the ground for a few minutes, Desta sat on the skin and gazed at the horizon above the eastern mountains. He looked so despondent and miserable that Ayénat wondered if he was going to be diligent in his assigned task.

"You will do exactly as we told you, won't you, son?" said Ayénat, her hand on Desta's shoulder.

Desta said nothing, with his eyes still fixed on the horizon.

"It's a very bad disease that is incurable once you become sick with it. The only cure is death, and you don't want to die, do you?" pleaded Ayénat, shaking him a little.

Desta moved his head slightly to mean "no."

Wretched as he felt, gazing at the blue sky above the eastern mountains soothed and calmed him a little. For Desta dying without touching that azure surface would be the ultimate disappointment. He thought he must do everything he was told not to die. "Can you answer me in words—that you will do everything as told to you?"

"Yes," said Desta firmly.

Desta's first trip to the bathroom produced the everyday variety—a soft rounded gray mass speckled with whole grains and fibers containing nothing of the animals his mother had described. Desta was revolted by the idea of poking it with a stick as his mother had suggested. He returned to his perch without touching it.

For the first hour or so, Desta was nauseated and retched several times but nothing came out when he staggered and sat at the edge of the goatskin. Intermittently, he managed to focus on a number of thoughts. On the forefront of his mind was Kooli's behavior and his ultimate demise at Damtew's hands. He remembered all the good times he had spent with the dog as well as the incident that happened to him.

When Kooli was a puppy and Desta not even two months old, a cow had stepped on one of his legs, fracturing it. Abraham had mended the leg by wrapping around it small bamboo strips with a clean cloth, but the dog was never able to stand up straight or walk normally after that. As a result, he limped along with Desta wherever he went, keeping him company and playing with him. That he would never see Kooli again made his eyes wet and his heart sink in sadness.

It was while he was in this melancholic state that Ayénat showed up. Desta straightened himself quickly when he saw his mother.

"Have you gone to the bathroom yet?" she asked gazing down on him.

"Yes—just once," he said grimly.

"Did you do what I told you to do?" said she in a stern voice.

"No, Ma, no."

"Why not? We need to know if the medicine is working. If we see something of the nature I described, we need to increase the dosage or use a stronger medicine."

Desta's spirit sagged.

"Where is it?" demanded the mother.

"No, Ma, No!" said Desta again, covering his face. The prospect of getting up and leading his mother to where he deposited his first excrement embarrassed him.

"I need to see it."

She paced around the perimeter of the acacia tree.

"Please stop, Ma, nothing happened. There is nothing of the animals you described in it."

"I need to take a look anyway, I will *not* go home until I see it, so get up and show it to me," she demanded.

Desta pulled himself up grudgingly. He took his mother to a cluster of bushes about thirty feet up the hill and showed her his mound, which now had taken on a darker hue and was under the flies' strict surveillance. Ayénat snapped a twig from a nearby bush, stripped its leaves, shielded her nose and mouth with her sleeve and bent over and studied the pile. Desta covered his face, leaving just enough room through his fingers to see what his fanatical mother was about to do.

With the stick she sliced the pile from the top into two halves, provoking the flies to rise and hover over the mess.

"Uggghhh," emitted Desta in disgust.

She pushed and spread the first slice, her small eyes intensely glued to the activities of her hand as if she were looking for some precious stone.

Desta continued to gaze at his mother through his fingers, grimacing and shaking his head. As he stared at his excrement, Desta was struck by how much of the mixed beans and whole grains he had eaten the previous night came out unscathed by the juices of his digestive tract.

The first half of the pile produced nothing. She needed to knock down the second half and look there too. Combating the flies, she pushed aside or turned over anything that looked suspicious or maybe a harboring of the tiny animals.

She found nothing there, either.

Ayénat sighed, dropped the stick, and uncovered her mouth and nose and said: "I didn't see anything so far. Continue drinking the whey. I will come and inspect the next batches."

Desta still felt nauseated but also tired and starved now. "How long am I going to be here?" he asked.

"Till sunset."

"Without food?"

"You can't have food till evening or the medicine won't work," said his mother fixing him with her deep-set eyes.

To Desta, evening felt like eternity. He closed his eyes and thought, *if I want to touch the sky, I must be alive. To be alive I must be cured of this disease.* He gritted his teeth, screwed his face, and marched back to his place of isolation.

"I'll see you in a while," said his mother and left.

The more he drank of the thin, grayish liquid, the more repulsive it became to him. Hunger had burrowed deep in his stomach, overpowering him as much as the monotony of imbibing the same fluid all day. Everything in his bowels seemed to have been washed out of him. He tipped the jar and poured himself another cup, brought it to his lips and downed the sickening liquid in one long, breathless chug.

The sun had turned west and began to hit Desta directly. He lethargically rose and moved the skin around where the shadow of the tree had rotated north. He left the jar where it stood.

The relocation of his seat afforded Desta a clearer and direct view of Saba and Yihoon's new property. He noticed that not only had nearly all the trees in the proscribed area been cut down, but Yihoon and his men had also chopped the branches into smaller pieces and the trunks into chunks and had piled them at multiple locations, readying them for fire. They also had created a footpath from the creek to the flatter, mid part of the property, where Yihoon would build the new home. Around this general area, he observed pockmarks in the earth where tree stumps had been dug out. Here and there he saw piles of bamboo and split wood which Desta thought were the building materials for their new home.

This observation brought back a flood of memories: the problems Saba had been having, Damtew and Asse'ged's threats to him, that man and Deb'tera

Tayé and how he, Desta, had been treated as an outcast because of his involvement in helping solve his sister's problems.

In the condition he was in, the last thing he wanted to do was torture himself with these bad remembrances. He thought a nap would help disconnect him from his recollections and help speed up the day. As he was about to lie down, he saw two figures shuffling on the path that went to Yihoon and Saba's newly cleared property. Desta couldn't make out the faces. The strong sun and the massive liquid he had been consuming had made him drowsy and his eyes blurry.

Squinting and moving his head to get a better look of the figures, he determined that they were his sister, Saba and her daughter, Astair. Desta sat up straight and watched the pair as they walked the trail that went to the creek. *They must be going to their new property*, he thought. Suddenly Astair noticed Desta and blurted, "There is Desta! Ma!"

Saba followed her daughter's gaze. A discernable grin crossed Saba's face when she saw him. They left the trail and walked uphill toward him.

"How are you Desta?" said Saba, halting several yards from him.

"I am not good but I think I will make it. . . . I am surprised to see you. What brings you this way?" said Desta.

"We heard you weren't doing well. Astair and I thought we would come see you," said Saba not moving from where they stood.

"Kooli bit my leg," said Desta in a weak, cheerless voice. "Baba and Mama think he might have been sick with the disease that makes dogs and people go mad. They were afraid I would become sick with it unless I got treated, so they gave me this nasty medicine this morning. Kooli didn't even go mad, but they killed him anyway."

"That is what Hibist told us," said Saba with empathy. "I am sorry to hear what happened to your friend. It's a bad, bad disease and they didn't want to take chances in case he bites other people too."

"Can you not come closer?"

"No, we don't want to cast our shadow on you. The medicine you have taken will not work otherwise. . . . We can come a little closer but not that close," said Saba as she took a few steps toward Desta. Astair did the same.

"Yes, that is what mother said to me this morning."

"I know I have not seen you for months, but we came here in part to thank you for being, hopefully, a part of the solution to our problems," said Saba, speaking as much in her beautiful brown eyes as in her melodic vocal cords.

"I have not done anything. I only repeated what the man told me. Hopefully all this will work."

"We know that. The man you talked about never revealed himself to anybody else but you. This means you are a special boy in our family," said Saba.

"I wish everybody else felt the same. More importantly, I hope that cloud man will not let you and me down. As you might know there are many people who think that I made him up. I didn't. I have seen and felt him in many different ways: my dreams, in person and even just in feelings. Baba had said that all I need to do is believe in him and he will do what he said he will do," said Desta in an eager and hurried voice.

"We know. For us even a change of the soil will probably do us some good. Things have gotten worse not better where we have lived."

"Things have gotten worse for me too. You know Damtew and Asse'ged—" Desta hesitated when he saw his mother rambling across the shoulder of the hill. "Don't go to the creek to fetch water by yourself. Send Astair to get water until you move to your new place. I fear the worst for you," he said hurriedly.

"Why did you say that?"

"I don't know for sure, but just do what I told you."

Desta's mother greeted her step-daughter rather indifferently.

"Be well. Hope to see you soon," said Astair, as she and Saba departed.

Ayénat grumbled about the visit. Desta had explained that he had not invited them. They came on their own.

"Where have you been depositing your stool?" said his mother abruptly.

"I have not had any, Ma. It's just the whey that is coming out and it's gone underground," said Desta, avoiding eye contact with his mother.

"Where did you go to the bathroom—the same place?" queried Ayénat again, tossing her head in the direction he had taken her the first time.

"No, Ma, why do you have to do this again? I am telling you, nothing came out of me but water—no dogs, cows, goats, sheep, birds, insects, nothing!" said Desta, exasperated.

"I need to see them for myself. Or I am not leaving," said his mother as she paced around the outer perimeter of the tree looking for Desta's excrements again.

Shaky and weak, Desta finally rose and staggered up the hill farther to the left from where he deposited his first excrement. Ayénat followed him with a piece of stick.

"There," he said pointing to the two patches of wetted ground. Traces of undigested food residue were left behind after the liquid had seeped through the dirt.

With the new stick, Ayénat poked and scraped the wet earth looking for any traces of animals—dead or alive—that might have come out of her son's body. She found none. She was pleased with her discovery. "In another hour or so, I will send Hibist to collect things from here and you will come home," she said.

Desta tottered back to his spot. The sun was already low and approaching the horizon above their home. Only slanted shafts were coming through the bushes. The shadow from the acacia tree was long and spear-like. Desta closed his eyes and waited for Hibist to come and collect him.

When he woke, he found Hibist had decanted the remaining whey and inserted the cup into the mouth of the jar.

"Good, you are awake, I didn't want to disturb you," said Hibist in her chirpy voice.

"I'm happy you are here finally. I get to go home and eat something," said Desta, groggy and sleepy.

"We have prepared fresh food and you can eat to your heart's content." Desta salivated with the thought of food. He couldn't wait to get home.

"Mama said you either didn't have it or are cured of the disease. She found nothing in your elimination," said Hibist, gazing at her brother.

"Mama will be proud of you," said Desta.

"What?"

"With your choice of words."

"Of course," said Hibist, confused."You always used that other word when we found the hyena's droppings," Desta said, grinning.

"Oh that." It suddenly dawned on her what the compliment was about. "Well, that was referring to the hyena. My brother deserves a little more dignity," she said, smiling broadly.

"Thank you. You are sweet."

Hibist lifted the jar with the rope and slung it on her back. Desta carried the rolled up skin on his shoulders. Although weak and emaciated, he still could manage. He teetered behind his sister. He was happy everything was finally over and he didn't have the disease. He hoped not, anyway.

FOURTEEN

Groggy and not fully awake, Desta raised his head from his goatskin sleeping mat and listened to the faint sounds of discussion taking place in the living room. From the snatches of phrases that reached him, the conversation had something to do with his dog bite and a further treatment he needed to have to ensure complete cure. A familiar male voice was recommending the additional treatment. Desta cocked his ears and listened some more. The voice was that of his maternal grandfather—Grandpa Farris, one of the boy's favorite relatives.

Desta spilled out of the raised bedding platform and landed on the floor. He wrapped himself in his gabi and went to greet his grandfather. He kissed the old man's knees first. His grandfather gently grabbed him by the chin and kissed him three times on the cheeks, grazing Desta's soft skin with his bristly beard. Desta sat next to him. His grandpa's coarse beard was the only thing he didn't like about him.

Zegeye Farris was a man of about five foot seven inches with a round face and dark, rough skin and fine features. His small eyes twinkled under heavy brows. He had a full head of hair that he kept short. He often came dressed in his long cream-colored breeches and light shirt over which he wore his gabi and black wool cape.

Grandpa Farris extended a hand and began caressing Desta's woolly hair. The endearing touch made Desta feel good, causing him to wish once again that his grandpa could live with them or that he had more grandfathers like him. While his parents were looking on, Desta explained to his grandfather how he had been bitten by Kooli and how his brother had killed the dog under his father's order. He also told his grandfather about the horrid treatment.

Grandpa Farris explained in his rough but gentle voice that Desta's parents had to do what they did because the dog's disease could kill unless treated immediately. To ensure complete cure, grandpa said that Desta now must also take the communion.

"What's the communion?" Desta asked.

"It's the blood and flesh of Christ," answered his grandfather.

Desta contorted his face and declared he was in no mood to eat someone's flesh and drink his blood. "Who is Christ anyway?"

"Christ is the son of God, who came to free us from our sins."

"What is sin?"

"A sin is like stealing, lying, killing and doing other bad things," said Grandpa.

Desta was quiet, trying to remember if he had done any of those things.

"Although we often do sinful things," continued Grandpa. "Christ can forgive our sins if we do good things."

"Is getting bit by a dog a sin, too?" Desta was asking when he was interrupted by his mother.

"Abayé, as you know, this boy could keep you all night with his questions. Let's stop here for now. Dinner is about to be served. Hibist, please bring water for their hands."

"It's good that he asks questions. That is how he learns about these things," said the grandfather, turning to his daughter. "He will grow up to be an honest and God-fearing man."

"Yes, but he never stops once he starts with the questions. Let's have dinner," said Ayénat.

FIFTEEN

"Why are these women standing out here by the trees?" Desta stopped in his tracks and stared at the veiled women who stood among the trees.

"They may be unclean," said his mother. "They may have recently given birth or they may be in their periods or have spent the previous night with their husbands," said Ayénat.

"Spending the night with their husbands makes women unclean?" said Desta a little louder than he intended to.

"Ssshhh. Do you have to know everything? Stop asking questions. Let's keep walking," said the mother, scowling.

A few yards later Desta saw men with their backs to the trees, their walking sticks planted on the ground, hoisting their arms. Their mouths were covered with the folds of their shemma or gabi edging their nostrils, leaving just enough space for air to enter and leave. A question danced on Desta's tongue, but fearing his mother would scold him, he swallowed it. Privately, he concluded that these men must be the husbands of the women they had passed earlier.

Since the evening when Desta's grandfather suggested he go to church to receive the communion as a supplemental ward against possible dog diseases, he had been secretly wondering what the interior of a church looked like and what it would be like to cross the Davola River for the first time.

From a distance, Desta was familiar with every nook and cranny of the land beyond the Davola—the corrugated façade of the mountains and their wave-like peaks and ridges that rose to the clouds and circled his world; the knolls and humps of earth that projected from the sides of the mountains and from lowlands like bumps from tree trunks; the deep and dark green canyons where he imagined creeks traversed down crooked and rocky courses; the legendary plateau in the south, beyond which the adults said lay a sheer cliff and where, according to them, enemies used to settle old scores by gagging and tying their victims and tossing them down the precipice; the smooth, immense rock that glistened and reflected the sun like a sheet of glass when wet; the hamlet of thatched roof houses that rose from hillocks, lowlands and mountain sides like mushrooms on dead wood trunks; and the two churches, on the north and south sides of the valley, enveloped by copses of verdure.

Visually, to Desta all these places were as familiar as the sun, the moon and the stars he observed when he gazed into the sky, but he had never had the opportunity to personally explore any of them.

He also was familiar with the various localities. There was the village of Avegira on the northern slopes below the Lehwani mountain ranges, Avinevra northeast, Dega Avesken directly east and Tuff Gumbla south of his home.

The crack of the shepherds' whips, the lowing of the cattle on the hills, the shouting voices of the farmers driving plow-pulling oxen, the cackle and laughter of the hyenas at night, the predawn deep and tearing guttural calls of the colobus monkeys; the medley of colors—the blues, reds, violets, greens and gold—that came and went with the change of the seasons and the pure, soothing fragrance of the air. All these things he saw, heard and smelt from where he lived, but he had never had a personal experience with any of them. This trip would give him the opportunity to see some of the places at closer range, to walk their grounds and to meet some of the people that lived on the other side of the river.

On the appointed Sunday, Desta was awakened by his mother and ordered to wash his face, put on the newly washed gabi and white shirt, and get ready to go to church with her. He would not be permitted to eat or drink anything until after he had received God's flesh and blood at church. The thought of eating God's meat and drinking his blood had revolted Desta, but Ayénat had explained that it was only symbolic. He would actually be eating bread and drinking water—holy bread and water, she had emphasized. As he prepared for the trip, Desta hung on to this notion and not to the other.

They took the dusty footpath around the wattled fence of their home down to the big open cattle field below. The trail sliced the field on the north side and snaked through a thicket of woods before it linked up with the major north-south caravan route that ran along the Davola River. After two miles on the main road, Ayénat and Desta turned on a side path. This path slanted along a gentle slope and came to a narrow flat land of farms, a cluster of homes and a cattle field. Half a dozen girls stood near the entrances of the houses and a similar number of shepherds in the fields stood in place and watched Ayénat and Desta shuffle past. A dog too sick or too tired to get up gazed at them listlessly, opening and closing its mouth as if trying to bark.

Desta lagged behind his mother briefly and studied his surroundings, the people and the animals. He wondered what disease had killed the dog's vocal cords. Since he was going to be a full-fledged shepherd in a few months, he wished he could talk to the boys to find out what it was like to spend all day doing nothing but watching after the animals. He had never met any boys from this side of the Davola before. He knew for sure they were not the ones that made those amazing sounds with their whips whom someday he had hoped to emulate. The other shepherds lived right across from his home.

I bet these kids are capable, too, Desta thought as he trotted to catch up with his mother. As he ran, he caught a glimpse of a long, narrow stretch of tree-veiled land that disappeared into a hazy horizon far in the distance.

"Mama, mama, mama!" shouted Desta as he ran breathlessly.

His mother stopped and waited for him.

"Is that all part of the earth?" he asked pointing and hyperventilating.

"Yes, a little ways from here is Danka. Then there is Fagita, and way at the end, where the haze is dark and thick is Kuakura–your father's birthplace," said his mother her small eyes dreamily probing into the landscape.

"Wow. Is that how big the earth is?" Desta gazed at the distance land in wonder. "I didn't think there was anything else beyond here."

"There is a lot more to the earth than we have around here," said Ayénat. "Let's keep walking, we can't be late."

Desta followed her quietly thinking about his discovery.

The path wound along a slope and dipped into a wooded gurgling brook, beyond which the terrain rose sharply. At the creek, another major trail came downhill from the right and joined the one they were on.

Once they crossed the stream, Desta limped ahead of his mother up the hill, dodging toe-bleeding rocks and rain-washed pits. Although his wound from the dog bite still bothered him, particularly as he climbed uphill, the excitement of seeing a church had masked much of the pain. He couldn't wait to get there. Ayénat walked as if she had stones attached to her feet. Desta had to stop and wait for her a few times. She breathed heavily, and a dew of sweat had dampened her forehead.

There were other people walking on the same path. Some greeted his mother with a slight bow of their heads without a word, others said good morning as they passed. Some of these people glanced sidewise at Desta and continued. Others complimented his lightness of feet as he hopped up the hill easily.

It occurred to Desta that he was the only person of his age—boy or girl—who was going to church. Undoubtedly, he was the only person from the valley who had been bitten by a dog and needed to eat God's flesh and drink his blood to be healed.

After the steep climb, the land leveled out and the path passed through what looked like a plaza or public gathering area. Here there were rows of stones, carved benches and large flat logs on either side of the trail. The ground of the plaza was compacted from heavy use but tufts of viridescent grass grew under the benches and around the rock seats. Ayénat explained that this was where large festivities, such as the church holidays and other events, were held. She also pointed to the north corner of the plaza, where there was a separate row of benches and stones. She said this was the place where his father held court on Sundays. Desta wished he could be here to see his father at such gatherings.

Farther north of the plaza, the land ascended gently for a short distance and then shot up to the sky to meet the clouds and high-flying birds.

"That up there is Lehwani," said Ayénat, pointing.

Desta tilted his head and looked through the tall oak trees in front of him. He saw a glimpse of the mammoth mountain's peak. Of course, he knew Lehwani from distance. He had seen its face for as long as he could remember, but never this close.

"Let's keep going", said Ayénat, turning around.

Desta trotted behind her again.

Past the plaza, the path entered a wooded ground, more like the familiar forest around his home. But Desta noted there were many things different about this place. Unlike the forest near his home, this one teemed with leafy undergrowths and had towering trees with large, brown, fuzzy trunks.

"Those are tsed. They make church walls and doors with them and they smell very nice," said his mother when she saw him craning his neck to check out the massive trees.

The air here was chilled and smelled sweet and earthy. The ground was damp and strewn with leaves—green, brown and yellow—which were cool and soothing to Desta's bare feet. Shafts of the morning sun had seeped through the trees and dappled the floor with light, making their walk colorful and pleasant.

After awhile Desta halted again. It was almost as if there were invisible strings pulling at his neck. This time he inspected the long, thin leaves of a plant.

"Those are kirkaha," said his mother. "We use them to make baskets, roofs and wall trusses. Let's move on. We can't be late!"

As they walked along the variegated path, Desta was struck by the hushed, enveloping tranquility which he never experienced when he hiked in the woods around his home. But the preternatural quietude was not to last. Reedy, trailing and melodic singing voices pierced the serenity. Desta at first was not certain whether they came from deep within the earth or from the far recesses of the forest. He stopped to listen. The voices trailed off and stopped as suddenly as they had begun. He walked for a bit and halted again when he heard the singing restart. To his ears, the voices sounded pure, beautiful and enchanting. The stillness of the place had amplified them, allowing the unadulterated notes of each singer's voice to permeate through the air, crisply and lucidly. They resonated deep within his senses. He was enthralled. He didn't want to move. He turned slightly and bent his neck to the ground. Cocking his ears, he tried to pick up the blurred lyrics that floated towards him.

"What are you looking at now?" asked Ayénat, retracing her steps, exasperated. Once near him, she too gazed down to determine the object of his curiosity.

"I am listening, aren't they beautiful—who's singing?" said Desta.

"My lord, I thought you discovered some exotic ants or something," said Ayénat, chuckling. "Those are the priests singing. You will hear them more when we go inside the church. Move on!"

As thick and lush as the forest was, Desta noted that the birds did not twitter and chirp, nor the monkeys made noises. To him, it was as if these animals were also enchanted by the liquid-like voices of the priests.

Desta chased his mother, keeping his ears cocked to the priests' singing. When they neared the church's entrance, something else hit his curiosity: the sweet, rich fragrance of the air had giving way to a pleasant but singular aroma of incense, which Ayénat said was burned by the priests.

They had seen so much along their walk. Ayénat had already admonished him many times for lingering and staring at things and people. For now, Desta just wanted to observe and record to memory what he was experiencing.

The path ended at a rectangular thatched roof house framed on either side by lofty woodcarvings that abutted the beginnings of mossy, crumbling stone walls. There was a line of people at the entrance. Desta and his mother had to wait.

Over the stone wall loomed the conical roof of a house much larger and more rugged than any Desta had ever seen. Atop its pinnacle rose a miniature, parasol-like roof whose eaves were skirted by tiny metallic chimes that quivered in the wind and shimmered in the sun. Inserted on the ferrule of this miniature roof was an egg many times larger than that of a hen's. Desta's eyes were not coming down from the roof until he found out whether it was a real egg or something else. This time, instead of asking, he gazed at the ovoid object for a long time and then turned toward his mother and stared at her. He did this so frequently that Ayénat finally broke her silence.

"That is an Ostrich egg," she said.

"What's an ostrich? Is it like a hen?"

"No, it's a big bird!"

"What is it doing up there?"

"It's to remind the parishioners that we should be as diligent and devoted to our religion as the ostrich is to her eggs. It's symbolic, like many things are in our church," said Ayénat.

Desta tried to visualize the bird that could lay that egg. *She must be as big as a cow,* he thought. He wondered where a bird like that lived. He wanted to ask his mother more about the bird, but he knew what the answer would be. He squelched his questions.

Once again, Ayénat scolded Desta for ogling everything he saw and hurried him toward the church entrance. Before she set foot onto the threshold of the gatehouse, Desta watched his mother touch the doorjamb with her forehead and lips three times. He had seen several men and women do the same thing before her. He just kissed the doorjamb once before he entered the gatehouse. The threshold was high and massive for Desta's legs. His mother hoisted him by the armpit so he could cross it. The two reddish brown wooden doors were also massive, as was the arcing capital above.

The interior of the gatehouse was a large rectangular room with benches around it. A dozen nuns in tight-fitting cotton skull caps and long girdled gowns sat on the benches, counting their rosaries. Some had russet glass beads; others had small tawny wooden ones. The slacked loops rested on their laps. Other women of different ages perched on these benches interspersed among the nuns with their heads veiled and bent in prayer.

Beyond the gatehouse, the church stood bound by a verdant, circular courtyard. Ayénat stopped at the center of the small house. Turning her face in the direction of the church, she crossed herself three times, bowing after each act, and prostrated on the floor after the third bow. She kneeled and planted her forehead on the matted floor for a long time. She was saying things in a hushed tone. Desta caught a few stray words. They were about his dog bite and asking God to heal him.

After she rose, Ayénat and Desta sat on an empty bench near the interior door, where they had a better view of the church courtyard. They needed to wait till Tamirat came to take Desta inside the church so he could receive his God's flesh and blood.

Tamirat soon appeared, dressed in a cloak that had red, green and gold colors with tongue-like strips cascading down his chest. On the cloak were metallic dots that glittered in the sun. Desta, impressed by his brother's apparel, battled a secret desire to touch the fabric and study the patterns and colors on it, but Tamirat immediately ushered him outdoors and across the amber-green courtyard, into the circular church.

As they hurried across the yard, Desta observed a great number of men standing around the stone wall, some reading books, others leaning on their walking sticks and appearing humble and repentant. At the far corners, tussocks of grass grew wild against the stone barrier and around some of the stone seats. Nearby, rose bushes with blood red blooms embowered the wall top in vivid contrast to the verdure beyond and the mossy gray stones below.

A woven bamboo skirted the exterior of the church from its eaves to the ground. They went through an open door and stepped onto a floor, twenty feet deep from the first interior wall. Soft animal skins and smooth palm leaf mats covered the grass-strewn floor. The aroma of the incense was overpowering and the ambience warm, serene and comforting.

Here too, there were mostly men with a few older women standing along the bamboo wall, some murmuring, others reading books or reciting something they knew by heart. Others still were kneeling with their faces on the floor.

Desta hesitated and his eyes lingered on the men and women who lined the walls or prostrated themselves on the floor.

"Come, come," urged Tamirat, standing before an immense set of closed wooden doors that rested on a massive threshold. These doors were framed with decorative arched headers and jambs.

High on the wall to the left of the door stood a man dressed in colorful brocade, looking down on Desta amiably. The man had wings that were partially unfurled. His head rested on a circular orange-colored disk and he held a sword in one hand.

Desta gazed at the man, wondering who he was and why he had wings like a bird and why he was standing on the wall with a sword in his hand. On the right wall was a pretty, big-eyed woman with a baby who appeared about six or so months old. She too had a disk around her head. There were also two people on either side above her shoulders, looking as if they were about to whisper in her ears. She looked reticent and virtuous as she stared into the distance. Only the baby seemed to look down on Desta. Both the man on the other side of the wall and the woman with baby looked unlike anybody Desta knew—their skin very fair, their hands soft and delicate, and their disposition unworldly. A string of queries brimmed in Desta's brain, particularly about the winged man, but it was not the time to ask them.

Tamirat had pushed open one of the doors and stood on the inner ledge of the doorsill. The boy hesitated—not wanting to walk on the beautiful mats with his dusty feet. When his brother waved at him to come quickly, he crossed the floor and joined him at the entrance. It was pitch black inside and Desta stood by the door staring at it.

"Where are you taking me?" Desta whispered, pensive and fearful.

"This is the interior of the church," Tamirat whispered back.

"Why so dark?"

Tamirat had no time to explain. He kept motioning his little brother to come in.

Desta heard muffled laughter from behind. He turned. A swarm of eyes were on him.

By the smiling faces and chuckling under the piled fabric beneath their noses, it was obvious to Desta that the onlookers must have found his skittish and tentative moves humorous. Tamirat glanced at the people and smiled too. He grabbed Desta by the hand and tugged him in. Desta closed his eyes and groped for the step and the floor with his feet.

"Why did you close your eyes? Open them, open them," urged his brother.

"What good will it do? I can't see anything in here anyway. I don't want to see where you are taking me."

"This is just another part of the church."

Tamirat closed the door and made Desta stand against the wall by the entrance. "Stay here until you receive the communion. I'll come and fetch you after the services are over."

Alone now, with his back pressed to the wall, Desta opened and closed his eyes, trying as hard as he could to see if there was anything discernable. The chanting and singing voices appeared to come not from deep within the earth but from deep within something in front of him.

He heard a rustling sound to his left followed by a guttural, throat-clearing type of noise. He turned to see. The more he concentrated in the direction of the noise, the more the darkness lifted. A dull and faded light seemed to have seeped in, not from any particular source, but somehow the darkness had transmuted into pale light on its own accord. Desta saw the dull white of someone's shemma. Or was it a gabi? He couldn't tell. He kept looking and looking. The figure became clearer and clearer, now more than an outline or a silhouette. It was a woman—an old woman, standing only a few feet from him, leaning on a cane. Her shemma now was a few notches lighter. She wore a gray skullcap. She eyed him from time to time as she said her prayers.

Satisfied that it was a human and not some monster, Desta turned and looked straight ahead. He could now see a curving, rugged wall with closed double doors behind an arched entry. The doorsill was similar in width and design to the ones he had already passed. There was another man, this time high up on the left wall. He could see, in the faded light, only the overall image of the man. He was on a cloud-white horse, holding a long spear that was wielded into the mouth of a beast the likes of which Desta had never before seen. The beast had a tail, a fat torso and a gaping mouth. Its teeth gleamed in the pale light, and frothy shadowed blood oozed out of the corners of its mouth. With his hair streaked back, the man appeared as if he had just flown through a strong wind. This man, like the others Desta had seen by the first entrance, was fairer than anybody he knew and had a golden disk behind his head.

The man's eyes were anxious and intense as he gazed at the animal he had vanquished. It all looked gruesome to Desta. Who was he? Why had he killed that strange animal? Desta looked away from the dead creature to see if there was a lamb or kid it might have killed that caused the man to attack, but there was no other animal. In the muted light, Desta tried to make out the details of the dark-gray beast. The more he kept his eyes on it, the clearer it became. It had a coiled tail and a sharp ridge that ran from its head to its tail. The feet beneath its metallic belly were stubby and clawed.

When Desta viewed the entire animal, he determined it was nothing but a lizard. He saw these creatures every day when he walked the grounds of his parents' property. But why so big? And what did it do to cause that man to so viciously attack? The lizards Desta knew were harmless animals. The adults never warned him against them. The snakes, yes. "Always carry a stick when you walk in the field or the forest," Ayénat had warned him. The stick was to be a protection against a snake that might rear its head and spit its venom if Desta ran into it by accident. Like the other people he saw earlier, this man was just as mysterious.

His thoughts drifted back to the singing voices. He now knew where they were coming from: behind the massive and lofty circular wall in front of him, the innermost chamber of the church.

Once his eyes adapted to the round hall, Desta could see more, albeit what he saw was still very dull and faded. More people—men and older women—in their white apparel loomed around him.

Desta was getting hungry. He wondered how much longer he would have to wait before the services were finished and he could go home and eat something. "When you go to receive God's flesh and blood, no food should have passed your gullet," Ayénat had said to him the night before. Now hunger pangs had begun to nibble at him.

The singers stopped and suddenly everything went quiet. Desta could hear only the occasional rustle and throat-clearing of the same neighbor. He was getting bored from standing alone in the shadowy place. He slouched a little as if to sit down.

"Mass is about to start. Stand up straight," commanded the woman.

Whatever that meant. Desta stood erect.

Mass started. Someone behind the thick wall before him began reading something, fast-paced and loud, as if intended for everyone outside to hear. Desta wondered if the women who had spent the night with their husbands, whom he and Ayénat first saw at the outer precinct of the church, could hear the man. He read and read and read and then broke into an almost seamless transition of singing in a trailing and smooth cadence. Shortly after the man was done, a younger, purer and intensely more beautiful singing voice took over. The progression of the voice was hypnotic and the feeling it aroused in Desta was thrilling. Desta wished he could sing like that.

As mass continued, a man in a long flowing gown with colorful brocade opened the door before him and came out, swinging an incense burner that hung from three metal chains with chiming trinkets festooned on them. The man was

escorted by a younger man dressed in red, gold and green, tinkling a bell. They
walked around the circular hallway, the man rattling the incense burner and
leaving behind and in front of him a swirling cloud of the sweet aroma. As they
circled the hall, they opened the doors to the outer hallway, trading the aroma for
light.

The mass was very long. How long, Desta didn't know. It involved singing,
reading, reciting and chanting. Occasionally one or two priests came out to fill
the air with the fragrance of incense. Everything was in the ancient language of
Ge'ez and Desta didn't understand a word they read or sang.

One of the priests who emerged from the sanctuary was the bearded man,
Aba Yacob, who had come to baptize Desta when Ayénat suspected he was
possessed by the Saytan. A young man who held a silver pitcher with one
hand and a bowl of similar make with the other was with him. The two stood
straddling the threshold of the inner chamber, where the bearded man washed
his hands with the water the young man poured from the pitcher. He shook
his wet hands a little and dabbed them dry with a white cloth he took from the
young man's shoulder.

During the service Desta noticed there were certain rules he must follow.
Not knowing what they were, he simply mimicked the old woman next to him.
When he saw her prostrate on the floor, he did the same, sneaking occasionally
to see if she was still in her supplicating position. When she got up, he followed
suit. When he heard the woman whisper prayers, he closed his eyes and prayed,
asking God to give Kooli a happy place in heaven. He repeated this over and
over and over. He wished Tamirat or Ayénat had given him a few lines of
prayers.

Near the end of the services, a sharp drum beat jolted Desta to attention. This
was followed by the tolling of a bell and by the appearance of the bearded priest,
accompanied by two more young people, one of whom was Tamirat. The priest
was holding something under the cover of a pale green cloth while the second
young man carried water in a silver vase. Tamirat held an umbrella and a silver
bell which he tolled continuously. Desta thought it odd for Tamirat to carry an
umbrella inside a house. A beeswax candle placed on a holder by the entrance had
brightened the room.

When Desta saw these people emerge from the room he threw himself on the
floor and covered his face, pretending to pray. To his embarrassment, when he
looked to his left to see if the woman had also dropped to the floor, he noticed

that she was still standing, saying her prayers, bending her neck a little.

A man came and picked Desta up and brought him before the familiar priest. Aba Yacob ordered him to open his mouth, then dropped into it a bead-sized, sweet tasting, warm bread that had the aroma of incense. The man who held water in the silver chalice tipped the chalice for Desta to draw from it, then he wiped the mouth of the chalice with white cloth.

The bearded man told Desta to cover his mouth before he walked to his place. Once back in his corner, Desta chewed and chewed and chewed on the flesh of God, trying to savor every bit of it. God's blood had barely wetted his tongue, but Desta kept smacking his tongue trying to determine the flavor of it.

He had thought he would retch from eating God's flesh and drinking his blood, but he actually enjoyed the bread and wished he could have more of it. He watched as more people, including mothers with babies, lined up to receive God's flesh and blood.

At the conclusion of the service, Tamirat came and they walked out into bright daylight. Desta was happy to be out in the cool open air. The courtyard was full of milling people. The two siblings joined their mother and walked to the chapel where, as Tamirat had said, they would break their fast. At the chapel, the bearded man who had given him God's bread and blood several minutes earlier and who a few months before tried to exorcise the Saytan out of him, sliced with a sharp knife the piled bread, two or three layers at once, into eight wedges and passed them out to the congregation.

Desta was still hungry. He couldn't wait till he got home so he could eat a big quantity of food.

SIXTEEN

First it was the vervets. Second it was Kooli. Now it is Hibist about to leave me. What have I done to deserve all this? Desta lay on his back, staring at the smoke-stained ceiling on which flames from the fireplace wavered, nodded and danced. Lately, he had been horribly preoccupied by Hibist's upcoming wedding. His nights had been sleepless; his days monopolized by his fear of loneliness and abandonment. *After Hibist is gone, who can I talk to when I have problems?*

The answer scared Desta. *Nobody!* There were no boys of his age nearby or any other closer siblings with whom he could share his feelings, thoughts and problems. He was an outcast to many of the family members. Hibist had been his support, his shield against anyone who criticized or scolded him and his dinnertime companion and hiking buddy.

With his father often gone and his mother too busy with her domestic chores to give him the attention and love he needed, Hibist had fulfilled the role of both. After the wedding, not only will he have lost Hibist but he would also be living with two complete strangers—the wives of his brothers, one of whom he honestly disliked. As the wedding preparations gathered steam, Desta became more and more depressed. He walked around listlessly with a dour face and red, somber eyes.

Two nights before the wedding, he woke again. A whispered conversation around the fire drew his attention. Two women were huddled there, tossing something that looked like a potato between their hands. He got up and tiptoed toward them. Hibist, who had her back toward him, was startled when she turned around and saw Desta's shadowed form. He apologized.

They were sucking the air nervously as they held the potato-like objects for a few seconds at a time between the tosses. Next to them was a wide-mouth metal pot holding more of the potato-like object.

"What are you doing? What is that?" asked Desta.

"It's *insocila*," said Hibist. She tossed the insocila from one hand to the other before she passed it to the other girl, their cousin, Genet.

"What is insocila?"

"It's a root that colors your hands magenta," said his sister, bringing her hand to the fire to show the stain.

"We have a long way to go, but it will eventually look magenta" said Genet.

Desta squatted next to the girls. "Why is she blowing air on to it as she tosses it?"

"It's hot," said Genet. "It was cooked to make the color come out more."

Hibist gave Desta the look. He stopped asking.

"It looks dangerous and hot to me, but . . .," Desta started to say.

"But what . . . go back to bed," snapped Hibist.

"Nothing, just, I hope you change your mind about going to live with a strange guy and his parents," said Desta, looking away.

"Desta, first, it's not my choice, our father and mother have arranged it. Second, I will come to visit you often. Mother said it's not very far where I will be going."

"Well, I just thought I would tell you what has been bothering me since mother told me what has been going on around here."

"Everything will be alright, Desta. Just think of it. You will have two for the price of one," said Hibist smiling.

"What I said was not a joke!"

Miffed, Desta trundled back to bed. He lay on his back and watched the flames from the fire flicker on the glistening bamboo, thinking about his sister and her nonchalance in the face of his heart-felt concerns.

When he finally drifted into slumber, Desta found himself in a dreamland. He was under the sholla tree below his home, alone, keeping an eye on the animals. Shortly after, there appeared the man in his usual cloud-like form. Desta was unhappy to be seeing him again and wondered why he kept doing this to him.

"You are way too stressed about your sister leaving you. Why??" asked the cloud man in a rather scolding manner.

Desta thought about the question for a moment. Then he said, "I don't know why you keep appearing in my life like this. I have been going through hell because of what you started. Could you please leave me alone?"

"That was not what I asked. Answer my question first."

"Well, what do you want me to do, dance and laugh when the person who has been closest to me is just about to be taken away?" Desta was surprised by his response. He didn't mean to be that confrontational.

"That is just it. You see, you have befriended monkeys, a dog and your sister all these years. You have to start to learn how to live with strangers—the new ladies that will be coming. There will come a time when you will live with nobody but strangers. This opportunity is given to you so you can start to adapt to change and learn how to live with your losses. Incidentally, you should also not expect your sister to be like Kooli—this point will be apparent to you later. She is only human and, as such, she doesn't have the profundity of feeling and loyalty that dogs have.

"I know you resent my appearing in your life again, but I am here to tell you, once and for all, that everything that has happened and will yet happen to you is for good reason. Those reasons will be explained to you in due time. For now, you have to be strong and accept things as they unfold in your daily life."

Desta stared at the cloud man, perplexed.

"Did you follow what I just said?" said the figure.

"I did, but what do you want me to do with all that stuff?"

"Just remember what I said, and everything will be all right—in the end," said the man. Then he slipped out of sight.

SEVENTEEN

Desta rose the following morning to something he had long been dreading. It was the day Hibist, Damtew and Tamirat were to be married. His home was swimming with people—aunts, uncles and cousins—as well as friends from around the valley and far away, some he knew, others he was seeing for the first time. Among the guests were a dozen or so children, a few around his age, others older or younger. Desta was amazed by the chaotic wedding preparations.

At the two indoor fireplaces, two women were busy baking injera and piling them in baskets. Outside, another pair tended large pots of cooking sauces.

The goats' and horses' stalls had been fixed up superbly for the event. Walls were sealed and draped with white cloths, the floors padded with dry grass over which were spread elegant cowhides and goatskins. White and black colobus monkey skins created accent, a great contrast on the walls and floors. *The goats and horses will never recognize their rooms*, said Desta after seeing the amazing transformation. He was equally struck by the number of antelope skins that adorned the floors in the rest of the house.

The big thatched tent was also decorated beautifully with large cowhides on the floor and white cloths hanging from beams around the perimeter. Ayénat told Desta that the skins had been stowed away for occasions like this. Some of the skins, particularly the antelope and colobus monkeys', came from Teferra's home.

At mid-morning, half a dozen men brought a gray, drooping cow and stood it before Abraham and two elderly men for the priest Yacob to bless. The cow was to be slaughtered for the wedding feast.

Enat, Desta's fifth oldest sibling, and Genet, the cousin, took Hibist to the back of the house, where warm bath water waited in a makeshift curtained room. Desta hesitatingly followed until Enat turned around and chased him away. More than this little rejection, what disturbed Desta was how happy

Hibist looked as they led her to the last bath she would be taking at home. This was not the first time she seemed happy. She had shown it all along.

He couldn't understand why his sister could be happy leaving him and their family to live with people she did not know. He thought her love was unconditional and would be forever. Was the affection she had for him only skin deep or was she that capricious? Here he was cheerless and depressed about her leaving, and she seemed completely oblivious. All the fear Desta had about her leaving now turned suddenly into anger. But just as quickly he remembered what that man told him in his dream: "You have to start to live with strangers. Everything that happened and yet to happen is for a reason . . Be strong. . . . Accept things as they unfold." The words comforted Desta.

I don't care about ever seeing you again, he said to himself as he returned to the house with his head held low.

In the afternoon, Desta was to guard the curtained opening of the grooms' room while his brothers changed into their wedding clothes. This allowed Desta to temporarily take his mind off Hibist.

Damtew wore full-length sky blue breeches, which were managed by opening the seams at the bottom, as his highly arched feet had made openings hard to slide through. Over the pants, he wore a knee-length white shirt that opened on the sides. A matching blue jacket went on top of the shirt. This dashing outfit was topped by a brand new gabi with thin, green borders.

Tamirat wore the same costume except his was all white, including the white priest's *timtem*—turban—that wreathed cleanly around his head.

They swathed their gabis around their bodies and folded and piled them tidily on their shoulders leaving enough room for their arms and hands.

Desta liked the way his brothers looked. Strangely, with their new clothes both appeared a few inches taller to him. No sooner had they emerged from their quarters than half a dozen smiling women gathered round. The women praised their looks and smoothed the wrinkles from their shirts.

The grooms stepped outside to meet their best men, their four or five extra groomsmen and the horse and mule team that would take them to get their brides. The best man from each group had a black cape and two khaki-clad topee hats that were to be worn by the groom and bride.

The grooms had to wait for the customary send-off ceremony. Surrounded by the onlookers, Abraham and Ayénat stood on the grass in front of the house with three elderly men, one of whom was Aba Yacob, the head priest.

The grooms stood like a pair of celestial bodies before their parents and the elderly while being blessed by each. Aba Farris, Ayénat's father, went first. He was followed by Aba Yisahk, Abraham's cotton-haired uncle, who, along with his words of good wishes, sprayed the grooms and those in close proximity with spit from his missing front tooth. Desta, who stood a few feet from Aba Yisahk, felt as if he were being pelted by a shower of soap bubbles. He shielded his face, squinted his eyes and wiped off the spit while others stood by, unmoved. The next speakers were Abraham and Ayénat. Abraham's speech was long and detailed, while Ayénat's was short and simple.

Aba Yacob said his prayers and blessings, wishing the grooms happy and safe trips over and back. He passed the cross over them and touched their foreheads and lips with it. The grooms, one by one, bowed and kissed their father's knee first, then their mother's knee, followed by the grandfather and uncle. The crowd clapped and the women let out a shrill "Lililililililililil!"

At the conclusion of the ceremony, the grooms and their entourages went to their respective brides' home to fetch them.

Enat explained to Desta that the horses were for the grooms and the mules were for the brides and the lead best man who would ride with them, ensuring their safety en route. Damtew and his group went north, toward River Davola. Tamirat and his entourage went west, to the mountains above their home.

Desta's preoccupation and thoughts of Hibist had temporarily been interrupted by the activities and excitement surrounding his brothers. Shortly after they left, he ran back to the house, nearly tripping, to look for Hibist. She was nowhere to be seen. Most of the women including his mother were still outside seeing to the departing grooms and their entourages.

Desta asked the first woman he saw about Hibist. The woman told him to ask the mother or Enat. He looked around for Enat. Remembering that she and Genet were giving Hibist a bath, he went to the back of the house. There was no sign of Hibist or Genet. The curtain was down, exposing the four poles and soggy earth, which exuded the fragrance of *Lux* soap. As he ran back toward the entrance looking for his mother, he saw Enat in the tent, with her back toward him, talking to her husband, Tenaw, and two other men.

Winded, he ran toward Enat. The men watched him as he weaved his way around the crowd toward them. Tenaw, who saw the men looking intently behind Enat, followed their eyes and saw Desta's panic-stricken face. Tenaw knotted his forehead and narrowed his eyes as he looked at Desta. Enat turned and watched the object of his interest. Desta, breathless, stopped in front of them. He hesitated, then blurted, "Where is Hibist? Where is Hibist?"

"You ran this hard just to ask that question? What's wrong with you?" scowled Enat, bending a little.

"I just wanted to see her before she left," said Desta meekly, stepping back, a little embarrassed. Others stared at him.

Enat excused herself and broke away from the men with Desta.

"Wait for me in the house. I'll be there shortly. Tenaw has bought Hibist's *she'etto* and I need to get it from him. Then you and I will go together to Hibist," she said in a hushed voice, her eyes warmly planted on Desta.

Desta ran back to the house with nearly the same speed. The people that saw him earlier followed him with their eyes as he snaked his way through the crowd.

Some thought he was happy for his siblings. Others wondered why there was such a distraught look on his face.

Desta stood by the entrance and waited for Enat. People were in and outside of the house but he was oblivious to them. Enat came swinging a fisted hand. "This will make Hibist smell nice," she said, opening her hand and revealing a small glass vial with greenish liquid in it.

Inside, Desta followed Enat to the corner back room which now was draped with cotton sheets, the entrance cordoned with a colored curtain that reached the floor. The room was scented with fresh aromatic grass and herbs and the floor was topped with the softest-looking goatskins Desta had ever seen.

Hibist sat in the middle of a small bench with folded knees, her white, embroidered gown spreading around her on the goatskin. On her long and elegant neck hung *telsome*, variegated shapes and sizes of silver jewelry festooned on bunched multicolored threads.

Above the telsome, a large silver cross on a black silk cord lay mutely in the dull lighting on her plump, olive chest. The elaborate needlework in red, blue, green and gold from around the neck opening of her white cotton dress had run down her bosom and was lost in the folds of the voluminous costume. A band of beautiful silver bracelets hugged her slender wrests and circlets of blue and green glass beads adorned her ankles.

Dark blue ground antimony mocked a sliver moon beneath her long lashes and a pair of large white orbs that shone more brilliantly than the burning beeswax candle affixed on the wall. One set of her tapering, exquisite fingers drooped lazily from a hand anchored to the bench, while the other was temporarily hidden somewhere in the folds of her dress. A pair of small cone-shaped silver earrings glinted in the candle light and complemented superbly all the items on her neck. Her soft, thick hair was trimmed evenly to a rounded mass and accented by a band of white sash that ran around the top of her forehead. Her fine nose and plump and rosy cheeks glistened from the same candle light that burned on the wall.

To Desta with all these adornments along with her quiet dignity, Hibist looked a very beautiful, young and becoming woman. She looked virtuous and chaste, just like the woman he had seen on the church wall with a baby in her arms.

Genet, the cousin who had helped Hibist put the henna in her hands, was massaging her feet and manicuring her toenails when Enat and Desta arrived.

Desta and Enat waited until the cousin finished with their sister. For a moment, Desta was so transfixed by his sister's transformation that he forgot about her impending departure. He stood by, happy they didn't chase him away. After the cousin was done, Enat handed Hibist the precious little vial from Tenaw.

The bride unscrewed the top and brought it close to her nose. "Smells beautiful," she said, pushing the vial toward her cousin for a whiff.

"You don't have to pass to me, I smell it from here. It's wonderful," said Genet as she inspected the label-less bottle.

Hibist was about to place her index finger on the opening of the vial and transfer the smell onto her neck, when Ayénat walked in and announced, "They are here, they are here. Are you ready?"

"Almost," said Genet.

Hibist gave the vial to her mother to smell the she'etto.

"Konjo she'etto. Who gave it to you?" said Ayénat.

Hibist pointed to Enat. "And Tenaw," she added.

"Excellent choice!"

Curious to see the men who would be taking his sister away, Desta ran out to find the groom and his company. In front of the house three of the groom's people were talking to Tenaw, who had been appointed by Abraham as their host. Several yards above the home, the remaining men stood around the groom. They had a lean gray mule with them.

Enat, in the meantime, had come out and was about to join her husband when Desta stopped her to ask who those men were. She explained they were the number one, number two and number three of the best men. Her husband Tenaw, as their attendant, would see to their needs during their stay, providing them with food and drinks.

He would also act as a go-between them and Hibist's parents, and coordinating the handing over of Hibist to them at the end.

Desta was crestfallen at the mention of Hibist being handed over to complete strangers.

Enat put her arm around him. "You should be happy for her, not sad. This is the best day of her life!"

"How can I be happy when they come to take away the only person that . . ." Desta hesitated, remembering his mother's admonishment about not showing his partiality.

Enat pulled him toward her, surprised by his emotional dependence on Hibist and the strength of the bond between them. She wished she could have been there for him too, but she had been married at age eleven, when Desta was just a toddler and neither of them remembered ever spending any time together. For Desta, Enat was little more than an acquaintance who came to visit on holidays.

Tenaw instructed the best men to bring the groom to the house. Then he dashed inside to ensure that the designated corner of the living room was not occupied by someone.

The men with the groom met with Tenaw just outside the front door. The muleteer tied the animal to a fence post and joined the rest by the entrance. Tenaw ushered them in and directed them to their pre-assigned seating area.

Desta was dying to see what Hibist's husband-to-be looked like. As the men walked past, both he and Enat watched their feet. Desta pointed to a pair of feet that were humped unusually high, their edges dry, scaly and chapped. "I think that's him," he said. "Let me run and tell Hibist."

Enat's hand grabbed Desta's delicate arm instantly like a vice. "Don't you dare!" She scowled at him severely.

"I don't want to see you near Hibist before she leaves with the groomsmen or I will tell Baba and Mama what you just wanted to do. If you wish to save your skin, I am sure you don't want me to tell them!" She turned and went into the house.

Desta bit his lip and walked off.

After the groom and his men were given food and drink, the best men rose and asked Tenaw if he would grant them permission to ask the parents for the bride. This request was swiftly administered. Abraham and Ayénat came and sat side by side on a high stool and received the three men and listened to their request. The three men entered into a verbal agreement before three witnesses, pledging that they would take care of Hibist until she was transferred to the groom's parents, and in turn, getting the in-laws to acknowledge that they received the daughter well and unharmed en route.

With these verbal vows made, Hibist was brought from the bridal room by Ayénat and Genet and handed over to the three best men. Outside, best man number one threw a black cape over her shoulders. He lifted her and set her on the mule, put the topee on her head, then hopped on the mule himself and held her securely.

As the bride sat on the mule all the guests clapped. The women began to dance and sing:

> The bride—the beautiful flower; the bride—the beautiful flower
> Be not afraid and let not your heart stir
> Your future will only be brighter and more beautiful than the one you
> are leaving behind.

They repeated this refrain as they clapped and danced, adding more lines as they went on.

The bride and the groom along with his best men and animals left shortly after the dancing and singing were over.

Enat located Desta who was leaning on the fencepost silently crying. She held him tightly and gently reprimanded him.

When the dancers and singers went inside, Enat brought Desta to the bridal room. She held and comforted him there for a while. She brought him food and water. Desta drank the water but barely ate the food. After his meal, he sat leaning on the wall, and thought about Hibist. He was exhausted. The many days of partial sleep had taken a heavy toll on his slight body and brain.

Somebody began beating the drum in the living room. The crowd gathered there, clapping and dancing and singing. Somehow in the din of the music, the commotion and the dance, Desta dozed off.

EIGHTEEN

Upon waking in the bright morning, Desta found himself surrounded by a great number of people who were strewn on the floor like wind-tossed bundles of wheat, fully clothed and draped from head to toe in their white gabis or shemmas. Some lay on their backs and snored, their cavernous mouths seeming to breathe air by the gallon. Others had assumed the fetal curl, their heads resting on their arms. They drew in air through collapsing nostrils as if sucking in a meager ration with a pair of thin straws, then dumping the waste by the bucket through flaring noses. Silvery liquid had leaked from the incontinent apertures from a few of the bowed sleepers, wetting their arms and the white goatskins beneath them. A few others were awake but groggy, eyes still partially closed. One or two ground their teeth and chewed on their cuds.

Now wide awake, Desta keenly observed his companions, mostly men, wondering where they had come from. Everything seemed like a dream. Where was he? The last place he had been, if his memory served him right, was in Hibist's bridal room. Where did she go? He remembered. She had been taken away on a mule by those men. She was married to that guy with the fat feet. After they had disappeared into the nimbus of graying dusk, he had hidden behind the fence, shedding pearly tears for the loss of his sister and closest ally, until Enat had come to get him.

He ran his fingers on the plush white bridal skin beneath him, wondering where Hibist was now and whether she was happy. Had she already begun to miss him and the rest of her family?

In his mind he saw the beautiful, sweet smiling face that came to wake him every morning before they went to milk the cows. He remembered the gentle tapping of her hand on his shoulders, her soft voice, the sweet things she crooned in his ears, the special foods she prepared for him and their dinnertime talks. The fun times they had in spring when they went to chase butterflies and picking flowers or gather berries, or collect figs from the sholla trees in the dry season. The laughter and carefree giggles they shared on their escapades. Now he would have nobody to do these things with.

Then he thought of his two other losses in the past four months. First, Kooli the dog had been killed, and then the vervet monkeys had fled after their trees were destroyed.

Now his non-human friends were gone from his life as well.

Desta tried hard to stem the tide of emotion that was surging through him but his feelings had gone beyond the watershed of no return. He placed his head between his knees and wept. The tears came silently, like a river that has spilled over its banks and flooded the land beyond. Finally, he stopped. He told himself he had to be strong. He had to move on with his own life. He knew he slowly would get over the absence of Hibist in his life. The cloud man's advice came floating to him once again: "Be strong—Accept things as they unfold."

Then he remembered something else. There were two girls coming, his brother's new wives, as Ayénat had said, "In Hibist's place." He wondered if they had arrived already. Slowly he rose and straightened himself, and hopping over the sleeping people, went to the living room. There were a few people sleeping here too. He saw his mother puttering in the kitchen. Without saying anything, he went outside to deal with his morning urges before searching for his brothers' brides.

Outdoors, Desta noticed that the guests who had slept in the tent were already up walking the grounds, leaning on the fence or sitting on the grass, swathed up to their noses in their gabis. The sun was high in the mountains. The morning was a bit nippy and dewy.

After addressing his personal needs in the backwoods, Desta returned and sat on the fence. There was a band of golden light high up on the mountain. He wanted to watch it come down, as he used to do when he was little, but shortly after he sat, a nimbus gray cloud spread over and veiled the sun, obliterating the golden light on the mountain. Desta perceived this spectacle as a metaphor for his own severance from someone he loved. He smiled at the irony, or was it a mockery?

Presently, he went inside to see if breakfast was being prepared yet. Having not had dinner the night before, he was hungry. He found Ayénat and Enat busy preparing food in the kitchen. From the hearth here, a great fire lit up and tessellated the wall of the adjacent room where Hibist last stayed.

After he ate, Desta asked if Damtew and Tamirat had returned with their brides.

"They are in there," said Enat, pointing to the big room by the entrance.

Desta looked toward the curtained entrance. Nobody was coming out or going in.

"Once they wake, you can go to see them—we'll all go to see them," she said.

Thoughtful and forlorn, Desta merely gazed at the entrance.

"Don't you want to see your new sisters?" asked Enat, peering down at him.

"I would rather see Hibist. These are not my sisters . . . but then again, I will have to learn to live with strangers," he said finally, remembering the words of the cloud man.

"Well, Hibist now has a husband and a new home. You'll get to see her when she comes on holidays and other occasions. But it's good to hear you're willing to give the new girls a chance," said Enat as she hurried back to tend to the sauce pot.

In the meantime, most of the guests had risen and there were a great number of them in and out of the house. A line of girls and boys had formed by the curtained entrance of the bride and groom's room, including Desta's nieces, Astair and Zena. Desta stood several feet away and watched the children as, one by one, they went into the room and then came back out. Some of those who came out went to the ones still in line and whispered things in their ears, giggling. Others seemed disappointed when they exited.

Curious, Desta approached a disappointed-looking boy and asked him what was going on.

"A man said he had to give a button, safety pin or money to see the brides," said the boy.

"You have to give something *just* to see them?" said Desta, wide-eyed.

"Yes. I didn't have anything to give and the man wouldn't let me see 'em," said the boy, pouting.

"You are not going?" a second boy asked Desta.

"He shook his head. I have nothing to give and I really am not that interested in seeing them just yet."

"You have that safety pin," said a girl, pointing to the metal device that was on the neck.

"I need it for myself, to take out the thorns from my feet when I become a shepherd," said Desta.

"You won't get to see them then," said the first boy.

"No, I won't since I have nothing else to give—unless somebody . . ."

"Somebody gave you something?"

"Yeah."

"I will be right back," said the boy and ran.

Desta watched the rest of the line of children. There was more giggling and laughter, and his curiosity was piqued.

The boy soon returned and handed Desta an item. "I had found this a week ago in our backyard. I gave it to my father to keep it for me. I was tempted to use it to see them but I will give it to you since they are your sisters-in-law."

Desta looked at the beautiful horn button the boy had given him. He would have liked to keep the button for himself, but he didn't want to offend the boy. Besides, he had no shirt to put it on. He might as well use it to see the brides.

Yet, he was hesitant.

"Go, go, go," said the boy, pushing him.

At the curtained entrance was a tall smiling man who allowed only one child into the room at a time. "Do you have your gift handy?" he asked Desta.

"Yes, it's in here," said Desta, showing him a closed fist.

"Go and talk to that man," said the gatekeeper, pointing to a second person who was sitting between the two veiled brides.

Desta was surprised to find that there were that many men in the room. He walked haltingly as he looked around the room. Most of the men were busy talking with each other and didn't pay attention to him.

Tamirat greeted him with a smile as he walked in. Damtew was talking to two of his best men. He glanced at Desta but said nothing.

"What do you have for a gift?" asked the second man, grinning. He said his name was Dawit.

Desta opened his fist and showed him his gift.

"Just one button?"

Desta nodded.

"That will allow you to see just one of the brides."

Desta was puzzled. The boy had not told him he would need to pay twice.

"If you want to see the second, you will have to give that safety pin," said the man, pointing to Desta's neck.

"No, that is mine. I will need it for myself."

"Which one of the brides would you like to see?"

"I would like to see her," said Desta, pointing to the veiled girl to the right of the man. She was the smaller of the two brides and Desta was curious about her.

Tamirat leaned over to the man and whispered.

"Okay, I will let you see both," said the man, smiling. "You will pay for this girl but not for Tamirat's. He will pay for you."

Desta smiled too as he crouched and prepared for the viewing of the mysterious little girl whose head and face were completely covered by the shemma.

Dawit held the edge of the shemma and slowly lifted it, taking as much time as he could without making it appear superfluous. Desta kept his eyes on the edge of the shemma not to miss every small revelation of the girl. First there came the feet—very fair and adorned with beads of silver anklets, nails trimmed but dry with cracks and chips in them. The feet, hennaed pure magenta, were flat and *not as pretty as Hibist's*, thought Desta. With the progression of the lift came small, hennaed hands, clasping her folded knees. Then came her arms and chest on which rose two small breasts like a pair of succulent pears. Farther up, there rested multi-color, bunched threads on which were festooned multi-piece silver trinkets with dangling chimes. Closer to her neckline hung a large silver cross on a black cord.

As the man continued to peel the shemma, there came the neck, chin—a cross tattooed on it—delicate and sensitive lips, rosy, plump cheeks, large and brilliant eyes and with a delicate beak-like nose, all in all presenting the image of a doll and not that of a girl. Her face was fair but had little expression. Her hair was black, thick and spherical.

The man smiled at Desta and said, "That is Damtew's bride. Her name is Melkam." Desta was surprised how small the girl was compared to her brawny husband. Dawit prompted Desta to introduce himself. "Hello, my name is Desta, I am your husband's brother," he whispered, his eyes planted on hers.

The girl merely gazed at him as if he were some curious object, pursed her lips, blinked and looked away.

Desta waited to see if she was going to turn back to him and say something.

"She is too sleepy to talk," said Dawit apologetically. "We will arrange for you to see her again tomorrow."

As Desta was about to go, the man said, "Don't you want to see the other bride? Tamirat has given you permission to see her free of charge."

"I'd like to see her then," said Desta in a low voice.

Tamirat's bride was leaning against the wall with her head slightly drooping. Dawit tapped her on the shoulder and whispered, "We have a visitor who would like to meet you."

The girl straightened her head, lifted the veil from her face and stared at Desta.

Taken aback and a little disappointed by the lack of suspense, he stared back at her, wondering if she would ignore him as the other one had done, or introduce herself.

"What did you say was your name?" said Dawit smiling, pretending ignorance.

"My name is Desta. I am your husband's brother," he said awkwardly.

The girl tossed her head down in a greeting, puckered her lips and smiled at him.

"My name is Amsale," she said, holding his eye.

Amsale's face was soft, her eyes big and intense. She had a narrow, aquiline nose, short jet black hair, low cheekbones and a curving chin. When she smiled there was a small glaring gap on the right side of her mouth, but her teeth otherwise were even and white.

Like Damtew's bride, Amsale was not predisposed to engage in a conversation with Desta. Dawit said she too was tired and he should come to talk with her another time.

Desta bowed and parted.

He was confused by the two girls—one was totally uncommunicative, the other a little friendlier but still unwilling to converse. *How could they possibly replace Hibist?* He remembered what Ayénat had said. He would be getting two for the price of one and twice as much love. *What a joke!!* Desta said to himself. At that moment, how he was already missing Hibist! And how he hated his parents for sending away the only person who loved him back!

The man's voice came to him again: *You have to learn to live with strangers.*

NINETEEN

For Desta, the second day of the wedding was much like the first. During the day people ate, drank, talked one-on-one or in groups inside the home, outside on the grass or in the tent. Some people walked about the property leisurely. Children laughed and giggled as they romped around the premises. At night, after dinner, people clapped, sang and danced to the beat of a drum until the wee hours of the morning.

By day, Desta sat and watched the people, feeling dreamy and melancholic. Nobody cared or had time to ask what was bothering him or why he was not playing like the rest of the children. Occasionally, he overheard relatives or family friends who knew about Saba and her family talk about him.

"How could they be so gullible to take a little boy's story as if it were God's word and uproot the entire family and cattle and resettle them?" commented one of the guests.

"They said the man he supposedly talked to was not even Saytan," remarked a second man. "They said he was some strange creature that happened to have human form. This shows that this idle boy dreamed up the creature in his daily fantasies and then recreated him for the Deb'tera."

With these comments some of them laughed hilariously between swigs of tella.

"In fact," said the first man. "It's known around the family that the boy has a bizarre imagination. He is able to see animal or human forms in the mountains, rocks and clouds."

"It's just a shame that the poor family has to be subjected to these crazy ideas, let alone be asked to abandon their home and farmland," said the second man.

Some of the people approached Desta and asked him directly to give them his account. To those who asked nicely, he told them precisely what he had seen and heard from the man by the river. Talking to these people gave him a respite from his thought of Hibist, a much-needed break from his depression. Talking about the cloud man always lifted his spirits a bit. His last advice, that Desta learn to live with strangers and everything would turn out okay, was reassuring.

But then when those drunk and boisterous men and even women approached him mockingly, Desta ignored them or walked away. He also heard women suck their lips audibly in empathy, "He must be really possessed by the Saytan to create such havoc in his poor family. Look at him; he seems so gloomy and unhappy."

"Well, have they not tried to exorcise it out of him?" asked one woman. "You know baptism by a good priest and taking the communion could help. Yes, he just doesn't look like a normal boy. Did you notice, his eyes are so sunken and it looks as if he has not slept or eaten for days."

"My understanding is that they had a priest out here to baptize him. He supposedly has even taken the communion. But from the looks of him, it seems neither has helped. Unless the family does something, I am afraid he will go mad. Or worse," said the second.

"Worse?" said the third woman, knotting her brows. "What would be worse?"

DEPRESSED BY WHAT PEOPLE WERE saying about him, Desta decided to stay out of the way until the guests had gone. During the daylight hours he went to his old playing grounds by the edge of the forest where he listened to the chirping of the birds in the trees and mourned the loss of Kooli and the vervets who would have been with him now in this place where they had shared so many fun times.

Desta could understand the loss of the vervet monkeys. They moved away because Yihoon and his henchmen had destroyed their habitat. They had become suspicious and mistrusting of humans. But Kooli's sickness and his ultimate demise in the hands of Damtew he could never understand. Why had a dog that had been healthy and friendly all of his life suddenly turn against him?

For weeks he had searched his brain to unravel the mystery. *What had caused Kooli to bite him? Why had the dog been sad and listless in the days before it happened? Did he really have the "horrible" disease his parents were so worried about?*

Desta lay on his back under the shade of the wanza tree, propping his head with interlocked fingers. Having had little sleep for the last two days, it felt good to rest in the shade and think.

He looked over at Saba's new place. The land was nearly cleared now. Here and there were fallen trees that had yet to be chopped up, gathered and piled like so many that dotted the hillside in miniature hillocks. Hibist had told him that Yihoon was planning to burn the piles. Desta hated Yihoon for doing that to the trees, for causing the vervet monkeys to flee. Desta also blamed the cloud man for causing all these problems, for approving Saba's move without concern for the helpless animals and birds that would be affected by the cutting of the forest. But Desta was afraid to hate the cloud man or say anything bad against him. He might exact a punishment on Desta.

Desta's thoughts drifted and he soon fell asleep. It was as if he had been decapitated.

His head dropped, rolled a little and rested on one side. His legs and hands went limp. He began to snore.

He was transported to another world, one with cinnabar green hills covered with flowers that filled his nose and lungs with the most redolent, invigorating and intoxicating fragrances. The sun gently caressed his back and neck as he galloped in the hills, his feet as light as feathers. As he ran he heard voices, soft whispers carried by the whoosh of the wind. They said, "Kooli didn't die of any sickness. He died for you."

Desta stopped to ascertain what he was hearing. The voice repeated, "Kooli didn't die of any sickness. He died for you."

"Why did he die for me?" Desta asked.

"Your family wouldn't have let you go beyond the Davola River if something drastic had not happened. You wouldn't have discovered the existence of other worlds if you had not left your birthplace," said the voice.

"He was not really sick then, when he looked so listless and lifeless, simply peering at people with those glazed eyes?"

"He was and he wasn't," came the reply.

The wind was blowing hard around Desta, fluttering his gabi about his body. He was astonished and transfixed by the revelation.

"He was sick because he knew how much you were hurting from all the things that had been happening with your family. He was not sick with any disease," said the voice gently.

"Kooli died for me? He sacrificed himself for me, so that I could discover the world beyond the river? Oh God!!"

Desta wanted to weep but tears refused to come. He thought of all the
wonderful things Kooli had meant to him, the absolute, ultimate devotion of
love the dog had shown him. The best he could do was cry. *I need to cry, I
need to show him how much I loved him, how much I will always love him.*
He squeezed his eyes shut as hard as he could again and again. Still no tears
came. *What kind of creature am I? What is wrong with me? Why can't I cry?*

He sat on a rock overlooking the green valley, closed his eyes and tried
to imagine what it might be like to be chased down, cornered and shot by
Damtew. He wanted to experience what Kooli must have felt in his last
moments, when the blast of the gun and the shattering impact on his body
were one and the same. But still he felt no emotion in the depths of his heart
or the far recesses of his consciousness. *What kind of cold brute am I?! Why
am I not capable of shedding just simple, ordinary tears for someone who
showed me the ultimate in love?* The more he thought about it, the more
desperate he became. He imagined Kooli looking down on him from the
heavens, gazing at him, seeing his gaping metal-cold heart.

*I am trying Kooli, I am trying. I am really not as emotionless as you have
found me*, said Desta in desperation.

He searched his mind for something else that might make him weep, but he
couldn't think of anything worse than being shot by Damtew.

*Just know that your friendship and companionship meant a lot to me all
these years*, he said to himself searching the sky for Kooli . . . *In fact I have
been heartbroken since you have been gone. I am not certain how my life
will be without you and Hibist."*

The voice in the wind spoke to him again. "Stop torturing yourself. Kooli
doesn't need your tears. His death was part of the overall scheme of things,
so you would get a chance to travel away from home, to see and discover
places, to learn about things, to be happy and to begin to think of a way for
your freedom. He didn't die so you could shade tears for him. But don't forget
the kindness, love, devotion and sacrifice he showed to you. He has set the
example for you. He wanted to teach you to be good and kind to others."

When Desta awoke, he found his feet and legs being devoured by a swarm
of ants—big, black ants whose sickle-like antlers had pierced into his flesh,
oozing blood in small, bead-like drops. He jumped and tried to brush them off,
but some of them had embedded their antlers into his skin so he had to pull
them off one by one. In doing so, the heads of some broke off and remained

driven into his skin; others came off with bits of his skin locked in their antlers. Meanwhile, more were scurrying up his torso and arms, climbing up and down the ridges and valleys of his gabi, looking for flesh to pierce. He removed the gabi and shook it.

Blood had oozed from the bites, as if someone had poked his arms, legs and feet with a needle, yet, curiously, he had never felt the stings.

It occurred to him that during the time he had fallen asleep; he had gone to a different world. He looked at the crop stubble in the valley and the seared grass beneath him. This was not the place he had been a few minutes before. All those beautiful green hills and mountains were mere manifestations of his dreams, as were the things that had happened there. Images loomed in his head and faded, becoming diffused and then turned clear again, like a misty landscape slowly coming into view.

He was amazed that he had slept through so many ant bites, yet when he remembered the sequence of events in the dream and the intensity of his feelings, he realized that his bodily senses had been overwhelmed by the power of the experience in the dream. As he walked home, he recalled the details of the dream: his inability to shed tears for Kooli and his various efforts to induce them. In the end, what he couldn't produce with his eyes, he was able to do with his body. He shed blood instead of tears for his best friend.

TWENTY

"This is the day of the Wedding Return," said Enat when Desta asked where his brothers and their brides were going. Enat explained that it was customary for the grooms and brides, along with their best men, to return on the third day of the wedding to the girls' families and stay there for a few days. "They will then come home and the two girls, as wives to our brothers, will become a part of our family."

"Does this mean, Hibist will come back too?" asked Desta anxiously.

"Yes, they should be here sometime later, before dusk probably."

Desta jumped to his feet.

"I am glad to see you happy for a change," said Enat with a wide grin.

"Seeing Hibist always makes me happy!" said Desta merrily.

"Just Hibist?"

"Well, others too, but this is the first time she has been away from me. I want to find out how she likes her husband and her new home."

"No matter. I am glad to see that handsome face awash with that beautiful smile. Do you know if you were not my brother, I would have killed to have you for one," said Enat, looking sideways at Desta's glowing face.

"Thank you. I am happy you are my sister too. I just wish I could see you more often. I don't even remember when you lived with us. I must have been very little," said Desta.

"I think you were three when I got married at eleven years old. Although I remember you very well, you probably don't remember me at all," said Enat looking far away.

"I have been close to Hibist because she essentially raised me. Mother and father were always busy with their things and never paid attention to me. Only Hibist did," said Desta, his face suddenly turning gloomy.

"Oh, I am sorry you feel this way about our parents. Yes, they had to take care of so many things to raise all of us," said Enat.

Desta and Enat were standing in the tent, watching the best men prepare the two mules which would be for the brides to ride on. Enat had told Desta that Damtew and Tamirat would be walking with their best men on the return. They would not be riding their father's horses with their brides on the return. Abraham didn't want to burden his son-in-laws with the added responsibility of caring for two animals or worse, hold them accountable if his beautiful horses got stolen.

Without much ceremony, Tamirat and his bride with their three best men went west, and Damtew with his men and bride went north. There were a few close relatives left among the guests and they too stood outside and watched them go. The elderly blessed and wished them a good and peaceful journey.

Shortly after the newlyweds and their entourages departed, Yihoon showed up with three men. He had come to find guests who could help him chop up the felled trees and collect them into a pile for burning. He found three young men who were willing to give him a hand.

These days Desta cringed every time he saw Yihoon. He wished he had not seen him this morning. To avoid making eye contact with his brother-in-law, in case he brought up the cloud man again and triggered more snide remarks about him, Desta ran into the house.

"Desta really doesn't like these new girls, does he?" said Ayénat to Enat a while later. "Have you noticed not long after they left he was grinning from ear to ear."

"I think the main reason he is smiling, more than not liking the new girls, is the intelligence I shared with him about Hibist's return today."

"Why didn't I think of that?" said Ayénat. "I can see how thrilled he must be with the prospect of seeing her."

"I think we should allow him to spend as much time with her as he wants," said Enat. "The more he learns about her new living situation, the better he will be in adapting to the changes."

"Yes," said Ayénat. "There was nothing to occupy him at the moment, as we have arranged for a young man to care for the animals through this month until Desta takes over."

That afternoon, Ayénat and Enat decided to serve lunch in the tent so that the house would be ready for Hibist and her people. The living room was sprinkled with fresh grass over which Enat spread the choicest goat and antelope skins. Abraham had a goat killed especially for the newlyweds and their company as well as for a few selected guests who might stay on for a few more days.

For Desta, the day felt as if someone held the remaining hours on either ends and stretched them. The closer the time got to early evening, the more slowly it passed. Every so often, Desta went out to look at the descending sun on the mountain above his home. The shadows moved ever so slowly.

"Stop running in and out of the house," said Enat. "If you don't watch the time, it will go much faster."

"I am afraid I might die before I see Hibist," said Desta, smiling but trying to be serious.

"Silly boy, if you calmed down and didn't think about her arrival, the time would fly. I have a solution. Here, go and pour this kettle of tella in each of the guest's cups and come back for a refill." She handed him a heavy tin kettle, the exterior of which was speckled with dried rivulets.

Desta staggered when he took the heavy kettle. Humping slightly, he wobbled to the tent, the tella spitting out of the spigot en route and landing on his feet and the ground. When he arrived, the guests had finished their early dinner, and Grandpa Farris was giving his blessings to Desta's parents, the absent newlyweds, the children and the livestock. He even said a few good wishes for happiness and prosperity for Saba and Yihoon in their new location. Desta wished he hadn't. A few people in the group turned and looked his way at the mention of Saba and her husband. Their stares made him feel like a criminal.

Shortly before dusk, two men arrived, chanting:

"Your son-in-law, the virile and the strong,

he has broken the silver bracelet."

They repeatedly chanted this catch line, one of them twirling a white handkerchief over his head. They were dancing in a circle when they arrived by the entrance.

Desta ran to get Enat to come and see these men. At first, he didn't know who they were.

"Those are the best men for Hibist's husband," explained Enat. "Our sister, the groom and the escorts should be somewhere nearby, waiting until the men return for them."

"What is the meaning of what they are saying?" asked Desta. "Why is that man carrying that handkerchief with red marks on it?"

"You are too young to understand," said Enat casually.

"What do you mean?"

"Everything is all right between Hibist and her husband. They are just pretending so that they can get a gift from Baba and Mama for the groom's accomplishment in bed. That red stuff is probably chicken or sheep blood."

Desta didn't really understand his sister's cryptic explanation but he didn't want to press her any longer.

Someone from the dinner crowd directed the two men to go to the tent, where Abraham and the guests were waiting. Desta and Enat watched them as they skipped, danced and sung, twirling the handkerchief over their heads. For a moment, Desta was not even thinking of Hibist. The novel chanting and dancing of the two men had captivated him.

The guests clapped as the men entered the tent, continuing their chanting and dancing. Desta and Enat followed them, watching with avid interest.

Shortly after the best men's entry into the tent, Abraham went to the house and returned with something in his hand. "It looks like Baba is going to give them some money," said Enat tilting her head to her brother. The father handed what he had in his fist to one of the men. Coins fell with a metallic clatter into the man's hand. Soon after the grandfather reached into his breast pocket and handed them something too. The rest of the guests gave whatever they had or could afford to give. Nearly all gave money. The cotton-haired uncle pledged a heifer.

Desta noticed Enat's eyes doubled in size when she heard the uncle's pledge.

"She was his favorite. He never gave us such a munificent gift," she muttered.

After collecting the gifts, which Enat said would be given to Hibist and her husband, the men went to fetch the groom and his bride, along with the third best man. Desta was not sure what he should say or do when he first saw his sister. He thought he would match her energy and enthusiasm, at least, at first.

The four men with Hibist arrived at the house. Hibist was still on the mule with the best man who had promised to care for her until she was finally handed over to her in-laws. The groom was on foot, along with the other men. The best man hopped down from the mule and helped Hibist dismount.

To Desta, Hibist looked tired and limp, as if she had not slept since leaving her home three days before. Enat embraced and kissed her first, followed by Ayénat and Abraham. Tired as she looked, Hibist managed to acknowledge every one who came to greet her. When it was Desta's turn, she planted three hard kisses on his cheeks.

She must have missed me as I missed her, he said to himself with pleasure. Content for now, he complied with the adults' order to get out of their way, although he was curious to know whose swollen feet he had seen when the groom and his best men first came to pick up his sister.

This time it was immediately apparent to him that it indeed was the groom with the humped feet. They were ugly with dry cracks, puffed and stumpy toes.

Desta couldn't imagine his beautiful sister sleeping with this man. *Could Hibist get his disease?* he wondered. He dashed across the doorsteps to Enat and pointed to the groom's feet as they walked in. "I was right," he said. "I was right when I told you about his humpy feet."

"Ssshhh," said Enat with a grimace after observing what Desta pointed out.

Ayénat had heard Desta and saw Enat's reaction. She pursed her lips as she came and stood near them. Her small eyes narrowed and dimmed ruefully. "He is very handsome otherwise," she said.

"Well, diseased feet can get worse," said Enat. "I am not sure if it's inheritable. If so, would you want a grandson or daughter with elephantiasis?"

"I don't know, daughter," said Ayénat, looking away. "I just don't know." Her eyes filled with tears that never fell.

"Tella, Tella," cried Tenaw as he came after sitting the guests. Enat rushed to the back room to bring tella to the men.

Ayénat stood where she was, transfixed as if she had been struck by lightening. "This is what can happen when you talk just to the parents," she said shaking her head. "We never met the son or had someone inspect his physical well being."

Desta remained where he stood, watching his mother and worrying for Hibist.

The following day, Desta rose early. He had expected Hibist might come and tap him on his shoulder and ask him to go milk the cows, but she had not come. In fact, she didn't wake until much later, leaving Desta to pace about the house in frustration.

When Hibist finally came to the living room, she explained that the previous night was the first night she had gotten a decent sleep. At her husband's place, the celebration and festivities had gone on all night so she had not been able to sleep at all.

After lunch, Desta asked Hibist if she would like to go for a walk. She agreed happily as this was the first day of freedom she had since she left home. They strolled to the forest boundary behind their house and back, stopping to rest under the gottem tree above their parent's home. The sun was already past the mid point in the sky and the shadow of the tree had rotated east, allowing Desta and Hibist good protection from the direct rays.

Desta gave a summary of his brothers' brides, describing how small, aloof and pretty Damtew's wife was and how unreserved yet unfriendly Tamirat's wife was. He told her of the boy who gave him the button so he could see the girls. He also told her about the all-night dances and prolonged feasting.

She in turn told him about her own experiences, how dark and small the room was where she, the groom and the best men had stayed. She had sat on an old balding cowhide that didn't have much padding of grass underneath. Because of discomfort she could neither sit comfortably nor sleep. The whole time had been an ordeal for her. She hardly met the parents of her husband and had no idea whether or not they were friendly. The only redeeming part was the best man number one. He was very nice to her and had tried to make her circumstances as pleasant and easy as he could.

"What has happened with you?" asked Hibist, changing the subject.

Desta shrugged, not ready to talk about his own current events yet. He was waiting to find the appropriate time to ask about her husband and maybe about his feet. Hibist was studying his face without saying a word, as if she was privy to the thoughts churning in her brother's head.

"I had a very interesting dream the other night," said Desta, brightening. "Well, actually it was during the day." He had been looking forward to sharing his dream with Hibist and hearing her thoughts.

Hibist, looking exhausted, sighed and shook her head. "How about if we do this tomorrow? I am really tired to be a good listener," she said. "Okay?"

Desta nodded, too disappointed to use his voice. *Why had she asked about me if she didn't really care to know?* he thought to himself.

TWENTY-ONE

"He has been distraught since you left," said Ayénat to Hibist on the second day of her return. "Enat and I had promised him he could spend as much time as possible when you returned."

"We spent a brief time yesterday. We can take another walk this afternoon," said Hibist, shrugging.

At lunch, Ayénat sat Desta and Hibist together. After they finished, she whispered to Desta, "You should invite her to go on a walk with you. She is leaving tomorrow."

This time Desta and Hibist went down to the field below the house. They walked to the Davola River, reminiscing and laughing about the things they used to do together. As they returned from the river, Desta tried again to tell her about his recent dream. Sensing his urgency, Hibist this time gave him her full attention.

Desta began.

"I took a nap in the afternoon above the barley field and I dreamt about Kooli. I have been missing him very much. I had been mystified by his behavior in his last days and why he attacked me—he was the dog I grew up with. I was worried about the supposed disease he might have contracted. You see, Kooli really didn't have a disease. He was not sick at all. He had sensed what was going on in my life, my troubles and he had become depressed. He was aching for me, the way I had been. He sacrificed himself for me, so that I could discover places beyond our parents' property. So I could learn about things and places far from here.

"I didn't realize there were more villages and land beyond our valley. By going to church with Mama that Sunday, I discovered the existence of those places. And what's more, Kooli was supposed to be part of the overall scheme of things, although I don't really know what that means. All this was revealed to me in my dream."

"Who was it who told you these things?" asked Hibist, puzzled.

"I heard it from the wind," said Desta.

Hibist stared at him. "The wind?"

"Yes! In my dream."

"I never could figure out the things you come up with," said Hibist, shaking her head.

"What I would like to know is what happened to Kooli's body?" asked Desta.

Hibist thought for a few minutes, then said thoughtfully, "As you know, Damtew killed him under Baba's orders. I think I remember where he disposed of him, but I am sure the hyenas must have consumed him by now."

"Can you show me where?"

"What are you going to do with him? He is a dead dog with hardly anything left of him probably."

"I want to thank him for being my friend all those years, for sacrificing himself so that I may advance in life. For being more compassionate to me than anyone else in my family, other than maybe you," said Desta.

Hibist hesitated and then got up.

They went along the north side of the house, down a steep grade where the earth formed a narrow cavity, about fifty yards above the northern creek.

They paced the ground in all directions. There was no sign of the dog's remains. Hibist paused, wondering if this indeed was the area where Damtew had dumped Kooli' body. They went farther down toward the creek. There, near a clump of bushes, was the skeleton of what appeared to be a dog. The legs were gone, and a few of the ribs were either crushed or broken off, but the skull and vertebrae were intact. Desta and Hibist looked down on the remaining bones silently. Neither knew what the other was thinking. Desta held back his emotion.

"I wonder if he was dragged here by an animal or if this was where Damtew left him," said Desta, finally breaking the silence.

"I am almost certain he was left here by Damtew. I remember saying to him that he either bury Kooli or place him near some bush. He said he wanted the vultures to spot him right away so they could eat him clean, and the odor would disappear quickly," said Hibist, struggling with her own emotion.

"If the vultures did eat him, we should see strewn bones," said Desta. As far back as he could remember he had watched vultures swoop down on dead animals and clean them to the bones within just a short time.

Hibist agreed. "As you might remember, Damtew wanted to club Kooli," said Hibist. "He didn't want to waste a precious bullet on a dog. But father said there was a lot of personal significance to that dog and he wouldn't allow him to club him.

So Damtew got the pistol and shot Kooli in the chest at close range," said Hibist, choking. "The sun was still out when he killed him."

Desta stood speechless, frozen in place, fighting the tears that coursed their ducts and gathered on his eyelids. He imagined Damtew bringing their father's pistol and shattering the heart of Kooli who had done nothing but love him and had shown it the only way he knew how. He had internalized Desta's pain, becoming listless, sad and angry at Desta for not fighting back, and finally had bitten him to illustrate what he should do to those who try to hurt him.

"His action was misunderstood," said Desta. "It cost him his life—and me his friendship." He finally let his tears flow. Hibist held him close and cried with him.

"He was always with me wherever I went," sobbed Desta. "He even slept next to me many times, despite the complaints I got from Ma. Really he was the only good brother I had. Would any of my brothers or sisters sacrifice their lives for me? Of course not! But Kooli did. I will remember him forever!"

"I understand how you feel," said Hibist, wiping away her tears. "I was one of those who criticized you for sleeping with Kooli. It's just not customary for people to sleep with dogs, but you did. But then again, you have always been different."

"I cannot tell you why I am the way I am, just as I can't explain how a dog could figure out what's inside your heart and grieve with you." Desta cried harder. With his sister and Kooli gone, how lonely he would be.

Hibist held him close to her chest once more, his tears soaking her new white dress. "Let's go. If we stay here longer thinking about all these sad things we are going to cry our eyeballs out," she said.

Desta sighed, letting his sister wipe his tears with the edge of her sleeve. "We shouldn't leave Kooli's bones here," he said, looking around. "I would like to bury them."

Hibist remembered a foxhole near the outer edge of their parent's property, by the kaga tree on the south side. She suggested they take Kooli there. Desta spread his gabi on the ground, gathered and placed every piece of bone he could find on it, folded them in and followed Hibist to the foxhole.

Once they found the foxhole, Desta held the opposite ends of his gabi and folded it to keep the bones in place, then poured them down the hole by letting go of the gabi with one hand.

Hibist suggested that they cover the hole with branches for now and come back the next day with a bowl to use to fill the hole with dirt, but Desta wanted to finish the burial.

He thought it would be better if they found a long log or several pieces of wood to fit into the foxhole and then covered them with rocks. They found three small pieces of logs and lined them over the opening, stepping on them to bury the ends into the earth. Then they filled the gaps with pieces of rocks and wood.

This done, Desta sat by Kooli's new grave and thanked him for being his best animal friend and for loving him and sacrificing his life on his behalf. He wished him well till they could meet again in heaven. Hibist looked on, touched by Desta's words and the feelings he expressed for his friend.

The funeral ceremony finished, Desta and Hibist walked north and then cut west to the footpath that crossed to the back of the hill that faced Saba's new property. Hibist chose this roundabout route because she did not want to dirty her new dress by crossing through the tilled soil. They walked in tandem, Desta behind his sister.

"I really admire Baba's humane choice of shooting Kooli instead of letting Damtew club him," said Desta.

"Well, for him it was more than just humane act," said Hibist.

"How do you mean?"

"Apparently, Kooli has been intertwined in his own life, keeping some sort of continuity between him and his lost father—Kooli's name, anyway," she said as they just turned the corner of the fence.

"Tell me."

"When Damtew asked him why he wanted to waste a bullet on a crazy dog, while in the past he wouldn't allow anyone to use his rifle unless they bought their own bullets," he said. 'Allowing you to club Kooli would be tantamount to carrying out the same act on my father.'

Hibist motioned Desta to sit on one of two flat rocks adjacent to the Abo bushes, beside the path, one of their favorite spots for sharing secrets. "I think we should sit here for a little bit if you want me to tell you the rest of the story.

I know you will find it very interesting."

"Baba was in a talking mood that night. He had been drinking for a while.

"He said when he was born his family lived in an isolated area of Kuakura, as they owned a huge amount of land. His father brought home a dog he named Kooli to look after Baba and his three sisters and mother. His father used to travel a lot. As it turned out, Kooli became Baba's best pal. They romped together through the open countryside and the dog kept intruding animals and humans at bay by night. Over time, Kooli and he became best friends. Kooli was with him when they scoured the countryside after his father disappeared. He nearly wept when he recalled this.

"Until Kooli died some five years later, he was the only symbol of connection between Baba and his father. After that, at least one of the dogs, if they had more than one, was called Kooli. And whatever dogs they got had to have similar color and basic characteristics as the original Kooli. Interestingly, the way your Kooli came into our lives had an uncanny similarity with the first one . . ."

"How so?" said Desta.

"Well, Baba got the dog right after you were born and the reason was, since we were here in this isolated part of the valley, he thought he would grow with you and keep you company in addition to guarding the family with the other dogs. Of all the dogs he named Kooli in the past, this one had the stronger symbolic value because it connected you and him the way the first dog connected him and his father."

"You know it all makes sense now," said Desta. "When I was little and I was playing with Kooli out in the field or in the grass above the house, father would sit and watch us, often smiling or telling me to be gentle with the dog. Sometimes he even played with us. And he always saved the entrails of a cow, goat or sheep and brought them to Kooli. Mother was horrified when I allowed Kooli to sleep next to me but father thought it was okay."

"Well, now you know. Let's head back home," said the newlywed as she rose.

Desta rose too and held his sister close. He kissed her cheeks and thanked her for being there with him.

As the last rays of sun on the eastern mountains brought closure to the day, Desta felt a measure of closure too.

TWENTY-TWO

The wedding that had caused Desta so much consternation had come and gone. Hibist and her husband, Zeru, along with their escorts, had stayed for three days and left. Damtew and Tamirat, who had spent those three days with their respective in-laws, were now back with their wives.

After the nuptials, there were more people living in Desta's home than he ever remembered. In addition to the two wives, Tamirat had become a regular member of the household. He had yet to go back and complete his schooling, but before that, as a future priest, he needed to cement his marriage by taking the communion with his new wife. For reasons not obvious to anyone, she, however, had not been cooperative in consummating this religious rite.

Desta was happy to have Tamirat at home. He was the only brother who had been neutral to the problems surrounding Saba's move. If the situation with Damtew and Asse'ged got worse, he at least would have Tamirat he could go to for help. Tamirat's presence at home also would give Desta an opportunity to get to know him better. Tamirat had started going to church school before Desta was born and they only saw each other when he came home for the holidays. For this reason, Desta had never had a close relationship with this third oldest brother.

Still, despite the many people around him, Desta had never been lonelier. There was a big void in his heart and in his home. It had begun as a good-sized dent with the departure of the vervet monkeys, then became wider and deeper with the loss of Kooli. Now with departure of Hibist, it had become an echoing void that no other human on earth could fill.

All his previous woes had been bearable because Hibist was there. Now with her gone, there was nobody he could turn to, not even his mother. She was always too busy to attend to his needs or listen to his problems. "Tell me later" or "I am too busy, go tell it to Hibist," Ayénat would say. Desta had stopped sharing his feelings with his mother altogether.

Since the wedding, Desta had been in survival mode. He took his meals, attended to the animals and slept. He talked little and smiled at no one.

Hibist and Ayénat had said the new girls would keep him company and care for him, but to Desta, his brothers' wives appeared too scared and out of place to extend friendship to him. Melkam, Damtew's wife seemed terrified of the mountains. Whenever she went outside she stared at them for a long time. She would study the ones to the east for a long while, turn to examine the ones to the north, then turn around once more and stare at the mountains above her new home. "This place makes me feel completely walled in," she complained. "Goota, where I come from, is flat as a baking pan. You can look any direction and you can't even see an anthill."

"I don't feel walled in," said Amsale, looking up at the massive edifices above the house.

"But I find them hell to climb up and down. You're lucky you don't have to climb these mountains when you go to your family. I nearly broke down the first time we went up this mountain."

"How I miss my family and the flat country!" said Melkam. "Do you notice the sun rises late and sets in early here?"

"Yes, I noticed that. I don't know how my parents found these people and this place. I certainly am not going to stay here the rest of my life," Amsale said, tossing her head with a frown.

The new wives did not attempt to disguise their distaste for their new home. Their foreheads were often knotted, their eyes melancholy and sad. They did the work given to them by Ayénat, Melkam more diligently than Amsale, but they talked very little to Desta or anybody else.

Their mutual, shared circumstances had caused them to bond with each other. They ate their meals together, and when Ayénat sat Desta with them for a meal, they talked in low voices, ignoring him. Often he finished his meal quickly and went to bed or outside while the girls were still eating and chattering.

"With the arrival of the new sister-in-laws, you will be loved twice as much," Ayénat had once told Desta. How hollow and ironic this comment seemed to him now. At a distance, he liked Melkam better. She was nearly the same size as he, innocent and shy and he could see himself being friends with her. Amsale, he didn't like at all. She was tall and pretty, slender with big severe eyes but her bearing was haughty. To Desta she projected the idea that the world revolved around her. She rarely spoke to him and he avoided her as much as he could.

Desta wondered if Hibist was happy where she was. Did she like her husband? Was she getting used to his feet? Was she scared she might get elephantiasis too?

His mother had been true to her words at least when she told Desta he would no longer have to get up in the morning to milk the cows. That job had been given to the new girls. Desta slept in a little longer. When he rose, he ate his breakfast of injera with leftover sauce from the night before, or if there were no leftovers, just the plain injera. With Hibist gone, he also lost his privilege of getting a tumbler of milk with his bread. In the mornings, Desta missed Hibist even more when he struggled to chew and swallow the dry injera without milk. When he didn't have sauce with it, he asked Melkam to give him water.

It was a Monday morning on May 14, 1956 when Desta became a full-fledged shepherd. Now Damtew was not only a married man but also a bona fide farmer, both of which he took very seriously. Desta noticed that since his brother had gotten married, his walk and attitude had changed. He pranced and swaggered around with self-importance. These changes in Damtew were demonstrated at no other time than the day he debuted as a farmer.

Impressed by his brother's weeks-long preparation with his farm tools with the help of their father, Desta remembered getting up early that morning to watch his brother's fervid activity. Desta didn't want to miss Damtew's formal entrance into the farming profession.

He remembered he was standing just outside the door watching his brother get ready with his farm equipment. Damtew had been up since before dawn, gathering the farm tools: some old ones and others that his father had recently made to complete a set for him, including the eight-foot stout, knobby wooden beam that would connect the hoe assembly to the yoke. One end of the beam was shaved flat into four even sides and trimmed to square corners. Two holes were bored into the flat surfaces. There were a straight sturdy wooden rod, one tip of which was attached to a gleaming metal plow tip, two wooden, perforated half wedges carved from a log, a short wooden dowel and a metal ring with a hook on one end.

Damtew inserted the dowel into the side holes of the long, stout beam and mounted the two wedges on the dowel on either side of the wood beam. He passed the hoe through the second hole of the beam, he pulled together the tips of the wedges and hoe and held them with one hand while he passed the ring portion of the metal hook to hold them together. Finally, he harnessed the hook end to the beam with multiple rounds of rope, creating one solid unit. He hoisted the whole assembly with ease and balanced it on his burly shoulder. He threw his whip over the other shoulder and drove the already yoked oxen pair to the lot behind their home. He was aware Desta was watching him. "Make sure the animals are safe and well looked after," he said, wheeling around.

As Desta watched his brother shamble away with his farm tools, driving his oxen, he had not even an iota of desire to become a farmer. But he was glad that now he and Damtew would have completely different jobs. He wouldn't have to bring lunch to him and Asse'ged again, as that would now be their wives' job.

Around the house Damtew became more bossy and demanding. Upon his arrival home from work, his little wife had to bring him his food promptly. After dinner she would perch on a small wooden stool by the fire, facing her husband, and place a large wooden bowl near his feet. Without saying a word, Damtew would lift a foot and place it in the bowl for his wife to wash it. She scrubbed the tough, calloused soles of his feet with her bare hands, and rubbed out dust or mud from in between his toes, and scraped the water off his feet with a cupped bottom edge or the curved top of her hand.

When she was done with one, Damtew lifted it carefully and put it on a dry cloth she had laid out in advance. After both feet were washed she would kiss the arched portion of the last foot or the big toe if she felt like showing affection. If she didn't kiss the foot, Damtew would leave it in the water basin till she did so.

AS TIME WENT BY, Desta had become more withdrawn. His interest in his surroundings had dramatically waned.

Both Abraham and Ayénat were greatly disturbed by Desta's despondency. Both saw the problem but they had no solution. One evening, they watched him disappear into the shadows of the back room right after he ate.

"Desta has been down in the dumps since Hibist left," said Ayénat, looking at her husband who was sitting across the fire. "I'm afraid things will get worse unless we do something." It was late Sunday and Abraham had just returned from church and was relaxing by the fire nursing his tella.

"What do you think should be the solution?" he asked.

"Obviously, we cannot bring Hibist back for him. But we should at least replace the dog. He needs a companion when he is tending the animals and it could help him adjust to the changes," said Ayénat, keeping her eyes on her husband.

"I have been looking for one ever since Kooli died," said Abraham. "As you know, I cannot live without one myself. In a strange sense the dog represents my father to me. And I don't want to bury him until I know for sure that he is no longer alive."

"Until you told us after Desta's dog died, I had wondered all these years why you kept calling your dogs Kooli. I thought maybe you had just run out of creative ideas," said Ayénat with a wisp of smile.

"Yes. Well, now you know. As far as getting a new dog, that exactly is my dilemma right now. None of the parishioners has puppies now. They keep telling me wait until spring."

"We are not going to wait until spring," said Ayénat. "We should get one immediately. Desta needs one when he is out there on his own in the field." She paused, her eyes fixed on the fire. "But Desta was traumatized by Kooli's death. I am not sure if he would want another dog."

THE NEXT DAY, later in the evening, after he put the animals away–the cattle in their pen, the sheep in their shelter, the horses and goats in their stalls in the house–Desta came and sat by his father's side.

His mother brought him half of a freshly baked injera, which Desta devoured with greed. He had eaten only his morning meal and was voraciously hungry when he got home.

Seeing how quickly his son ate, Abraham told Melkam to bring him more. Ayénat interceded saying he should wait until dinner was served instead of filling himself with plain injera. Abraham overruled her.

Desta munched on his second portion of injera more slowly than before. His eyes were on the fire, watching the column of swaggering and nodding flames.

"What do you say we get another dog–another Kooli, Desta?" asked Abraham, glancing at his son.

"What for?"

"To replace the old dog."

"I am not interested in any other dog. I only knew one Kooli and he is gone. I'm not going to get another dog so I can forget the Kooli I had," said Desta firmly.

"Your mother and I thought that with Hibist gone, we would get another dog to keep you company. We couldn't keep Hibist past her marriageable years, but we can get and keep a dog until he gets old and dies," said the father.

"I don't need another dog to keep me company. The Kooli I had has always been and will always be my company. He is always in my thoughts. I cannot trade him for another so that I can forget him,"

Ayénat, who had been listening to the conversation, came from the backroom and stood across from them. "Don't you think it will help wean yourself off of all these thoughts you have of Hibist and the old Kooli?"

"Why should I exchange the person or the animal I loved with another person or animal so that I can forget them?" said Desta, angered by his mother's pressure.

"I know you have wanted me to replace Hibist with the new girls. I am not lonely or in need of company. I am happy keeping my memories of Hibist and Kooli."

Abraham and Ayénat looked at each other. She shook her head indicating to her husband that he should leave Desta alone. He nodded.

"Can I get another Kooli for myself then?" he asked, smiling.

"By all means, but may I ask why?" said Desta wishing to hear from his father what Hibist had already told him.

"I got your Kooli for me as much as for you. At the time you were born, the old Kooli had been dead two months. I waited to get the new one at the same time you were born. I had done the preparations in advance, so by the time you were born I had the puppy ready to pick up. Remarkably this Kooli was uncannily similar to the one my father gave me when I was born. For that reason I was as much attached to him as you have been. That is why I didn't have the courage to shoot him myself when we mistakenly diagnosed his condition. It was a misjudgment, a rushed judgment and he was killed," said the father nearly overtaken by emotion.

Desta listened quietly. His eyes filled with tears, too.

"Hibist and I found his bones and buried him in a foxhole we located at the other end of the property," said Desta, wiping his tears.

"Good boy, I'm proud of you," said Abraham patting his son on the shoulder. "I was not aware that you did that. It was in my thoughts to do that but lately I have not even had time to have a proper meal at home. Thank you for doing it for both of us."

"You are welcome!" said Desta. "I couldn't sleep at night knowing that his bones were left scattered to desiccate in the sun."

Abraham proudly gazed at Desta.

Ayénat listened quietly. She was pleasantly surprised to see such a sensitive part of her husband. That rugged, impenetrable persona he projects is just a veneer. He has such sweet side as well, she said to herself. At that moment, she felt as if she had met her husband anew.

While the parents and Desta were talking, Damtew walked in huffing and puffing. "What is wrong?" asked Ayénat, looking toward him.

"Asse'ged and I ran into Yihoon. He wants us to help him with their move next Saturday."

"Well, what did you say?" asked Abraham

"Asse'ged said maybe. I said nothing."

"Mum is the answer to your sister who solicits your help?" said the father, staring at his son.

"If I had said 'yes,' I would be lying about my feelings. If I had said 'no' without adequate reason, he would be offended. I took the safest route and said nothing," blurted Damtew.

"You mean to say, after all these months, you're still hankering for that piece of property? What happened to compassion, love and support for your sister, your nieces and their father? Why wouldn't you see it as merely a good neighborly gesture to say, 'Yes, I'll come.' You should know this, Damtew. Your pouting, reeling, sizzling in anger and holding grudges changes nothing. They will not lose anything but you will. When the time comes for your own needs, nobody will help you. You'll reap what you sow. I am afraid for you," said Abraham as he rose to leave.

"Aren't you going to eat dinner?" asked Ayénat.

"Our son has killed my desire for food. I'd better just go to bed," he said as he shuffled to the sleeping quarters.

Damtew sat next to Ayénat in silence. Desta watched his brother's reaction. The heavy breathing had died down. His face was pensive but not contrite. He narrowed his eyes and looked into the fire he was not seeing

"You should listen to your father," said Ayénat. "What is done is done. If you don't support them in their move, you will have animosity not only from Yihoon but also from Saba, their children and surely from your father. You don't want to have a bad reputation in the family."

Damtew just stared into the fire, but his face was more relaxed and his eyes softer. "I guess you are right. I'll have to grit my teeth and do what you are telling me to do. But it won't change how I feel about their move to that place," he said finally.

TWENTY-THREE

When Yihoon came to the house that Saturday morning to solicit assistance with his move, the sun was struggling to break free from the charcoal gray clouds that hung ominously over the eastern mountains. There was dampness in the air from the previous night's rain and the ground was wet and soggy.

Abraham had just returned from relieving himself and was about to go inside when he saw Yihoon a few yards away. "Good morning, Yihoon. What brings you here so early on this chilly morning?"

"We are scheduled to move to our new house today. I came to collect Damtew and Asse'ged and whoever else I can find to help."

"Oh, yes, Damtew had mentioned you would be coming. Is everything in the new house complete?"

"Most of it. All we have left is the partitioning of the rooms, the raised platform beds, the sealing of the exterior walls and a few miscellaneous items."

"Good. You can do those slowly, as they are not so critical. You wish to beat the rain, don't you?"

"Exactly, Baba. In fact I am already behind with my farming. The house has occupied all my waking hours."

"Come in. Let's see if Damtew is still here."

"He is. At least he was a little while ago," piped up Desta, who had overheard the conversation. He was returning to the house after releasing the cattle from their pens.

"Desta, good morning! Here we are, ready to move to the new place you have recommended!" said Yihoon, grinning.

Abraham was looking at Desta keenly.

"I didn't recommend it. The cloud man did," said Desta in a low voice.

Seeing the fear in his son's face, Abraham came to his rescue. "No matter who, this was the only option. Let's see how your family would fare in a year or two."

"I know. I had to tease him a little bit," said Yihoon, his grin widening. "As much as there was anxiety at the beginning, now both Saba and the children are very excited. I suspect the animals are happy too. I saw some of the goats leaping for no reason, the sheep were running in circles and the donkeys were braying merrily."

Desta burst out laughing as he imagined the animals' antics. Abraham smiled at the glow of mirth in his son's face.

Desta was ready to ask about the cows when his brother-in-law hurried off to find Asse'ged.

"I'll tell Damtew to wait for you," said Abraham, heading into the house with Desta.

Having become a full-fledged farmer and no longer responsible for tending and managing the animals, Damtew didn't rise early on weekends and if he did, he sat leisurely by the fire and watched his little brother run around getting the animals ready to be driven to the field. When he felt generous and particularly when their father was around, he would help Desta with the morning chores.

When Abraham and Desta returned, Damtew was sitting by the fireplace with his arms crossed on his folded knees staring into space.

"Yihoon was looking for you to help him with the move. He's gone to collect Asse'ged. He should be here in a few minutes. Be ready to go with him," said Abraham, looking down on his son.

Damtew grunted.

"So . . . what's your story?" glared Abraham.

"He is not outside now waiting for me, is he? I'll go when he comes back and calls for me," mumbled Damtew, looking away.

"Get dressed and wait for him outside," ordered his father.

Abraham went to the closet and took his knee breeches, cream-colored long shirt and khaki coat from an old wooden box. While he put on his clothes, he watched Damtew who kept staring into space, pursing his lips and at times curling his lower lip and biting it.

When he noticed his father's eyes were still on him, he rose begrudgingly and went to his loft. He returned after putting on his work shorts and an old worn sleeveless jacket and shuffled out to the fence. When Yihoon and Asse'ged arrived carrying three leather sacks and chatting, he grew increasingly dark and gloomy. He coughed out a curt, "Good morning," in reply to Yihoon's friendly greeting.

Handing his supply of leather sacks to Asse'ged, Yihoon went inside the house and re-emerged with more sacks. Then all three departed for Yihoon's home. Damtew followed several feet behind his brothers, head down, staring at the earth as if he were angry at it.

When they crossed the creek, Asse'ged and Yihoon remarked on the amount of rain that had fallen the previous night as evidenced by the amount of debris littering the flooded embankment.

When they arrived at Yihoon's home, the brothers were relieved to see that there were two additional men to help as well as a few draft animals. One of the men had gathered all the farming equipment—the hoe, yoke, *weggel*—and had piled them outside on the grass. In the cow's pen were two pack mules and three donkeys feeding on hay through an opening in the fence.

When Yihoon and the two brothers entered the house, they found Saba and the two children squatting around a broken black object, letting out disappointed cries and talking among themselves. Having come from the morning's bright sun, it took a moment for the men to see that Saba, extremely upset, was crying over her broken pan.

"There is no other baking pan. That was the only one we had," said Saba, gazing at the men.

Damtew wanted to say, *Maybe something is telling you to stay put.* But he didn't have the courage.

Yihoon looked away shaking his head. "We will be happy once we leave this place behind."

"The irony of all this is last Saturday I was going to buy a new one," said Saba. "I thought it would be a good idea to bake our first injera at our new place with a new baking pan, but I couldn't find the size and quality I was looking for. And now we don't have any pan at all! What does this mean? Does this portent something bad? Why did it happen on our moving day?" Her eyes ran from her husband to her brothers as she became increasingly distressed. "I mean, not having our means of survival. Without a baking pan we can't bake our food. Without injera, our staple diet, life would be near impossible."

"It means nothing. It's just broken clay," said Yihoon, annoyed by his wife's suggestion that her broken baking pan was a bad omen. "We have to get going."

"You can look at it positively, too," said Asse'ged with a faint grin. "Symbolically, it could mean that you are breaking free from the life you have lived here in the last four years."

In the larder, Yihoon instructed Damtew and Asse'ged to fill the sacks with grain, tie them with the cords he handed them and arrange them neatly in piles outside. They would be loaded on the pack animals later.

Asse'ged and Damtew wiggled the circular, interlocking, walls of the barrel-like granaries, removed the top two rings and took them outside. Damtew, with basket in hand, scooped the grain and poured it into the sacks that Asse'ged held open. A few minutes later, Yihoon brought his two men to do the same thing in the other granaries.

From three different granaries, each containing barley, rye and teff, they filled and tied a total of fourteen sacks. Then they took the sacks outside and arranged them in three rows.

In the meantime, Saba had moved the broken pan out of the way. She and her girls were filling large and small bamboo baskets with pots and pans, clothes and other miscellaneous household items, and arranging them tidily outside to be taken to the new house by the men.

In the bedroom, Astair and Zena argued about who should roll the animal skins. Zena didn't have the strength to roll, but she nevertheless insisted that only she should do it. A fight soon broke out but was as quickly neutralized by the arrival of their father, who ordered his little daughter to leave so that the older, stronger girl could do the job. Zena left pouting nearly in tears. Yihoon took her outside and sat her near the piled household goods with a stick to chase off any goats that got too close.

The warm morning sun had heated the wet ground and the dung in the cows' pen and steam was rising from the ground. The air was redolent with dung odor and the flies were a cloud of torture for every living being around the property. The men became accustomed to the strong odor of steaming cow dung, and after awhile they did not even smell it.

In the thick gottem tree above the spot where Yihoon had stationed Zena, a handful of finches twittered while a group of wrens sounded songs of joy. Zena was enchanted by the birds and soon stopped her pouting.

Saba too was pleased to hear the chatter and beautiful melodies coming from the thick green foliage of the gottem tree. She had been preoccupied with her broken baking pan, worrying that it was a bad premonition. The way it had broken was so unnatural that she wondered if some evil force had been responsible, perhaps the Saytan that had told Desta they must leave this place. The entire time she was too confused and worried to accomplish much. She just moved through her house mechanically, randomly gathering things and taking them outdoors.

Now hearing the birds imparting such happy notes calmed her. Her father, who was an accomplished bird song reader, would find these pleasant notes as a positive sign, she thought. Emboldened by these thoughts, she concluded that whoever that spirit was—bad or good—maybe he didn't want her to bring her old baking pan, to the new place. *The fact that it broke so precisely was to show me that it didn't break just casually. It had meaning and purpose*, she said to herself.

By early afternoon, all the grain had been transferred to the sacks and piled up like flood barriers. Yihoon and the four men sat next to the sacks to take a break and Saba brought them lunch, injera piled on a mosseb with a generous amount of shiro wat in the middle of it. Astair staggered behind her mother with aluminum kettle filled with tella. Zena followed with a stack of four horn cups and two clay cups, which she passed out to the men. One cup she set aside for her mother.

Damtew and Asse'ged downed their drinks in one swig, as if they had just arrived from a scorching desert and had not had a drop of liquid for days. The other men also drank their tella in one continuous chug but stopped after they drained the cups half way.

"That is the tella I prepared for your wedding, Damtew, did you like it?" said Saba, surprised he had finished it so quickly. She ordered her daughter to bring more.

"It's not too bad," said Damtew, looking away.

"Well, thank you for the compliment," said Saba, simulating a smile.

"No, it's very good, Saba. It obviously has aged a little, which makes it even more enjoyable," said Asse'ged genuinely.

"Thank you, we don't have much left and I am not sure when I can brew the next one. We have to wait for another major event I guess," said Saba. In the meantime, Astair had brought another kettle of the brown drink and poured a second round. This time, the men drank leisurely, eating their meal at the same time.

The sun had descended halfway between its zenith and the top of the mountain above them. Yihoon studied the façade of the mountains to the east. There were many lots that had been tilled already. Some of them still had their previous season's stubbles. The rest of the land was mantled with either a thin veil of newly born grass or the forest green of the vegetation that lined the deep creeks.

Yihoon wished he had started his farming early like the other farmers whose soil would be ready for planting as soon as the rainy season was in full swing in another three weeks or so. He had so much to do with the house before he could even think of tilling his lots. He sighed deeply. Saba, who was sitting next to him tapped his knee and said, "What's wrong? We should be finished moving by Tuesday, so don't get stressed."

"It's not that, I was just thinking of the farming I have yet to do. I am already behind with it."

"We have enough grain for at least six months. If we get half of what we harvested last year, we should be okay."

"Thanks. That helps ease the pressure," he said, resting a hand on her shoulder.

"How are you feeling, guys?" said Yihoon, turning to his helpers.

"We are fine. We should load the animals soon, as the day is passing rapidly," said Asse'ged as he placed his empty cup next to the mosseb.

They loaded the donkeys with just one sack of grain each. The mules were loaded with two sacks placed on their backs crosswise. Asse'ged and Damtew each carried one of the rings of the granary on their shoulders, each driving a donkey. The other men carried the smaller sacks on their shoulders and drove the mules. Yihoon shouldered one of the remaining adobe rings. He looked awkward as he teetered along behind the men and the animals. Saba carried some of her pots and pans. The children were left behind to tend the remaining household items and sacks of grain.

At the new place, they quickly unloaded the pack animals and brought the sacks inside, then left to fetch more. In two hours the sun would slip behind the mountain.

With the second trip they were able to move the rest of the grain.

On their third trip, Damtew and Asse'ged took the last of the granaries. The other men and Yihoon carried furniture and skin mats, leaving only their bedding and the cooking pots they would need to prepare their meal that night.

By the time the sun had finally set, they were done. Yihoon and Saba thanked Damtew and Asse'ged and invited them to the big housewarming party they planned to hold the following weekend.

TWENTY-FOUR

Before they could move into their new house, Saba and Yihoon needed to have it blessed by the head priest of their church. On the morning of the move, they gathered the last of their belongings and left for their new place. Deb'tera Yacob, the head priest from the Avinevra church was coming early in the morning with holy water to bless the house before the family moved in.

When they arrived, the priest had not yet come, but Saba was happy to see her father and stepmother strolling toward the house, particularly happy when she saw that Ayénat was carrying the new baking pan she had promised her when Saba's old pan broke. Shortly after, Teferra, Asse'ged and Tamirat arrived with their wives. Enat and Hibist who lived far away with their in-laws couldn't come. Damtew claimed to have been struck down with a severe headache and didn't attend.

Aba Yacob was the last to arrive. He apologized for being late, explaining that he had been reading the Bible and praying over the small green bottle of water to make it holy. Saba was grateful. Ayénat thought it was wonderful of him to rise early to bless the water especially for their ceremony. She was hoping to have a few drops dabbed on her face and body and maybe even have a sip of it.

The priest stood by the entrance of the new home. He took his Bible from its leather case and began reading. The family stood around him, listening attentively, but they didn't understand a word of it since everything was in Ge'ez, the ancient church language which only priests could understand.

After the reading, the priest crossed the entrance, tipped the little green bottle over his cupped hand and sprinkled the water in and around the entrance, saying things nobody understood. Then he went inside followed by Saba, Yihoon, Astair and Zena, Grandma Azal—Saba's mother—and the rest of the family. He continued pouring water into his cupped hand and throwing it around the interior of the house as he recited his blessings.

Lastly, he poured a bit of water into the cupped hands of the four family members, telling them to rub themselves with the water and drink it if they wished. Then he handed the bottle with a small amount of the remaining water to Ayénat, which she accepted graciously.

Before they sat down, Abraham whispered something to Tamirat and signaled to Asse'ged and his wife. They left the room but returned minutes later, Asse'ged with a jar of tella, Mulu with a mosseb of freshly baked loaf. Amsale brought knives and Tamirat, the last to show, came trailing behind him a beautiful lamb.

Saba gasped. "Baba, what an unexpected thing!" She spoke with her big eyes as well as her mouth.

"It's not so much. We wanted you to have a happy beginning in your new house," said Abraham in a low voice.

Everyone, including the priest, turned and looked at him with admiration.

"Where had you hidden these? When did they come?" asked Yihoon excitedly, grateful for the thoughtfulness of his father and mother-in-law.

"Ask Asse'ged and Tamirat. The job was delegated to them," said the father with a smile.

"We brought them early this morning," said Asse'ged. "We hid them behind the house."

"That is incredible. Beyond our wildest expectations . . . thank you both," said Saba, glancing at her father first, then her stepmother.

With these niceties, Tamirat brought the sheep to the entrance of the house. The men and priest followed him. They stood around the sheep while the priest said prayers, passed his gleaming silver cross over the sheep. Once done, Tamirat grabbed the animal's legs and flipped it onto its back. Asse'ged grasped the mouth, held it tight, and pulled it back to expose the neck. Amsale passed the big knife to Yihoon. Yihoon crouched, said his own prayer, then rose and placed the sharp edge of the knife over the lamb's neck. A torrent of blood gushed out and sprayed everywhere, causing the people to jump out of the way. After the sheep came to a complete quiescence they went back to their seats.

Saba, thrilled by the unanticipated gifts from her father and stepmother, quickly made a fire. She placed her new baking pan on the three stones, covered the top with two fistfuls of gomen-zer, put the lid on the pan and let the oil-rich brown seeds burn until they turned black, until the poppy-red color of the pan itself became black. The process would cure the pan and make it ready

for baking injera. Saba wanted to make the first injera in her own pan in the
new house but had seen that possibility crumple along with her broken pan just
a few days ago. Now, with a brand new baking pan, she made her first flawless
injera. She couldn't be happier. She placed the steaming, pancake-like flat
bread on a straw tray and brought it to the priest for blessing. The bearded man
cut it with a knife into small wedges and passed them out to everyone.

That night, with tella from Ayénat, Mulu and Saba–all left over from the
wedding–and injera baked in the new pan, the whole family had a big feast.

Desta was the only one who couldn't attend the housewarming party, as he
had to attend to the animals. But Saba sent Astair with a separate basket of food
for him, saying that all this happened because of him and she hoped she would
return his favor in a grand way when she had her first baby.

Late that night, Abraham walked home behind Ayénat, secretly praying that
Saba would soon bear his first grandson.

TWENTY-FIVE

"Here, put on your sheepskin," said Ayénat.

"I don't want it," said Desta.

"You need it for the cold. It'll keep you warm and protect your gabi from the rain. Here. Take it."

"I don't want it. The gessa is enough protection against the rain."

"Every shepherd wears a sheepskin. What is the problem with you?"

"I am not every other shepherd, and I am not a sheep."

"Here, put it on, before I put it on your face."

Desta grabbed the sheepskin and threw it on the stubby fire log. "There! That's where it belongs!" he cried as he dashed out of the house and into a cloud of flies. This was May, the fly season.

Ayénat watched him go, stunned by his unfamiliar behavior.

AFTER DESTA BECAME a full-fledged shepherd, he had begun spending his days—from dawn to sunset—with the cows, sheep and goats. Every day Desta rose in the morning at daybreak and released the goats, the sheep and the horses from their stalls in the house and let them wonder off to graze nearby until the cows were milked and he'd had his breakfast.

After his morning meal, Desta collected his gessa, whip and stick and put on his sheepskin like a cape over his gabi. Mindful of Damtew's instructions, he left to gather the animals and drive them to the larger pasture below his home. As the custodian of the animals, he had to keep an eye on the kids and baby lambs at all times and maintain a close watch on the cattle, particularly the bulls and lead cows while they were still in the fields.

May was the beginning of the rainy season. The sporadic short showers that had begun in late April would become more regular and steady as the months advanced. Since the arrival of the rains, Desta had watched the mountains, canyons and flatlands become greener and greener by the day, advancing from thin and mossy film in early May to richer and thicker emerald grass and foliage in June. After three months of hiatus, the farmers and their oxen were back working their fields, getting them ready for sowing in late June and early July.

Within a few weeks, the once motley of white stubble patches would be transformed into a quilt of burnt sienna in a sea of green. The hushed, lifeless world of the previous three months, when the predominant sounds of the valley were the echoes of wedding and funeral drums, the lowing of home-bound cattle in the evening, and the occasional cries of hawks and other birds, would come alive with new energy and activity.

Since he had become a shepherd, Desta had noticed that there were a greater number of cattle, sheep and goats grazing in pastures all over the valley and more shepherds tending to them. He had watched from a distance as they cracked their whips, played hockey, ran in the open fields, laughing and shouting. He longed to join them, to run and laugh and shout alongside them, but he knew there was little chance of that happening. Not only were the other shepherds far from him geographically, they were also far away as people. He had never met them and didn't know how they would treat him.

As he observed the external changes that were taking place around him, Desta realized that changes had taken place within him as well.

His fear of what his brothers might do to him because of the land their father had given to Saba had been more or less assuaged. Damtew and Asse'ged appeared to have finally accepted the loss of the coveted property. Being busy with their work, they were less menacing to him.

To his surprise, he had also slowly come to accept his own losses: his sister, his dog, and his monkey friends, all of whom he kept close in his thoughts and memories.

He was happy to be free of the paralyzing fears and melancholic thoughts of the previous months. The only one that still came in waves was the possibility that Saba might lose another baby, and this he kept under control by pushing it to the back of his mind every time it popped up.

Desta's preoccupation at present was not sadness or fear but hatred. He hated his job. It had not even been thirty days since he debuted as a shepherd. It felt like a year, long enough for him to realize how hard it was to be a shepherd and how difficult the cows, goats and sheep were to manage.

It was a late afternoon, during the first week of June, when Desta, donning his small papyrus gessa, had taken shelter under the spreading branches of the sholla tree. Sitting on a foot-long flat, gray rock, he watched the rain come down in slants and pummel the ground, generating misty sprays and covering the field in front of him with white haze. The leaves chattered and the branches squeaked and clashed in the violent wind. The black clouds above the eastern mountains cracked into lighting and the wind howled and moaned as it came through the deep curving gorge of Davola high in the eastern mountains.

This was the first rainstorm Desta had experienced outdoors and he was terrified. His feet and hands were cold and numb. The blood from his toes and fingertips was drawn away, causing the skin to sag and dimple. Fortunately, the small gabi and the sheepskin had kept his body warm, and the gessa and the branches and leaves above shielded him from the rain.

The animals too had taken shelter from the pelting rain. The sheep huddled behind him on the other side of the tree trunk, the goats gathered under the gottem tree several yards from him and some of the cows clustered in the middle of the field ruminating while others continued to graze unfazed.

This was the type of moment, undisturbed by anyone, when Desta usually escaped into a dreamland of imaginings. Today, he was reeling with hatred and anger instead—for both the animals he was tending and the adults who ruled over him.

Of the animals, he found the goats to be the most unruly. They seemed to never obey him. This was proven by their behavior that morning. After he drove all the animals down, the goats managed to enter a forbidden section of his parents' property, where the bushes were thick with thorns and the ground littered with the long needles. Desta would need a stiff cowhide armor to go in after them.

Standing outside the bushes for nearly an hour, Desta shouted, begged and cracked his whip at the goats. He might as well have been a rock or a tree. They simply went on nibbling at the freshly sprouted leaves as if they were delicacies not to be missed. Damtew's words came to him: *When the sheep or goats are in these woods, they will be in imminent danger of losing their babies.* Having given up trying to get them out, Desta kept shouting, hoping at least to scare any predator that might be lurking nearby. In the end, having cleaned out all the fresh buds, they came out on their own accord.

Desta had noticed that the bulls and some of the cows didn't obey him either. No matter how much he shouted at them when they went astray, they never even turned to look at him. He remembered when Damtew was tending them, they would turn when he shouted at them from a distance. For Desta, they wouldn't turn unless he cracked his whip in front of them. He figured the reason: he was not as big as Damtew, and they were not intimidated by him.

The sheep had their own idiosyncrasies. He observed that these animals went in packs following a leader. They also moved in the direction their face was pointing. They had no sense of home once in motion. They simply kept walking. Desta had to constantly keep turning them around and keep an eye on them at all times.

By the time the rain stopped, the sun had swung over the western mountains and was sliding downward in a silver glow amidst patches of charcoal gray luminescent, gauze-thin clouds. It was at times like this before his shepherd days that Desta would retreat into a dreamland of fantasies. There was no dreamland trip for him now.

After the rain stopped, Desta parted his gessa and stood it up to dry. Stiff, cold and depressed he watched as the goats and sheep shook the rain drops from their bodies and filed out from their respective shelters. All around the valley the farmers, shepherds and animals had come out of their coverings. Desta could see their movements and began to hear their shouts as they resumed their activities.

Out in the open, Desta sat on a large granite outcropping that jutted out of the earth like a disc, trying to shake off the dampness from his clothes and body with the help of the dull, waning sun. His mind returned with its earlier preoccupation about his career and fate as a shepherd—this job his parents had foisted on him and he had willingly accepted, thinking about the fun he was going to have spending his days with the animals.

Desta's mind leapfrogged backwards to the good old days, when he used to entertain his family and guests after dinner with his dance.

The dance, called "Skista" involved the movement of his body above the waist, particularly his shoulders. With the adults clapping their hands, Desta would stand akimbo and shudder and see-saw his shoulders from right to left, or shake his whole body in a frenzied vibration. As the clapping got louder and louder, Desta got more and more into the dance. Occasionally someone would beat an upturned metal pot to accompany him.

His dance always concluded when someone engulfed him in their arms after they noticed he was tired. How Desta missed the good old days of his childhood.

TWENTY-SIX

Desta sat under the eaves of his home, shrouded in the pitch black darkness of early evening, cold, worried and shivering. The sheep he looked after were lost without a trace and Desta blamed himself for their loss. Afraid he would be punished, he was sitting there half listening to the rain pelt the thatched roof over his head while at the same time straining his ears to discern the words and fuming notes delivered by his father to the occupants of his home.

Desta had never heard his father so angry.

"How could you sit on your fat ass all day? My sheep! Gourmet meals for the hyenas! Oh my, oh my, how could this happen? The whole pack, decimated by the cackling hyenas . . . oh my, oh my . . . my cursed children . . ." Abraham's voice went up with every word and phrase he uttered. Desta looked through the crack in the wall and could see his father pacing the living room, around the fire, past his stool. Every so often he stopped and held his head with one hand and stared into the fire. And then he paced around it again saying "Oh my, oh my, oh my . . ."

Desta could not see his mother. Melkam and Amsale were huddled together behind the parapet but he could see only the tops of their heads.

Abraham leaned over the parapet and said, "Has anybody gone looking for them?"

"He and Asse'ged," said Melkam meekly. Desta thought the "he" she referred to was her husband, Damtew. Melkam, like her mother-in-law, never called her husband by his first name.

"What about that lazy, tailed one?"

"We have not seen him since we learned of the sheep's disappearance," said Amsale. Abraham grunted and walked off.

Desta knew he was the "tailed one." He did not dare go near the door, let alone go inside.

After a while, Desta couldn't see his father anymore. The flames in the fire had gone out, leaving only a smoldering bit of wood. The smoke lazily twirled and swayed as it dissolved into the darkness.

Although he couldn't see his mother, Desta thought she probably had dissembled into the darkness too and into the larder. Hibist once told him that the best way for a woman to escape a beating from her husband was to quickly run into the larder. "No pants-wearing man would dare go in there and drag her out to beat her. It's a woman's sanctuary of safety," she had told him. Desta had never seen his father beat his mother. He rarely even saw them having a normal conversation. Their communication typically involved a "yes" or "no" to a question one or the other asked or just short phrases and sentences. The few times he had seen his father angry at his mother, he had done all the talking.

Desta heard the popping noise of someone walking on the muddy path that came around the cattle pen. He turned to inspect. It was Damtew, wrapped in his gabi, his face a mere blur in the shadow of the night.

Desta swallowed his saliva and held his breath as he watched his brother head straight for the door.

"Any good news?" asked Abraham in an angry tone. His voice had come from the back room. Desta thought he must be lying in bed.

"Asse'ged and I scoured the perimeter of the field as well as across the creeks and canyons. We saw no sign of the sheep."

Desta's heart sank and his stomach tightened. He heard the howling of a hyena and was not sure where it came from. He cocked his ear and listened. It was coming from high in the mountains above their home. Desta was relieved. This hyena probably wouldn't get to the sheep as they had been below their home when they disappeared. Shortly after, he heard another howl. This one came from somewhere in the woods across the Davola River. This hyena was closer, but the sheep had disappeared on this side of the river, so chances were the second hyena would not get to them either. He was not certain if hyenas could swim cross a teeming river. It had been raining most of the afternoon and the creeks and Davola were roaring.

After retuning from his distraction, Desta brought his face again to the hole in the wall and watched the activities inside the house. Melkam went to the father-in-law and asked if he would rise for dinner. He said he had no appetite for a meal and told her to go ahead and serve the others.

For a moment it seemed Damtew was the only one who was hungry. Melkam disappeared to the kitchen and returned with food in a basket and set it before

Damtew. He tore off the injera, rolled the wat with it and placed it in his mouth, tilting his head like a chicken that tosses its head after it has sucked up water.

Desta's stomach growled. Melkam went to the kitchen and returned with a folded injera in her hand. Amsale was right behind her. The two girls shared a stool together as they joined Damtew. Desta's mouth salivated as he watched them eat.

But something was strange about the scene. Where was his mother? And why hadn't Damtew asked about *his* mother, considering the two were very close.

Desta knew his mother had probably taken refuge in the larder. He walked along the perimeter of the curving wall and sat near a small aperture in the wall of the larder. He pressed his face to the hole to see what Ayénat might be doing in there.

By the slumbering fire from the kitchen, he saw the silhouette of his mother arranged in a position he had never seen her before, other than that time when he and she went to church to receive a communion for the dog disease.

Her knees were planted on the ground, her back bowed into an arc, face near her knees. She was holding her head with both hands and reciting something in a hushed voice. He could only hear a smattering of her words.

"Good Lord . . . guard those sheep from the hyenas . . . return them safely— Lord, please do. Please Lord, send your angels to guard those sheep."

"Please lord, keep Desta safe . . . return him home . . . Desta safe . . . from wrath of his father . . . us too . . . Please lord."

Melkam appeared in the larder with the empty basket from Damtew's meal, nearly tripping on her mother-in-law's skirt which lay spread on the floor. Ayénat gathered and tucked it while her head was still resting on the bare earth. As soon as Melkam returned to the living room, Ayénat raised her head, sat up and said a few last words, crossed herself, got up and walked off in the direction of the living room.

Desta quickly went by the front entrance, where he could see through the gap between the doorjamb and the post next to it. Melkam came to the entrance saying that she needed to close the door.

Her mother-in-law looked at her incredulously. "Close the door?"

"Yes, the hyenas are howling and I am afraid," Melkam said timidly.

"What about Desta?" said the mother, looking at the daughter-in-law in disbelief.

"Ahh, I, I . . ."

"I know. You forgot he was out there . . . He probably is hiding around here someplace. Don't close it yet."

"I think you should leave him out, Mama. It will be a lesson to him," said Damtew.

"I hope you are kidding," said Ayénat, glancing at Damtew's shadowed face.

"No, I am not," replied Damtew, looking away.

Ayénat kept her eyes on Damtew as if waiting for him to turn and face her. To Desta the figures standing by the fire were merely silhouettes.

"I knew it, Ma; I knew something like this would happen," said Damtew finally turning to his mother. "Desta never took his training seriously. He never had an interest in what I was teaching him. He's too dizzy dreaming about all kinds of wild things. The best way to teach him a lesson, so that he will remember it every day, is to leave him out in the cold. The sound of the hyenas will help shake him up . . ." Damtew didn't have to wait for Ayénat's response. Her face had spoken volumes. He merely shuffled off to his loft.

"I never thought you were that heartless, Damtew," said Ayénat and turned to her daughter-in-laws, who were sitting by the fire in the kitchen. "Don't lock the door," she said. "Close it yes, but don't throw the pole across."

Having heard his mother and feeling safe from his father's fury, Desta decided to make a discreet entry into the house.

"Good, you came as I suspected you would," said Ayénat in a whisper when she saw Desta.

"Let's go straight to the fire in the kitchen. Your hands are terribly cold, you need to warm them."

She hid him with her skirt as they walked past the dying embers of the fire in the living room.

"I will take care of him. You go to bed," said Ayénat to Melkam and Amsale who were standing by the parapet, surprised Desta had materialized out of the darkness.

As he waited for his mother to bring him something to eat, Desta's teeth chattered and his body shook. The fire seemed to have made his chills worse.

"I am not going to ask you to explain how the sheep got lost tonight," said Ayénat when she returned with his food. "It is a moot point now and I don't want to wake your father. Here, have your dinner while you are getting warm."

"Your father, as you must know, is very mad. I am not sure you want to be within close range of him when he wakes tomorrow morning. I will give you a goatskin and my old gown and you can sleep in the larder. Get up early before dawn and go hide in the woods. I will have the cattle driven to the field for you by the girls. They will bring your breakfast there as well."

The flames on the fire had gone out. The ash-crested charcoal embers glowed with the wisp of fresh draught from the door and dimmed when the breeze subsided.

Desta wolfed his food ravenously, his eyes on the fire, half listening to what his mother said. He was afraid to think what would happen if the sheep had been killed by the hyenas.

He pushed the basket aside, chilled. "Can I sleep by the fire instead?" he asked.

"I wouldn't take that chance if I were you," said Ayénat. "I will give you enough gabi; it is better that your father not see you."

Ayénat prepared Desta's bed in the area where she had been praying. She spread straw from the horses' stalls and threw a goatskin over the top, then covered him with his gabi and her own heavy old gown.

"Remember, you need to rise early and go hide in the woods. Bring the gown with you to keep warm," she said as she tucked the clothes around him.

Soon after his mother left, Desta arranged himself into a ball and thought about the sheep's disappearance. Nothing like this happened to him before and he had no idea what the consequences would be. From his mother's behavior, he could only conclude that the retribution, to both of them, would be severe.

IN THE MORNING, Desta followed his mother's advice, but with a slight modification. As soon as he got up, instead of just hiding in the bushes, he went searching for what might be left of the sheep, any bones, a trail or spattering of blood on the grass, shreds of skin or severed heads with gaping mouths and glazed eyes. He walked the entire perimeter of the field until his bare feet and hands ached from the morning chill and his mind went numb with worry.

Around the area where he had last seen the sheep Desta went deep into the woods searching in crevices, under big trees, and any other place the sheep may have taken shelter from the rain. He imagined them huddled under a tree, some sleeping on the ground with their feet folded under their bellies, others standing chewing on their cuds, eyes half closed in a dream-like state.

Nowhere did he find the missing sheep.

Exhausted and scared, Desta sat on a rock near the gottem tree in the south of the field, waiting for the sun to come down from the mountain and warm his body. His feet and hands were the coldest. To warm them, he sat squatting on the rock, tucked the edges of his gabi under his feet and buried his hands in the folds of the cloth.

He was rocking back and forth listening to the tumult of thoughts that came and went in his mind, when he was distracted by voices that came from behind him. He turned to see Asse'ged and Yihoon emerge from the woods at different points along the south end of the field. They were walking toward each other, searching the area around them.

Desta wanted to run and hide, but running would make him more noticeable so he stealthily ambled to the tree and stood close to its trunk.

Asse'ged and Yihoon scanned every corner of the field, then slowly approached the gottem tree.

Desta froze. He clung to the trunk hoping it might save him.

Asse'ged spotted him first. "What are you doing here?" he demanded. The whites of his eyes were red as if he had not slept all night. But then, he wouldn't have slept. Three of the lost sheep were his.

"I woke up early to search for the sheep," said Desta timidly.

"What do you think happened to them?"

Desta shrugged and looked away.

"Where were they when you saw them last?" asked Yihoon.

"They were exactly over there," said Desta, pointing to the north side of the field. "And when you woke from your long sleep, they were gone, right?" said Asse'ged, looking at Desta disdainfully.

"I didn't sleep."

"How could they just disappear into thin air if you were keeping a good watch on them?"

"I went to gather some goats that had strayed into the woods. By the time I came out, the sheep were gone."

"They were on that side of the field?" said Yihoon, pointing to the location Desta indicated.

"Yes, over there. They were grazing facing the river."

"Let's just hope that at least some of yours and mine were spared from the hyenas' jaws," said Asse'ged glancing toward the brother-in-law.

Shortly after Asse'ged and Yihoon left, Melkam arrived with the cattle and goats. On one arm, she had carried Desta's breakfast in a small basket. He anxiously opened it and found a folded half moon injera with a spoonful of the leftover shiro wat—ground peas sauce from their previous meal. She sat by his side watching as he devoured the cold meal.

"Both Baba and He looked everywhere in the foothills and returned without finding any sheep—dead or alive," said Melkam, as Desta was swallowing his last piece of the injera.

"But if Ma's prayer works, maybe they will come home alive. She has been on her knees since the day broke."

"Do you think they will?" asked Desta. "I heard so many hyenas howling last night. I hate to think it but . . ."

Melkam looked at Desta severely. "When Baba and He returned empty handed, Amsale and I thought the hyenas must have killed the sheep and dragged them into their holes in the forest. How else can you explain the disappearance of the entire fold without a trace?"

"I don't know," said Desta as he wiped his tears away.

"You should pray," said Melkam as she gathered the basket and rose.

Desta blew his nose with the tip of his gabi. "I don't know how. And what good will it do now if the sheep have already been eaten by the hyenas?"

"Just say, 'God, please bring the sheep home alive, God, bring the sheep home alive.' Repeat those words until you get tired," said Melkam.

The rest of the morning and into the afternoon, Desta kept repeating the words Melkam had told him. "God, please bring back the sheep alive . . . God, please bring back the sheep alive. . . ." But how could God, bring back sheep that were already in the bellies of the hyenas? He was not expecting a miracle.

Late in the morning Asse'ged and Yihoon returned. Neither had any sheep with him. Desta scurried into the bushes and hid. He didn't want to talk to them.

"No trace of the sheep?" Yihoon asked Asse'ged when they met at the common footpath.

'No sheep dead or alive," said Asse'ged with a deep sigh. "And, obviously you didn't either."

"No, but I asked the villagers to let us know if they come across any lost sheep," said Yihoon in a grim voice.

"You must believe in miracles," said Asse'ged sarcastically. "How can you expect to find them alive if we've not found them by now?" He stared around the eastern sky. "I hope you are right, but I still feel like we've wasted good hours of farming before it begins to rain."

Desta was hiding less than fifty feet from the two men. He slowly emerged from his hideaway and looked up at the winter sky. It was shrouded with spreading sheets of ominous clouds.

THANK YOU, LORD! Thank you, Lord! Thank you, God Almighty!" Ayénat was saying when Desta woke early in the morning on the third day of the sheep's disappearance.

He shook his head, trying to come out of his deep sleep. He cocked his ears and listened to what his mother was saying.

"From way over there? It's amazing!"

"We were amazed ourselves. . . ."said an older deep voice.

"Who found them?"

Desta couldn't believe his ears. "The sheep were alive!" He bolted out of bed and ran to the door, where his father and mother were speaking with an old man and a boy. The sheep were gathered behind them.

"My son here found them in a cave up on top of that mountain," said the man.

"This is nothing short of a miracle," said Abraham. "First, how in the world could they have been spared from the hyenas for two nights? And how is it possible that they went all the way to the top of the mountain, crossing the rough waters of the Davola River?"

"We are at a loss ourselves," said the old man.

"When you pray for the help of St. Mary and her son, anything is possible," said Ayénat. "I've been praying for these animals to return safely ever since they disappeared and look what happened. This is a true manifestation of the God All Mighty!" she said triumphantly.

"They had gone all the way up there," repeated Abraham, pointing to the distant mountaintop.

Desta followed his father's finger, shaking his head incredulously.

"Yes, all the way up there!" said the old man. "The amazing thing is that my son came to tell us about these fat antelopes. He wanted me to go and shoot them. When I went with my gun, they didn't look like antelopes but sheep. Having heard about your lost sheep from Yihoon, we thought they must be yours so we brought them home last night and boarded them with ours."

"I am sorry you had to travel so early in the cold morning," said Abraham.

"We wanted you to have peace of mind, knowing that your sheep were alive and well," said the man, looking at Ayénat, then Abraham.

"Would you come in and have something to eat before you go?" asked Ayénat.

"No, no, we have to go. We have work to do. Thank you for the kind offer," said the man as he rested his hand on his son's shoulders, urging him to go.

"I have pledged two shillings to St. Mary's church if the sheep were returned to us. I'll give them in your name," said Ayénat as she watched the father and son shuffle down the path.

"That is kind, you really don't have to. All we did was bring back your sheep."

"For boarding them and the trouble you have taken to bring them to us in these cold hours."

"If it pleases you, Weizero Ayénat . . . May God bless you and protect your sheep."

After the man and boy had gone, they counted the sheep and discovered that two baby lambs were missing. Abraham thought maybe they were eaten by a fox or had drowned when crossing the river. But he was still very grateful that the other thirteen were returned alive. He thought about what Asse'ged had always told him. "We are not a sheep family, why don't we get rid of them?" It was on this day that Abraham decided to give the sheep to somebody who knew how to raise them.

After the others went inside, Desta remained outside, staring at the massive, granite rock that capped the mountain facing his home. It was under this rock that the boy found the sheep, the same granite rock that had first captivated his interest in touching the sky. On a wet and sunny day, the face of this rock flashed like a sheet of glass, illuminating the valley with reflected light. Desta was grateful to the mountain for sheltering the sheep for two nights and dreamt once again that one day he could climb to the top and let the clouds flow through his fingers.

TWENTY-SEVEN

It was before dinner time when Abraham walked in trailing behind him on a leash, a tired and wilted brown dog. Ayénat, anticipating his arrival, had been cleaning the house and preparing dinner. Desta sat at his usual place at the foot of his father's long stool. Melkam and Amsale had finished milking the cows and were helping Ayénat in the back room. Damtew sat on his own stool, next to Ayenat's, quiet, wrapped to his nose in his gabi like a crowned spirit.

"This dog is to replace the one we mistakenly lost. It should keep you company in the field," said Abraham as he handed Desta the leash. "Maybe now you can be a better shepherd in its company than you have been."

Ayénat had stopped her activities and had come to look at the dog. Melkam and Amsale too had come to see the dog. Damtew didn't move. He simply stared at the dog and Desta.

"But I don't want a dog, Baba," said Desta, dropping the leash.

"It's a gift from my sister, Welella. She got him from a friend over a year ago as a puppy because it reminded her of the first dog I had as a boy. When she heard that we had lost our Kooli, she decided to give it to us." Abraham looked at the dog as he talked.

Ayénat said, "That is very nice of Welella. Desta, I know how distraught you have been since Kooli died. This dog can be good company and help you gradually forget your old dog."

"But I don't want to forget Kooli," barked Desta, staring at his mother.

"By the way, Welella calls him Tizitaw, but I've renamed him Kooli," said Abraham, looking at his son appealingly.

"There you go!" said Ayénat brightly. "With the identical name as your old dog, it's like you never lost him. You will remember your old dog every time you call his name."

"Baba, I know for you the only way to keep alive the memory of your father is by having a dog named Kooli. For me the only way to keep alive the memory my Kooli is to not replace him with another dog with the same name," said Desta in a firm voice.

"Desta has a point. For how long will you keep getting a dog called Kooli?" said Damtew, pulling the pile of gabi down from his mouth.

Desta was surprised that Damtew had come to his aid.

"Until my father returns or we find out exactly what happened to him," said Abraham, tossing his head a little and looking at Damtew. He too seemed surprised by Damtew's question.

"Do you think your father might still be alive?" Ayénat asked, glancing at Abraham.

"Miracles do happen, don't you think?" said Abraham, thinking of the recently lost and miraculously recovered sheep. But the father was also thinking about the dog and Desta at the moment. The little boy's reaction toward the dog had surprised and disappointed him.

For what seemed a long time, no one spoke.

"I think you are right about the miracle part," said Ayénat finally. "It's good that you still have hope. How old would he be now?"

"I don't know exactly, probably 68 or 70. He could be living like a monk in some church. I just wish we had followed up on the three leads we had about his sighting in Lalibela years ago," he said his voice trailing away. "But enough of this. It's dinnertime and I'm hungry."

While Ayénat and the girls were getting dinner ready, Abraham leaned over to Desta and said in a low voice, "I brought the dog as much to remind me of my father as for you to have a companion while you are tending the animals. You don't have to associate yourself with him if you don't want to. He can just be a guard dog in the house.

"That's okay, Baba. I'll just keep the memory of my Kooli deep in my heart so this Kooli will not come between him and me," whispered Desta, happy his father had shared such personal information with him.

FOR ABRAHAM, the new Kooli turned out to be a good guard dog as well as a continued link to his father. Kooli yelped at visiting guests and barked furiously at night, protecting the animals from hyenas that approached their pens.

It seemed to Abraham that more and more hyenas were invading his property. Only recently a pack of hyenas had killed and devoured an old cow that was accidentally left out.

He was sitting with Desta at his feet, across from Damtew, when he heard the sound of a racing pack of hyenas not far from the home. He thought at first that Kooli, who was barking furiously, was chasing them, but then it became apparent that the hyenas were after Kooli. Abraham hastily put on his trousers and a heavier gabi, grabbed his rifle and headed for the door.

Ayénat discouraged her husband from going out, but he didn't listen to her. Desta and Damtew also tried to discourage him, fearing he would be attacked by the hyenas, but he merely told them to shut the door behind him. Kooli was happy to have human reinforcement. He whimpered at first then barked with gusto as he ran to Abraham.

"Come take the dog inside," Abraham said to Damtew. He grabbed Kooli by the skin on his neck and gave him to his son.

The half moon was hardly visible, buried by the heavy cloud of the winter sky. Desta and Damtew stood by the door, staring into the near pitch black darkness and worrying about their father who had been now completely swallowed by the shadow of the night. Ayénat and the girls were also by the door.

"Nothing will happen to him," said Damtew, reading his mother's worried face. "It's crazy to go after a pack of hyenas in the darkness," said Ayénat gazing sideways at Damtew. She had her fingers on her mouth.

"He has a gun," said Damtew. "What can happen to him?"

Desta's eyes went from his mother to Damtew and then to the dog. Surrounded by people, Kooli now was quiet.

"Sshh, listen," said Damtew, cocking his ear.

What they heard was a huge pack of cackling hyenas stampeding down the hill above their home as if they were being chased by a furious beast. Within that instant, the group's concentration on the rushing hyenas was interrupted by a deafening blast that silenced the hyenas as if it decimated them all. They listened and peeked out to the black void, but all was silent for a few seconds until the dog began to bark again.

"Did Baba kill all the hyenas?" asked Desta, looking up to his mother. "There is no more running."

"I don't know. We'll find out when he comes," she said.

When Abraham returned, his wooly hair was curled and matted by the damp winter air and his gabi hung cockeyed. He held his rifle with one hand, barely off the ground. "Did you kill them all, Baba?" said Desta anxiously.

"I probably killed one but scared the others off," said Abraham with a grin. Desta thought his father's smile was sweet even with one chipped tooth.

Desta couldn't wait to see the dead hyena. All his life he had heard the hyenas' terrifying calls and marauding cackles in the night but had never actually seen one. Hibist had once told him that hyenas were ridden by *Budas* to gravesites to dig out buried people and share the flesh with them or to carry the dead bodies to the budas' homes so that they could eat them over time. Budas, she had told him, were people who were possessed by evil spirits that caused them to prey on children and adults alike.

"WHAT ARE YOU DOING HERE on the doorstep so early?" said Abraham when he saw Desta sitting on the threshold wrapped like a cocoon with his gabi from his neck to toes.

"I was waiting for you to rise so we can go and look at the dead hyena," said Desta.

"I am anxious to do that myself because I'm not completely certain that I killed one," said Abraham with a faint grin.

After his father returned from his morning ritual in the bushes, the two of them went to look for the dead hyena. For what seemed a long time to Desta, they looked everywhere—under the trees, in the bushes that lined the southern creek, all the ravines—but they found nothing, not even a drop of blood or a spent bullet. As they continued to search, Desta noticed that the question mark on his father's forehead became more and more pronounced.

"I was certain—not completely certain, that the bullet hit flesh," said Abraham as they walked home. The question mark on his face had turned into widespread puzzlement.

LATE IN THE DAY Melkam came running, out of breath, to the field where Desta was tending the animals.

"Go, go, go, run, run . . . to where they are farming behind the house," said Melkam, grabbing Desta by the arm and pushing him.

"What is going on?" asked Desta, pulling out of his sister-in-law's grip.

"Baba wants you to come quick. They found the hyena. He's is not dead yet, Baba wants you to see it before he finished it off. Go, run . . . It's crippled . . . It has been trying to drag itself away. I'll keep an eye on the animals until you get back. Run now and come back soon."

Excited by the prospect of seeing a hyena, Desta flew.

When he arrived at the periphery of the farm, he was panting and breathless. He coughed and held his chest, trying to calm himself.

"Here is the hyena we looked for this morning. See, I told you I had hit him," said Abraham with a smile when he saw Desta.

Desta was gasping too hard to respond.

"Why did you run so hard?" said Tamirat. "He wasn't going anywhere, silly."

"I didn't know what to think. Melkam rushed me to get here."

Desta stared at the wounded animal. "It looks like a dog! I thought it was much bigger than a dog, at least from the way it howls at night."

Damtew had pinned down the hyena. Its eyes, pained and watery, had glinted toward Desta when he arrived. The earth around the hyena's feet was scraped and dug up from the animal's struggle to free itself before it finally resigned itself to its fate. One of its hind legs was broken and hanging, the other was under a rock slab.

"Hyenas are not big but they have strong jaws," said Abraham, staring down at the vanquished brute.

The hyena had a round, spotted belly and legs and its brown hair was frizzy, showing a dandruff skin below. Flies were busy sucking its nose and gaping mouth and the blood crusted wound on its right hind leg. Its tail was streaked with blood and mud, and the flies were hunting for food there, too.

"It's very ugly," said Desta. He couldn't quite imagine how Budas ride it to gravesites or load it with dead bodies.

"Hyenas aren't known for their beauty or personality, but they are powerful beasts," said Abraham. He was twirling a crooked stick with one hand. "This is where the bullet entered, he said, pointing to the wound area with the stick."

Desta squatted to study the bullet hole.

"It shattered the thigh bone, came out and grazed the skin of the belly," said his father.

"What amazes me is how in the world could you shoot in the pitch-black of the night and bring down a hyena," said Tamirat.

"I had a lot of practice during the Italian war. Do you think I got those medals for nothing?" said Abraham with a grin and a glimmer of pride.

"I am proud of you, Baba, people can't hit their targets in the broad daylight let alone in the dark," said Damtew. He was recalling his own experiences with a gun. "You know that well, don't you Damtew?" said Tamirat chuckling.

"I must admit it was very dark. Some luck must have been involved also," said Abraham with humility.

"You deserve another medal for this one," said Tamirat.

"I have enough. I pass the baton to you two . . . three," he said, looking at Desta. "We should all go back to work. Desta, now that you know what a hyena looks like, could you go and get me my pistol?"

"What for?" said Damtew.

"We need to finish him off."

"This is not Kooli, you know. I can do it in a flash with my own sheer power," bragged Damtew. He slid the pole toward the hyena's neck, straddled it and pressed down hard. The beast kicked with his unharmed hind leg and sleep-walked with the front two for a few seconds, then its mouth gaped open, a clear liquid oozed out, and its tongue hung from the corner of its jaw.

Desta looked at his brother and shuddered.

TWENTY-EIGHT

Desta was in the field tending his cattle when he found himself under the breath of a fuming, tall balding man, who accused the cattle of destroying half of his crop. "These are your cows and bulls that decimated my three months of sweat," said the man, pointing to a dozen cattle he had brought back to Desta. He demanded to know which farming field his father was working that day.

Shaken, Desta looked toward the animals the man had brought. Sure enough, they were Lomee, the bull, and a few other young bulls, and cows that had crossed the river to graze on the freshly grown crops.

"My Baba has gone to court and won't be back for two days," said Desta.

"Never mind, I will come another time. . . . Haven't they told you that this is a very critical time for all shepherds to keep a constant and close watch on their animals?" Desta looked down at his feet.

"Can you answer the question?" said the man, tapping Desta's head with his work-worn hand.

"Yes, my brother had told me all about it, but I am also tending the sheep and goats. I have already been in trouble with them so I was keeping a close watch on them instead. There has not been a problem with the cattle all this time," said Desta in low voice, his eyes flickering between the man and the animals he had brought back.

"If you are tending the cattle, you should do so with the utmost care as well. Now your father will have to pay for the losses I have suffered," said the man and shuffled off.

Desta watched him go, angry at himself for allowing this to happen again with the animals he was tending.

TWO DAYS LATER Desta and Damtew drove the animals across the River Davola to their parents' old property. There was a big field that had been left fallow and was thick with newly grown grass. They needed the animals to cut it down. Part of the land was also currently being farmed.

Desta and Damtew had just finished eating the lunch that Damtew's wife, Melkam, had brought for the workers when their father arrived. Desta was about to walk off to his animals, when Abraham signaled that he should come because he had an important question to ask him. Desta walked over to his father obediently.

When Desta reached his father, Abraham grabbed him by the arm with the power and sudden swiftness of a predator stocking its prey. "Tell me," he said glaring down on Desta. "What were you doing when the bulls and cows crossed the river and destroyed Gizaw's crop?"

Desta was more mortified by his father's eyes than by his tight grip or harsh voice. As he looked into the big, intense eyes bearing down on him, Desta tried futilely to pry open the hand that had locked on him.

His father tightened his hold as he repeatedly demanded an answer to his question.

Desta stammered, stuttered to say something, but no clear words came out.

"You must have been dawdling your time away doing nothing but staring at mountains and the sky, huh??" demanded Abraham still bearing down on his son. "I think it's time you should be taught a lesson, Desta," said Abraham as he shook his arms and pushed him down onto the tilled soil. Before Desta could rise and run, the father brought out his horse-riding whip from under his gabi, uncoiled it and began to slash his bare buttocks and legs. When Desta tried to get up and run, his father pushed him with his feet and continued to slash him,

"Because of your irresponsibility and lazy habits, I am going to have to pay money that I worked so hard to earn," he kept saying as he struck him.

People on the farm as well as neighbors, who saw and heard Desta's wails came running to rescue him. Every time one of them tried to grab the father's swinging arm, he would scold them and threatened to lash them, too. Fearing for themselves, these people simply stood back and watched with their hands on their mouths, their faces gripped in horror.

To protect his face, Desta buried it into the freshly tilled earth, forcibly inhaling the aroma of the soil as if it could pervade his body and deaden his senses. Desta had now given up the idea of getting up and running. He merely lay there waiting for his father to kill him.

Once Abraham was satisfied with the seven lashes he delivered on his son, he coiled the whip, tucked it under his gabi and sauntered off. When he turned and saw one of the women bystanders had come to pick up Desta, he came rushing back and said, "I don't want any of you here to do anything for him. This was meant to teach him a lesson."

"But he is only a small boy, Abraham," stammered a woman whose voice was familiar to Desta.

"It's when they are small they should be taught responsibility and accountability," said Abraham looking down on Desta with severe eyes. "Just a month ago we nearly lost our herd of sheep, last week the goats destroyed my young crop and two days ago I've learned my cattle went across the river and destroyed Gizaw's crops. He has demanded that I pay for his losses or he will take me to court. We are having all these problems because of this lazy, dawdling and useless product of mine." His anger seemed to surge again, getting stronger with the itemization of Desta's failings.

As he lay in the dirt feeling a burning sensation on his tender skin, Desta's fear of his father was renewed. Seconds ago when the beating stopped, he had dared to think he might live. Now Abraham's return and renewed fury caused him to cover his face with terror. He wished the people would go away so his father would leave again.

"None of you here are to help him. He needs to lie here until sunset, hopefully thinking about the causes of this punishment," said Abraham looking around at the women.

All the women just stood there, looking down. For what seemed like a long time, everybody was quiet. Desta could hear Damtew's whip cracking as he drove the plowing oxen. He slowly lifted his head and looked to see if anybody was still there.

He saw three women. One was Melkam. The second was Mawa, a woman with whom Desta had a love-hate relationship because whenever she came to visit, she always kissed him intensely on the cheeks, particularly if his parents were watching. The third woman he had never seen before. She was tall and good looking and had lines of tattoos around her long neck. He remembered she was the woman who tried to intercede when his father was beating him.

Desta put his head down and lay on his belly with his face in his hands. Now that everything around him was quiet, he began to feel the stinging sensation of the lashings. "Could you please cover my legs and thighs with soil? The cool earth may help sooth the burning," said Desta in muffled voice.

He heard the women softly speaking.

"I can do it," said Mawa finally. "Abraham has disappeared behind the hill."

She lifted Desta's legs and pushed away as much soil as she could manage. Then she dropped his legs in the small trench she had created and began pushing the fresh soil on top of his legs. Desta sighed deeply when he felt the cool earth on his naked legs.

"Not too much, not too much—you don't want to crush them," said the third woman.

"I am fine, I am fine," said Desta soothed by cool dirt.

Damtew had come over. Desta heard him tell the women to get back to their work.

"This is interesting! Whose idea was this?" Desta heard Damtew say.

"His own," said Mawa.

"Why? Now he wanted to be buried alive? He should get up and go to his job," said the older brother.

"His legs and thighs were burning from the lashes. He wanted to soothe them with the cool soil," said the woman with the tattooed neck.

"He deserves it! I told him from the beginning how important it was for him to be attentive with those animals. Let's just hope this will be a good lesson for him. If not, I'll have my own share of his little body," said Damtew with bravado. "Tell him to get up and go to his job."

Desta cringed at the thought of being beaten by Damtew.

Eventually everyone left and Desta fell asleep, comforted by the cool soil. When he woke, he lifted his head and looked around. He saw the woman with tattooed neck squatting next to him.

"Are you feeling better?"

"The soil was good. Can you help me take it off?" asked Desta. "I think my legs have gone to sleep."

"It's as if you have been eating the dirt, my little one. You have soil all over your face, lips and nose. Let me clean them for you," said the woman as she used the ends of Desta's gabi to brush the dirt off his face.

Desta dragged his legs slowly and sat up.

Damtew and his wife had left the farm. Desta slowly rose, trying to see if he could go home also. He found that his legs wouldn't take him a few yards, let alone the long stretch of hilly and winding paths to his home. The tall woman, who introduced herself to Desta as Degay, offered him a stay at her house until he felt better. Mawa had left earlier, saying she would try to return to check on him later. Having not much choice, Desta limped alongside Degay the hundred feet to her home. That she had been there sitting by his side the whole time made Desta feel closer to this strange woman than to his own relatives.

Once inside, she laid him on a furry sheepskin by the fireplace and quickly made a roaring fire to warm him. The tickling sensation of the fire on his half-naked body made Desta feel at ease and relax.

She gave him a warm tumbler of milk with injera that helped kill his hunger and quickly put him to sleep.

When he woke the following morning, Mawa was there sitting by his side. "Are you feeling better?" she asked tapping Desta on his leg.

"I am still sore where Baba lashed me and I can't walk normally," said Desta, his face partially buried in the extra clothes Degay had laid on him.

"I came to take you home. Your mother must be wondering why you didn't come home last night," said Mawa.

"I just saw him struggle to go to the bathroom," said Degay. "I am not sure he can walk the full distance yet."

"We have the monthly association get-together at my brother's house today, Ayénat and Abraham will be there," said Mawa.

"In that case, Desta, Mawa will take you to your mother this afternoon at the gathering. Till then, rest here," said Degay, her soft beautiful eyes resting on him.

WHEN MAWA TOOK DESTA to the Association meeting, they found the house teeming with people. He remembered many of the people he saw because they were the same people that came when it was his parent's turn to host the monthly meeting. The adults gather and discuss community affairs, followed with a dinner party at these meetings.

Ayénat, dressed in her flowing and voluminous, embroidered gown, was sitting at the edge of the living room, talking with two women. Desta remembered neither of the women. Higher up in the living room sat about half a dozen men, among whom was his father. He sat in the middle, holding a hot discussion about a court case he had won.

Desta didn't want to cross to the other side of the living room to his mother, afraid his father would see him. To ease matters, Mawa thought it would be better to invite Ayénat outside so she could see the condition of her son. Not wanting other people's attention, she took Desta behind her brother's house and sat him on a peeling log and went to fetch Ayénat.

"Oh my Lord, my Lord!" cried Ayénat. "This is not what Damtew told me had happened." She ran her fingers on Desta's legs, thighs and buttocks. Desta stood and held his gabi up as his mother inspected his body.

"What did he tell you?" asked Mawa knotting her forehead and looking down on Ayénat.

"He said their father had spanked Desta for allowing the cattle to destroy Gizaw's crops and that Desta had refused to come home because of it. I figured he would come home eventually," said Ayénat, after a quick glance at Mawa. Her eyes and hands were still inspecting Desta's body.

"As you can see, this is not mere spanking," said Mawa. "This is a beating that turned the inside of the boy's skin out."

"It seems to me he found a reason to vent his repressed anger once again. I remember he had done this once to Damtew," said Ayénat. Her eyes filled with tears. Mawa shed a few of her own. Desta just wanted someone to hold and comfort him. Neither of the women did.

"What is he angry about?" asked Mawa, surprised.

"It has something to do with his father and a lost item. Don't ask me much as I know very little about them," said Ayénat, looking away.

"Ma," Desta said turning around with a severe face.

"Yes, dear,"

"I want to see Hibist."

"We'll invite them after the new year—in two to three weeks."

"I want to go see her tomorrow. Take me with you when you go to church," demanded Desta.

Ayénat looked at Mawa and then Desta.

"He must be missing his sister. I think you should fulfill his wishes," said Mawa after a long pause.

"But he can't even walk in this condition," said Ayénat.

"Yes, I can! It will be worth all the pain to see my sister again," said Desta emphatically.

Baffled, Ayénat looked at Mawa as if soliciting her input. "But . . . but we don't have anybody to attend to the animals. Damtew and his wife have things to do at church in Avinevra."

"I'll loan you my son," said Mawa. "As you know, he is the same age as Desta and a good shepherd too."

"Will you, really? Desta has been asking me about seeing his sister all winter, but I couldn't take him because we have nobody to attend to the animals," said Ayénat.

"I know Koomay will be happy to do it," said Mawa.

"In that case, you have my word, Desta. I will take you to see your sister tomorrow. But we have to be thankful to Mawa and Koomay for enabling you to make this trip," said Ayénat, glancing at Mawa appreciatively.

Desta smiled at Mawa.

"I am happy to see him smiling, finally. I need to go for a little while," said Mawa as she rose. "I will see you two later before you go home. I may even bring Koomay so that he can come with you this evening." Desta hobbled in front of Ayénat as she led him into the house to join the gathering.

DESTA ROSE EARLY IN THE MORNING, put on his shirt and wrapped himself with his gabi. The anticipated trip to Hibist's new home had him turning and tossing most of the night. Although he felt much better than he had the first night after his flogging, it still hurt to walk. Somehow, he needed to make his body tolerate the discomfort.

His mother was dressed and ready to take him to see his sister. It had rained the previous night and there were several pools of dirty rainwater in the hoof marks in front of the house. Much of the sky was veiled with piles of charcoal gray clouds with light silver tint on the edges.

Ayénat and Desta took the footpath that went north along the River Davola. As they hiked, Desta noticed that like the many streams that fed into the River Davola, several other footpaths fed into the main caravan route that went alongside of the river; something he hadn't noticed when he and his mother had gone to church for his communion. They passed many people who were walking in the opposite direction and others who joined them from the side paths. Desta kept track of the details as they walked, asking little but paying attention to everything.

When they reached the neighborhood where Hibist lived with her in-laws, a shepherd boy called Tilahun helped them identify the house. The moment she saw the visitors, Hibist came running.

"This is like a dream! I am so happy to see you," said Hibist, her face radiant. "I'd never have thought you would come to see me. All through these dismal months of the rain, I kept wishing the days would go faster and the work would be over so we could come and see you."

"That was our plan too, to invite you in September after the holidays were over, the farm work was done, until harvest, and the days brightened a bit, but we had to . . ." said Ayénat, glancing toward Desta.

Hibist followed her mother's eyes to Desta, her face faintly crinkled into a question. "Come in. My in-laws have gone to church and He is out to help his brother with something." Desta noticed that like Melkam and Amsale, even his mother, Hibist didn't call her husband, Zeru, by his first name. She, instead, referred to him as "He."

They walked along a broad and knobby log that was laid over the island of mud just outside the threshold. Desta thought this was better than having to hop from stone to stone as they did at home. Here you wouldn't have to worry missing the stones, especially at night. Hibist brought out a brown goat hide for her mother and brother to sit on. Desta surveyed his surroundings. The house was smaller than theirs at home, and he noticed that there were no stalls for animals. He wondered if Hibist's in-laws didn't have animals or if they kept them elsewhere as they did at home for all but the horses and a few goats.

Hibist brought leftovers of the food her mother-in-law had prepared to take to church. She gave Desta a loaf with a tumbler of milk. It seemed like the old times again to Desta, and he realized how much he missed his sister for these kinds of special treats.

Sitting by her mother's side, Hibist complained about how hard she worked every day, from milking the cows, working in the field, grinding the grains, fetching water, cooking, doing laundry and washing her in-laws' feet at night.

The foot-washing work intrigued Desta. He wondered if she washed her husband's feet also, like the girls did at home, but she didn't say.

It was past midday when Hibist's in-laws returned. The couple was pleased and surprised to find Hibist's mother and brother at their home.

"This boy here has been despondent for many weeks," said Ayénat. "Recently he threw a fit, demanding to see his sister and I decided to bring him, hoping to cure him of his melancholy and temper tantrums."

"We are happy you are here," said the mother, who had introduced herself as Marta. "Separations can be hard with siblings. We'd have liked my son and your daughter to come and visit you but we have been so busy that we'd have been working on Saturday and Sunday with our farms if we didn't fear God or being an outcast in our community." Marta was a diminutive woman with a pretty smile and big soft eyes. Her husband, Nega, was her opposite. Tall and big framed, he said little and rarely smiled.

"Hibist, why don't you take your brother outside and visit with him for a while?" said the mother-in-law.

Desta was thrilled. He liked his sister's new mother immediately. Hibist didn't hide her excitement either and quickly seized the opportunity. "Let me show you my neighborhood," she said as she rose and took Desta by the hand. They hadn't even reached the door when she put her arm around his shoulders, just like she used to do. It felt wonderful to be held by his sister again.

They walked through a passage past a smelly cow pen and a farm field thick with corn that was a foot taller than Desta. Farther out were several fields of barley, rye and teff, some of which, Hibist pointed out to Desta, were theirs. "That is where I sweated all winter," she said in a begrudging voice. Scattered over a wide area were houses bordered by green corn or luxuriant potato fields.

Once they cleared much of the bordering crop fields, Hibist led Desta to a dark granite rock that stood on the side of an incline amidst lush green grass around it. They sat side by side overlooking the wide, panoramic view in front of them.

"That, over there in the thicket of juniper trees, is our Church, Ginda-temem Mariam," Hibist said, pointing to the west.

Desta studied the wooded grove at the foot of a rocky mountain. He wondered if this church looked like the one in Avinevra, where he went for his communion.

"Over there, in the north on top of the plateau, live my father-in-law's brothers with their families." As Desta followed his sister's pointing hand, he caught sight of some boys driving their cattle to the open fields. He wished he could meet the boys and talk to them . . . ask them if they liked being shepherds.

Hibist continued. "Over there is Danka, bordered by the tail end of the mountain Lehwani, which we have back home, above the Avinevra church. Farther out there in the haze is Fagita. Way beyond it is Kuakura, Baba's birthplace." These are the same lands, Desta first saw, thanks to Kooli, when he went to the Avinevra church for his supplemental treatment for the dog disease.

Seeing that Desta was only half listening, Hibist changed the subject. "So how do you like your new sisters?"

Desta stared away for a bit, deciding what to talk about first—his father's beatings or how much he hated his sisters-in-law. "I don't like them," he blurted.

"Why is that? What did they do to you?"

"They didn't do anything to me but they are not friendly. They are always with each other. They don't give me any food when I come home from tending the animals."

"Have you tried to be friendly with them?" asked Hibist. "Have you spent time with them?"

"I am not unfriendly. I've no time to spend with them. I get up, spend all day with the animals, come home, eat my dinner, go to bed and get up in the morning to repeat the same thing all over again, seven days a week," said Desta resentfully.

"And your Kooli is no longer there. I can imagine how lonely you must feel," said Hibist.

"And you are not there to talk to me when I have problems."

"I know. I enjoyed being there for you when you needed me," said Hibist. "I will tell Mama to tell father to get another dog."

"As matter of fact, he did. But I have nothing to do with the new Kooli. The only Kooli I had and will ever have is gone," said Desta. "But what I asked mother to bring me here today is to talk to you about something else, something that happened to me recently."

"What happened to you?"

"Look!" said Desta as he stood and pulled up his gabi and shirt.

Hibist covered her mouth, Desta's lash marks were still crusted with blood, the ends of some beginning to peel. "How did this happen?"

"Father beat me for allowing some of the cattle to destroy someone's crop field."

Hibist stared at the numerous trailing lash marks, some crossing each others, other parallel or at odd angles. They were on his thighs, legs and buttocks.

Desta watched his sister's face as she examined him, to see how much sympathy she still had for him. In no time, he saw tears pool in her eyes. Pearly drops rolled down her cheeks and landed on the neckline of her dress.

Hibist wiped away the tears with the back of her hand. "I never thought father had it in him to beat you like this," she said finally.

"I never thought he would do this to me either. I am always afraid of Damtew and Asse'ged—not father," said Desta.

"Yes, I've always been worried for you about Damtew. I've watched his behavior and attitude change after Saba and her family were given the new property," said Hibist, looking at Desta. Her face was still somber. Tears smeared her long eyelashes.

"I thought I was going to die when he was beating me. He chased away the people who came to help. But after he left a tall woman with tattoos around her neck came and took me to her house. She fed and comforted me and kept me overnight. Her name is Degay and she lives in a nice house on our old property. I had never seen her before. Do you know who she is?"

"From what you described, I think I do," said Hibist. "She is father's distant relative. Mother and us girls don't like her, but I am glad she cared for you."

"I don't know why you don't like her. She was so nice to me," said Desta. "Anyway, you know what my greatest fear was when father was beating me?"

Hibist shook her head.

"That I would die before I touched the sky," said Desta his eyes filling with tears.

His sister tightened her lips and crinkled her forehead and looked away. Tears suddenly welled up in her eyes too. To Desta, she looked as if she was gripped by something horrible.

"I didn't mean to horrify you with my tale," he said apologetically.

"Oh no, I am just sorry all these things happened to you."

"I made mother bring me here because I want you to hug me and tell me that it will be all right. I am so afraid of father," said Desta, coming closer to his sister.

Hibist held him tightly. "Yes, it will be all right, I am sure father didn't mean to hurt you."

"In some ways, I wouldn't mind dying," said Desta. "Because then I would get to join Kooli. Mother once told me that when we die we will be with the people and animals that we loved."

"We don't want to die until God calls us," said Hibist.

"I just don't want to die before I go to the top of the mountain and let the clouds flow through my fingers," said Desta brightened by the prospect.

"I'll see if I can take you when I come to visit," said Hibist, herself smiling.

"Would you? It would be sooo great!"

A young man was shuffling toward them. "Mother wondered where you two had disappeared to," said Zeru, Hibist's husband.

"We didn't disappear. We were here reminiscing about home and things," said Hibist as she rose. She helped Desta dismount from the rock on which they had perched.

Zeru bent his bulky frame and kissed Desta on both cheeks, a total of three times. He then put his arm around Hibist, who, in turn put hers around Desta, and they walked home.

TWENTY-NINE

For Desta it was as if the stars had come down from the sky and begun crawling on the sides of the hills and the grounds around the villages. It always seemed that way every year on this day. Everywhere there were lights—small twinkling ones and large, bright and flaring orbs; some darted about, others moved in arcs, and still others were stationary. "Everybody is out with their cheebos," said Abraham, rushing into the house.

In the pitch black darkness, from a distance, Desta could only see the lights and not the bearers of them, almost as if the lights had a life of their own.

The thirteenth and the shortest month of the year was just over. The New Year had arrived. By the Ethiopian calendar this was September first.

A commotion in the wee hours of the morning woke Desta. He had risen, wrapping himself with his gabi, and had run outside to watch the spectacle. At the time the family woke, it was several hours before dawn and an hour or so before the rooster crowed. Desta ran back inside to watch what his brothers were doing.

"This year we are beaten. I was planning to do this before I went to bed, but I was tired and forgot," Damtew was telling Tamirat. Both were in the flour milling room, making their cheebos from dried twigs that Damtew had stowed away near the chicken coop months ago for this occasion. He had brought them down the night before and left them at their present location to build his long torches from them.

"I know, you are a farmer now. You have more things on your mind." Tamirat was saying.

"Yeah, but more than that, these things are not as important to me as they once were, I guess" said Damtew.

"I agree these events are more thrilling for boys like Desta here," said Tamirat glancing toward his little brother, "but still I don't think I'll ever outgrow celebrating the New Year."

After he finished his cheebo, Tamirat put together a dozen of twigs, tied them at several places and handed a spindly bunch to Desta.

Ayénat came in and urged the two brothers to finish quickly because she thought Teferra and his wife would soon be there with their cheebos burning to celebrate the New Year. She had seen two lights coming down the hill across the Davola and wanted Damtew and Tamirat to be ready with their torches when their brother and wife arrived. "I am surprised Asse'ged is not here yet," she said. "He should be arriving shortly as well."

"As I have said every year, hold your cheebos as low to the floor as possible until you clear the eaves," said Abraham when he found the brothers still bustling in the milling room. They both did as instructed. Tamirat lit Desta's cheebo outside with his own.

Abraham held his torch up in the air and watched Damtew and Tamirat go around in circles and up and down the hill, saying *"Eyoha Abebaye Meskerm Tebaye.* Hurray the New Year has arrived." At times Abraham, too, paced and moved his torch-bearing hand up and down, singing "Eyoha Abebaye Meskerm Tebaye." Desta followed suit but stayed close to his father.

The two wives came out to watch their husbands' jubilant moves but were soon swept up by the spirit of the moment.

"Abeba Ayehi wey, Have you seen the spring flowers?" crooned Amsale, remembering the melodic, timeless New Year's ditty.

"Lemlem," chimed in Melkam.

"Balenjerochè koomoo betera, My dear friends stand with me," continued Amsale.

"Lemlem," harmonized Melkam, as she clapped.

Amsale began to clap, too, in tempo with Melkam.

"Inchet se'biray, bet iskisera, Until I gather wood and build my home," intoned Amsale.

"Lemlem," replied Melkam.

"Inquan bet ena, yelegne Attir, I have no wood for a fence let alone for a house," said Amsale, still clapping.

"Lemlem," replied Melkam.

"Iwichi adralehu kokeb sikoter, But instead I spend the night outside counting the stars," said Amsale.

"Lemlem," hummed Melkam.

"Iwichi aderay sigeba bêtè, Tikottachigen injera enate, When I come home at dawn my stepmother scolds me for staying out in the cold."

"*Lem . . . lem*," replied Melkam, absentmindedly. Her eyes and mind had wandered off to the earth-borne stars near the villages across the river.

"Look at all those lights," said Amsale, interrupting the song and throwing Melkam off cue.

They stopped clapping and stood next to each other, enchanted by the lights in the rest of the valley. Their eyes darted from one village to another and from the south end of the valley to the north.

Desta wished Amsale and Melkam would sing the beautiful refrain once more. He remembered Hibist singing the same lyric again and again, adding more lines as she went on, at the New Year's celebration, Desta standing beside her chanting "*Lemlem.*"

"We don't have anything like this from where I come from," said Melkam, turning to Amsale.

"We do, but you just don't see these many lights for either trees or hills cover us," said Amsale.

"That is what I mean, where we are the land is flat and the houses are buried in the trees, so you don't get to see much light," concurred Melkam.

Not long after the family began celebrating, Teferra and Asse'ged arrived with their wives, each carrying a roaring torch. Their arrival was followed by Yihoon, who came by himself. The men gathered together and danced.

Ayénat stayed at home, for the most part, preparing the New Year's *goozgoozo*. This was a double-ply injera that she made by placing an already baked injera over one that she just poured and spread on the baking pan and letting the two bake together until the lower layer was cooked. When they were baked, she took them out and placed them on a basket to cool while she made a few more batches. She smeared these injera tops with ground pepper paste, with her fingers. On top she spread a thin layer of home-made cheese and garnished it with liquefied spiced butter and basil pesto.

Desta salivated the night before when he thought of goozgoozo. In the morning, after the torch dances, he came inside and found piled goozgoozo on a basket. "If you don't give me a piece from that pile right now, I am going to die," said Desta, half grinning

"My Lord, you act as if you have not eaten for days. What is the matter?"

"I don't eat goozgoozo everyday and it happens to be my favorite food."

"Here, take this slice to stop you from dying," said Ayénat, throwing a side glance and a smile at her son.

Desta wolfed down the small wedge his mother gave him.

After their cheebos were nearly gone, Abraham and the brothers put them out in the wet grass and came inside—wet, sweaty and weary. The women too came in, following their husbands. Yihoon went home with his cheebo still burning.

Abraham cut the layers of goozgoozo into wedge-shaped pieces and handed them out. He started with his oldest, Teferra and his wife, Asse'ged and his wife, followed by Tamirat and Damtew and their wives, and finally Desta. Abraham and Ayénat were last.

DUTIFULLY DESTA RELEASED the goats and horses and let them graze on the grass near the house. Damtew had helped release the cattle and driven them to graze above the house where it was safe from wild animals and where there were no crop fields that needed to be guarded from the cattle.

When the sheep were released, one lamb was not allowed to go with the rest. Damtew grabbed it by the scruff of its neck and dragged it into the house. It kicked, bleated and struggled, forcing him to pick it up and carry it in his arms. As he tied the unruly animal to the corner post by the horse's stall, its bleating grew stronger and mournful. "Bahahaha, bahahaha, bahahaha," it cried repeatedly.

The men and some of the women had sat in the living room around the fireplace. Ayénat ordered Melkam to roast coffee. Using a wrought iron pan, she washed three handfuls of coffee beans by scooping them in her hands and rubbing them together in water to remove the dead skin. She rinsed them three times, then placed the pan with the coffee beans in it on the three stones in the fireplace. With a wooden spoon she continuously stirred them, releasing the blue-gray smoke and the rich aroma of roasting coffee. When these beans became dark brown, Melkam removed the pan from the fire and transferred them onto a straw tray to cool. After the roasted beans cooled, she poured them into a wooden mortar and pounded them with a pestle.

Desta, sitting by the side of his father, kept an eye on the bleating lamb. At times it stood and chewed its cud, staring at the door. At other times, it stopped chewing and stared far away as if something was going through its head. Then it shook its head, bleated and began to chew again. With the passage of time, the sheep's eyes took on a somber hue. They saddened Desta and he began to feel sick.

Abraham ordered Desta to give the lamb some food. He pushed a small basket of barley seeds in front of it. The sheep nibbled some indifferently, then raised its head and began to bleat again. Desta saw a clear liquid fill one eye and plummet onto the freshly cut kettema beneath its feet. He wished he could tell someone how he felt. He wished Hibist were there.

After the first serving of the coffee, Abraham announced that it was time to kill the sheep. Damtew and Tamirat rose. Damtew removed the leash and pushed the lamb toward the center of the entrance and stood with it a few feet from the threshold. Abraham took two large knives from a basket Melkam brought and sharpened them by grinding them against each other. This sound always sent shivers up Desta's spine. It was only when his father was about to cut meat or kill an animal that he made those shredding sounds with the knives.

Damtew grabbed the animal by its feet, hoisted it a little and flipped it onto its back, all in one swift motion. The lamb struggled to escape. It freed one of its hind legs and Damtew grappled to hold it. Tamirat came to his rescue. Abraham said a prayer and mimed a cross over the sheep's neck, then, he grabbed the mouth and pulled it back to expose the throat. He rested the sharp edge of the knife on the sheep's pale neck and went to work. A torrent of blood gushed out in two different directions. Tamirat dodged it just in time, but Damtew and Abraham received a blood bath. The red frothy liquid hit the father's face and arms. Damtew got hit on his chest and his brand new blue shorts. Desta had to contain a giggle. Melkam came rushing with a pitcher of water and a cloth.

All eyes were on the vanquished lamb that lay on its side still struggling to live. It had kicked its hind legs violently right after the neck was severed; then, it seemed to sleepwalk with its front legs. They moved briskly at first, then slower and slower until finally the sheep was dead.

"Baba, you have a long life to live," said Asse'ged who had kept track of the time it took before the sheep finally rested in peace. The animal's glazed eyes stared blankly up at the smoke-stained bamboo ceiling.

Desta hated his father for killing the beautiful lamb. He went outside, hid in the apiary and cried. Later as he returned to the house, he wondered where the life that moved out of the sheep's body had gone.

After all the blood had been drained out of the sheep, Abraham handed the knives to the brothers and told them to skin it. Damtew undertook the task with pleasure. He stuck the tip of the sharp metal deep underneath the skin near the cut by the throat and worked his way down to the anus of the sheep, splitting it into two halves. Then he cut a circle near the ankles of one of the front legs, tipped the knife into the skin and sliced it down to the chest to join with the vertical cut he had made earlier. He did this with each of the legs.

Tamirat tied the hind legs with a rope and hooked them to a noose that hung from a crossbar above them. Blood continued to drip from the severed neck. Once the skin was removed, Damtew cut open the belly, releasing a translucent, convoluted mass. The metallic smooth flesh containing the stomach and the intestines, hung down, dragging the rest of the body with it. Damtew cut them out and handed them to Desta telling him to take them outside and disgorge their contents, then wash them completely in the creek and bring them back.

Afterwards, Damtew reached deep into the cavity of the animal, incised and pulled out two pieces of flesh, one reddish brown, that trembled to the touch, the other pink and foamy. He dropped them in the basket, covered with false banana leaves.

Desta returned with the cleaned tripe and intestines and gave the tripe to his mother.

Ayénat chopped the tripe and liver into tiny pieces and sautéed them with chopped green onions, green peppers, salt and garlic. This was the family's first meal from the lamb that was sacrificed in commemoration of the New Year.

The intestines were thrown to Kooli. Mandefroshi, also known as Mandy, the cat, came to snatch some but Kooli growled at her and she ran back and hid in the mill room. Tamirat called her back and gave her a half slice of the spleen, which she grabbed greedily and dragged away to her hideout. Once she had her fill, she kept the remaining bit by her side. Later Kooli came to steal it but she hissed at him furiously and he backed off.

"Give a good portion of *dulet* to Desta," said Abraham when he saw Ayénat dishing out the sautéed mixture on their mosseb. "This is the only portion he will be getting for the day. The rest of us have two more sheep to kill and will have more than our share to eat."

After eating the minced liver and tripe with spiced butter, salt and pepper, Desta watched the family leave for the next round of activities, which would take place at Saba and Yihoon's house, since Saba was the next oldest of the family members, and later at Asse'ged's house. Although he was missing out on the festivities, Desta was actually pleased he didn't have to go to Saba's house. At one point or another, somebody would raise the question of her future baby, and pretty soon everybody's eyes would be on him. He didn't want that. He would rather stay away. Thanks to his father, Desta, had a good portion and was content when he left his home to tend to the animals.

The day was glorious. There were puffy clouds here and there in the sky but there was a lot of blue in between. The valley was hushed. It was always like that on the holidays. Desta liked it when it was quiet. He could be more attentive to his duties that way. Today though, his mind kept drifting back to the celebration of the New Year. This was the first time Desta was to have his New Years dinner without Hibist—and probably the first when he would not receive special treats.

He wondered how much meat he would receive for dinner. In previous holidays, he and other children always received bones with hardly any meat on them or just a few boneless cubes of meat. Desta often got a piece of vertebra. The few morsels of meat on these bones were always stuck in the crevices and very hard to dig out with the teeth or tongue. He often ended up bloodying his lips or poking his tongue with the sharp pollard ribs. If he were lucky enough to receive a bone with marrow in it, Desta was in seventh heaven. If he didn't receive one directly from his father, there arose rather humiliating situations, where Desta allowed himself to receive discarded bones from certain family members. When his father, Ayénat or Teferra gave up a bone because they couldn't get to the marrow without cracking it with a stone, Desta would readily accept and crack it open between two rocks and slurp out the marrow. He wouldn't accept such bones from Damtew, because he never liked him, and sometimes even from Asse'ged. He would take one from Tamirat, but he was very stingy with his bones.

In past years, regardless of what bones Desta got, Hibist always saved a hunk of meat and gave it to him privately. This year nobody would do that for him.

When Desta returned at the end of the day, he found his mother, Melkam and Amsale busy preparing the New Year's dinner. "This is just to tide you over until dinner is served when the rest of the family arrives," said Ayénat as she handed him half a freshly baked injera. He had been looking forward to eating meat, not plain injera, so he set it aside. He didn't want to fill himself up with something he ate every day. That night all he wanted to eat was meat.

After the rest of the family members returned from their day-long rounds of killing lamb, eating its dulet and drinking coffee, tella or in some occasions honey wine, dinner was served. The adults ate together from two separate mossebs. Desta, Astair and Zena sat around one large old platter, loaded with injera and sauces.

After the adults finished eating their injera, Ayénat brought the pieces of meat she had siphoned out and kept in a bowl. She poured them into the middle of their mosseb for Abraham to pass out as he saw fit.

Slightly inclined over the mosseb, Abraham gathered all the meat with bones and placed it on a pile. In the meantime, Ayénat gathered all the cubed meat and put it onto a separate mound.

Abraham then sat back, inspecting the people at the two mossebs. Then he went to work, judiciously deciding which of the boned meats to give to whom. Desta remembered in the past it was always by age, the importance of the people to his father, and whether they were guests or family members that he decided whom to give which meat with bone.

After all the boned meats were passed out to the men and their wives, Abraham moved to the mound of cubed meats. He quickly and randomly picked three or four cubes and he passed them out to Desta's group. Before they received their portions, Desta and the rest of the children had to rise, stand erect, extend two touching hands and bow immediately after they received their meat.

Desta received two large cubes, which he at first thought were equivalent to the three small cubes the other children received. That was all the meat he probably would eat till another holiday, like Christmas or Easter. He might get some morsels in the next one or two meals, but the lion's share was always consumed at the main New Year's dinner.

For Desta, the New Year's dinner meat he received was adding insult to injury. Not only did he not receive a bone with marrow in it, he didn't even get a good portion of the cubed meats. A later glance at Zena's three cubes confirmed to him his two were not equal to hers. This meant what he received was the lowest amount of all the people at the dinner party.

Later, as he lay in bed, the chorus of marrow-slurping men and women haunted him. He wished he had protested the injustice. None of the children at his table had received meat on bones, and the portions they received were considerably less than what the adults were given.

He wished he were an adult. He wished he could get his parents to kill another lamb and feed the children with its meat and bones for days to come. More to the truth, he wished Hibist were there. She would have saved a chunk of meat on a bone with a juicy marrow in it and given it to him when no one watched. Now he might never get bone with marrow and a hunk of meat till he became an adult.

THIRTY

September

Desta was standing by the entrance of his home about to go to attend to his
animals when Tamirat walked in. The brother didn't appear to be his normal
self. He neither smiled nor greeted anyone when he entered the house. He
had not been at home for a few days and everybody, including his wife, had
wondered where he had gone.

"Where have you been, stranger?" said Ayénat, who was standing by the mill
room.

"I went to talk to my *mergeta* on the matter you and I discussed a few days
ago," Tamirat said, glancing briefly at his mother. "While I was there, he talked
me into helping them with a new school room they're building. I also had to
tidy up the lesson I started with him before the wedding, until I go back next
year to continue my studies—after, hopefully, we have done this communion
business."

"Regarding the communion," Ayénat said, "I think you should have
consulted your father before you talked to your teacher; after all it's a family
matter. Although I could see that the mergeta could be a good counselor as well
in this particular situation."

For nearly four months, Tamirat had been confronting a problem that was
poised to destroy his career, shatter his dreams and break his father's heart. His
wife, Amsale, had refused to receive the communion with him so that he could
become a full-fledged priest after he finished his studies. This sacramental rite
was one of the laws of the Orthodox Church. Any married priest was required
to consummate it in order to maintain his title of priesthood and remain a
member of the church. If divorced, the man had to become a celibate to remain
in the elite profession of priesthood.

Tamirat did not want to become a celibate in order to continue with his
priesthood if he and Amsale separated. But the alternative—leaving priesthood

and remarrying—would be hard on his father who dreamed of seeing his son as
a qualified priest.

For a twenty-year-old man who had barely discovered the wonderful world
of manhood—the mysteries and joys of his body—to suddenly abandon
them and devote the rest of his life to the service of God seemed to Tamirat
the ultimate punishment. Then, of course, there was the idea of procreation,
progeny and living to eternity through the seeds he would sow, none of which
would be possible for a law-abiding celibate who had had a failed marriage.

For the past five Sundays, Amsale had made every conceivable excuse
she could concoct for not going to church with her husband to receive the
communion. Knowing that they were not supposed to eat or drink anything
before they went to receive the communion, she used food and water as
excuses for not going to church on the first three Sundays. On the fourth one
she blamed her period. Women who had their periods were prohibited from
entering in the inner sanctuaries of God's house where they went to receive the
communion. Tamirat had not seen a drop of blood anywhere, but he did not
challenge her. On the fifth Sunday, she was struck down by a severe headache
and couldn't make it to the door, let alone walk the long distance to church.

Tamirat's patience had finally run out. When Amsale insisted that she was
afraid of taking the flesh and blood of Christ without the presence of her
immediate family, he went to consult his teacher. Unfortunately, the mergeta
had no explanation for his wife's problem, except that she was perhaps too
young and afraid to get involved with something that dealt with God. He
recommended patience.

Ayénat thought the girl might be possessed by Saytan and suggested Tamirat
take her to one of the famous priests at the big churches to have the sacred
liquid poured over her body, but Amsale violently opposed this idea. Ayénat
also supported the idea of him going to her village and trying to take the
communion there.

Although Tamirat knew that even his father did not have the power it would
take to change Amsale's mind, he still wanted Abraham's advice on the matter.

It was not too long after Tamirat had arrived home that Abraham walked in,
coincidentally, followed by Amsale with a jug of water on her back. Tamirat
sought eye contact with his wife, but she went past them with her head down.

"Can I talk to you for a few minutes outside, Baba?" said Tamirat in a
whisper after Amsale was out of sight.

They stood leaning against the wattled fence outside. Abraham was disturbed by Tamirat's cheerless, desperate face.

"Everything all right?" asked Abraham in low voice.

"I have been having a problem with Amsale," said Tamirat in a somber tone. "She won't come to church and take the communion with me."

To Abraham, his son looked as if he had not slept for days. His fair skin was dry and blotchy and his small eyes dulled with sadness.

"I'm aware of that," said Abraham. "I thought in time she would change her mind."

"I have tried five times, Baba but she keeps coming up with excuses. Now she says she wants to go home and take it in the presence of her family. Should I do this?" Tamirat looked into his father's deep brown eyes as if the answer to his problem might be found there.

"Let me ask you something man to man" said Abraham. "Is everything okay?" I mean, you know. . . ."

Tamirat kept his eyes on his father, suppressing a laugh.

"Yes, of course," he said finally.

"I had to check, you know . . . a man's sexual impotence can be a real problem for women, young women," said Abraham thoughtfully.

"You don't think men would have a problem with a sexually inhibited woman?" said Tamirat nervously.

"Well, men in your situation—I mean priests can put up with the problem because divorcing would bring nothing better. The companionship can be just as important as having a sexually-satisfying relationship."

"I am glad you brought this up," said Tamirat. "I am terrified. My marriage with Amsale might not work. She seems to have a heart of stone and a closed mind that no amount of talking and pleading will crack open. To be honest . . ." Tamirat couldn't finish his thought. The rest of what he was going to say would break his father's heart. He let it die on his tongue.

"If there is no real problem like I thought, the rest of it is fixable," said Abraham. "We can get her parents involved, if worst comes to worst. If she prefers to do it in the presence of her family, that is understandable. Make a plan with them first and go."

"I am scared, Baba. I'm afraid if we divorce, I may have to give up my career as a priest. I am in my prime. The idea of becoming a celibate in the name of the priesthood . . ."

"Tamirat, go to her parents, as she has requested. Stay for a week or two, or more if you have to, and come back once you have received your communion. All this other stuff—divorce, celibacy—is rubbish. The girl has hesitated, and now you have gotten all worked up and started to feel as if your world is coming to an end. She is only eleven years old, for Christ's sake! What does she really know about life and such things as communion?

"Go and do it at her parents' if that is what she wants. You have plenty of time to finish school. Don't rush her. Make an ally out of her parents—they can be the key to her heart."

Tamirat looked away for a long time. Deep down he thought he could never pry open the door to Amsale's heart. As young as she was, she still manipulated him in ways a woman much older would.

"Do you hear me?" said Abraham, watching his son's mournful face.

"I heard you. I will do my best."

"Don't be pessimistic. You are dealing with emotions—feelings. Feelings can change at any time. Once she is in the company of her family and friends, her resistance might melt away."

"Like I said, I'll give it my best."

"In that case, you will go at the end of the month, after you have celebrated Meskel with us," said Abraham. He tapped his son's shoulder and said, "Come, let's see if your mother has some breakfast."

THIRTY-ONE

Desta sat in the open meadow keeping an eye on the animals and enjoying the caressing morning sun as he thought about all the things that had happened since he became a shepherd—since his quiet, happy and carefree life of the prior years had changed.

He thought of the long, mind-numbing days spent watching the animals grazing in the field or nibbling on young leaves in the bushes; the cold, wet months that sent him scurrying for shelter when it rained; the chill mornings that caused his bare feet to sting and his fingers to go numb; the threats of Damtew and his father, some already meted out and others still hanging over his head like dark winter clouds.

Then he thought of events: the weddings of his siblings and the loss of his best sister; the dog disease scare and the ordeal he went through to cure himself of his supposed illness; the loss of his best friends, Kooli and the vervet monkeys; the disappearance of the sheep and their miraculous return two days later; the beating by his father that had left deep scars on both his body and mind; and the New Year's celebration, its lights, blood, festivities and the skimpy amount of meat he was apportioned at the big dinner. When he thought of all these things, Desta felt very old. So much had happened to him since he became a shepherd.

What Desta saw around him brought back tender memories of happier times. The spring season had awakened and every weed, grass and bush was alive with dazzling color. Virtually everywhere there were whites, yellows, golds and blues. In the backyards, fallow lands, virgin hills and valleys, under bushes and in meadows, the spring season had dug up colors it had stowed away in its bosom through the rainy season.

This was the time of the year when he and Hibist had had the most fun. As far back as he could remember they had roamed the countryside in spring time, chasing butterflies and gathering flowers for the bouquets they would hang around the center roof-bearing pole of their home. It was during this time when Desta's desire to go to the top of the mountains took a paralyzing hold on him, when he wanted so badly for someone to take him to the highest peak so he could spend all day being close to the pristine azure sky. But now with Hibist gone, there was no one who would listen or care enough to even promise to take him there one day.

Sitting here, looking at the amazing array of flowers and the deep blue heaven above, Desta felt he could not bear the pain.

IT WAS WHILE DESTA was entertaining these thoughts his brother Damtew walked up cradling a newly born kid. The kid's mother, a wedding gift from Ayénat, was right behind him, bleating incessantly and nudging at him. The beautiful male kid was Damtew's pride and joy. He loved talking about him and showing him off.

"I am going to the river to introduce my kid to the swimmers," he said, towering over Desta with the kid in his arms. "Do you want to come along?"

Desta said "no" with a grunt and shake of his head.

"I want you to bring him back with the mother after I finish introducing him to the boys. I plan to stay around for a swim," said the brother commandingly.

Desta explained that he needed to stay with animals, but Damtew persisted by arguing that they could drive the goats to the river embankment so that they could keep an eye on them while Damtew was showing the kid to his friends. Since they would be close to the crossing route of the Davola, the possibility of the cattle crossing the river unseen would be remote.

Desta drove the goats close to the river as instructed by his big brother and followed him to a group of boys and men gathered on the embankment of the river.

As they walked, Damtew crooned steadily to the skinny gray-colored kid. The mother, still following them, sounded more desperate with every step but she still managed to snip grass along the way.

Desta was amazed by his brother's devotion to the kid goat. *Where did this love and compassion come from in a man like Damtew?* He wondered how he would treat his own child if he was so insanely in love with a scrawny baby goat.

There were about a dozen men and boys on the bank where the river had carved a half moon against the embankment, creating a large pool. Several boys had spread their gabis on the grass and were lying naked on their bellies, feet stretched out, water glistening from their backs. Others were dry and basking in the sun. A few sat up, wrapped in their gabis, watching the boys in the water.

"What do you have there?" said one of the men, as Damtew and Desta strolled toward them.

"This is my new baby—baby goat. His name is Habté. Isn't he handsome?" said Damtew as he slowly lowered the animal to the ground. The boys on their bellies rolled over and sat up. They crossed their legs, shielding their fronts, and directed their eyes to the animal. The men who had been watching the swimmers also turned to gaze at the curious creature.

"He looks alright, how old is he?" asked one of the men.

The mother goat had begun nuzzling her son as soon as Damtew dropped him. The kid staggered quickly toward her dugs and began to suckle contentedly.

"Born four days ago. He is not strong yet, but I think he is going to be a beautiful goat," said Damtew, trying as much to assure himself about the attributes of the animal as to reject the lukewarm comment from the man.

"All baby goats are skinny and rickety like him when they are born," said the second man. "He has long legs and a long torso and neck, and I think he certainly has the potential to be a handsome goat."

Damtew glowed. "I think you are right. What I see is not what he is now but what he will be when he grows up. I have always wanted to have a big mookit, like my father's goats. This one definitely has the makings," said Damtew looking at the man who had made the supportive comment.

A couple of the boys stood and patted the animal as he nursed on his mother's teat. Others looked at him indifferently. Desta's eyes kept stealing toward the boys in the water. They seemed to glide easily and freely in it, making swimming seem easy and fun.

"Does Desta know how to swim?" asked the man who had first greeted them. He was Mogus, a distant relative who lived across the river.

"Not really. I have tried to bring him here before but he repeatedly refused," said Damtew gazing down on his brother.

Desta silently acknowledged that this was true. Although he enjoyed spending time with Hibist, he wanted to spend as little of it as possible with Damtew.

As he continued to watch the swimmers, two more boys dropped their gabis and ran to the embankment and jumped into the deepest part of the pool. They disappeared momentarily, then resurfaced and began swimming naturally and easily. Desta stared. "He seems very interested. Why don't you show him how?" said Mogus.

"Does anybody have a rope?" asked Damtew, looking around.

"Here, I have one," said a brown-skinned boy about Desta's age. "I am still learning myself. . . . I am getting better but continue to bring this rope in case I need it." He handed the rope to Damtew.

"What do you think?" said Damtew, turning to Desta.

"It looks fun."

"Yeah, it's fun," said the boy who gave Damtew the rope. "At the beginning it's hard, but as you do it over and over, it gets easier—that's when it becomes really fun."

Desta couldn't see what was so hard about it. It seemed easy enough.

"Someone had better go with him and get him started. You just can't throw him by tying his body to the rope," said Mogus.

Damtew hesitated. Desta told himself *If he was going into the water, it wouldn't be with his brother.*

"I will teach him how to float and kick his feet," said Mogus, smiling. "It will give me pleasure to be the first to teach your brother."

"Great! I'll have the pleasure of navigating him with the rope from here," said Damtew grinning at Desta.

Desta dropped his gabi and was ready to go into the water.

Mogus led Desta to a spot where they could climb down on a few rocks that jutted out of the wall of the embankment. Mogus went first, holding Desta by the hand as they rappelled down one step at a time. Once they were in the shallow section of the water, Damtew threw one end of the rope to Mogus. Mogus tied it around Desta's waist, slung the loose end between his legs and tied it to the main part of the rope, making Desta feel as if he were a bucket that could be dropped and lifted in the water with the lever of the hand.

While Damtew held the rope securely from high on the embankment, Mogus held Desta by the waist and moved him around the shallow portion of the pool, telling him to kick his feet and push the water away in front of him with his hands and arms.

For Desta, kicking his feet in a rhythmic and coordinated manner like the other boys seemed daunting but he was determined to give it his best.

"Good, you are getting better," said Mogus as Desta became less afraid of the water and slowly began to float on his own.

Sitting on the ledge, his feet dangling down, Damtew monitored Desta's progress. Every time he felt his kid brother could handle it on his own he tugged the rope, trying to pull him out of Mogus' hands. "Not yet," Mogus would shout when he felt the tugging and Damtew would stop.

The longer Desta stayed in the water, the more comfortable he became. Mogus sensed his confidence and finally loosened his hold.

Desta struggled to keep afloat, when Mogus noticed he was swallowing too much water or seemed about to go under, he grabbed him. "Let him go! Let him go! I am holding him," Damtew shouted. Mogus let Desta go.

The instant Mogus let go of Desta, his brother dragged him to the deepest part of the pool and relaxed the cord. After struggling to keep afloat, Desta went down. Damtew kept him in the water for a few seconds, then pulled him up. For Desta, powerless to save himself, it was terrifying. The more he fought to stay up, the harder it was to stay afloat. When he opened his eyes, he saw smoke gray liquid he was drowning in. Then he felt the tug on the rope and he was momentarily out of the water again. He took a huge gulp of air and furiously fought to keep afloat.

Amidst his struggles and the swishing of water in his ears, he heard a roar of laughter from the people high up on the embankment. Then he felt the rope slacken again and he slowly sank back under. He couldn't breathe. The water was choking him. This time there was no tug on the rope. He was going to drown. He thought of the sky and knew now that he was going to die without ever touching it. He frantically tried to catapult out of the water, but with nothing to push against, he merely sank farther and farther down. Out of desperation he even grabbed the cord that held his beads around his neck.

Then, thank God, there was another tug on the rope, and he heard a din of laugher once again. Out of the corner of his desperate and water-drenched eyes, he saw Mogus swimming toward him, coming to rescue him.

To his horror, before Mogus reached him, he felt Damtew dragging him away and slackening the rope once again. He gulped a great quantity of air and held his breath. This time instead of sinking, he found himself being dragged along underwater. When he came up for the fifth time, he saw he now was at the other end of the pool.

Mogus was rushing toward him and shouting at Damtew, but Damtew

and the other boys were laughing. Desta saw a rock and grabbed onto it but
Damtew jerked the rope with such force that he plunged right back into the
water.

When finally Desta came up for the sixth time, it was because Mogus was
holding the belt of the rope and swimming ashore with him to the other side of
the river.

When the man pulled him out of the water, Desta wrapped his hands around
his neck and wouldn't let him go. Mogus repeatedly assured him that he would
not let him get into the water again. He quickly untied the rope and threw it
away. They were alone on the grassy beach. Mogus laid Desta on the ground.

Shaking uncontrollably, Desta gasped and heaved until a mixture of mucus,
food, blood, water and saliva gushed out. Mogus tapped him on the back and
tried to pacify him with kind words. After several minutes Desta recovered,
comforted by the warmth of the strong sun and soothed by the sibilant sound of
the river. Mogus and Desta rose and crossed the river to collect their gabis and
join the group.

They arrived amidst a fiery argument between the two older men and
Damtew.

"How else is he going to learn? He needs to be pushed. The harder he tries to
keep above water, the sooner he learns," Damtew was saying.

"You don't teach a small boy by terrifying him," said one of the men, glaring
at him. "You should be punished by your parents."

"My intention was not to terrify him, but to challenge him to learn faster," said
Damtew. "Besides, we have not had such a laugh for a long while. Isn't that true,
guys?" He turned to his friends, who responded with another peal of laughter.

"You should tell your parents what he tried to do to you," said Mogus as he
watched Desta wrap himself in his gabi to go home. "I will tell them too when I
see them."

Mogus escorted him past Damtew and Desta walked briskly away.

"Where are you going? What about the animals?" Damtew ran after him and
grabbed him, dragging him back.

"You have terrified the little boy, you scoundrel. Is that the way you treat
someone who is going to care for your baby goat?" Mogus said angrily.

"I wish he could do it again," giggled one of the boys.

Mogus gave him a look that instantly caused him to shut his mouth.

"This is just one installment of the payback for all the havoc he caused in our family," said Damtew with an evil grin.

"Go tell your parents," said one of the men.

"What will they do to me?" bragged Damtew. "One of them is a good ally of mine. The other is careless. I run the show."

The men looked at each other and then Damtew. The boys continued to giggle under the cover of their gabis, as they looked at each other and then Desta.

Desta wanted to run home and tell his mother what Damtew had done to him, but after hearing what his brother said, his heart sank and his feet now could only walk. With Hibist gone, there was no one he could go to.

"WHAT BRINGS YOU HOME SO EARLY? Where are the animals?" said Ayénat, frowning.

"Damtew almost killed me . . . I was afraid he might actually do it if I didn't come home," said Desta, tears filling his eyes.

"What?"

"He took me to the part of the river where people swim. He wanted to see me learn how to swim. He attached a rope to my body and kept bobbing me in and out of the water. Every time he dropped me, I struggled to keep afloat but I just sank down more. It was like having a nightmare." Desta fought his tears.

Ayénat listened keenly. "He probably thought it was funny. For him everything has to be entertaining. I will talk to him when he comes back," she said casually.

Her hollow words hurt Desta even more. "Damtew said you don't care what happens to me. Please tell him not to kill me, at least, not before I touch the sky." His tears overflowed.

"That is rubbish. I don't love any one child less than the other. Stop that foolish talk. I don't want to hear it again," barked Ayénat.

That evening when Damtew came in after putting the animals in their stalls, Desta heard Ayénat stop him in the living room and say, Desta told me what you did by the river. If you do it a second time, I will never let you in this house again and I'll let your father handle you in whatever manner he chooses."

Her words were harsh, but not harsh enough for Desta. He wanted her to beat Damtew, to whip him until he bled. But she couldn't do that. Damtew was too big for her to handle. *He was too big for anyone to handle*, Desta thought.

THIRTY-TWO

"I hope you will be that caring and attentive when you have your own baby," said Ayénat when she saw Damtew caressing and talking to his baby goat outside.

"This is like my first baby. I love him like my own. Do you see how beautiful he has gotten in just a couple of weeks," boasted Damtew as he ran his fingers over the goat's dove-gray hair.

"This is nothing short of obsession. Your life revolves around him. I am anxious to see the tenderness and affection you will bestow upon your own children. I think it's a good sign . . . I commend you," said Ayénat before she crossed the doorsill.

Desta couldn't believe that someone so cold and brutal could be capable of such tenderness. It was almost as if the baby goat had transformed Damtew from a cruel animal into a gentle and caring human being.

Every evening, the first thing Damtew did was pet his goat and bring him a basket of grain. Desta had even seen him share with his goat the roasted barley that Ayénat gave him for a snack. Worried the goat might become hungry at night, he also brought him hay and left it for him to graze on. He even made a bed of hay for him to sleep on at night. The other goats, including his mother, slept on the bare floor and never got any extra grain or hay.

One night Abraham scolded Damtew for feeding salt to the kid goat, saying it was not good to do that at such a young age. He said salt was good only after the goat's testicles were maimed so the goat could become a mookit.

Damtew explained that his goal was to get the goat to become big as soon as possible, maim his tentacles and turn him into a mookit. He planned to sell him for a lot of money that he and his wife would use to buy things when they moved into a house of their own.

"That is a good goal, but you can't hurry nature. Yes, feed him well but don't give him salt just yet," said Abraham.

Secretly, Damtew still fed the goat salt occasionally.

Within two months the once scrawny little animal had grown into a handsome and rugged beast.

"Just like his grandfather the Billy goat that sired the mother," commented Abraham. "Although you wouldn't know it by looking at her, she is so diminutive and skinny." He eyed her sympathetically. "The grandfather of Habté was the most beautiful goat I ever had. I wish I had not turned him into a mookit. He would have produced many a handsome goat like this one. Sometimes when the need for money looms before our eyes, we can be shortsighted. Don't repeat my mistake."

"Is she the only one he fathered?" asked Damtew, studying the pathetic animal.

"She had a twin sister, but we sold her. I wish we hadn't. She would have given us more offspring of the same pedigree."

"How can such a beautiful creature be extracted from a sickly-looking goat like her?"

"That's what I mean," said Abraham. "I repeat: put off the idea of turning him into a mookit. He could sire many more future mookits if you breed him for a few years."

"I'll see. Maybe we can get two baby goats out of him before I turn him to a mookit," said Damtew casually, more to satisfy his father than meaning it. Because it took at least three years for a new mookit to fully mature, he had wanted to turn Habté into a mookit as soon as the prized animal got big enough.

"I mean that," said the father, sensing Damtew's insouciant reception to his earlier comment.

"Okay, okay. We'll decide when the time comes—you and I," Damtew said, grinning.

Abraham threw his hand in the air and walked into the house.

EVERY GUEST OR FAMILY MEMBER who came to visit, *not only* had to meet the goat *but also* feel his translucent coat. "What have you been feeding this goat for his skin to be soft and beautiful like this? Can you give me the recipe?" people would say.

"No special food, but I have been giving him a lot of tender love and affection," Damtew quipped. And invariably he added, "You know, I've discovered goats can be like humans. The more you love them, the more beautiful they look every day."

Desta nearly puked when he heard his brother say this. *Which human being have you shown love to, to come up with such an idea?* he said under his breath. *You never showed affection for your little wife. Your love for the animal is for selfish motives, for the money you will make by turning it into a mookit and selling it. You're greedy. It's why you're holding a grudge against me because Saba got the land you coveted.*

But Desta also wondered if love indeed could cause animals to become beautiful. Undeniably, this goat had become the epitome of beauty. Unlike other goats that were feisty and testy even when they were fed, the kid goat hung around and sniffed at people. The love he received from his master seemed to have rubbed onto him as well.

"Take good care of Habté," Damtew invariably ordered Desta after he finished petting and talking to his kid. He would linger and contentedly watch the little goat strut away with his mother.

Damtew's extreme devotion to his animal had made Desta doubly conscious of the importance of protecting the kid from any preying animals. When he did his head counts at the middle and end of the day, he always started with Habté. Once he saw him in the pack, his mind was immediately at ease.

THIRTY-THREE

November

This must be the rain that everybody had been talking about—no, terribly worried about! thought Desta as he watched the sky over the eastern mountains become progressively somber. "If the rains come in early November, we'll be finished," his father had said a week ago. The unwelcome rains, especially the spate of downpours that sometimes came during this month, could cause the grains from the un-cut fields to be stripped out of their husks and collect on the ground to become feed for the birds. Those fields that were already cut and left to dry would mildew and rot—making the grains useless to humans, cattle or birds.

Desta jumped when he heard a huge crack followed by a flash of light. Soon the entire face of the mountain had been swallowed with boiling vast clouds, below which the rain poured abundantly. Not too long after, the same clouds were driven across the Davola River, black and ominous and water clogged, turning the day into night.

Desta saw the farmers on the mountains scurry to take shelter in their homes or under the nearest trees. He knew he had to do the same because the rain was rapidly advancing west. As the rain began pelting the earth around his feet, he ran to the sholla tree for cover. Under the largest bough he stood and watched the rain come in sheets first, then turn into showers of rocks that shredded the leaves in the tree and pocked holes in the earth. Deceived by the many sunny days, Desta had forgotten to bring his gessa. He wrapped himself tightly with his gabi and stood shivering with his back pressed to the tree trunk.

He had never seen the *berredo*—hail—come like this even in the whole rainy season. Once, a few years ago, he had been safe at home, watching a similar hailstorm assault the bare earth. When it was all over, it left piles of white watery pebbles all over the field. He remembered they stung his fingers when he scooped them up. This time he just wanted to survive the bombardment.

Some of the cows had come to the tree for shelter too. He watched them shiver, grinding their teeth on their cuds.

Seeing the cows reminded him of the goats he should have been checking. He had not gone to see them for a long time. Captivated by the gathering storm, he had completely forgotten about them. He prayed they were safe and the sheep had stayed where he could find them again.

When the storm was over, the entire field was being blanketed with a rushing, rusty flood that came from the mountains above. Brown water had pooled in depressed areas, small gullies trundled down the beaten footpaths and a river of the rainwater coursed along flood channels around the field. On the higher grounds and around trees the white rocks were piled in patches.

The sky cleared and white light draped the valley. Daylight had returned, although dusk was just around the corner.

The cattle came out of their shelters, shook their heads and bodies violently to rid the rain from their skins. Desta scampered nervously to the woods and was relieved to find the goats congregated around one of the sholla trees, their rears butted against the trunk, facing outward, ruminating. Their eyes were bright and alert. Desta walked around the tree and cracked his whip to drive them back to the field. They filed along the footpath into the open field. Desta hissed a sigh of relief. He drove them toward where the cattle were, because pretty soon the evening would fall and he had to take them home. As he walked toward the tree where he took shelter to pick up his stick and whip, he remembered he had not made a head count of the goats. He collected his stick and returned to them. He raised his index finger, poking the air as he counted.

He counted twice and each time he came up short of one goat. Halfway on the third attempt something dawned on him. *No . . . no . . . no . . .* he said as he continued with his count once more. *No . . . no . . . no . . .*, he repeated as if the word would be the answer for the terror that was slowly gripping him. *Please God, not Habté, please God, don't do this to me . . .* He ran back to where he had found the goats. He circled the tree, looking in all the directions around it. Thinking the goat might have drowned, he walked along the bank scanning the creek. There was no sign of Habté.

He scurried back to the goats, praying he had miscounted or would find Habté hiding behind his old shaggy mother. He counted again and he looked under the belly of every goat. No sign of the animal. A new thought. Maybe he had become separated from the pack when the others ran to the tree for shelter.

Maybe he was under some acacia tree, wet, shaking from the cold. He felt a moment's relief, until he pictured the little goat huddled under a tree alone, struck repeatedly by the rocks of ice. *How could he survive that?* He couldn't. Desta remembered how those white rocks had torn up the earth. *The body of a delicate young goat . . . no way*, he said to himself.

He had to keep looking. He walked the length of the acacia thicket, bending low occasionally to see if the baby goat might be hugging the tree or lying on the ground.

And then he found him. At the area where the acacia bushes ended, near where the southern creek joined with the River Davola, in the thick undergrowth beneath the tall trees, there he was, lying motionless, neck twisted, belly torn open, skin hanging in tatters from his small ribcage. His eyes were glazed and lifeless, his long neck and torso, his beautiful face, the repository of many handsome goats to come, ambushed by an unidentified animal.

Desta crouched near the goat, dazed, not thinking yet of what Damtew or his father would do to him. He was concentrating on the beautiful kid goat, *the irretrievability, the finality, the lack of explanation, the absence of one shred of redeeming value to his senseless death*. He sat there for a long time, looking at the goat's soft, gray coat, slicked by the rain and pocked by the hail. His skin glistened. A portion of his bottom leg and tail were buried under the piled hail.

From the wound marks, Desta thought the attacker probably had grabbed him from the back first. Once he had brought him down, he switched to the neck and killed him by cutting off his air supply. Damtew had once explained to him how most predators kill goats and sheep. Desta couldn't understand why the animal had not torn away the legs or any other part of the body. He thought maybe the sudden arrival of the rain and hail had scared it and so it went for what it could get quickly and easily—the gut. Now that the rain had stopped, it would probably return to finish off the rest.

The evening was rapidly advancing. Desta needed to deal with the problem quickly. The skin for sure, in its condition, would have no salvage value, either for home use as a mat or to be sold in the market. The only value it might have would be to Damtew as a memento of sorts. But did he want Damtew to have such a memento that would likely forever cause him to blame Desta and treat him more hatefully? No.

He needed to move the body, to hide it someplace. He made a lasso of his whip, slid it on to Habté's neck and brushed the hail off from the body. Then, he pulled him out to the field struggling over rocks and pieces of wood that made the journey difficult to negotiate. When he was out in the clearing, he had to decide where to hide the body. First, though, he needed to find a place to spend the night himself. Going home now would be foolhardy. Damtew and his father would be furious when they found out what had happened to Habté. One would start beating on him, and the other would finish him.

He thought it would be safe for him to spend the night tying himself to a branch in the sholla tree. With this in mind, he dragged the goat behind the bushes on the north side of the tree where he could keep an eye on him from his perch in the tree and shout at any animal that might come to steal him. He hid the carcass behind a row of abalo bushes and covered him with branches from the bushes.

The evening was getting on very quickly. Desta gathered the rest of the animals and drove them home. He put the cows in their pen, the goats, except the mookits, in their stalls in the shed. The mookit goats he brought into the house and drove to their quarters, behind the horses' stall. Then, he demanded that his mother give him food because he was hungry and would die immediately if he didn't have it. Ayénat looked at him quizzically but when she saw the disturbed and wild look in his eyes, she hastily brought him a half injera. "This should save you from dying and tide you over until dinner time," she said as she handed him the bread.

Desta wolfed down the food in a few large chunks. Realizing he would need more food to last him for a day or two, he had to wait for an opportune moment and then see what he could do.

He watched Melkam go to milk the cows with his cousin, Genet, who was visiting. Ayénat was busy in the mill room grinding something. Desta grabbed the bar of salt and dashed to goats' stall as if he were going to feed the mookits with it. On his way he detoured to the larder where he folded several pieces of injera, stuffed them in his pouch and returned the salt bar to its place. From the bedding area, he gathered his father's old gabi, folded it three times and threw it over his own. Then he yanked one of the ropes that hung from a beam above the entrance and slipped out of the house.

Trying to avoid any possible contact with Damtew or their father, Desta leaped over the garden fence, dashed across the fallow potato field, crossed a grove of bushes and emerged near where the sholla tree stood. Its leaves were rustling in the evening breeze.

He slung his bag over his shoulder and scampered up the heavily branched tree as he had done many times before when he was collecting figs. He went as high as he could and found a strong bough among the thickest branches. He straddled the vee of the bough and secured his body by using the rope to tie himself to one of the branches.

He waited.

He thought through the scenarios of how the absence of Habté might come to light. Damtew, soon after he came home, would go to pet and caress his little animal, as he always did before he had his snack or dinner. Not finding it, he would start looking in all the possible places where it could be, his face darkening as he continued his search. He would go outside and call after Desta after Ayénat told him she had seen his little brother a short while ago. At the same time, Damtew would continue to search for his goat in the cows' pen and in the bushes behind the house as he called for Desta. Lost and confused by his predicament he would walk down to Asse'ged's house to share with him what was going on.

IN THE MOONLIGHT—thank God there was a full moon—Desta saw something or someone moving along the southern end of the property. Holding his breath, he watched as Damtew's hulking form came into view. He was with Asse'ged. They were heading for the thicket of acacia trees, where the goats often grazed. They were talking, but Desta couldn't make out what they were saying. After covering the full length of the thicket and not finding anything, they hiked across the field toward the sholla tree.

Desta's hands began to sweat and shake like the wet leaves around him as he watched the pair approach his hiding place. His heart pounded and his mind raced, but he kept his eyes on his brothers. *They had come across the track he had made when he dragged Habté's dead body and were following it*, he thought.

"Where are you going?" asked Asse'ged when he saw Damtew heading toward the tree.

"That big tree is one of the places Desta takes shelter when it rains. I am just . . . uhhh . . ." Damtew sounded confused and lost.

"Do you think he would still be here?" asked Asse'ged. "There is really nothing you can do tonight. Tomorrow, in the broad day light, we can do a better job of searching. Let's go home."

Damtew walked to the tree anyway. He circled it, slowly, looking up to the branches as if he sensed something. Desta stopped breathing. His heart skipped several beats. He clung to the branch tightly and closed his eyes and prayed. He heard a faint voice, not Damtew's or Asse'ged's. He couldn't make out the words, but somehow the voice calmed him and reassured him of his safety.

"It would be comforting to think my kid goat got mixed in with the neighbor's goats, like it used to happen to us in the old days. But I am sure nothing like that happened here, as our goats almost never cross the river," said Damtew, nearly choking with emotion.

"Don't torture yourself. Let's go home," begged Asse'ged.

As they walked Damtew was fuming. "I've been telling you that son of a bitch was created to bring mayhem in our family and misery to me. If my goat was killed by an animal, I swear I will kill him. Baba can shoot me afterwards. I don't mind dying."

"I know how you feel but you can't jump to conclusions that quickly. Don't become a martyr over a baby goat," said Asse'ged.

"It's no small matter. You have no idea what the goat means to me. I have so many grand plans with it for me and my future family."

"Okay, okay. Let's go home. I am cold."

Desta lost them to the woods below Asse'ged's home. He began to breathe normally again, barely.

His buttocks and legs were aching and his feet had become numb and heavy. His clothes were drenched from the tree's water-clogged leaves and his own sweat. Even his glass beads from his neck felt cold and weighty. To comfort himself, he loosened the rope and stood up. He folded his gabi several times and wedged it into the cleft of the branches for a seat. For a cover, he swathed his father's old gabi around him. "Now, I can hopefully sleep better," he said as he secured himself once more with the rope.

It was not long afterward that he heard the first howl of a hyena. It came from the southern end of the valley near the church. His heart jumped. He had not thought of the hyenas till now. But what could they do to him? Hyenas can't climb trees.

Another hyena howled back across Davola, near the foothills and Desta trembled. He cocked his ears to listen for more. He parted a handful of leaves and peered through the branches. The moon had been freed from the clouds and everything around him was bathed in its comforting cool light. At least he could see if some animal came near the tree.

A third hyena responded to the calls of the other two. This one, to Desta's surprise, came from exactly the area where Desta had found Habté's body. *Oh my God, he must have smelled the blood and is now looking for the body,* he told himself, terror running through his head. His heart raced as if he were chased by a hyena himself. A fourth howl came from directly below Saba's new home. The one at the other end of the field howled again. Desta wondered if he was telling them he had found the remains of some food and they should join him.

The chorus of calls continued. Desta kept his eyes and ears on the hyena that howled at the other end of the field. Not long after, he saw him sniffing the trail and coming toward the tree. After each howl, the hyena whimpered and growled as he chased the blood trail.

Soon Desta discovered that the hyena was accompanied by two more. He kept his eyes on them. When they got to the tree, they circled it three times, frequently stopping to look up and sniff. Desta wondered if it was true that hyenas couldn't climb trees. He thought they must have smelled him to be circling around instead of following the trail of blood.

Desta prayed and petitioned the help of all the angels—Michael and Gabriel, followed by the saints: Mary and George. While he was praying, a story his father once told came to him.

A long, long time ago, our country used to be ruled by a python. Every year, the tax paid to him was in the form of a girl or a boy. They needed to be the first born, and a lottery was held to determine who would be fed to the python that year.

The last year the lottery was cast, the name of a beautiful girl called Saba was drawn. Her father was a poor farmer. The only unattractive parts of her were her feet. They were not only ugly but curved out in opposite directions. She was an outcast and had no friends. All her relatives shunned her. When she was picked to be taken and delivered to the python, the father, grieved, but the rest of her family were happy to get rid of her as she shamed them. The father, full of tears, brought Saba early in the day and left her under a giant oak tree, the place the python came looking for his meal on the appointed day and time every year. Afraid, she climbed the tree and waited. While in the tree, she prayed and prayed, tears washing down her cheeks.

The python finally came, crushing everything in his way. He slithered his giant body around the tree, disturbed that his food was not there. When he looked up, he saw the weeping girl. He was pleased. He lifted his giant head, extended it through the heavy branches, struggling to pass it through. When his mouth was close to Saba's feet, he opened it, trying to grab them and bring her down. At this instant, St. George came flying in on his white horse and lodged his gleaming spear into the gullet of the python. The beast struggled mightily to get the spear out of its mouth, but the more it fought, the deeper the spear went into his mouth and belly. He died finally, blood frothing from his mouth.

Saba climbed down from the tree smiling. As she landed on the ground, her feet accidentally stepped on the python's blood. To her surprise, soon after, her old feet dropped off like the skin of a snake and were replaced with new, beautiful ones. She became the first ruler of our country.

Now, sitting on the sholla tree, Desta concentrated on praying to St. George. *Save me, St. George. Please come flying in on your white horse the moment one of the hyenas attempts to climb the tree and kill him with your spear.* Then another thought came to him. Did he really want the hyena killed? Or Damtew?

He thought for a moment. Hyenas didn't climb trees, so he probably was safe. From Damtew he would never be safe. He had promised Asse'ged he was going to kill Desta anyway, so why not get him first?

The thought of St. George ramming his spear into Damtew's gaping mouth horrified him.

He had seen the same image on the church wall when he went for the communion, the same man on the horse vanquishing the marauding beast, blood gushing out of its mouth, tongue twisted, eyes glazed in agony. He quickly brought down the curtain in his brain to hide the image of Damtew with the spear in his mouth. "If you wish bad things to someone, bad things will happen to you," Ayénat had once said.

The wind began to blow and shake the leaves around him, and a velvety soft voice came to him. "Don't despair. Everything will be all right," it said. Desta thought he must be hallucinating. He held his breath, cocked his ears and listened again. The wind was still rustling, agitating the leaves around him.

Drops of the earlier rain landed on his face and his father's gabi. He heard no voice or message again. He thought his mind was playing tricks on him, but then he remembered the cloud man appearing and saying things at unexpected moments, particularly when he was in trouble. Still it had been several months since he heard anything from him. He thought he was done with that.

When he looked down he saw no hyena, but there were disturbing cackles coming from the area where he had hidden Habté's body. He wondered if the hyenas found the goat and were fighting over the body. He parted the leaves to look.

He was right.

One hyena was dragging Habté's body out into the open, trying to appropriate it for himself. The other two were chasing him. After a few minutes of the chase and dance around the flailing carcass, the first hyena dropped it and all three hyenas began snatching, chewing, and crushing the bones. Horrified, Desta wished he were strong enough to bring the goat up in the tree with him or that he had a gun so he could shoot the howling beasts. Shortly, more hyenas arrived, but the first three had already devoured Habté. The others paced around, sniffing the blood and scavenging for any remaining morsels. Eventually the original hyenas vanished. Even more trotted to the scene of the feast, sniffed around and, finding nothing, vanished into the woods, also.

Desta could not sleep. He was terribly uncomfortable and afraid that if he didn't keep awake, he might fall and be eaten by the hyenas. He checked to ensure the rope was still tightly knotted. As his fear subsided slightly, he became aware of the dampness of the big gabi. There was nothing he could do about it now. He pulled his coverings closer to try to keep out the biting cold. He had to bear it till dawn, which he thought was probably a long time away. His heart dropped and his stomach lurched at the thought.

Throughout the night, he nodded, waking when his head banged the branch that was his perch. Each time this happened, he reminded himself, *I can't afford to fall asleep, I can't afford to fall asleep* . . . He shook his head to drive the sleep from his brain.

Once he was alert, he parted the leaves in front of him and peered to see if there were any animals or monsters trudging through the field. There were none. Just the yellow moonlight draped over everything he could see in the valley. Distant trees and bushes appeared as mere shadows and the grain lots up on the mountains resembled huge gray sheets spread out to dry in the moonlight.

The quiet of the night was broken occasionally by the howl of the hyenas, the whisper of the leaves in the tree, and the increasingly aggressive wind, which seemed engaged in a duel with the fall of Davola up in the mountain. The sound came in waves and at different pitches, which Desta thought was a result of the wind disrupting the steady fall of the water. Even now, the sound was comforting to his ears.

While Desta listened to the pulsating sound, he thought of something very important that he must keep in mind: his goal of going to the mountaintop to touch the sky. He *must* not die. The more he thought about his goal, the more alert he became.

He parted the leaves once again and peered out to the yellow world, straining his neck to get a good view of the mountains. He saw snatches of the sky near the top but couldn't clearly see the horizon. It didn't matter. He knew what he must do some day.

He thought of his trip to the mountaintop. He knew he had to go when the day was gorgeous and sky very deep blue.

What would he need to bring? Several things: a stick to use to touch the sky at places where he couldn't reach it with his hand, a bucket of blood and a tied bunch of straw, which he could use to paint the sky, something sharp to widen the holes in the sky, a sack to collect clouds in, water in a canteen, and loaf of bread in his pouch. With whom would he travel? That was obvious. It had to be Hibist.

While Desta was planning his journey, a rooster from his home tore the silence with his ritual call announcing the impending arrival of day. Desta knew it would be a while yet before the night faded into day but he was glad to know the bulk of the dark hours had already gone into obscurity. It would not be long now before the sun made its way to his valley, and he should prepare to dismount from his perch before dawn and find a safer place to hide.

He had to fight off the urge to give in to sleep. He began to nod again, but woke every time he heard the rooster crow, then just as quickly his head swayed again. He went through this cat-and-mouse game until the morning's silence was rent by the racing guttural calls of the colobus monkeys. This was it—dawn was imminent.

Desta untied himself from the bough, leaving the rope attached to the top branch. He rose slowly, stiff and achy all over. He attached one end of the rope to the sack that held his food and slowly lowered and dropped it. He threw down his father's gabi and wrapped himself with his own. He scanned the field and all areas around him, then he gingerly climbed down the trunk of the great tree. Grateful for the shelter it had provided him, he kissed the tree's trunk three times.

As he stood at the foot of the tree, he noted that there was still darkness. The ravines and the canyons up the eastern mountain appeared black as if smudged with charcoal. The ones on the western land masses were not as black. The thought that there could still be hyenas lurking around gave Desta the chills. *I have to be brave*, he told himself. Now the question was where to go.

He remembered that the shed in Saba's old place was still packed with hay. He thought that would be a safe and a warm place to sleep. But he had to see first if there were any remains of Habté.

The entire goat had been devoured. The only things left were the crushed jaw with the teeth intact and fragments of the skull. Desta kept shaking his head as he inspected the ground for any more remains, a token, a memento for him to keep. Tears kept coming back as he thought how the beautiful goat had ended up as a meal for the hyenas.

He didn't have time to reminisce about Habté. He had to leave the area before Damtew came looking for his goat. He gathered up his sack of injera, his father's big gabi and the rope and scampered across the field in the cover of the predawn pencil gray hour. Through the woods and across the creek he went. As he walked, the things Damtew and his father used to say about Habté came back to him: its pedigree, the future father of many handsome goats, the money Damtew would receive after he turned him into a mookit and sold him, the things Damtew and Melkam would buy when they moved into their own home.

What worried Desta most was how the loss was going to affect Damtew. Although Damtew had also received a heifer and young male bull from his parents when he got married and Melkam had brought her pair, none of those animals mattered. His happiness revolved around Habté.

Through that goat, Desta had seen the human side of Damtew. He was capable of showing love and feeling love. He remembered too how Damtew had talked and smiled when he walked around with the goat in his arms. It was as if with Habté, Damtew had found the freedom to feel and express his happiness. But now . . .?

Desta couldn't imagine what *now* might mean. He didn't want to imagine what would happen to Damtew. Would he kill himself? Would he turn into a worse beast than he already was?

Desta was afraid to answer those questions.

At the shed, Desta discreetly pulled out a few bales of hay and made room for himself to rest.

He looked across the creek toward his home. He saw a figure in white exit the house and disappear to the back. Desta thought it must be either his father or mother going to the bathroom.

He couldn't afford to be seen. He snuggled into the pocket he had created, using his father's gabi for a pillow. With him in it, the pocket quickly became warm. Desta thanked Yihoon for not taking the hay and demolishing the shed. As he tried to fall asleep, he wondered what he would do the following day.

Having heard Damtew tell Asse'ged he would kill Desta if something had happened to his goat, Desta knew there was only one answer. He had to run away from this place. He had to disappear completely.

THIRTY-FOUR

When Desta awoke late in the afternoon, groggy and confused, the sun was already setting. Unidentifiable noises drifted back to him from somewhere in the distance. At first he thought this was the second day and that he had slept through a day and a night. After he was fully awake, he realized it was still the same day. Once this was clear in his mind, he wanted to find out about the strange and disconcerting noises.

He tilted his head and listened. The noises, faint at first, were getting louder. It sounded as if they were coming from his home. He wondered if Damtew was having a mental breakdown and the family members had gathered to console him. Or, God forbid, he had gone berserk and killed someone. No matter what happened, Desta resolved not to move from his hideout.

He was terribly hungry and thirsty. He nibbled on a bit of injera, but this only made him thirstier.

When darkness finally fell, he crawled out of his berth and scurried to the creek for water. He cupped his hands and drank. The water tasted wonderfully soothing to his parched throat and mouth. He ate part of his injera and drank some more water.

Feeling better, he went back to the shed. As he walked he thought about what he needed to do next, whether he should stay in the same place or find a nearby tree to spend the night in.

He was not going to go home for sure. Tomorrow before daybreak he planned to go to Hibist. She would keep him safe and give him food and shelter. For tonight, despite his worry that the hyenas might find him, he thought he could sleep better if he remained in the hay shed. He closed off the opening as much as he could, allowing only an opening for needed air into his chamber and went back to sleep.

When he woke the following morning, it was still dark, but he needed to get going soon before anybody woke and saw him leaving his hideout. He transferred his remaining injera to his gabi, then stowed his father's gabi and his pouch in the pocket in the hay. He no longer needed them since he was going to Hibist's house. They would only be an encumbrance.

After filling his stomach with dry injera and creek water, he walked along the tree-lined banks of the creek. Birds chattered and twittered their predawn songs. Two dik-diks bolted from the side of the bushes along the river and dove into the tall weeds on Saba's old property. Startled, Desta jumped and nearly fell on a pile of dried agam thorns that stood up from their stems like porcupine needles. He needed to walk carefully on this unbeaten path.

He was happy when he finally connected up with the caravan route near the confluence of the creek and the Davola River. The day had not fully broken yet, but it was visible enough for him to travel without tripping. As he walked along the rocky road, he noticed hyena tracks in the dusty route. He wondered if they had come back the second night looking for another dead goat in the field where he tended the cows.

As he walked farther down, he saw farmers driving their oxen and carrying their tools on their shoulders. Blue smoke rose out of the thatched-roof homes that stood in clusters along the foothills and mountainsides. He saw little boys like him driving their animals to the fields, cracking their whips. *That would have been me, if I were still at home,* Desta said to himself.

He couldn't wait to see Hibist. He was sure she would be very surprised to see him, coming alone all the way from home! And he couldn't wait to eat a platter full of food and drink a big tumbler of cold milk.

As morning advanced, Desta saw more and more boys along his route. He worried about whether they would stop and beat him up. He had heard stories about groups of boys doing all kinds of things to other boys they found traveling alone.

Some of them stopped him and asked where he was gong. He told them he was going to see his sister not far from where he was, but he wouldn't say why he was traveling without an adult. Some thought he was a runaway and invited him to come to stay with them for a while. Desta firmly declined, and they let him go.

He traveled all morning, passing many men and women—some dressed in nice white clothes as if they were going to church or a wedding. Others were in their work clothes. Some of the men stopped and asked him where he was going. He told them he was carrying a message from his mother to his sister who lived a short distance away.

Desta was thrilled when he saw the tall, packed juniper trees at the foot of the rotund mountain west of the River Davola. He remembered that was his parents' church, although they more often attended the old church closer to their home. Hibist's house was a short distance from the church.

Excited, Desta picked up his speed. He left the main caravan route and took a smaller side street that went in the direction of the church. Shortly after he had turned onto this route, he saw a group of boys playing a bead game. He had never seen the game played before, but Hibist had once told him about it when she gave him her bead necklace.

He stood and watched them briefly. They stopped what they were doing and stared at him. Desta counted. There were five boys. Two of them looked big and menacing. The other three appeared to be about his height, weight and age, but unthreatening.

"Stop! Where are you going?" asked one of the big boys, walking up to Desta. He had a cleft lower lip and, mean looking deep-set eyes.

Desta kept walking, keeping his eyes on the road.

"Didn't you hear, he told you to stop?" said the other big boy. He had a huge shaved head and ugly, crooked teeth.

Desta froze. The boys surrounded him.

"Do you want to come and play a game of diba with us?" asked the boy with the cleft lip. Desta noticed this boy's eyes were on the beads he wore on his neck.

"I don't know how."

"We'll teach you. It's fun," said the boy with the big head. Desta observed that he too was looking at his beads with interest.

"No, I need to go. My sister is waiting for me."

"C'mon, just for a little bit," said the boy with a cleft lip, tugging Desta's gabi.

The other boys watched, their eyes running from the boy with a cleft lip to Desta.

Desta yielded to the pressure, partly because he wanted to know how to play the game and partly he was scared what they would do to him if he didn't.

He noticed that on a sloping ground they had shaved the grass, smoothed the surface and drilled a hole the size of a shilling. One of the kids stood some distance away with the bunch of beads in his hand. He moved his hand back and forth several times, his eyes fixed on the hole. Then he threw the beads.

A few beads fell into the hole and others scattered around it. He collected the ones in the hole and held them in his hand.

Another boy collected the scattered beads, stood at the same spot as the last player, aimed at the hole, and threw them.

Three beads fell into the hole. He claimed them, leaving the others. A third boy rose, aimed and miraculously threw all of the remaining beads into the little cavity. The big boys, the ones that had been eyeing Desta's beads, stared in shock.

"Would you like to play?" asked the boy with the big head. Desta found him to be less menacing than before.

"No, I don't know how and I have no. . ." Desta began to say as he pushed his gabi farther up his neck to hide his beads.

"We can teach you, very easy . . . and you have plenty around your neck," said the boy with the cleft lip in a sweeter tone.

"No, my mother will kill me, if I play with these."

"No she will be happy because you will win and bring home a bunch more," said the boy with a big head.

"I can help you untie them from your back," said the boy with a cleft lip.

"No, I can't, I don't want to . . ."

"Look, the rule is, any boy that is alone and passes by this road, must either play with us and go home with dignity or get a bloody nose and have his beads ripped from his neck," said the boy with cleft lip.

Desta looked at their feet and contemplated the ultimatum given to him. "So, what do you say?" said the boy with the big head.

"I guess okay. Just two games," said Desta in a meek voice.

"Everybody has to have a set of beads to play with. I will help you untie your necklace so that you can have yours," said the boy with the cleft lip.

"O . . . O . . . Okay," said Desta fearfully. He remembered Hibist tying the cord that held the beads tightly. She had wanted to make sure that her gift would be kept safe. These were the same beads she had worn as a little girl. She had given them to him when she discovered one day he had nothing around his neck, which she told him was un-Christian.

To Desta the sentimental value of the beads was more important than his Christian-hood. They were reminders of his beloved sister.

A boy with a split lip quickly untied the knot and looped the cord over the cleft of his thumb and index fingers, holding the ends so the beads wouldn't fall off. Considering how fast he untied the cord, Desta thought he must have cut it with a blade.

"You need to have at least three beads to start the game," said the boy with the cleft lip as he discreetly stripped a bunch of them off the strand and handed the rest to Desta. Desta observed his act in horror. The others covered their mouths with their hands to keep from laughing.

"Now take out three and let's play," said the same boy.

"This is how it's done, let me show you," said the boy with the big head as he snatched Desta's beads and stripped another bunch from the opposite side of the cord. "Look." He fashioned his fingers into a cone by bringing them together. The stacked beads rested from the tip of his fingers to the middle of his palm. He laid his thumb over the stacked beads so they would stay in place as he moved the hand back and forth, aiming for the hole.

"Do you understand?" said the boy, looking at Desta.

Desta shook his head. He looked at the hand that held his beads wondering if the boy was going to give them back to him.

"Good! Now take three off your necklace and let's play," said the boy with the big head.

The three small boys could no longer contain their laughter. They began to giggle, covering their mouths.

The boy with the split lip gave them a glare and their giggles vanished instantly.

Upset and afraid to show it, Desta pulled three beads from his necklace and held them tightly in his hand. He tied the cords and slid it up his arm and under his gabi. More than half of his beads were gone.

The boy with split lip collected one bead from each of the players and gave the first shot to Desta. For the others he drew a lottery for the order in which they would throw the beads. Desta's shot scattered around the hole. Only one bead fell in. He retrieved it and stood by the side. He bit his lips and watched the boy with a split lip as he gathered the scattered beads and walked to the marked spot to throw them.

His throw netted him three out of the remaining five.

One of the smaller boys had his turn and he threw. He got one in.

The fourth player tried the one but didn't get it in.

The fifth hit the bull's eye. Nobody even saw the bead disappear into the hole. The others looked at him in awe. Desta was impressed.

On the second round Desta lost the bead that he had gotten in on his first try.

He took his necklace off his arm, untied the knot and began to put the other two beads back.

"You're not leaving, are you?" said the boy with the big head.

Desta nodded.

"The rule is any kid that passes by here must at least play three games before he leaves," said the boy with the cleft lip. His eyes were hard and menacing.

Desta yielded.

On the third round he played again and lost.

"I need to go. I have already played three times and lost each time," Desta said politely.

"Well, since you are not good at this game, you deserve to lose what you have left. If you remained and played, you would lose anyway. Save yourself time and give us all those beads," said the boy with the cleft lip. He stepped up to Desta and looked down on him threateningly.

"No, I can't . . . I won't," said Desta. He attempted to run but the boy with the big head tripped him. He fell, hitting his forehead on a rock. He began to bleed.

"See, all this could have been avoided if you had given up those beads peacefully," said the boy with the cleft lip. He reached for Desta's arm, slipped off the necklace with the remaining beads.

Desta began to cry.

"Here boys, you take your shares," said the boy with the split lip as he passed out Desta's beads. "Each of you gets three. The rest will be shared between me and my buddy." He tossed his head toward the big-headed boy. "Now you must run from here or we'll beat you up," he told Desta.

Desta got up and scampered, half walking, half running, occasionally looking back to see if they were following him. He kept dabbing his head with his gabi to stop the bleeding.

Once he was far enough away, he slowed and began to walk normally. His earlier excitement at the prospect of seeing his sister was now dampened by the loss of the beads she had given him. He also was now "Islam," since there was not a single straw in the area long enough for him to regain his identity as a Christian. Worse, the link with his sister had been broken. Every time he missed his sister, he would reach for the beads, comforted by the knowledge that he was wearing the same necklace that had once graced his sister's beautiful long neck. *Now they were gone, what would she say when she found out? How upset would she be to know that her beads had been divided up by kids in her neighborhood, while he was on his way to find safety and comfort in her home? He would have to be sure to keep his neck covered.*

Another thought came to him: *Maybe Hibist's husband and family could recover the beads.* They might know the boys' families. This gave him a slim glimmer of hope. For now, though, he must walk quickly to get to Hibist. He would tell her about the beads when the time was right.

As he walked two horsemen galloped past him. He looked to see if there were any more on the way, wondering if something was happening someplace that called for their participation.

Instead of men on horses, Desta saw a lone figure walking toward him briskly. As the man came nearer, he noticed that the gait and figure looked more and more familiar. The closer he got, the clearer the image became.

"Oh my God! That's Asse'ged!" said Desta, halting in his tracks.

He had to make a quick decision: run and hide or stay put. The impulse to run outpaced the consideration to stay put. But where could he hide? Everything around him was farmland, and the grains had already been harvested, leaving only short stubbles. To the left side of the road, a few yards from him, a big rock jutted out from the flat earth as if it were some strange outgrowth. Desta scuttled toward the rock, finding scanty dried grass behind it. He could see a lush bush of Abo behind a fence that bordered a farmland and, beyond the bush was a house that looked not more than a year old.

Desta lay flat on the ground behind the rock and closed his eyes, listening for Asse'ged's footsteps. Although his brother had been far away when Desta first spotted him, he might have seen him as he dashed to the rock. The thought caused his heart to race. Every time he heard a bird rustle in the bushes behind him or the buzz of an insect, he held his breath and cocked his ears. It seemed a very long time that he lay there waiting for Asse'ged to pass. He was contemplating whether it would be safe to rise and look for his brother along the path, when Asse'ged materialized behind him.

"You thought I didn't see you, did you?" he said as he grabbed Desta by his foot.

A hyena or a leopard might as well have grabbed him. Desta was terrified and speechless. Not only did he think his brother didn't see him, he also didn't hear the slightest sound of his steps, crashed leaves or anything that could have alerted him.

"Come out of here, let's go home," said Asse'ged as he tugged on Desta's foot.

"Let go of me," said Desta as he tried to slip out of his brother's hold. Asse'ged stared at him.

"I am not going home, even if you threaten to kill me," said Desta sharply.

"Look, nobody will hurt you," said Asse'ged pleadingly. "Right now, everybody is worried that you might have drowned. Mother is beside herself. Many people are blaming Damtew because they thought you were afraid to face him as the result of his lost goat . . . Everybody will be so happy to see you."

Desta didn't move.

"You look so weak and emaciated," Asse'ged continued, finally letting go of Desta's foot. "Your forehead is bloodied and swollen. Looks like you must have just fallen and hit something . . . I bet you have not eaten for the last two days. Let's see if we can get some food for you from that house over there."

Desta stared at a line of ants that had ringed the base of the rock.

"Let's not worry about going home. Let me see if I can get you some food . . . get up," said Asse'ged, grabbing his brother by the hand.

"I can wait until I get to Hibist's house." said Desta sullenly.

"She is not there. She and her husband have left for his aunt's funeral. Mother sent me yesterday evening, thinking maybe you might have gone to be with Hibist. I slept at their house last night because I was tired and it was too late to walk back home."

Desta's gut tightened into a ball. "You are lying!" he snapped.

"Why should I lie? If you want we can go back and you see for yourself. Actually, I can go home, and you can find out for yourself that you have no place to go . . . the dogs there are ferocious."

Desta's eyes filled with tears. "I won't go home," he cried. "I want to kill myself!"

Surprised and frustrated by his brother's reaction, Asse'ged looked away for a few seconds. "I have a suggestion," he began to say turning to Desta. "I know you want to kill yourself. That is fine. I will teach you a quick way to do it. But before I do, you need to eat some food. You will need it for the rest of your dead life. You know there is no food like here in heaven. Whatever we eat just before we die, will be the one food we'll have the rest of our dead lives."

Desta had never heard anybody say that before. He certainly didn't want to have dry injera for eternity. He stared into the distant haze to the place Hibist said was their father's birthplace, the place where his grandfather had vanished, the ancient family coin was stolen. He weighed his options. Was he really ready to give up his dream of getting to the top of the mountain?

"What do you want to do?" asked Asse'ged in a resigned tone. "Want to come with me and let's see if there is someone at the house that can give you food?"

Desta couldn't sacrifice his life just yet. Despite the struggles and the pain, he had to keep living until he had touched the sky.

He staggered to his feet and hobbled behind his brother. Asse'ged climbed over the wattled fence first, then reached over and helped Desta. They crossed a stubble of teff field. When they reached the entrance of the home, Asse'ged called to see if anyone was there.

A woman in a long old gown came out. She was slender, maybe in her thirties with a dark olive complexion and pretty, almond eyes. Her hair, soft and curly, was piled in large loops like Saba's. It would have bounced as she walked and glinted in the light had she washed it, and combed it out and touched it up with a tad of butter, like Saba always did, thought Desta.

"My little brother here is very hungry," said Asse'ged, resting his hands on Desta's shoulders. "He has not eaten for a few days. Could you be so kind to give him something? A glass of water and piece of injera will do."

"Oh, I am sorry to hear that. Please stay for a moment. I don't have anything freshly baked yet, but I'll see what I've got," said the woman as she disappeared into the house.

To Desta's delight the woman came back with a tumbler of milk and two full size injeras with thick, yellow split pea sauce. She set the platter on a chopped log and went back inside and came back with two wooden stools for them to sit on while Desta ate.

Then she vanished again, returning this time with a tumbler of tella for Asse'ged. Desta downed the milk in two long swigs and tore into the injera, scooping the split peas with it. The injera tasted old and dry, but not as dry as the one he had been eating for the last two days. *This injera was heavenly in comparison*, he thought.

Asse'ged watched his brother eat. The cut on Desta's forehead had crusted with blood and was swollen like a bump on a log.

"I brought the food for both of you, please help yourself also, sir," said the woman as she brought a kettle of tella to refill Asse'ged's tumbler.

"I just wanted the boy to have his fill first. Thank you," said Asse'ged.

"Was there something wrong with him that he had not eaten for so long?" asked the hostess, looking down on Desta with empathy. Her dark eyelashes were long and glinted in the sun.

"One of the animals he was tending was killed by a beast, and he ran away, afraid someone might spank him, I guess," said Asse'ged, glancing toward Desta.

The woman sucked her lips in sympathy. "Does he get spanked that badly for him to abandon his home for these many days and without food?" she asked with her eyes still on Desta.

"No, not really . . . He is just a sensitive and adventurous boy . . .," said Asse'ged.

"Ahhh . . .," she said thoughtfully as if she doubted the truthfulness of Asse'ged's response.

Desta fixed his eyes on his brother, wondering what other lies he would tell.

"Just to show you how adventurous he is," Asse'ged continued. "We live in a place called Jomer. Have you heard of it?"

"No, I haven't," said the woman.

"You have not missed much. It's the kind of place you would want to run out of as soon as you arrived," said Asse'ged with a grin.

The woman looked at him quizzically.

"It's a bit far from here. All you see around you is a wall of mountains. We have a sister here, and Desta came all the way from there to here . . . alone. Don't you call that adventurous for a little boy who is only eight years old?!"

"He came all the way here by himself and he is only eight years old?"

"Yes. He is very close to his sister and apparently he had wanted to come to see her for a long time. With work up to our necks, we didn't have time to bring him. When we failed him, he decided to brave it on his own. Unfortunately, he didn't even get a chance to see her this morning, as she is gone to a funeral with her husband.

"When he didn't come home two nights ago, our mother sent me yesterday suspecting he might have come to his sister. I ran into him just now as he was heading to our sister's house."

"That is too bad," said the woman. "Sibling separation can be very hard, particularly on young ones like him. You should invite her or bring him to her often. After the harvest, it should be easier for both of you."

"We think so too," said Asse'ged, motioning to Desta to get up. "Thank you for your kind help. He should make it home now with a renewed energy."

Desta did not take his eyes off Asse'ged. He was disgusted by the way his brother had distorted the truth.

"Let's go," said Asse'ged, resting his hand on his shoulder.

Desta jerked his shoulder free.

"Thank you again. May God bless you and your family," said Asse'ged, turning to the woman.

"May your trip home be safe and free of obstacles! Take care of the boy," she said.

"Will do," said Asse'ged without looking back.

As he walked behind his brother, Desta sizzled with anger. But what could he do? His world was run by the adults who didn't care for him other than the animal herding job they had given him. He would rather not go back and face Damtew again, but he knew he must if he wanted to travel to the place of his dreams one day. He couldn't allow his fears to sabotage his goal. Strengthened by these thoughts, Desta walked home with less apprehension and worry.

THIRTY-FIVE

When Desta and Asse'ged returned home, there were about a dozen people huddled around Ayénat on the grass outside the house. They appeared to be consoling her. Some were her friends from across the Davola River, including Mawa, Mogus and his wife, Yisehak and his wife, Maray and a few other people Desta didn't pay attention to. Yihoon, Melkam and Mulu were also there. Damtew was sitting several feet away from the group wrapped in his gabi, his chin buried in the turns of the fabric, his eyes boring into the dirt near his feet, which he was poking with a stick.

"There is Desta with Asse'ged!" blurted Melkam the moment she saw the pair. All turned to the two brothers who had just come around the fence. Damtew gave Desta a hard, cold stare.

"Just like I thought," said Ayénat with a half smile. She rose to meet them. Others did as well. Mawa dashed before Ayénat and kissed Desta intensely on both cheeks. Desta cringed as Mawa held him close and showered him with her exaggerated affection. She was always doing this to him when Ayénat or Abraham were watching, and he hated it. In the old days, he would run and hide the moment he saw her outside. Now he had no choice but accept the assault stoically.

"You found him at Hibist's?" asked Ayénat once Asse'ged had stopped near them. "No, he was on his way there," replied Asse'ged.

"Where had he spent the last two nights?" asked Ayénat, wide-eyed.

"That you will have to ask him."

The other women gazed at Desta with wide eyes too.

"As you can see, he is pretty emaciated and tired," said Asse'ged. "I think he can use some food and sleep before you ask him too many questions."

"Melkam," said Ayénat, glancing at her daughter-in-law. "Could you please prepare Desta a good lunch and give him a cup of milk? He looks like he has not eaten since he left home two days ago."

Desta followed Melkam into the house. Coming in from the bright sun, he found the house dim and the sitting area barely visible. He groped with his feet for his father's bench and sat on it. In due time his eyes adjusted to the lighting and everything was clear to him.

While he was eating, Desta overheard Ayénat's thanking God for bringing him home safely and thanking Asse'ged for his willingness to go to Hibist's to look for him. Shortly after, the people wished her well and left. Asse'ged and Mulu left too.

As Desta was finishing his meal, Damtew and Ayénat walked in and stood before him, the brother morose and gloomy like a winter cloud.

Desta shrank and looked away.

"Can you tell me what exactly happened to Habté?" asked Damtew, his voice laced with anger.

"Right after the hailstorm, I found him dead by the creek, near the Davola," said Desta, looking down at the fireplace.

"You mean to tell me the storm killed him?" growled his brother.

"I don't know. But he was dead with his stomach open. It seemed like some animal got to him, but I am not sure whether before or during the storm," said Desta, now looking at his mother and wishing she would tell Damtew to leave him alone.

"The storm didn't kill any other goat. It obviously must have been an animal that killed him because you didn't keep the animals out of the bushes, as I repeatedly told you to do," continued Damtew.

"Nothing can be done now, stop asking him questions. Go attend to your things," commanded Ayénat.

"I just want to know the story behind what happened to my goat," muttered Damtew.

"Nothing what you say or hear from Desta will bring him back," consoled Ayénat. "Please go out of the house for now."

Desta shrank farther and farther into himself as he listened to his mother and brother. He wished he had refused to come home with Asse'ged. He couldn't imagine living with Damtew after this. His brother would probably bring up the lost goat every time he got mad. Desta would rather run away again than live with his brother. But where could he run to? And how could he run away now, before achieving his life's dream.

"I need to take a nap now, Ma," said Desta as he rose. "I've not slept much for two days."

"You think I'll forget this?" said Damtew, watching Desta head to his bed.

As Desta crawled into bed, he watched Damtew and Ayénat go out of the house. She was saying something to him, but Desta couldn't hear the words. He covered his face and closed his eyes, wishing sleep would come soon and take him away from this place he called his home.

THIRTY-SIX

January 1957

It was early morning, January 21, the day of Timket, Epiphany. Desta had just come out of his house about to drive the animals down to the field when he saw Yihoon emerge from around the house with a broad smile on his face. Desta's father was squatting in front of the house, feeding his two mookit goats a mixture of salt and grains.

"I came to share good news," said Yihoon. "We think Saba is pregnant."

"Congratulations! What great news!" said Abraham, looking up to Yihoon.

"This was the second month Saba has skipped her period. She feels certain she is pregnant," said the son-in-law, beaming.

Both men glanced at Desta but he quickly left to get the animals, avoiding eye contact.

"I'll see you at church," Yihoon said, hurrying to catch Desta. "Let's hope your man's suggestion works. A little prayer to him could help. I hear you're always in contact with him."

"No, I have not even seen him in my dreams for a long time," said Desta, trying to distance himself from Yihoon and Saba's problems.

"We made this move, in the process creating enemies out of your brothers, because of what he suggested," said Yihoon.

"What do you want me to do now? I don't want to hear it," snapped Desta, suddenly engulfed by fear remembering what Damtew and Asse'ged had done to him in his dream.

"I just thought you might pray for us; ask for the help of that man so our dream of having a baby—a boy—is fulfilled. "

"Pray for yourselves. Don't drag me into your mess again," retorted Desta, running away from Yihoon.

When he looked back, he saw his brother-in-law walking slowly, head bent to the ground.

This news had put a damper on Desta's spirits that day. He was afraid that for the next seven or eight months he would be plagued by worries that Saba might not carry her baby to term. For now he didn't want to think about it. He drove the animals to the field and sat on his usual perch by the sholla tree.

In the dry season, there was nothing in the valley that was new or changing to keep Desta's attention. The days began to warm soon after the sun cleared the eastern mountains and the temperatures progressively rose through the day. The clouds visited the valley only sparingly and even then, mostly in wisps and sheets, not interesting enough to spark his imagination. *It's all for the better,* he told himself. As much as he loved the company of the clouds, he certainly didn't want a repeat of what happened the last time he was distracted by them.

Damtew and everybody else believed, rightly so, that the reason Habté had been killed was because Desta had not kept an eye on the goats in order to move them from a place of danger.

"I can't believe you are still here while my beautiful Habté is gone," Damtew had told Desta privately. "My dreams became a meal for some wild beasts, thanks to you! It's only because I gave my word to Ma that you are still walking these grounds . . . some day it will happen," he had fumed.

The little brother's hairs stood on their ends. As usual he said nothing. He simply looked down at his feet and walked away slowly.

Desta now certainly was more attentive of his duties than he ever had been in the past. When he was not walking around and checking on the animals, his days were filled with mind-numbing boredom. He even got tired of looking at the beautiful blue slate above, his private passion for adventure.

BUT TIMKET was always an exciting time for Desta. Two or three weeks in advance, everybody in his family washed the clothes they would wear on the holiday, folded them and put them away. The women stashed nice-smelling grass and herbs in the folds of their dresses and put them away in wooden boxes. The men buried their folded trousers and jackets a few days before the event between layers of kosso leaves and placed slabs of stone over them. When they removed them on the day of the event they found them soft and neatly pressed.

Desta remembered Hibist's glee on Timket last year. She wore a long white dress with blue, green and red embroidery around the neck and a large strip of the same handiwork and colors running down in the front and terminating in the shape of an intricate cross. Over her shoulders she wore an equally decorative shemma. She was only ten years old but to Desta she transformed into a beautiful young adult when she dressed up. Mother often said Hibist was mature, both mentally and physically, way beyond her age. Desta knew that. It was these qualities in her that made him respect and love her more than any of his other siblings.

"I wish you were old enough to come with me," she had said to him last year on Timket morning.

"I am so anxious to go," he had replied.

When she returned she told him the details of what happened. He closed his eyes and remembered what she had said.

"When we arrived the priests were already doing mass by the river. They and a great number of the lay people camped on the bank of the river, singing and praying and chanting all night.

"The priests were dressed in long vestments of beautiful brocades of gold, blue, green and red and other colors like amethyst, purple and lavender. One man carried on his head the *Tabot,* wrapped in beautiful and rich colors of the ones I mentioned earlier. Several of the priests and deacons congregated around the Tabot carrying colorful umbrellas that shimmered in the bright sun.

"Around the pool by the river stood the crowd dressed in all white waiting for the head priest to bless the water and sprinkle us with it. Aba Yacob had several rounds of white timtem around his head. He moved forward and dipped his large silver cross three times into the water, blessing it; then he cupped one hand and scooped the water and threw it around the congregation in sprinkles. After that more of the regular priests began to do the same thing, and everybody else, particularly those in the younger crowd, began scooping the water with their hands and throwing it onto everybody who was there. You should have seen it. It was quite a riot.

"After the water blessing ceremony, the priests split into two groups and lined up in rows facing each other in front of the priest who carried the Tabot and others who stood around him carrying the shimmering umbrellas. They were now poised to start the Dance of David. One of the priests began to beat the kettle drum in a slow ponderous rhythm. The priests in the two rows began to sway from left to right, tinkling rattles and moving prayer sticks in tempo with the beat of the drum. As the drummer picked up speed, the priests also picked up momentum, and now in addition to the left-right swaying, they added back and forth movements, advancing toward each other and receding, still keeping time with the drum, the rattles and the prayer sticks.

"After the first dance was finished, the priests, still dancing to the drum beat, led the crowd in a procession back to the church. Once the priests and the Tabot reached the church grounds, the crowd dispersed."

Hearing Hibst's story, Desta couldn't wait until he was old enough to go to Timket with her. This year, not only was his sister gone, he couldn't leave the animals. Besides he didn't have the white clothes needed to go to this beautiful event.

On this Timket day, Desta sat at the far corner of the field, watching as the rest of his family marched down the road to attend the ceremony. Strangely, he didn't wish he were with them as he would have if Hibst were there. He was thankful to be left alone so he could escape to his thoughts and daydreams undisturbed by anybody. For all he cared, they could go away forever.

THIRTY-SEVEN

The Annual Saint Mary's Celebration of their church was the only time when relatives came in great number from near and far. It happened on the twenty-eighth of January, and Desta always awaited the day with great excitement. He got to see his uncles and aunts, as well as cousins and family friends. During that time the house teemed with people. They went to church dressed in white or the best of their clothes and brought food and drinks to be served to the people who came to celebrate the holiday at church. At home, people ate, drank and danced.

Desta's cousin Awoke, who lived across the Davola River with his parents, had come to the festival with them. Awoke was five years older than Desta and treated him more like a kid brother than his equal. He was much bigger too. His family had a lot of cattle and he had grown up drinking a great quantity of milk, a precious commodity in Desta's home, where his mother preferred to use it to make cheese and butter.

Awoke had brought with him a small square pamphlet held together in the middle with a thin thread. The morning after the holiday celebration, Desta found his cousin sitting between two boys by the fence reading something in the pamphlet to them. Intrigued, Desta stood before them and watched. With a thin amber straw, Awoke was pointing to letters in the pamphlet and calling them out. The two boys' heads were nearly touching Awoke's as they followed the movement of the straw and repeated what he was reciting. Desta was transfixed.

Once Awoke finished reciting all the letters, he asked Desta if he would like to learn the alphabet. Desta immediately accepted the offer and sat beside him. Awoke took Desta through the entire alphabet and then did it a second time. Desta was thrilled. The two boys left. This gave Desta an opportunity to ask what seemed to him was a miracle.

"How did you learn to read like this?"

"I can read too, but I was just showing you the alphabet so that you can actually read pages like this," said Awoke as he flipped to the third page. He began to read "Abugeeda . . ." To Desta nothing of what he read sounded like Amharic, the language they speak.

"What did you just read?" said Desta.

"This page contains letters arranged in such a way as to make your learning how to read faster. They don't mean anything," said Awoke.

Desta repeated the question: "but how did you learn to read?"

"Oh, on my own," was Awoke's quick reply.

"On your own?"

"How?"

"A relative who is a Deb'tera taught me the alphabet a couple of times. From then on I taught myself not only to read but also to write."

Desta couldn't quite conceive how it was possible to remember all those letters so that he could read a page like the one Awoke just read.

"Look I can write my name too," said Awoke, taking out a stubby golden wooden piece with a thin gray rod inside it.

"This is *Irsas*," said Awoke dangling the golden rod before Desta.

He flipped to the back of the booklet and carefully and slowly wrote his name.

"This is my name written out," said Awoke with a touch of pride.

Desta just looked at Awoke as if he were some supernatural being.

"You can learn to do it too. It's easy!" said Awoke, noticing the surprise on Desta's face.

"How can I? I have nobody that can teach me and I have no book like that," said Desta looking far away—almost doubting his ability to remember all those characters so he could read that third page in the pamphlet and write his name.

"I will teach you. You can use my Fidel—this book is called Fidel," said Awoke. "I want to . . . I would like to . . . I would love to . . . but . . ."

"But what?"

"But you will not be here all the time to teach me," said Desta. Actually he really meant to say *how much room I have in my head to remember all those letters. I may need someone to be here to show me over and over again until I can remember them all.*

Desta didn't have even a vague notion about what learning the alphabet and knowing to write his name or words could mean to him. He had never seen anyone read a book before. He had never even seen his priest-to-be brother, Tamirat, bring and open a book at home. He probably would never have the opportunity to read and write like his cousin. His cousin was much more advanced than he and probably it would take him a long time to read and write like him . . . He wondered if it would be worth the effort.

Awoke promised to teach him.

While they were engaged in this conversation, his mother, Maray, came and took Awoke away.

The next day, they saw each other again down by the fence at the end of his parent's property. Desta was tending the animals.

"I want to write my name . . . I can write my name . . ." Desta kept saying as he hopped on the railing of the fence and jumped down. He would hop on the railing again and repeat his mantra and jump down.

He did this act repeatedly. Awoke was watching him secretly.

"Yes, you can. I will show you how . . . It's easy."

Desta stopped, enthralled by the sudden vision of Awoke.

Awoke and Desta sat with their backs touching the fence. The cousin opened his little book and began reciting the alphabet again. Desta repeated.

$$ህ \quad ሁ \quad ሂ \quad ሃ \quad ሄ \quad ህ \quad ሆ$$
Hä Hoo Hē Hä Hā Hĭ Hō

$$ለ \quad ሉ \quad ሊ \quad ላ \quad ሌ \quad ል \quad ሎ$$
Lä loo Lē Lä Lā Lĭ Lō

$$ሐ \quad ሑ \quad ሒ \quad ሓ \quad ሔ \quad ሕ \quad ሖ$$
Hä Hoo Hē Hä Hā Hĭ Hō

$$መ \quad ሙ \quad ሚ \quad ማ \quad ሜ \quad ም \quad ሞ$$
Mä Moo Mē Mä Mā Mĭ Mō

. . .   .

As Awoke kept going down the first page and the next, Desta immediately started to see and hear the pattern.

"Once you know the first letters, the rest are easy. They are merely a variation of the first," said Awoke.

"I see and hear that," said Desta excited. All of a sudden, what seemed to him a great task at first became a very easy and doable task.

"Just remember all you need to memorize is the thirty six letters here on the first column," said Awoke running his finger.

"Yes, I see that."

Just after four recitals of the entire alphabet, Desta already remembered about a quarter of it.

Telling Awoke to fold the booklet, Desta closed his eyes and recited them.

"You see, I told you it is very easy. I must admit, you are also a fast learner," said Awoke sending a ghost of a smile over his big face.

"Thank you. This is great!"

"At this rate you should finish the whole alphabet by this afternoon. That way I will give you the book so that you can repeat them on your own and memorize them well," said Awoke.

"I would love it!"

By the end of the day, to Awoke's great surprise and Desta himself, the latter had memorized nearly all the alphabet. As promised, Awoke loaned his book of the alphabet and left with his mother.

Desta couldn't resist the question that had been circulating in his brain since he began learning the letters.

Desta ran after his teacher and asked him to stop.

"Can I ask you something?" said Desta.

Awoke gave his approval.

"What good will it do me learning the alphabet and knowing how to write my name?"

"I will give you the same answer that the Deb'tera who taught me gave me. The first good thing it will do for you is, you don't have to use your thumb to sign your name. You will actually be able to write it yourself. The other is, if you want to writer a letter or receive one, you don't have to travel a long distance looking for a priest to read or write it for you. You can write or read it yourself."

Neither of the answers Awoke gave satisfied Desta. He might never need to sign his name, read or write a letter. Even then, for something that he would use maybe once a year or maybe never, he would waste his time learning the Alphabet.

"You are not convinced by the answer I gave you, huh?"

Desta nodded.

"In that case give me back my Fidel,"

"No, no, I want to learn it. I was just wondering what I can tell people if they asked me."

"Tell them you plan to become a priest someday."

"That is easy. I can do that. Thanks. See you next time."

Desta ran back.

THIRTY-EIGHT

Desta could not be grateful enough to Awoke. He had given him his new passion: learning the alphabet. Wherever he went, he took his cousin's Fidel with him. Whenever he had free time, he opened the little booklet and recited the letters. He even brought it to bed with him, visualizing the letters as he drifted off to sleep.

Desta had completely memorized all the letters of the alphabet by the end of the first week. He almost could recite it backwards too. The next task was to remember the shapes of each letter in the first column and all the special attributes of the derivatives. He observed that they all had essentially the same pattern—all he had to do was remember the descending characters on the first column and memorize the shape and extensions of a few of the first rows. The rest followed suit. Then he could combine the different characters to write words and names.

After he had spent a few hours studying the shapes, he put his learning to a test. He closed his book. With a dry but firm straw, he wrote his name on his thigh, ደ(de) ሰ(sä)ታ(ta). The letters were halted and squiggled, but the basic shapes and patterns were legible. When he opened the book and compared them, the first and last letters were correct, but the middle letter sä should have been Si. He nonetheless was thrilled.

He was pleased too with the wonderful contrast of the scratched white letters against his dark skin. From now on, his thighs would be perfect writing slates. He erased the middle letter with spit, waited for the skin to dry and wrote the correct replacement. "That is my name," he said, shaking his head and biting his lip. It was a miracle. For a long time he stared at the three letters as if they might evaporate into thin air were he to remove his eyes from them.

Desta then tried the names of his brothers and sisters. He wrote Hibist's name right below his. He got all her letters correct except for one. He rubbed it out with spit and wrote the correct letter. To his surprise, all of Hibist's letters were from the sixth column of the alphabet. Below Hibist's name he wrote Enat's. He got all the letters right. Over the next two days he wrote the rest of his family's names on both thighs and legs, putting Damtew' s name at the very bottom, and in the process turning his body into an exotic work of art.

"What have you been doing to your body?" said Ayénat when she noticed the bizarre and cryptic lines on Desta's thighs and legs.

"Oh nothing—just scratch marks from my nails and the dry grass where I lay in the field," said Desta.

"Does your body itch? Let me see," said Ayénat, grabbing his arm and inspecting it.

"Not a lot."

"You don't have those horrible scratch marks here," she said, twisting his arm.

"It's the grass, Ma . . . where I had no cover when I lay on it. Let me go," said Desta, pulling away.

"Be careful. Spread your gabi so all your limbs are protected."

The last thing Desta wanted was scrutiny like this. He had not shared what he was doing in his spare time with anybody. He instinctively knew that none of them, except perhaps for his father and Tamirat, would approve.

To avoid future scrutiny, he needed to find a different surface to write on.

He had seen Tamirat take dictation from his father for his court cases with blue ink from a small blue bottle. He wrote the dictation with a sharpened split-tipped reed on a large white paper that had many faded green lines with double red ones on the top. All he had to do was find these three items and he would be ready.

He knew more or less where his father kept the white paper—folded several times, in a straw box, mixed with old court documents. Desta probably would be able to steal one or two sheets from that box, assuming he could find it.

He knew he would be breaking one of God's cardinal rules. But as he would probably steal food if he were really, really hungry, stealing paper when he wanted to learn to write was probably the same. If he could do one, he might as well do the other. He would ask God's forgiveness later or make up for his sin by doing something really nice that would make God happy. He remembered a remark his father had once made: "Even in the act of transgressing one of God's rules—like stealing, if you pray, he could still help you in accomplishing your mission, although he might yet punish you in the end. Desta thought that so long as God helped him find the box and steal the paper, he could find some other way to make it even with Him. Besides, it was likely to be a long, long time before he died. Maybe, God would forget by then.

What else could he do? His father wouldn't give them to him. Abraham always treated his papers as if they were made of gold. Desta had no option but to steal.

The reed would be easy. He could make it from one of the thin bamboo plants that grow so plentifully along the Davola. But the ink was a different matter. He had never seen where his brother kept his blue bottle since they always chased him away, saying "this doesn't concern you, go attend to your business," before their father finished his dictation. He thought and thought but still couldn't think of a way to get that bottle.

The next day a light went off in his head. He and Hibist had sometimes used charcoal to paint their faces. He could try grinding charcoal, mixing it in water and using it as ink.

Desta went to work. He gathered all the cold charcoal he could find from the fireplaces and ground it to fine powder using two small slabs of stone. Then he mixed the powder with water in a small horn drinking cup. This cup became his ink well.

Now he needed to find the oval-shaped straw box that contained his father's paper supply. Ironically, the beautiful little box had been made by Damtew when he used to tend the grain fields. Now nobody was allowed to mention the box in front of him because he was ashamed of it—ashamed, Hibist had explained to Desta, "of having engaged in a woman's work."

Desta had witnessed his brother's reaction whenever their father took out the paper box. If there were people around, Damtew would get up, glaring, and leave the room.

"I wish you could find something else to store your paper in. Don't you need something bigger?" he heard Damtew say once when Abraham and he were alone.

"Why? It's very special to me because you made it," said Abraham." As to its size, it accommodates my papers just fine once I've neatly folded them."

Desta wished he could bring the box out every time they had guests in the house and tell them who made it. He would have loved to watch Damtew crawl into his skin with shame and seethe in anger.

But he was not thinking about tormenting Damtew. He just wanted to remember which granary their father had put the box in. There were three of them, standing in a row and dividing the living room from the larder, just behind the bamboo partition.

In the past, he remembered Abraham had always put it in the middle one.

When the grain was low and Abraham couldn't reach the box from the outside, he would lift Desta and drop him into the granary to retrieve it for him.

When nobody was around, Desta climbed onto a stool he took from the corner in the larder, slid the granary lid to the side and groped inside with his hand. The grain had been gathered a month ago and all the granaries were nearly full. He felt around, searching, and searching. And then he felt it.

Desta took the box to the light by the entrance, untied its cords and opened it, flipping quickly through the folded papers until he found a thick packet of squarely folded blank sheets. He carefully peeled off two sheets, then folded the remaining six pages along the original creases. Hastily, he closed the box, tied the cords and dropped it back in the granary. He slid the lid back on and put the stool back in its place. *The perfect crime*, he thought with a smile.

Folding the gleaming blank pages along the creases, he tucked them under his arm and ran out. He was ecstatic. Now he could write on real paper!

For starters, he wrote the names of his immediate family, putting his own name on the very top, then Hibist's, then Enat's, then Saba's, followed by Tamirat, then Teferra, then Asse'ged and finally Damtew. He wrote his parents' names in a separate column, his father followed by his mother. For the in-laws he had a separate column as well.

Then he began copying words from Awoke's Fidel. He didn't understand what he was writing but he faithfully transferred each letter as he saw it from the page in the booklet onto his writing paper, leaving the spaces between the words. He remembered the characters of most of the letters, but he couldn't combine and read them the way Awoke had done. For now, though, he was content with his efforts.

Desta was writing furiously, deep in concentration, when Asse'ged materialized out of thin air.

"What are you doing?" he asked, glaring at his little brother.

"Nothing," said Desta, startled. He quickly folded his page and put it underneath him.

Asse'ged saw the little book, the ink cup and the bamboo pen. "Let me, let me see . . . how . . . where did you get all these?"

Desta scrambled for a safe answer.

"Let me see that paper you hid!"

Desta shook his head.

"Either you give it to me peacefully, or I will help myself."

Desta slowly pulled the paper out and handed it to his brother. Asse'ged looked at it, silently reading—or pretending to read.

Desta had once heard their father say that when Asse'ged was in church school, he had mastered the alphabet in a few days and was learning to read and write twice as fast as the average student.

Desta had long wondered if Asse'ged could still read. This was the test.

"What have you written here?" said the big brother, dropping the hand that held the paper. His eyes bore down on Desta.

"Some of them are names. Others are just words I copied from this book," said Desta, pointing to the little booklet.

"Whose names have you got here?"

"Everybody's in our family."

"Am I here?"

"Yes." Desta got up and pointed out Asse'ged's name.

"Way at the bottom here—how come?" he said with a little smile.

"Not for any particular reason."

"Let me see the book."

Asse'ged leafed through the pages, finally coming back to the beginning and stopping at the alphabet.

"You know I once knew all these letters. Some of them I still remember— Ha, Le, Ma . . ."

"You skipped the second Ha," corrected Desta proudly.

"Oh, yeah." He began reciting again. As he got farther down on the page, he couldn't remember many of them. Desta kept correcting him.

"See, I have forgotten," he said as he handed him back the book. He narrowed his eyes and looked away. "What I want to know is, how in the world did you learn to write? Did Tamirat get you started? . . . Where did you get all this stuff?"

"Awoke Yisehak taught me the alphabet. The rest I did on my own."

Asse'ged's eyes grew bigger. "Does Awoke know how to read?"

"Yes. Some Deb'tera had taught him how. But he said he learned a lot of it on his own too. He told me I could as well. All this stuff is his. He loaned it to me."

Asse'ged's eyes grew wider still. He looked away again and thought for a long time. "I hate to tell you this," he said looking back at Desta. "It's a complete waste of your time. As the keeper of the animals and a future farmer, you will never get to use what you learn. Like me, you will pretty soon forget it all, and the time you spent learning it will be a waste."

"I hope to become a priest."

Asse'ged snickered.

"Like Tamirat?!" Asse'ged shook his head. "Listen, Desta, Tamirat got to go to school because I could become a farmer and Damtew could be a shepherd. Baba and Mama could afford to send Tamirat to school. But, you—we have no one else to tend the animals. Stop fantasizing! You need to give all this back to Awoke and concentrate on keeping the animals safe and out of the crops."

Desta pressed his lips together and looked away. He wondered if he should believe what his brother was saying.

"I need to go," said Asse'ged. "Don't let others see what I just saw. You'll be in real big trouble."

As he watched Asse'ged shuffle away, Desta thought about what he had said and realized sadly that his brother was probably right. No matter how much he desired to learn, he had no say in the matter. He had to do whatever the adults chose for him.

He put his face down on his gabi and wept until his eyes stung and his cheeks were flushed red. When he stopped crying he dried his eyes and vowed to continue his reading and writing. He was not going to let anyone deter him from learning.

But I've got to make sure nothing like this happens again, he told himself.

For the next six months, whenever he felt safe, Desta practiced his alphabet. He copied all the pages in the booklet, at least 50 times. Awoke brought him more paper and blue ink of his own. Awoke also taught him the Amharic numbers and Desta practiced writing these as well.

Right before the New Year, at the end of the thirteenth month, Awoke brought a prayer book to Desta. He had read it several times himself and had decided to loan it to his cousin. Desta didn't yet know how to read. When he did, he did so slowly. But he had mastered enough of the alphabet to write with consistent accuracy.

The new book had black writings and red writings. Awoke had told him that the red writings were the words of God. Skipping the black ones Desta read all the red words. What he read didn't make sense to him, but he continued reading anyway.

These activities kept his eyes and mind from wandering aimlessly around the valley. His surroundings were there but only as a backdrop to what was going on in his mind. The dramatic cloud scenes, the rainstorms, the flooding of the fields and the roaring noises of the waters in the rivers no longer captivated him. Instead, it was the little Fidel and prayer book that claimed a seductive hold on Desta.

THIRTY-NINE

The spring season had arrived. Flowers had begun to invade the fields, mountainsides and backyards. Some of the farms were veiled with sprouted grains—some short, others as tall as knee high. It was the time of year when in the past Desta would have let his eyes feast on the surfeit of colors, reminiscing on the days and years past when he roamed the hills and valleys with Hibist.

But he was a student now, and his love and interest were in his Fidel, and writing and reading. His involvement with his studies was so great that the animals he was tending had taken a more secondary role.

Having assured himself the goats were safe and the cows were in their grazing grounds, Desta retreated to the shade of the sholla tree to practice his handwriting. Writing cleanly and neatly was as important to him as reading. He had heard his father comment about the handwriting of the priests who took dictation from him. Desta hoped that if he wrote well, someday his father might ask him to take dictation for his court cases.

He took his writing things from his little pouch and spread them in front of him. He had his blue inkwell, his bamboo pen, a writing sheet, his Fidel and a new book of biblical verses Awoke had loaned him.

He had just finished copying a line and was about to dip the pen into the inkwell again, when he noticed Damtew out of the corner of his eye. He was driving some cattle toward Desta, the three cows and the bull which were the most dangerous crop raiders. Desta froze, his hand suspended in midair above the inkwell, his eyes fixed on Damtew and the animals. For a moment he lost his senses, then he knew exactly what had happened. The animals must have gotten into someone's crops. He had overheard shouts earlier but he'd thought they were coming from the boisterous shepherds across the creek. The shouts must have belonged to the farmer whose grain fields were being destroyed by the animals Damtew was now bringing back.

Desta panicked. He tried to gather his things but his hands kept missing them because at the same time he kept his eyes on Damtew. His brother was walking toward him like a wild beast that was stalking its prey.

Desta managed to put all his writing materials in his pouch and scrambled to his feet before Damtew got to him.

"Desta, I found these animals on the other side of the river. I just wanted to make sure you didn't lose sight of them," said the big brother in a benign voice.

Desta knew better. Despite Damtew's friendly tone, he sensed danger as a dik-dik would sense the imminent threat of a stalking leopard. He slipped the loop of his pouch onto his arm, spun it around and ran.

He sprinted up the field as if he were going home, then cut to the right into the bushes. When he looked back he saw Damtew charging towards him.

He slipped underneath the blackberry bush and saw what looked like the start of an animal path. The thorny bush tore at his exposed skin as he dove through the narrow opening, ripping bloody gashes up and down his arms and legs. Ignoring the pain, he fought his way through the opening and struggled out of the path.

Realizing the portal was too small and thorny for his big frame, Damtew ran around the bushes to the spot where Desta, if he was trapped in the bush, would likely emerge.

But Desta had already escaped the bushes and was flying down the path. He skirted their parents' property and headed, without thinking, in the direction of Saba's new home.

He glanced back as he ran and saw that Damtew was following him. He also heard Asse'ged's voice. Standing high up the hill where they were weeding a crop field, Asse'ged shouted to Damtew, telling him which direction Desta was running. When Desta looked back a second time, he saw to his horror that Damtew was rapidly gaining on him.

Desta crossed the creek that bordered Saba's new property and was halfway to her house when Damtew caught up to him. At the same time, he noticed Saba had come out of her house and was shouting at Damtew to stop. She was attempting to run toward them, but her big belly slowed her down. She moved like a mountain, calling out to saints Mary and Michael for help. Desta wished she would appeal to Saint George, the swift, spear-wielding equestrian who could come flying on his white horse and stab Damtew in his gullet. On the opposite side of the creek on the higher ground, Asse'ged continued to urge Damtew on.

Desta was still in motion, sweaty, out of breath and terrified when Damtew kicked him with all his force, causing him to fall flat on his face. He rolled down the slope, hitting rocks, logs and tree stumps. When he came to a stop, he scrambled to his feet and made a desperate attempt to keep running, but he was too weak to get very far. Damtew caught up and kicked him again.

Desta could still hear Asse'ged's voice of encouragement although most of it was drowned out by Damtew's kicking, shouting and swearing. While he cowered on the ground, gasping in pain, his brother snapped a long slender branch from a nearby Abo bush, stripped its leaves and began to whip him. Desta covered his face and eyes in terror-stricken resignation. Damtew was going to kill him, as he always had threatened to do.

As Damtew kept lashing him, his body rapidly lost its sensation. His mind was alert but he no longer felt the searing pain of the branch tearing into his skin. This was what it *felt* like to die. Now he would never go to the mountaintop.

He could still hear Saba's pleadings. The horse-riding saint never came, but Damtew finally stopped whipping him. He heard a rustling sound and slowly lifted his head a few inches off the ground. He saw Damtew opening his pouch and taking out his folded papers. He slipped the handle of the pouch onto one hand and held the opened pages with both hands, staring at what Desta had written. Desta knew Damtew had never seen the alphabet, let alone learned to read, but his brother kept looking at the page before him, as if studying the characters or admiring the handwriting. Completely absorbed in it, he became quiet and calm.

The longer his brother stared at the pages, the more curious and worried Desta became. Maybe Baba had sent Damtew to church school once too and he did know how to read. If so, once he got to the bottom of the page and saw his name was last on the list, he was likely to renew his attack on Desta.

He slightly raised his head and turned it to see if Damtew was holding the page the right way up. He saw the blotch of spilled ink at the bottom of the page. The blotch had been at the top of the page when Desta had spilled the ink. Damtew was holding the page the wrong way up. He was not trying to read it. Desta was relieved but confused. Why was Damtew so engrossed in his writing if he didn't know what it said?

Desta watched his brother nervously, trying to gauge his emotions. He was still and quiet, but his jaw was tense. Desta watched and waited, barely breathing.

Then it happened. Like a sudden crack of thunder on a sunny day, Damtew exploded in anger. Shouting and swearing, he furiously tore at the pages, shredded them into tiny pieces, which he threw at Desta's prostrated body. Then he pulled out Awoke's book of verses and Fidel and shredded them, too, ripping out several pages and showering Desta with their confetti. A scrap of paper with God's word fell on the ground right before Desta's eye. He wished he could read what it said but the writing was in Ge'ez, the church language that nobody other than priests understood.

Damtew used the bottle of ink for his grand finale. He opened it, held it high over Desta and proceeded with the show. "This is what you deserve, our priest-to-be. I heard all about it. This is what costs when you dawdle away your time instead of attending to the animals like you're supposed to." He slowly poured the blue liquid over Desta's body. Then he hurled the empty bottle away as if he were throwing a rock and crushed the writing reed under his feet.

Desta tuned out the rest of Damtew's tirade. He didn't care anymore. He just wanted to die. He didn't even care about going to the top of the mountain.

With a final kick to Desta's ribs, Damtew left. All was quiet again. Unable to move, Desta remained curled in the dirt, waiting for death to take him.

Dazed and disoriented, he waited, but death didn't come. Slowly, he began to feel the effects of the beatings. His legs and arms felt as if steaming hot water had been poured over them. His pulse pounded in his temples. His heart raced. He heard footsteps and he felt the presence of a big figure hovering over him. Was death, at last, arriving on foot?

"Thank God, you are alive!" said Saba. She squatted next to him and put her hand on his shoulder. "Desta, are you okay? Talk to me."

Desta didn't answer. He couldn't answer. He felt as if his vocal cords had collapsed.

"I'll send Yihoon to help you get up. I am too weak to do anything for you. I am sorry. If it were other times, I would have run like a gazelle to protect you, but there are two of us here and I couldn't endanger the precious baby. I'll be back."

Desta's pulse began to tame. He waited, afraid to move, for Saba's return. He tried not to think about what had just happened to him, about what Damtew had done to his books and papers, about what might come next.

Finally, Saba returned with Yihoon. They sat on their heels next to him. They talked in hushed voices as if afraid to wake him.

"Desta, this is Yihoon. Are you okay? Can you say something?" said the brother-in-law, shaking Desta lightly.

"I feel pain all over. Can you please take me home?"

"We came to bring you to our home."

"No, I prefer to go home. Can you help me walk?"

"I will carry you if I have to."

"Check to see if there are any broken bones before you pick him up," said Saba.

"Let's see, can you move this leg?" said Yihoon touching Desta on the top leg.

"Clean the ink off first," said Saba.

The brother-in-law snipped a couple of leaves from the Abo bush behind them and wiped off the rivulet of ink from Desta's thighs and upper body.

Desta slowly stretched his leg and with the help of Yihoon he lifted it. "And the other?"

Desta rolled on his back and did the same.

Yihoon was satisfied with the condition of Desta's legs. "How about your arms?"

They were okay too, although they were bloody and blistery along the lash marks.

"Your back okay?"

With Saba's help, Desta slowly sat up. He nodded.

Yihoon turned to Saba. "Go home. We don't want any more drama with you here. Lie down. I will return soon."

"I would have loved you to come to my house but with the condition I am in, I would not be much help. I will come and see you tomorrow, God willing," said Saba, kissing Desta on the forehead.

Yihoon, half carrying him, half walking him, brought Desta home.

When Ayénat saw them approaching the house, she dropped what she had in her hand and came running to the door. "What in the world happened to him?"

"Damtew had a field day with this small body," said Yihoon. He helped Desta cross the doorstep and sat him by the fire.

"Oh my, oh my, oh my," said Ayénat as she ran her fingers over Desta's body.

"It's a shame, really a shame, a grown, big boy like him to be abusing a fragile body like this," said Yihoon, gesturing with his hand toward Desta.

"He is such a Saytan. I don't know why he won't stop harassing him," said Ayénat, wiping tears and cleaning her sniffle with the back of her hand.

"Either you have to put a stop to this, or he is going to kill the boy one of these days," Yihoon warned.

"It's not as if we have not told him. We have, many, many times. Yet he is unrelenting."

"I have to go," said Yihoon abruptly. "As you know Saba is near her term. We have been on pins and needles, as you can imagine."

"I understand. Go. The fact that she has carried the baby this far is very encouraging," said Ayénat.

"That is how we feel too. Desta had something to do with it, a lot has to do with it, and we are grateful," said Yihoon.

Desta hated having his name linked with Saba's situation but at the moment he didn't care to concern himself about it.

"Let us know as soon as anything begins to happen," said Ayénat. "Her father knows good medicine for fast delivery, you know."

Yihoon nodded. "I'll send one of the girls the moment there is any movement." He turned to Desta and patted his head. "You are a strong boy. I am proud of you. You handled it like a man."

DESTA HOPED his mother or father would punish Damtew, make him bleed and cry and suffer, the way he had done to him.

He stayed up as long as he could, waiting, but Damtew didn't come home. When he woke the next morning, his brother still was not there.

Although Desta never counted on his father to do anything, he wanted him to see what Damtew had done to him. He limped to the bedroom to see if his father had slept in, as he sometimes did on Saturday mornings or when he arrived late from a trip, but Abraham wasn't there either. He asked his mother where his Baba was. She said she had expected him to be home the day before, but he hadn't come. She thought he would come later that day because he had an important appointment at church the next morning.

That day Desta didn't go to attend to the cows. He didn't know who took care of them and he didn't care. All day he waited for his father. He waited for Damtew too. He wanted to witness the whipping his father would surely give him.

Damtew never came.

Abraham did come, however, late in the evening. The moment he arrived, Desta hobbled to him and kissed his knee.

"Bless you," said Abraham in a low voice, lingering a little until Desta let go of his knee. He appeared haggard and heavy-eyed. He had his usual post-trip, not-disposed-to-talk look.

Desta sat by the fire, waiting for the right moment to display his wounds, but the fire was low and the room too dark to give a good showing of what his brother had done to him.

Noticing Desta's restlessness, Ayénat said softly, "Better wait until tomorrow morning."

Desta reluctantly agreed, but only because Damtew was not there to be punished.

WHEN DESTA ROSE THE FOLLOWING MORNING, he found his father dressed and ready to go to church. He was going out when he saw Yihoon at the door, asking Melkam if his father-in-law was at home.

Abraham hurried to the door to greet Yihoon. "Anything wrong?" he asked urgently.

"Saba's in labor. I came to see if you could bring your medicine," said Yihoon with apprehension.

"Era—you're not kidding?"

"No, she just started. Knowing her, she will probably go on for a while. We thought the sooner you bring the medicine, the better."

Abraham looked disheveled. "You caught me just in time, I was just about to . . . tell me, is it the time?"

"Our counts tell us it shouldn't have come for another week or so," said Yihoon. "There was a disturbing incident yesterday that may have accelerated things." He looked away, worried.

Desta was all ears. *Better if the news came from somebody else's mouth,* he thought.

"What happened?"

"Desta was severely attacked by Damtew. Saba heard his cries and saw what was happening. She ran to help him but she slipped on a rock and fell. Even so, she still managed to reach him and got me to bring him home."

"That's right," whimpered Desta, pulling down his gabi to show the wounds on his shoulders and arms. "He'd have killed me if it were not for Saba. I am sure of it. You can see for yourself."

"What did you do to deserve this?" said Abraham, looking down at Desta's wounds with awe.

"Era, era, era, who can believe this . . . who can believe this?" he kept saying, as he ran his fingers over Desta's hands, arms and legs.

"No one deserves this kind of punishment, no matter the crime," said Yihoon.

"I am sad to see this. Don't worry, Desta, he will have a piece of my mind and hand, but I have to go now," said Abraham as he patted his son on the head.

Desta wished his father wouldn't leave. He wished he would stay home, all day if necessary, and beat up Damtew when he eventually came home.

"Yihoon, I didn't finish what I was going to tell you. I was just about to go to church to seek the Lord's assistance in resolving a property dispute. I was planning to hold court after the services but now that plan appears about to change. I'll dispatch Asse'ged to tell them what happened. Let me swap my clothes and I'll be right back," said Abraham as he disappeared in the backroom.

"Desta, I don't know if you heard, but Saba is in labor," said Yihoon, after his father-in-law was gone. "Can you contact that man again and pray to him for his help? We are all worried, especially since we think it's a week or more early."

"I've not seen him for a long, long time—since that water treatment by that priest—and I don't even know who he is—an angel or a spirit or something else," said Desta. "I can pray to God, yes, but him—I don't even know what to call him."

"Okay, just pray to God," said Yihoon, seeing his father-in-law return in his regular clothes.

"Let's walk by Asse'ged's house and get him to relay a message to those parishioners," said Abraham.

After the two men left, Desta went to bed. He curled up, closed his eyes and thought about his beating and the news about Saba. As he started to analyze the coincidences, his mind flooded with questions.

Why did Saba go into labor early? Why was he the cause of it? Why did he run toward her house when he saw Damtew coming for him? Was there someone, like a Saytan, that made him go in that direction? He tried to piece together the events that had unfolded right after Damtew began to chase him. His initial intention had been to elude his brother by ducking into the woods but Damtew was a faster runner. He was on Desta's trail and could see exactly where he was going. When Desta slipped into the blackberry bushes, Damtew could have caught him if he had dared to follow but he chose a safer route instead, allowing Desta to buy time and cover more distance. When he finally emerged near the potato field behind his house, it had been easier to run around the fence where the grass was short than to wade through the grown potatoes. From there it was an uphill run to his house, so he had simply kept running along the foothills to get as far away as he could. He had chosen his path instinctively, not thinking of Saba or her house as he ran. She just happened to be there at the right time and place.

Was it merely an unfortunate coincidence that Saba had fallen while she was running to rescue him? Or was it part of a greater design? Was he going to be the cause of another miscarriage even though he was the reason Saba and her family had moved to the new place in hopes of having a healthier baby there? Was that man really a Saytan, as his mother had suspected? Would he cause Saba to have another miscarriage, even in this new place, and cause everybody to blame Desta?

Or was Desta in a fantasyland, as everybody had said when he first saw the man by the river? Was that man indeed a figment of his imagination? He shivered at his thoughts.

He could almost hear what Damtew and Asse'ged would say if Saba had another miscarriage. "See, we told you so. He made up that man! Now we have lost our land, all because of his lies."

Curiously, Desta had not seen the man or dreamt of him for over a year, ever since the night he was in the tree after Damtew's kid goat was killed. Even then, Desta had not been certain it was him. He thought he heard a voice that reminded him of the man's voice, but the voice was thin and the leaves were rustling so much that he couldn't be sure. If that had been him, why would he want to support someone so mean and dangerous as Damtew? Was he more aligned with Damtew than with Desta? If so, maybe he *really* was a Saytan.

The more Desta analyzed things, the more convinced he became that there was something terribly twisted that he couldn't quite explain.

But he also found one silver lining, albeit a flimsy one. If Saba lost her baby, he could blame Damtew. *Saba would not have fallen if she hadn't been trying to rescue me,* he would argue. *And if she hadn't fallen, she would have had a normal baby.* That was it! He would stick to his guns on this point.

That settled, he calmed himself and waited. His entire body ached and his open wounds stung terribly, but as badly hurt as he was physically, he was even more battered emotionally. He tried to sleep but no sleep came.

Melkam was the only person in the house. She brought food and water when he needed it but didn't try to comfort him. In early afternoon, Ayénat returned. Desta searched her expression for any clue about Saba's status. He covered his face and watched his mother through small apertures in his fingers.

He removed his hand from his face. "Everything all right with Saba?" he asked softly.

"Not really."

His stomach tightened. "What is happening to her?"

"She has been in labor all day, but the baby hasn't come. Some of us had to leave because we couldn't do anything more for her."

Desta relaxed a little. No miscarriage yet.

LATER IN THE EVENING, Abraham came home, looking ragged and exhausted. "I tried every treatment I could think of but nothing worked. Saba has been pushing all day, yet there is no sign of the baby."

"She is in the Lord's hands. We just need to be patient," said Ayénat.

"I need to take a nap and then go back to them," said Abraham as he clambered to bed. "If I'm not up by midnight, please wake me."

Desta's spirits flagged again, more so now that his able medicine-man father, who had helped hundreds of other women deliver babies, couldn't do it for his own daughter.

"The moment I placed that particular root by the manure portal of the house, the baby came flying out," he had heard him say many times.

Desta wondered if Saba's baby had no wings.

After Abraham went to bed, Melkam brought Desta his dinner of freshly baked injera with shiro wat. He was hungry but his mouth was sore and his jaw felt dislocated. When he fell after Damtew kicked him, he had managed to bite the interior of his cheek, and it pained him every time he moved his mouth.

He carefully ate a few bites and drank his cup of water. Then he pushed the basket away and lay back on his pillow. Next door Abraham began to snore. Desta wished Melkam would go over and shake his father a little to make him stop so he could fall sleep himself. He had been mentally and physically exhausted. Somehow his ears went deaf and he fell asleep.

At midnight he was awakened by Abraham as he prepared to go back to Saba's house.

"Lock the door," he heard him say to Melkam as he left.

Drowsy and half conscious, Desta rested his head, begging sleep to come once more. He drifted back to unconsciousness but was awakened again about an hour later. This time it was Ayénat who had come home. Asse'ged was with her but he didn't come inside. Desta heard his voice as he said good night to his mother at the door.

IN THE MORNING DESTA was awakened once again by noise and
commotion as Ayénat prepared to go to Saba's house with food and drinks and
some clothes that Desta couldn't identify as he drifted back to sleep.

The next time he woke up was several hours later when Melkam came
with his late breakfast. He forced himself to eat, despite the severe pain in his
mouth. His jaw had gotten worse overnight. With a little substantial food in his
stomach, Desta slept well till mid-afternoon. When he woke, a face he had not
seen for a few months was peering down at him. It was Astair, his niece.

"My father wants to know if you could come and pray with them. He wants
you to pray to that man who sent us packing to this new place," said Astair.
There was a somber note to her voice and frown lines on her forehead.

Desta didn't like what he heard. He was sure the line Astair just said was
hers. Yihoon would not solicit his help and at the same time load his request
with a veiled incrimination.

"I am sorry, I cannot come. Tell him that it has been very difficult for me to
go to the bathroom, let alone travel that far. But I will pray here where I am,"
said Desta, studying his niece's face.

"Is that the best you can do for my mother, father, Zena and me—after . . .
after making us believe in that man you concocted and causing us to move from
our good home?" scowled Astair.

Lacking the energy to argue, Desta said nothing. Astair's eyes bore down on
him as she waited for his reply.

"Sit down. I want to show you something," said Desta, finally. Astair
crouched.

Grimacing from the pain, Desta sat up, leaned onto one elbow and peeled his
gabi from his legs and lower thighs.

Astair cringed. She covered her mouth and gazed at Desta's legs, eyes
fluttering as if she was trying to keep from crying.

"I am sorry, I . . . I . . ." Astair turned away. When she turned back her face
was streaked with tears. "I didn't mean to accuse you . . . but after all those
miscarriages, one more would be too much to take. We thought it would work
this time because, well, in part we believed you. Sort of. And as Grandpa said,
we had nothing to lose by moving. But we are afraid it might not happen this
time too . . ." She broke down again, sobbing out loud.

"I understand," said Desta. "I am not offended or upset. I just am sorry I can't come to pray with all of you."

"You know," said Astair after a long pause. "You know they had always wanted to have a boy after us girls. That was why they kept trying all these years even when nothing worked. We are scared to death it's going to happen this time too. I am frightened for my parents. Their spirits will be broken forever. I am afraid Mother might kill herself." She struggled to continue through a new surge of tears. "And we won't be immune from their sadness—my sister and I. Our hearts will ache. Our spirits will be dampened every time we think of our mother and what she has gone through."

Desta wished he could get up to comfort his niece. Knowing he couldn't do that, he just listened, letting her purge what had been dammed in her heart. That was how Hibist had always let him deal with things that made him cry. He thought it would help Astair too.

After a while, she wiped away her tears and said softly, "I'm sorry I said those things. I'm not mad at you."

"I understand," said Desta. "I am very sorry for your mother, but as far as this baby is concerned, you don't know yet."

"I know but she has been in labor now for a day and half. Everybody is sitting around her, saying, 'push, push . . . keep pushing' but nothing happens."

Pulling his leg slowly, Desta sat up and leaned against the hard leather pillow.

Astair helped him with his legs. "What I was also going to say, regarding what happened to you . . . My parents feel that mother's premature labor was probably caused by her fall and the stress she experienced when she saw what was happening to you. She was very sad and upset afterwards. She cried and cried till her eyes were red.

She said she was crying not only because of what she saw, but also for dragging you into her problems. We know what has been going on. Damtew, and I think Asse'ged too, have held grudges against you because we have taken the property that was supposed to be theirs. We have heard from Asse'ged's wife what Damtew has been saying and doing to you."

Desta nodded, scooted down to comfort himself and waited for her to continue.

"One of the reasons we have pretty much stayed away from this side of the creek was that we didn't want to aggravate the problem by being a reminder of it," said Astair. "We thought if Damtew and Asse'ged didn't see us, they would eventually forget their hankering for the place. We were heart-broken when Damtew's goat was lost and you ran away. Oh my God, mother was so worried for you. We also heard what happened to you when Damtew took you to swim. Asse'ged's wife said Damtew bragged how he enjoyed terrifying you."

"I feel sorry too that we have not seen each other for a long time," said Desta. "I thought it was because I was spending so much time with the animals and was never at home when you might have visited.

"No, we just decided it was better to stay away."

"You know, no matter what happens to me, or what they do to me, my greatest fear is to die without touching the sky. I fear Damtew is determined to kill me before I can reach my dream." Desta was now lying on his back staring at the ceiling.

"We are aware of that also, how important it is for you to go to the mountaintop. My mother always said she wished she could help but because of the way things are now between us and everybody here, she has not done anything about it."

"So long as I am safe from Damtew, I will eventually get there. I am sure of it."

"I think so too," nodded Astair.

"Tell me," said Desta, turning his head. "Who else is at your house now?"

"My grandma, Azal, Asse'ged and his wife, your parents and Damtew."

"Damtew is there?!"

"Yes, believe it or not . . . Mama and Baba were surprised too. He wouldn't want to miss mother's miscarriage, I guess. He came with Asse'ged. He was sitting at the far end of the house, wrapped with his gabi to his nose. If it didn't look bad, we would have liked to kick him out."

Desta thought for a moment and said, "You know he has not come home since he beat me. He must have been staying with Asse'ged these last two nights."

Astair rose to go. "I better get back."

"You understand that because of my condition I cannot be there to pray for your mother, but I will do it here. Tell your father and mother what I showed you. Whether it is to God or that man, I will do my best. Tell your father loud enough for everybody to hear. The reason I couldn't come to pray with them is because of what Damtew did to me. He is the one to blame for your mother's premature labor."

"I am not sure if I can say all those things when Damtew is right there listening, but I will tell them what I saw and what you told me regarding the praying. I need to run now. They are waiting for my return with you."

Astair hugged and kissed Desta, then hurried off.

FORTY

Desta woke at midnight to the touch of his father's hand. In the background
Ayénat was talking to Melkam excitedly. She was thanking God, Saint Mary
and a number of other saints and angels and telling Melkam what had happened
with Saba. Desta slowly adjusted his eyes to the light by the fireplace and
shook the sleep from his consciousness.

"You will be happy to know that Saba finally delivered—a baby boy! She
has named him Desta."

At first Desta thought he was hallucinating. "What? She gave birth to a live
baby?" He turned to his father.

"A beautiful baby," said Abraham, smiling. "A little smaller than he should
have been, but considering he arrived two weeks early, he still is healthy and
lively as they come."

"I am so happy for Saba and . . . ," said Desta

Abraham smiled again. "I know. We are all happy to bring that string of
losses to an end. You are a part of it, Desta. You should be happy for yourself
too. Your credibility had been under scrutiny for so long."

"I hope I can live in peace and everybody will leave me alone from here on."

"I understand you have been teased and I was not always here to look after
you. Not only should the teasing stop—I'll make sure it does—they should hold
you in high esteem for your ability to connect with people of the underworld to
help us solve this problem. And to think I resisted it because I never believed in
such things. I am humbled.

"Now I have no reason to doubt that there exist entities that can solve human
problems if properly sought by the right individual. I feel and taste the true
meaning of your name today. I called you Desta—happiness—because we had
the gladdest of times when you were born. Today, tonight, I feel the happiest
because you helped unravel the problem that had plagued us for so long. I
won't suggest it was a coincidence that Saba had a normal baby after they

moved to their new place, as others are apt to say. No matter what, you are still the reason that we are all happy tonight."

Desta was overwhelmed by his father's effusive praise for him. He rolled over onto his side. Just then, he saw Abraham staring at the fire obliquely, swimming in thought.

His father turned and said, "I have not forgotten what Damtew has done to you. But because of this thing with Saba, your mother's and my attention has been with your sister. I'd whip him if that would please you, but I think I can punish him in ways that would be just as severe or worse. Justice will be served in either case. I assure you!"

"My wish is that you please tell Damtew to leave me alone. I can't wait till he moves out of the house like Asse'ged."

"You have my word," said Abraham. He rested one hand on Desta's shoulder and tightly pressed his lips against the boy's forehead. "I am proud of you, son. Good night."

Desta couldn't believe his father's sudden display of affection and such a show of excitement. *I hope from here on, he gives me a meatier part of the chicken,* said he to himself with a smile.

He was very happy for Saba, Yihoon, Astair and Zena. And he was happy for himself. He hoped the dark cloud that had hung over his head for the past twenty-four months would now quickly dissipate. He hoped now his brothers and the rest of the family would leave him alone—and maybe even be nice to him a little.

With these expectations, Desta saw new opportunities for himself. He hoped to be able to practice his reading and writing without harassment. More importantly, maybe now he could convince one of the adults to take him to the top of the mountain. And if they would not take him, he would ask them to find someone to tend the animals, so he could do it on his own.

FORTY-ONE

December

The sun rose over the eastern mountains like a crowned spirit. A thin, gauze-like cloud had veiled its path, causing it to glow like a lantern and the shadows from the mountains to become one indistinguishable blur. Desta studied the sun and its camouflage with great interest.

It was early Saturday morning. Abraham had just returned from his morning outing when he ran into Damtew at the entrance. Desta was sitting by the fireplace eating his breakfast before he left with his animals. He could see and hear the two men from his vantage point.

"I need you to attend to the cattle today as I need Desta to help me at the nursery," said Abraham.

Damtew looked at his father as if he had lost his mind. "Since when I am demoted to a shepherd?"

"This is no demotion. Since you have no farming today and we don't have anybody else to be with the animals, the responsibility rests on your shoulders."

Damtew mumbled a few more words, but Desta couldn't make them out. His brother's face spoke volumes about the gravity of his displeasure.

Desta too was stunned by this sudden decision of his father. He had never spent any time with his father. The prospect of spending the day with him both excited and puzzled him. *What would he be doing at the nursery? What would they talk about? Would they spend the whole day together?* The thought was a little frightening. For Desta, his father had always been merely a figure in the house, someone who went away on business trips or for court matters for several days at a time, came home for a few days and then went away again on one or another trip.

Desta had noticed that his father had been smiling often since his grandson was born. He flashed his chipped tooth at everybody but was particularly generous with Desta.

After breakfast Abraham put on his old khaki shorts and his old gabi, and they left for the nursery, which was located on an irrigated land by the banks of Davola.

Known as "The Onion and Garlic Field." It was the only irrigated land in the valley, mainly because Abraham had devised a method of diverting the river water to grow the two cash crops all year round. Every year a large quantity of garlic and onions were produced and taken to the market, thanks to the hard work of Abraham and his helpers.

Abraham and Desta walked to the onion and garlic farm on the same footpath that went to the Avinevra church. Desta noticed details about his father's physique he had never paid attention to before: the high arches in his feet, his long shapely legs, straight back, broad shoulders and his towering height. He also noticed how unique his father's walk was: his steps measured and decisive, his gait smooth and graceful. There was a language to his walk that made Desta happy. He hoped to be like him when he grew older.

To his surprise, Desta felt very comfortable being with his father. His earlier fears rapidly faded from his mind.

"Desta," said his father without looking back.

"Yes," said Desta, trotting a little closer, glad to hear his father's great voice.

"I want you to know I am very, very happy with what you have been able to do for your sister."

"I didn't do anything for her."

"I didn't mean it that way. You're the reason through whom Saba was able to have her son—and me, my grandson. Without you, we wouldn't have this child. I am sure of it. Because we had tried everything and nothing had worked."

"I am happy it worked finally. I was not sure of it myself. Because everybody said I had imagined seeing that man by the river, in the end, I started to believe maybe they were right."

"I know. We all had our doubts because what happened to you was not something that occurs every day."

They walked along the trail from their house to the caravan route that ran along the flat land next to the river. As they walked the main road, they passed a number of market goers; their donkeys loaded with sacks of grain, stacks of animal skins, or freshly fired pottery. Many stopped, bowed to Abraham, kissed him three times on the cheeks and chit-chatted before continuing on. One woman kissed his knee and thanked him profusely for helping solve a property line dispute. Some of them patted Desta's shoulders or head and imparted endearing words to him as his father looked on.

Desta realized for the first time how important his father was for all those people. This discovery made him even more proud of his father.

They reached the onion and garlic field after they crossed the Davola and walked north a few hundred yards. The field was huge—how huge, Desta didn't know—divided into two halves, one for garlic, the other for red onions. A third, much smaller patch to the west of the onions was covered with straw. In one part of this patch, young plants of varying heights stood bunched together.

Desta trailed behind his father as he inspected the larger field. The onion stalks were partially dried and fallen. The garlic plants were already dry, their bone-white skins gleaming in the morning sun. Several canals ran the full length of the field. Along these canals, at discrete points, were large holes, which Abraham said were watering depots. It was from these watering holes that workers would water the growing produce with wooden bowls. With Desta following behind Abraham, they paced the entire perimeter of the field. "Once in a while we have pedestrians who help themselves to a few heads of onion and garlic," said Abraham. "So far so good this year."

After the inspection tour, they stopped at the straw-covered beds in the small field. There were seven beds in all, each about three feet wide by seven feet long. Abraham bent over near one of them. He lifted the straw and peered at the sprouted green things.

"These are new beds of Bahar Zaf," he said as he fingered the green sprouts. The soil was damp and there were also sprouted weeds along the border of the beds.

"What kind of tree is Bahar Zaf?" asked Desta, intrigued.

"It's a type of tree that grows fast and tall and has a certain aroma that is pleasant. Those over there I planted a few months ago. They are already tall enough to be transplanted, but I can't do that until the wet season comes. These here are a different variety and they should be ready to be transplanted to our property by June, along with the others. They will be the only trees still standing when I am gone. 'Those are Abraham Beshaw's Bahar Zaf,' people will say when they look from far away."

Desta walked over to the brownish-green leaved, smelly plants and inspected them. They were unlike any other plants he had ever seen or smelled. "Can I come with you when you plant them?"

"Yes, just remind me. It will have to be on a weekend so we can get Damtew to attend to the animals."

This suggestion pleased Desta, to see Damtew become a shepherd one more time.

"We need to open the canal and bring water for them," said Abraham as he rose. Then he added, "Let's first close off the part of the canal that goes to the rest of the field." He lifted a wooden board from the side of the water course and inserted it in two vertical grooves in the canal, blocking the waterway. Then he walked toward the bank of the river with Desta in tow.

He lifted a large, rectangular wooden board that was wedged near the gate of the canal. Desta watched the released water rush through.

"I will wait here," said Abraham. "You go and watch as the water depots fill and let me know when they are done."

Desta loped along the canal gleefully, chasing the headwater as it surged, picking up straws, leaves and loose dirt and carrying them with it. When the water reached the nursery area, it flowed along the channels to the nursery and began filling the watering holes.

Desta shouted to his father after the holes were filled to their brims. Abraham closed off the gate and walked briskly towards Desta. He straddled the water hole and began to scoop and throw the water over the sleeping, sprouted Bahar Zaf—eucalyptus—with an old wooden bowl that he held with both hands.

Desta couldn't help but ask his father why there were seven beds—and not six or eight. He knew his father had a superstitious proclivity toward the number seven, just as his mother liked the number three. Hibist had told him about both, but he wanted to hear it firsthand.

Abraham stopped from his task to answer Desta's question. Desta couldn't tell if it was water or sweat that hung from his father's forehead.

"Seven is a lucky number—my lucky number," said Abraham after catching his breath. "Besides, it has religious significance. It's a number that has been revered in our family, something that has been passed down for generations—who started it and how far back it goes, I can't tell you. We did everything in sevens. Seven also has a personal meaning to me—bad or good. I was seven years old when my father disappeared, which was bad. You're the seventh of my children, which is good.

"In fact, the reason that man was revealed to you and not Astair was probably because you're the seventh child. I am almost certain of it," said

Abraham, still standing with the wooden bowl in his hand.

"Are all these seven beds filled with Bahar Zaf?" asked Desta.

"Yes and no. Yes, because I have the germinating seeds in all the beds. No, because they're only thinly sown, to allow the making of the seven beds. Not all of those I sowed may germinate."

Abraham continued watering the beds. Once done, Abraham stowed the bowl in a grove of bushes near the nursery and invited Desta to sit with him under the oak tree near the river for a while before they headed home.

They sat on a rock facing the river. The shade of the tree and the cool breeze from the river were soothing. The sound of the river added a tranquil effect. The late morning sun, filtering through the branches, threw a shower of yellow light on the ground under the tree, reminding Desta of the butterflies he and Hibist used to chase in the meadows in the spring season. He was momentarily transported back in time, eyes fixed on the butterflies, ears turned to the sound of the river.

Abraham too was reflecting on things, sorting and processing his thoughts, saving some in his mind and discarding others. "Desta," he said, glancing toward his son. "One of the reasons I invited you to come with me this morning was to share my thoughts with you about your sighting of that man. Now that what he foretold has come true, I need to tell you something that happened to me."

Abraham stopped when he saw a massive, membranous sac of frog eggs floating in the water. Desta followed his eyes and saw two fat, white-belled frogs leap and dive in the shallow water. Immediately, they began their guttural rattle, which seemed to awaken others in the vicinity as a chorus was soon formed.

"They must have sensed there was an audience around and wanted to show off their vocal skills," said Abraham, grinning at Desta.

"I didn't know so many frogs live in a river," said Desta, fascinated by the sound.

"Only in the dry season. This is where they lay and hatch their eggs," said Abraham. "Anyway, to go back to what I started to say, there are things I wanted to share with you while they are fresh in my mind.

"The revelation of that man by the river reminded me of an experience I had years go, right after I got married. I have never shared this with anybody other than my mother because what happened was so odd and I thought nobody would believe me if I told them."

Desta was looking at his father and listening.

"I loaded two horses with a great number of young tsede trees and took them to the church of Ba'tha Mariam in Kuakura, my birthplace. I wanted to plant them on the church grounds in the memory of my father and got permission to do so from the head priest. I was alone, feverishly planting these trees. On three different occasions I felt a hand touch my right shoulder and I heard a voice whisper, 'Good job, good job, I am proud of you.'

"When I turned around, I saw the phantom-like image of an old, old man with a long white beard. The moment I focused my eyes on him, he vanished. At first I was so spooked, I wanted to leave the church yard immediately. But then when I thought about it, the voice was kind and did nothing but praise me. It was a long journey from home, the trees were precious and I had only one day to plant them. I worked from dawn to sunset without even taking a lunch break.

"By the time I finished and walked out of the woods, I had this great sensation of joy—joy from accomplishing my mission on behalf of my father. I was also happy to know somebody here on earth saw the value of my efforts and complimented me."

"Who do you think he was?"

"Mother said it could be a *Goossa*—an old monk who has taken the form of a spirit and who roams the forest. But she also thought he could be a family guardian angel who was pleased with my work and came to acknowledge it. For all I know, it could have been either one." He paused and smiled at his son.

"Coming to your own experience, Desta, I think the man you sighted could be our guardian angel, not an alien spirit. You were the channel through whom he chose to solve our problem. You should feel blessed and happy that he chose you."

Desta smiled. He felt blessed indeed. The fact that his father had had a similar experience made him feel that much more special. His head was light with happiness.

"Baba, you always do things in the memory of your father. How come you have not gone looking for him? If he is still alive, it would be great to meet him."

"You know, I have been thinking about that lately, that it would be nice for him to meet all his progeny, particularly an 'oddball' like you," said Abraham, smiling and stealing a wink at Desta.

"I would love to come with you if you go to look for him."

"The journey is too long and tiring. You are not ready for such a trip. But if I find him, I'll bring him home with me, even if I have to pay with my shirt for transportation. In the meantime, we just need to pray to God and to our guardian angel to help us find him," said Abraham looking away thoughtfully.

"If I ever see that man again in my dreams or in person, I'll definitely ask him for his help."

"Good . . . We need to go home now. The sun is getting stronger. We cannot do anymore watering," said Abraham as he rose.

Abraham's sudden change of subjects had caught Desta off guard. He had a few more questions to ask about his grandfather, but he knew his father always clammed up whenever the conversation turned to his own father. Desta was not going to press him with any more questions.

Abraham went to the nursery area after telling Desta to wait for him in the shade. He wanted to ensure that everything by the onion and garlic field was in order—that the canal opening was tightly closed, the wooden bowl was stowed and the nurseries were sufficiently covered. He brushed off the mud from his feet on the green grass at the edge of the river and joined Desta on the main caravan road.

As they walked Abraham once again told Desta how proud he was of him and how happy he was they had spent some time together. Being chosen, he told his son, is an honor and a privilege that carries with it responsibility and accountability. He should feel humble and modest about these advantages. He should not talk to strangers or even his family about his experiences, as they could become jealous of him. If those who knew what happened to him teased and harassed him, he should simply ignore them and walk away.

Desta acknowledged his father's advice but this sudden outpouring of interest and concern for him had become overwhelming. His throat became lumpy and his eyes began to gather tears. To Desta these tears were both of happiness and anger. He was happy that he finally seemed to have an ally in his father but angry that his father had not been there to defend and protect him all along. As his father continued to express his admiration and appreciation, the dam broke loose and Desta openly cried.

Abraham was startled. "I am sorry, son. I didn't mean to make you cry," he said, as he held him close. "I hope those were tears of joy. I feel blessed myself to finally have the child of my dreams, somebody special, who someday is destined to do great things."

That day Desta came to realize how capricious the adult world was and what a precious commodity love was in his household. It had to be earned and was not freely given. He couldn't imagine what the outcome would have been if Saba had had another miscarriage.

FORTY-TWO

January 1958

Desta remembered that it had been nearly nineteen months since Tamirat had gone to his in-laws so his wife and he could have their communion together on her home turf. The progress report that periodically came through Amsale's cousin, Tenaw, the husband of Desta's sister, Enat, was not heartening. Things had turned for the worst. Instead of being cooperative, Amsale had drawn a line in the sand. She had become even more resolute not to take the communion with her husband, and when the pressure from her relatives had mounted, she had gathered her personal things and run away.

Tenaw told them that Tamirat had taken refuge with his cousin, Kiwin and her husband, Brihan. He had been praying day and night that God would intercede to bring the girl back and save his marriage. *If you really wanted me to be a service to you to the end of my days, please save my marriage,* Tamirat had pleaded with God, Tenaw related one evening when he came to update Ayénat. Only Abraham was not privy to this story because Desta's mother feared it might upset him. Abraham had long wanted to have a priest son that would make him proud.

Tenaw reported that Tamirat had told him that he could not bury his young feelings of the flesh and accept the idea of being a celibate the rest of his life without having sired progeny that would carry on his line. His brother-in-law had resorted to desperate measures, he said.

He had gone on a hunger strike. He had taken to standing on one leg where he prayed every morning from before the rooster crowed until daybreak. He read the Bible every evening and morning. He went to church every Sunday and prayed in a very secluded place in the woods—away from the distraction of people, particularly young women—where he felt he would have purer thoughts, which, in turn he hoped, would give him quicker access to God.

When nothing happened, Tamirat had to come to terms with his predicament.

Having given God a chance to mediate, having done everything he could to immunize himself from guilt and regrets, he had no choice but to divorce the girl, remarry and lead a lay life.

A LITTLE OVER a year and a half after leaving home, Tamirat returned as a divorcee with a new wife, five years younger than he, named Bogay. Although the marriage was arranged by his cousin Kiwin, Tamirat had met and approved his bride-to-be as he had not done when Ayénat arranged his marriage to Amsale through her son-in-law, Tenaw.

Bogay's sunny personality, voluptuous figure, and big brilliant eyes that shone like polished silver were captivating, and Tamirat took her as a consolation gift from God. Her fair skin was pure and attractive and he could easily imagine the beautiful children they would produce in due time.

He was anxious to introduce his new bride to his parents. Uncertain how his father would react to his decision to leave the priesthood, he waited to bring her to meet his parents and also a good many of his relatives at their annual church holiday. Given the holiday occasion and the presence of many people, Tamirat thought his father would take the news less severely.

When Tamirat and his new wife arrived home late in the afternoon, his parents' house was full of relatives and friends. Desta, who was playing with a few children outside, came running to greet his brother and the new wife.

It was Ayénat that Tamirat and Bogay met next. The mother was outside giving orders to helpers who were setting up dinner mossebs and benches. She immediately broke off from the people she was talking to and stepped aside to receive them. Since they were not expected, she was pleasantly surprised to see Tamirat and happy to finally meet his new bride. They kissed three times on both cheeks. She was asking why he had not returned home in such a long time, when other relatives, led by Enat and Genet, came running.

Ayénat thought her son looked well and much happier than when he had left home a year and a half before. There was a glow to his fair skin and he appeared at ease. The more she studied his new wife, the better she liked her. Not only was Bogay very pretty but she was also polite, with a reticent disposition. Ayénat wondered why Providence had not led them to her when they were looking for a wife for Tamirat the first time. The young woman appeared to be a perfect priest's wife, for a son who now could never be a priest. She could only pray that her husband, who knew of his son's divorce but not his remarriage, would take the news lightly and would feel similarly disposed to accept her.

TAMIRAT CAUGHT sight of his father as Abraham was returning with a group of men from a private meeting at the back of the house. He immediately broke away from the people that had circled him and walked over to meet his father.

Abraham's eyes lit up as if Tamirat were a vision, but they dimmed quickly when he thought of his son's divorce. "Era, where did they find you today?" he said in a tone tinged with irony. He clasped his son's chin with an extended hand and kissed him on the cheeks three times. The men who were with Abraham also kissed Tamirat and asked about his well being, his new life as a married man and his school.

Abraham listened coolly as Tamirat responded to the various questions, offering a particularly vague answer to the one about his married life. The news of his son's divorce was still fresh in his mind. He was eager to learn what Tamirat had decided about his future career as a priest, but such a personal question would have to wait until the right moment. For now general questions about his well being and the well being of Kiwin and her family would have to suffice. As they strolled back to the house, Tamirat answered all the questions and also conveyed Kiwin's good wishes and regrets for not coming to the festival.

As they approached the home Tamirat glanced around nervously, looking for his new wife. It appeared that his mother and sisters had wisely vanished with her, wishing to defer the introduction of Bogay to his father until a more suitable time.

At dinner, Bogay sat with Enat and Genet in the back room while Tamirat ate with his two uncles and their wives in the living room. After dinner, Ayénat arranged for Tamirat and his wife to sleep at Asse'ged's house. She didn't want Abraham to discover Bogay until they were ready to formally break the news to him.

It was mid morning. The sun shone over the eastern mountains. A few puffy clouds hung above the pass south of Lehwani. The guests draped in their white gabis sat out on the grass like a flock pelicans, enjoying the pleasant morning. Tamirat stood by the fence, impatiently waiting for his father to break free from three men he was talking with.

Noticing Tamirat's restlessness, Abraham hastily wrapped up his conversation and strode toward his son. He was eager to have a private conversation about everything that had happened since he left home over a year and a half ago.

They greeted each other, and Abraham smiled a little, barely showing his chipped tooth. Tamirat returned the smile but his was artificial and nervous.

"As you must realize, I am keen to hear a firsthand account of what ultimately happened with Amsale," said the father.

"Not one you would want to hear, I am afraid," said Tamirat, looking away, his face knotted.

"I have heard fragments of it, so it's not entirely news to me. Let's go to the back woods where we can talk without distraction."

When they were beyond earshot of the guests, they sat in a clearing where they had a good view of the Davola River and the mountains beyond.

"What exactly happened after you got to her parents'?" asked Abraham, eyeing his son anxiously.

"She continued to give me a string of excuses about not wanting to take the communion with me. When her father finally put his foot down and threatened her with punishment, she gathered up her personal things and disappeared in the dead of night. Nobody knows where she went." Tamirat shook his head, remembering his frustration.

"She had procrastinated and prevaricated for several weeks. I prayed daily for God's intervention but in the end it was all to no avail. After she vanished, I stayed with her parents for two weeks, hoping she would return. She never did.

"When the situation seemed hopeless, I left the in-laws and stayed with Kiwin and her husband for the next seven months. For the first five months I prayed, rising early in the morning and standing on one leg, petitioning God to save my marriage so that I could be of service to Him. It seemed He didn't really care because my wife didn't return to me or to her family.

"After I gave up waiting for her, I prayed for two months more, again rising early in the morning and standing on one leg asking God to take away my desire of the flesh, to give me strength so I could lead a celibate life and serve Him. But the more I beseeched Him, the farther away He felt from me, as my desire for a female companion became even more consuming. It seemed He didn't care what I ended up doing with myself.

"When I finally told Kiwin and Brihan, what was going on, they said it was not meant to be and I should stop torturing myself. They suggested I . . . I . . ." Tamirat couldn't go on with his story. He looked away and struggled to compose himself.

Abraham waited for his son to finish his thoughts. "They suggested what?" he asked finally.

Tamirat turned around and studied his father's face. "I know you are not going to like what I am about to tell you because this is not what you have wished for me all along. I have given it my best effort, but as Kiwin and Brihan said, it just was not meant to be." He looked down at his feet.

"You mean you will no longer become a priest?" said Abraham, his face nearly bloodless.

"I am afraid that is so, Baba . . . I am sorry . . . I just couldn't spend the rest of my life a celibate . . . I am now remarried—her name is Bogay."

Abraham thought for a long moment. "You know, if your twelve years of education were going to end like this, you could have saved yourself the hardship you went through to earn it." He planted an elbow on a knee and played with his goatee. "You could have prepared yourself for the farming life."

"I am very sorry . . . It was not my intention. It was bad luck that brought Amsale into my life—to disrupt my career and bring sorrow to our hearts— yours and mine, Baba. I knew this would sadden you. That was part of the reason I prayed all those months and why I didn't invite you and Mama to my wedding to my new wife. I thought it would be hard for you to take, to see me abandon my priesthood."

Abraham was silent for a long time. His face looked darker, his eyes— somber and metallic—stayed fixed on the distant mountains, his lips and tongue seemed to have lost their mobility. "I am just sad to see your career and my dream of having a priest son end like this because of a twelve-year old girl," he said at last, fumbling with random thoughts that came to his head. "What is the background of your new wife?

"She is the daughter of Belay Zeru and Alem Nega. Her parents are Kiwin's neighbors."

"At least she comes from a good family. I know the mother," said Abraham.

"I just wish you had fixed me up with Bogay the first time around."

"It was all your mother's handiwork," said Abraham bitterly. Flooded with emotion, he rose to head home. "Let's go back now. There may be people wanting to see me." He was hurried and businesslike, anxious to end their conversation.

Tamirat followed his father, thoughtful and cheerless.

When they arrived home, a crowd of people came to greet Abraham. They were all well-wishers, new guests who had come for the festival.

Tamirat dropped back when he saw the people and cut to the north side of his parents' house. He knew some of them but purposely avoided them, fearing they would ask personal questions. He didn't want to disappoint any more relatives with news of his abandoned career.

IT WAS LATE MORNING when Abraham excused himself from his guests and went on a walk to the southern creek. Tamirat's bombshell had bothered him a great deal. He needed a private time and place to think through what had been going in his mind. The sun was intense, but the cool breeze from Davola River had tempered the air enough to make the walk bearable. Across from the creek he could see Saba's old property. Only the old hay shed was still standing with a few bales of hay in it. Where Saba's house used to be, tall grass with a mixture of daisy, pansy, daffodil, dandelion and other flowers had grown during the rainy season. Now the same outgrowth had dried and was matted down. Abraham stopped for a moment and studied the vacant land wondering what its fate would be in the years to come. Nobody had walked over it or even allowed animals to graze on it since the family left. But the tableau distracted him only briefly from his greater concern: Tamirat's abandoned career and what it would mean to Abraham.

"The sons of fire are ashes," Abraham kept saying under his breath as he walked, his eyes on the path, his mind far away. He couldn't fathom how, out of his four grown sons, all of them mentally and physically healthy, none had inherited his own drive, ambition and motivation to stick it out no matter what the circumstances. In his mind, he itemized the many things he accomplished: his medal–winning feats during the Ethio-Italian war, his innovative and enterprising business skills, the oratorical and verbal abilities he brought to his mediation and courtroom work and the logic and strategic acumen he applied to win cases honestly and ethically before the most corrupt of judges. He thought of the many decisions he had made to provide his family better living conditions and opportunities, his dogged determination to see anything he started through to completion, his vigorous cauldron of a mind that never ceased to spin out ideas . . . Yet, sadly none of his grown male progenies showed any of these attributes.

As he strolled along the path that led to the creek, a few hawks circled overhead, beaks pointing to the ground, eyes scanning the earth. Several yards from him, on a scraggy bow of an oak tree, he noticed a trio of vultures. *They must have been feeding on the severed head of a cow we killed for the festival a few days ago,* he thought.

He wished his children had the vigilance of a vulture and the eye of a hawk to pursue life goals that could distinguish them above the common folk of the valley. It was not as if he hadn't pushed or motivated them, perhaps too hard at times, he thought, remembering the beating he had inflicted on Desta after the boy let the cattle plunder their neighbor's crops. But still, his intentions had always been good. From the time they were little he had always tried to steer his sons in directions that would bring honor to the family and distinction and respect for themselves. Of the four grown boys, two he had wanted to become accomplished horsemen, *like your grandfather,* he remembered saying to them. The other two he had wanted to become priests, the only high-status profession available to them in the valley.

To his disappointment, none of the boys had a desire for horsemanship, and of the two he sent to church school, one had dropped out after only a few months and now the other had abandoned the profession after committing twelve years of his young life to it. He had banked on Tamirat to be the one who could make him proud, the one who would fulfill, in some way, the aspirations he had for all his children. Now that dream would never come true.

This realization was a big blow: to his personal pride, to his wishes and hopes, to his sense of fulfillment as a successful parent. He had wanted to give his sons opportunities he didn't have, to create a good foundation for them and their children. He felt now as if he had failed twice—once, on his own and now again through his children.

It was past midday, and the heat was getting increasingly intense. He moved to the canopy of the acacia tree a few yards from the path and stopped. He sat on the dried pale grass. His eyes caught blackberry vines drooping from a kaga tree at the edge of the woods. There were berries at different stages: green and pink ones on the lower branches; lush, ripe and dark blue ones higher up and seared, dried ones near the top. He salivated and swallowed, remembering that he had not eaten that day. Studying a swarm of bees paying homage to the sky-blue flowers, Abraham prayed to God for the wisdom and steadfastness to endure his personal hardship.

When he took his eyes away from the bees, his anger and disappointment with his children had abated. In his mind, he looked for the qualities and attributes they had instead of the boxes he had tried to place them in.

He knew that Teferra, the oldest, had inherited his abilities as a marksman, but what good was a sharpshooter in peacetime? The Italians had long since gone home, and there was no other war in the offing. Admittedly, Teferra had become a great hunter. He had accumulated enough antelope skins and colobus monkey skins to furnish every home in the valley and the walls of his home were decked out with antlers and antelope heads. *But hunting trophies was nothing but fodder for his own vainglory*, thought Abraham. The activities themselves would not bring him public recognition, honor and respect to him or his family.

Asse'ged's redeeming attributes were his verbal and interpersonal skills. Abraham could see that someday he could become a good defender of the family's multitude of properties against encroachers. He could also get involved in community activities as an arbiter for quarreling families, as Abraham himself had been doing. Yes, there was hope yet for Asse'ged.

Tamirat, with his ability to read and write, could assist Abraham as reader and transcriber of court documents. He could also hire himself out for people who need these services, putting his education to use in a way that would be helpful to the community.

Damtew was a natural farmer. In just one year at the profession, he had significantly increased grain production. With his physical prowess and athleticism, he could have been a fine horseman, but he had never shown an interest in that, nor was book knowledge something that suited him. He was a poor conversationalist and he lacked intellectual curiosity.

As he finished going through his male children in descending order, he came to Desta, almost as an afterthought—a scrawny, precocious little boy who probably wouldn't amount to anything. He could never see Desta as a horseman. He was far too small and not especially athletic. Nor was he good priest material. To prepare for priesthood, it took a great deal of self-reliance, including having to fend for himself by going around to neighbors and asking for food, after finishing his daily lessons. Desta was certainly too small and sensitive to endure the hardship and hunger of a church school.

Abraham had never accepted the allegation that Desta was a curse to the family because he asked endless questions and was always daydreaming, but when he thought about his youngest son's size and physical limitations, he could only conclude that Desta would never be in league with his other children. If he couldn't count on his four strapping older boys to make him proud, how could he expect much from his skinny eight-year-old oddball? He couldn't.

His mind returned to the very capable, near-priest son who could no longer be the symbol of his dreams and aspirations. Tamirat, he had to admit, was as good as dead to him now. With a rush of resignation he felt the heavy blanket of despair descend on him once again.

No longer would his heart leap with joy and his head inflate like a balloon on Sundays, as they used to when Tamirat sung the hymns in the inner sanctuary of their church. During mass, his beautiful singing voice reverberated through the layers of walls and filled the air outside for the hushed parishioners all around the church to enjoy.

"That is your son, isn't he?" someone who stood next to him would ask. Abraham would acknowledge with humility but inside he would be bursting with pride. On other occasions, he would hear parishioners talk among themselves, wondering whose liquid voice that was that graced them that morning. "That's our son," he would say casually.

No longer could he dream about his son sitting at the head of the table during big festivals at home, blessing the food or reciting prayers. Now he would have to continue to depend on an outsider to perform these sacred duties. Perhaps worst of all, at his own funeral one day, it would no longer be his son leading the procession. Again, he would have to depend on the services of an outsider.

It hurt him to be powerless to change things, unable to put them back the way he wished them to be. But he could not undo what was done. He couldn't change the church laws so that Tamirat as a remarried man could continue with the priesthood.

He had to accept that all the hopes and dreams he'd had for his son and himself as another vanished vision. Tamirat, his bastion of success and pride, had failed him. He hung his head, hurt and disillusioned.

He wished he could talk about his feelings with someone who would not be judgmental of him or his children, someone who would truly understand what it meant for a father to lose hope in his son. A friend would not do, nor would a relative who had no personal interest. It would have to be someone who would share the burden and disappointment. That person would have been his father.

Abraham thought he would have been able to share his feelings and thoughts openly with his father. Had his father been around from early on, he would have given him pointers that could have made him a better father and would have encouraged his grandchildren to follow in his footsteps as accomplished horsemen, artists and businessmen. He wished his father were there with him under the cool shade of the tree, talking with him about these painful, personal matters. But that was not to be!

As in the past, he needed to rest his head near a gurgling water to help calm his nerves and soothe his mind. Abraham rose and continued on the path. He entered the wooded creek and walked upstream along the embankment until he found a convenient place to sit near a waterfall where the water gurgled soothingly as it flowed through the gray rocks. He sat on a moss-fringed slab and laid his head on a massive boulder.

He closed his eyes and listened to the water for a long time, letting the soft sound drown out his thoughts and tranquilize his senses.

When he finally opened his eyes, he felt as if he had awakened from a deep dreamless sleep. He cupped his hands and drank from the cool spring water. Refreshed, he rose and headed for home.

As he walked, he felt free and unencumbered. It was as if he had washed off all the visions and expectations he had for his sons in the cool water of the creek.

FORTY-THREE

April

The long, flesh-melting days of fasting were over. People could eat any food they deemed fit any time of the day other than Wednesday and Friday, the two regular fast days of the week. This Easter, three lambs lost their lives and their meat fed three households for a whole week. The families went to different homes for dinner for three nights over five days. The only family members that were not included in the circuit were Teferra and his wife, Laqechi because they lived farther than the rest and nobody wanted to walk home after dinner from their home. They did come for dinner for the first meal at their parents' home.

Desta got lots of attention and adulations, especially from Saba's family, although he received only cynical remarks from Damtew and a few nods of acknowledgement from Asse'ged and Teferra.

Typically, the third and the last dinner was served at Asse'ged and Mulu's house, but this Easter Abraham and Ayénat wanted to give a fourth dinner for an important announcement Abraham was going make to the whole family. For three days the family speculated as to what the announcement would be. Damtew and Asse'ged guessed that their father had recently come into possession of a new land and wished to divide it between them as a replacement for the one he gave to Saba and her family. Saba and Yihoon thought maybe their father wanted to give a great bash in celebration of his first healthy grandson. Some of the women thought he wanted to honor Desta with something special, a piece of land, a cow or a mookit goat, for helping solve Saba's problems. Only Abraham and Ayénat knew what the announcement would be and they weren't saying anything.

AT THE FOURTH DINNER PARTY, everybody was on pins and needles. They couldn't wait until dinner was finished to hear the announcement Abraham was going to make.

Upon completion of the meal, Abraham gave a long blessing of the food that had been consumed, the individual children and animals, their future harvests, and their healthy and happy passage of the upcoming winter into the New Year in September. The last blessing was showered on the newly born baby, his mother, father and sisters. "May he be a happy and healthy baby, may God bless him and care for him, may he grow to be a good, obedient son . . ."

After he wrapped up his long-winded blessings, Abraham took a long pull from his tella, cleared his throat and began to speak. "We invited you here tonight to share with you a long overdue journey I have finally decided to make," Abraham began to say.

"Journey? Journey? Journey?" exclaimed a few of the men and women, obviously disappointed.

"This journey had long been deferred. I wish I had done it a long time ago, as soon as I became old enough to make the trek."

"Ahh, I know," grunted Damtew, looking at Asse'ged.

His older brother nodded. Only Saba and Teferra seemed in the dark.

"As the only boy of my father, and after having fled from jealous neighbors, I didn't want to leave my mother alone while I went on a trip to an unknown land hanging on a flimsy and conflicting lead." He paused, gazing out at the group. "Some of you look confused. I am referring to my father. Your grandfather. As most of you already heard bits of the story, he was lost to me when I was only seven years old. He disappeared without a trace. Along with him also vanished our ancient family coin. It was rumored then that he had been given a mind-altering herb by invidious neighbors, which caused him to go mad and leave his family. Since my mother was left alone with four small children and no close relatives nearby, the perpetrators thought they could take over our lands and steal our cattle.

"My mother, bless her soul, was wise enough to flee from the neighbors and area. She didn't want to witness the scrambling for her property or watch something happen to her children. We gathered our cattle and the rest of our belongings and went to settle in Avinevra near her relatives.

"Over the years, we talked to people who claimed they had seen my father in Lalibela. They said he asked specifically for those who came from Kuakura and told them his name and about the family he left behind. We heard these rumors from three different people, but the accounts varied. Two said the man was from Agew Mider and their descriptions of him and what he said were different from the first.

"As I said, with these conflicting accounts, I couldn't leave my mother and go on a two-week journey. And she wouldn't have allowed me to leave either. Be that as it may, it has bothered me all these years that I did not make the extra effort to find out what really happened to him. Now, I will try to do what I should have done long ago. I will try to find my father.

"I guess you might say, my own mortality is becoming more real as the years go by. It's a shame my father lived without knowing what became of his children or meeting his grandchildren. The recent arrival of Saba's new baby has brought so much joy in my own life . . . It's this kind of pleasure my father never experienced."

Abraham went silent, his eyes glistened with tears. The women silently cried and sniffled. The men tipped their heads. Instantly the room had become a room of mourners. Nobody dared to speak.

Finally, Abraham cleared his throat again and continued. His voice was ragged, his eyelashes still wet.

"Only Ayénat knows some of the story of my father's disappearance. As we grew up, we couldn't talk about what had happened because it was considered a shame for a father to abandon his family. But we knew he had not intentionally left us because he loved us. I remember how he carried me on his shoulders, with me grabbing onto his thick hair as we wandered in the fields. My sisters had similar stories. We have no doubt about how much he loved us. We were also certain he was not murdered. We scoured every corner of the place around where we lived but found no dead body or skeleton; nor to this day have any human remains been found in the area.

"Mother had said there were neighbors who had sore eyes for the amount of wealth we had and lifestyle we led. They wanted us to go away from the area, you see. . . . And what's more," Abraham continued after a pause. "For lack of adequate proof, we couldn't sue these people. . . . And I was denied the dream I once had of taking the law in my own hands by going after the criminals and reclaiming the coin. By the time I was ready to fulfill my dream, the perpetrators had died."

Abraham went silent once more.

"And they did take over your parents' land shortly after you moved to Avinevra, didn't they?" asked Teferra, trying to get Abraham to continue with his story.

"Sadly, yes. And it wasn't a small amount," replied the father.

Abraham sighed. "How we all would have loved to have had him in our

lives, to talk and share his life experiences, to receive his parental advice. . .
Anyway, I wanted to share with you my plans of going to investigate once and
for all if your grandfather might still be in Lalibela—alive or dead and buried."

"When do you plan to leave?" asked Yihoon.

"Next Saturday, assuming your mother will prepare enough dabo kolo for me
to eat for a couple of weeks."

"Can one of us come with you?" asked Asse'ged.

"I need to do this by myself. This is a personal mission because I have held
it so long in my heart. My Dama is strong enough to carry me there and back."

"How long will it take to get to Lalibela? Do you know how to get there?"
asked Teferra.

"They say a good two weeks on foot, perhaps about half that time on a
horseback. I know the general direction but not the exact route," said Abraham.

"They say Lalibela is beautiful," said Ayénat. "The pillars are made of
iron and the walls from stones. Every year people travel long distances to pay
homage to God and receive his ultimate blessings there. I wish I could come
with you."

Abraham just shook his head.

"Another thing," said Yihoon. "How old do you think your father is now if
he is alive?"

"I would think about sixty-eight or seventy."

"That is not so old," said Saba. "There are many monks around here that are
much older than seventy."

"I was just thinking, that if you find him and he wants to come home with
you, you are going to need the help of at least two strong men and a horse,"
said Yihoon.

"First things first. I need to make this investigatory mission for now. God
willing, if he is still alive, then we can arrange to bring him home.

"If you all have nothing planned next Saturday, do come and send me off.
Also in the meantime, if all of you women would be interested in contributing
dabo kolo for my trip, it would be appreciated. I know it's a tedious job for one
person to make it."

"We would be very happy to do it," chirped the women in unison.

"The night is getting old for now, and you all had better get to your homes.
The baby should get to his crib," said Abraham, pointing to his new grandson.
For the first time that evening, he smiled.

FORTY-FOUR

The appointed Saturday for Abraham's trip to Lalibela arrived gloriously. The sun rose and beamed brightly over the entire valley. The interior of his home was brightened with filtered light through apertures in the walls and the opened front entrance.

"What a day! This should be a good omen," said the traveler as he crossed the doorstep.

Inside, everybody was busy making dabo kolo for him to take on his trip. They put a small amount of oil in the palm of one hand, pinched the viscous dough with the other and rolled them between their palms. Once a near perfect sphere was achieved, they dropped them on the hot baking pan. Five women were gathered around the two fireplaces, working feverishly to finish the rolls so Abraham could leave before the day got hotter.

They had been baking since the early hours of the morning and had produced only about a hundred of the apricot-size rolls. They were made from wheat flour spiked with spiced, ground red pepper and salt. Desta and some of the women found them irresistible. A sizable number had already been consumed by the bakers under the pretense of trying to see how they tasted.

A late brunch of injera with lamb sauce was served to Abraham. Saba and Mulu brought their contributions of the dabo kolo and mixed them together in a large basket, making them appear more like freshly harvested apricots than bread rolls.

Ayénat transferred the rolls into two separate cloth sacks, making sure they were of more or less equal weight. *That way they would balance well on the horse's shoulders*, she thought.

"Don't give me too much," said Abraham. "They can be cumbersome to me and the horse. I just want a few to munch on whenever I am really hungry. Knowing how it goes on trips like this, I will probably end up being fed by strangers I meet."

Abraham put on his brown breeches and donned his khaki coat over his older, sweat-stained shirt. "This one is good for the trip. I will bring one extra that I can change into, once I arrive there," he said when Ayénat balked about the advisability of bringing such an old shirt. He assured her that he would wear his new shirt once he got to Lalibela.

On top of the coat he put on his new, month-old gabi. He neatly folded his extra clothes—an extra set of breeches and lighter and newer white shirt and placed them under the saddle seat cover.

The horse was fixed up nicely. The sacks of dabo kolo were hanging from the pommel on either side of the horse's shoulders.

Then came the troubling part for Abraham. Just about everybody wanted to send along something as a present for the grandfather. Saba had prepared three symbolic discs of bread for her father to share with a cup of water when they first met. The breads were to be consumed in the names of the Father, the Son and the Holy Ghost. Teferra brought a new gabi, Asse'ged a thick cotton skull cap, Ayénat prayer beads made from beautifully carved wood. Desta was not to be left out. He threw his safety pin into the mix.

"What good will that do for him," snapped Damtew. "He probably is not walking on thorn-infested fields."

"Actually that is probably the most useful gift you can give to an old man," said the father, glaring at his older son.

To his satisfaction, Abraham found most of the gifts to be simple, practical and light enough to carry with him. Only Teferra's gabi was too bulky to take along. He suggested Teferra think of something else that would be manageable to carry.

Ayénat had bought a pair of scissors for her own father but had not given them to him yet. She suggested Teferra buy them from her and send that instead of the gabi. Everybody thought it was a good choice and Teferra agreed. Saba's breads were put into the dabo kolo sacks, two in one, and the third in the other. The rest of the items were carefully folded or rolled in a cloth and given to Abraham to carry in his coat pocket.

They gathered outside, some by the horse, others around the father. One by one he kissed them. Saba wept openly. The in-laws pretended to cry. Ayenat's forehead was knotted with worry, but didn't cry. Asse'ged grumbled, wishing he could join Abraham in this expedition. Teferra complained too, saying he wished his father had planned the trip well in advance so that one or two of them could join him. Desta held the horse's lead and watched as his father was kissed and hugged. "Need to leave, need to leave," said Abraham heading toward the footpath that would take him to the main caravan route along the river.

Desta went ahead of him, leading the horse. The others followed the father. When they reached the middle of the field below the house, they said their final goodbyes. Abraham bent over and pressed his lips on Desta's cheeks. "Be good. We can talk more when I get back," he said holding Desta's head and shaking it a little. "Got to go."

He took the lead from Desta and mounted the horse. He put on his hard topee hat, uncoiled his leather whip and started the horse in the direction of his journey, waving his hand as he galloped away.

The family stood without moving until Abraham disappeared into the woods at the north end of the field. Then Ayénat invited them to come home for coffee and a breakfast of leftover dabo kolo. They all strolled back to the house in silence, heads hanging and lost in their thoughts.

After everybody left, Desta cried, *not* because his father left *but* because of the special intimacy they had shared before he mounted the horse. He had never known this kind of closeness with his father before.

NOT LONG AFTER ABRAHAM LEFT, a horseman emerged from the same section of the woods Abraham had gone into a while ago. Desta was the first to see him. He wondered who the unfortunate visitor was to be arriving after his father had left. He kept his eyes on the figure as it came nearer, then he realized with a surprise that it was his father. "I wonder what he's forgotten," he said as he ran towards him.

The horse wasn't galloping as it had been when they left. Dama walked almost a solemn walk, almost as if he was feeling his master's emotion.

"What happened?" said Desta as he ran up to his father.

"The birds, son, the birds."

"What about the birds?"

"I need to go home now, son. I will tell you later," said the father in a monotone. "It's complicated and I don't feel like explaining it here."

Desta didn't want to push him.

When Abraham reached home, everybody came out running. They all looked puzzled. "What did you forget?" asked Asse'ged breathlessly.

"Are you feeling alright?" asked Teferra, looking at his father's somber face.

"I am fine," said Abraham as he dismounted the horse.

But he was not fine.

Damtew took the horse's lead and stood by. The others looked at him anxiously, wondering what had happened to cause his sudden return.

"Are you afraid of making this trip? Or are you not feeling well?" asked Ayénat studying her husband's troubled face.

"Damtew, remove the harness and the bags from the horse and let him free. I will make another attempt at this tomorrow. Nothing of what you are asking, Ayénat. Let's all go inside, and I'll tell you."

Abraham sat on his stool and the family congregated around him, anxious to learn about the mysterious return.

"I hadn't even gone past the woods at the edge of our property before they began chattering doomsday at me," Abraham began.

"Who . . . what are they?" said Teferra, baffled. Everybody looked at each other, wondering if their father had lost his mind.

"The birds. I had lived in the forest long enough, studied bird language long enough to discern their presentments. During the Italian invasion when we all lived in the forest fighting the enemy, it became routine for my comrades to come and ask me what a certain bird was saying. I could tell, you see, whether we were going to have a good or bad day just from listening to the birds as we traveled through a place. The last time I heard the birds talk to me as they did today was when my friend Gdaff got shot, killed right in front of me. I had just finished telling him, 'Watch out, watch out, someone is either here or at the next corner,' when someone shot him. He was just a few feet away from me. I heard the birds and recognized the danger just moments before he died. Today I had nearly the same experience. I know I would be a fool to proceed with the birds ranting at me as they did."

"Maybe today was not meant to be the day for your trip. We should be thankful you have the gift to know enough to get out of harm's way," said Asse'ged.

"After you left, we were sitting here, talking about your trip," said Yihoon. "After so many years of not knowing your father's whereabouts, to go so far now, we thought it was dangerous. . . ."

"Frankly, I've been very uneasy about the whole thing since you announced it last week," said Teferra. "I certainly concur with you about this guardian angel that protects us. He must have been trying to communicate with you through the birds about something dangerous that might have been lying ahead."

"I don't know what it was but I just didn't want to take chances when I know better."

"As the saying is, we don't want to lose what we have got in trying to find that which we have not had," said Asse'ged.

Abraham could see the changes in his family's faces—from shocked to somber and now to relaxed. They realized some higher personality may be trying to save him from danger. They were glad he had to stay clear of it.

"You know, something just occurred to me," said Abraham, looking away, his eyes narrowed.

Everybody was hushed.

"I had meant to bring my gun and had forgotten. I wonder if those birds were trying to remind me about it. It's the only formidable weapon I have for self-defense against some dangerous animal or a *shifta*"

"That may well be it," said Asse'ged confidently. "Your guardian angel must have been trying to warn you not to take such a long trip in unknown land without some sort of protection."

"Even a shifta would think twice if he saw you had a gun at your side," said Teferra.

Satisfied by this interpretation of the birds' mysterious chattering, the two older children got up to leave with their wives saying they would come back the next day to send him off once more. Abraham discouraged them, saying he planned to leave at the break of dawn to cover more ground before the sun heated up. Damtew went out without telling anyone where he was going. The women got busy with their work.

Abraham took his pistol from the wooden box where he kept it with his clothes and the coin box. He polished and oiled it and loaded six rounds of shots in its cartridge. He counted another seven bullets and placed them in the bandolier that would be strapped around his waist along with the gun in the holster. As he was engaged in this activity, he kept thinking of the birds' chattering. More and more he became convinced that his family angel was trying to protect him and he was grateful.

FORTY-FIVE

The following morning, Abraham rose before dawn to make another attempt at his journey to look for his long lost father. Ayénat rose too and prepared him freshly cooked shiro wat with injera for breakfast. Damtew harnessed Dama, hung the bag of dabo kolo from the pommel and had the horse waiting outside.

After a quick breakfast, Abraham strapped his holster on his waist and slung the bandolier with the bullets over his shoulder. He kissed his family goodbye and mounted his horse and left. There was a metallic glow around the horizon over the eastern peaks. The valley bottom was still dark but not prohibitively so.

The birds twittered and chirped—a full chorus of them, welcoming the new day. Abraham kept his ears cocked, trying to recognize any of the doomsayers of yesterday as he proceeded along the wooded path near his home, but there were too many mixed up songs for him to pick out the bad omen birds. He nevertheless was relieved once he cleared the woods and left the birds behind.

By the time he reached Timbil, the dense forest at the south edge of the valley, the sun had risen, washing the treetops and mountain flanks with thin golden light. The air was cool and invigorating.

Abraham was glad to arrive at the forest when visibility was good. In this forest, too, were a great number of birds chirping and twittering. As he rode along and the sun rose higher in the sky, there were fewer birds but he could hear more and more of the portents. Hidden in thickly leafed trees and bushes, these black and grey birds tweeted and cheeped sad and disturbing notes.

"No matter what you tell me, I am not going to return home this time!" he said to them.

The journey was not without surprises. Dama's hoof beats and occasional snorts sent a wild boar charging away from the side of their path, causing the horse to rear, nearly throwing Abraham. Farther down the path, a pair of grazing antelopes flew off when they saw them, again startling the horse.

Occasionally, Abraham heard other animals run off through the dry leaves. Each time the horse would jerk to a halt, ears pointed and stiff like a pair of horns. Meanwhile, the portent birds kept up their heckling.

If only those damn birds would stop, thought Abraham, increasingly annoyed. "I have my gun this time and I will defend myself till death, so stop bothering me," he shouted at them.

As the birds' calls multiplied, he began to wonder if the sounds were in his head or if there really were that many birds out there determined to torment him. The one that annoyed him the most was a white-tailed, gray-feathered pest that kept flying back and forth across his path, relentlessly, as if trying to physically block his passage.

Eventually he lost patience. *I need to be rid of you once and for all,* he decided as he stopped his horse and dismounted. He tethered the horse to a young koma tree and went looking for his tormenter.

He had last seen the bird perched on the bough of a broad-leaved tree a few yards away from the path. When he returned to look for it, the bird flew to a gottem tree across from a gaping ravine, burying itself in the tree's thick olive green leaves. Although mostly hidden in the leaves, the bird kept sounding its calls. Abraham thought it must be mocking him. He walked on, looking for a way to cross the ravine. A few feet farther on he saw an uprooted fallen tree that had fallen across the chasm. He gingerly crept along the trunk to the other side, then whipped out his gun and paced quietly toward the gottem tree.

With its head covered in the leaves and its tail flashing, the bird continued its chattering of bad things to come. Abraham inched his way closer, treading softly on the dried leaves that blanketed the forest floor. When he was in close range, he aimed at the bird's white tail and pulled the trigger. A branch splintered in half, and leaves rained down. Abraham scuttled to the foot of the tree, hoping to find his dead enemy, but he found no bird, dead or injured.

Cursing his failed shot and wasted bullet, he made his way back over the ravine and stomped up to the tethered horse. Clearly frightened, Dama reared and pulled at the lead, forcing Abraham to tone down his anger. He patted and crooned kind words to the horse until he relaxed and stood calmly as Abraham climbed back in the saddle.

For awhile, everything was tranquil and Abraham didn't hear birds. Hoping his gun blast scared them away, he relaxed and prepared to enjoy his ride.

His sense of peace didn't last long. Shortly after he began riding, the same bird reappeared, resuming its chatter of doom. Soon several others joined in and before long, every tree and bush seemed to harbor portents of evil things to come.

As if to compound his distress, a pair of crows suddenly appeared on the left side of the road. *These are real messengers of death, aren't they?* he said to himself.

"This is it!" he shouted. He dismounted Dama and led him away from the chattering birds and the crows, back in the direction they had come from. He hitched him to a tree once again and returned to the path, bringing with him not only his gun but also the bandolier with the extra bullets.

The crows were hopping around, snatching meat from a carcass of a small animal they had found by a cluster of abalo bushes. With his finger on the trigger, Abraham walked surreptitiously toward them. He took cover behind a big oak tree, aimed and shot, hitting and killing one of the crows.

With a mixture of satisfaction and anger, he went around the forest looking for his tormenters, shooting randomly at every bird he spotted. He ran from tree to tree, bush to bush, shooting again and again but not managing to hit another bird. When he finished the bullets in the chamber, he reloaded another set of six.

The birds flew from tree to tree ahead of him, mocking his futile efforts with their incessant chatter until finally, exhausted, sweaty and angry at himself, Abraham conceded defeat.

He staggered back to his horse and crumpled onto the trunk of a fallen tree. In his present state of mind, he knew he couldn't go on. He hadn't the physical or emotional energy to continue to battle the birds, at least not on that day. Abraham rose wobbly to his feet and headed to his horse. To his shocking discovery Dama was gone, spooked he thought by the bizarre behavior his master had displayed. A piece of the broken lead was attached to the tree where Abraham had tethered the horse. Abraham sat on a stone under the tree. The thought of walking home defeated was overpowering. He was stuck, unable to go forward, unwilling to go back. He sighed deeply and buried his head in his hands. It seemed to Abraham there was something or somebody that kept interfering with his attempts to do something on behalf of his father. He wished he knew what or who that was.

He could walk the hour-long distance to his home once he had recovered from his present anger and disillusionment.

While he went on his killing rampage, he liked the large warka tree under which he stood as he pointed and shot at the birds. While here, even in his madness, he remembered how church-like the tree was. Its giant trunk, its long and stout limbs, its thick and drooping leaves, and its cool and enveloping serenity were inviting. Abraham decided to retreat under this tree and think through what had just happened to him.

He rose and made his way back to the great warka tree. He needed to rest, to calm himself, to think things through about his madness, but his aching head and chaotic emotions clouded his ability to focus on anything but his overwhelming sense of failure. The possibility that he would ever complete this trip and find his father and learn about the whereabouts of the coin seemed to be, once and for all, beyond his grasp. Strange thoughts began to play in his head. 'What does this journey matter?' 'Why do I matter?' he asked himself. He didn't have a good answer. Increasingly, he believed there was no good answer. All the anger and frustration of his earlier years he had toward his parents' old neighbors suddenly surged through his head and blanketed him.

A dead and decaying tree lay on the path nearby. Its wood was rotten and crumbled, its bare branches covered with moss. Abraham pictured his own body, lifeless like this tree. Unlike the tree, however, he wouldn't have the luxury of surviving even one night before the hyenas and leopard made a feast out of him.

He spread his gabi under the warka tree and sat down. He set aside his gun belt and bandolier, pulled out the gun and opened the cylinder to see how many rounds he had left. He lost track of the number of bullets he had spent, chasing after the birds.

It was empty.

He removed the one remaining bullet from the bandolier and inserted it into the chamber. He held the gun in his right hand. It felt cold, heavy and powerful.

He raised the gun and brought the muzzle to his lips. He smelled metal tinged with body odor.

He opened his mouth and inserted the metal tip into it. He closed his eyes and counted to three: one . . . two . . . three . . . He pulled the trigger.

To his dismay nothing happened. He pulled the curved metal trigger again. And again. Nothing.

He opened his eyes. Unlocking the cylinder, he took the bullet out and shook it. It had powder. The trigger mechanism seemed fine. Baffled, he put the bullet back into the chamber, closed and locked it.

He heard a noise and looked up. He couldn't believe his eyes. His tormenter was back, perched above him in the warka tree. The bird began twittering and flashing its tail, ridiculing him. "I cannot believe this," said Abraham. Without thinking, he rose, lifted his gun, aimed and fired. The blast was deafening. Shocking. He saw a cloud of feathers, then spattered blood on dried brown leaves and fragments of the dead bird.

He was stunned. "How did this happen? My last bullet, the one meant for me, ends up taking the life of my enemy? "Who can explain this mystery?"

He returned to his berth and sat. His senses came back. He felt alive and triumphant. Now maybe he could even move forward with his mission, another time since his horse was gone, no doubt already safely at home. He needed to go home too, but first he needed to rest. He closed his eyes. The birds were singing happy notes now. The leaves rustled in the wind. He was at peace.

DESTA COULDN'T BELIEVE HIS EYES. After he returned from checking on the animals, he found Dama grazing with the other horses and cattle, still fitted with his saddle, reins and dabo kolo sacks. Abraham was nowhere to be seen.

Desta slowly approached the steed, keeping his eyes on the image he thought might be an hallucination. But he was not hallucinating. His father's horse was here, unaccompanied by his master.

He ran for home to see if his father might be there. But if he had come back, why would he leave Dama with his saddle on? It didn't make sense.

"Is Baba here?" he called when he saw Ayénat outside the house.

"Do you think he would have flown over and back from Lalibela in one day?

Horses are not airplanes, you know," said Ayénat, puzzled by Desta's anxious look.

"Well, Dama is here—with everything on him still. I found him with the other animals."

Ayénat jerked her chin toward her chest in surprise. "What?"

"Yeah, Dama is here . . . with everything on him."

Ayenat's hand flew to her chest. "I wonder if he fell off and is need of help somewhere along the road. Go tell Asse'ged. I will send Melkam to Yihoon."

Desta took off at a sprint toward Asse'ged's house.

"Where did you say Dama is?" shouted Ayénat after him.

"In the field with the rest of the animals," Desta shouted back, still running.

Ayénat was standing in the field by the horse when Desta, Asse'ged, Damtew, Yihoon and Melkam arrived.

Kooli was with them. They looked at the horse and each other, mystified. Asse'ged grabbed Dama by the reins and hastily looked through Abraham's supplies. The extra clothes, the gifts and the dabo kolo were still there, intact.

"He must have been thrown off the horse and hurt himself," said Yihoon.

Asse'ged pulled the horse. "Dama is one of the most docile horses you could ever ride. I don't think he threw him, although I suppose he may have fallen off accidentally." He checked to see if there were any scrape marks on the animal's body.

"What else could have happen to him? It's not as if he had enemies waiting to ambush him. Everybody loves him here," reasoned Yihoon.

"Regardless, we need to find out," said Ayénat, turning to Damtew. "He should not be far because they left not too long ago."

"Let's go," said Asse'ged.

"Go and stay at home, in case he comes," said Ayénat, turning to Melkam.

Everyone went except Desta. He had to stay behind to attend to the animals. Kooli trotted behind the group.

As if searching for a stolen cow, they kept their eyes on the horse's tracks. Occasionally one of them left the trail to check around the bushes or big trees. As luck would have it, there were no other horse hoof tracks going north, although there were quite a few going the other way.

The longer the family walked with no trace of Abraham, the more somber they became.

"Really, I had my misgivings about Baba making this trip alone," said Yihoon. "Those birds warned him yesterday. It seems he didn't even have to leave the valley before something happened to him."

"This is not his first trip out of the valley, for chrissake!" blurted Asse'ged. "What should happen to him?"

"It's not that," said Ayénat. "I just think there's something strange associated with your grandfather and that coin. He vanished without a trace. The coin was stolen by those horrible neighbors, so we think. Now a simple attempt to look for him is met with trouble from the start."

"We really don't know what happened to him. We shouldn't jump to conclusions," said Asse'ged calmly.

"No matter, it's still trouble!" cried Ayénat. "The horse came home and your father didn't!"

Part way through the Timbil forest, they lost the horse's tracks. The hoof marks went off the road into the forest and disappeared in the leafy floor. Try as they might, they couldn't pick up the trail. The forest floor was too covered with dead leaves for the hoof prints to show.

"What do you think happened here?" said Yihoon, at a loss.

"It seems to me the horse must have turned around from here because there are tracks going the other direction," said Asse'ged.

"What happened to your father then?" said Ayénat.

"That is the question, what happened to him?" said Asse'ged loudly.

"Do you think there is some foul play here?" said Ayénat, turning to Damtew

"I doubt it, Ma. . . . We can't be sure, of course," said Damtew.

"If the horse returned from here, let's see how he got back on the road," said Asse'ged going off by himself. He saw faded track marks going into the woods and followed them.

The hoof marks led to a tree where Asse'ged concluded the horse must have been tethered, judging from the trampled ground and undergrowth. When he closely inspected the ground, he found tracks going back to the road. It seemed to him that the horse had been led outside the path for some time before it got back on the road father down.

Happy with his discovery, Asse'ged motioned for the others to join him. Once again, they followed the tracks.

WHEN ABRAHAM WOKE, he found Kooli breathing down on his face, licking his cheeks. "Get away, get away," he said, pushing the dog aside. Kooli's whimpered, wagged his tail, waiting for the rest of the search team.

"Kooli sounds like he's found something," said Asse'ged. He looked off in the direction of the dog's whimpering.

"God help us," said Ayénat right behind her son.

Asse'ged saw his father first. He rushed to his side. "What are you doing in here, Baba? Are you alright?"

"Well, I am still alive if that is what you mean."

"What happened to you?"

Ayénat, Damtew and Yihoon pushed past Asse'ged, encircling the father in a lunar arc.

"Are you alright?" Ayénat asked, her voice shaking.

"I had a battle with the birds and I lost," said Abraham in a defeated voice, his eyes fixed on the ground near his feet.

"How did you get in a fight with the birds? This is sheer insanity!" said Ayénat as she sat by him.

"They got in my way. They kept pestering me, torturing me with their forecast of doom. I decided to silence them once and for all." He nodded at his gun, lying by his side. "In the end, used nearly all my bullets and didn't get anything but a damn crow."

"Mama, is right, this is insanity. What is happening, Baba?" said Asse'ged, kneeling down, his eyes boring into his father's.

"How is it that a person of your stature would get in a fight with air! That is what they are, air," said Yihoon.

"I can't tell you why, but I did it," said Abraham gravely, placing the gun in its case.

"Let's go home now. We are just glad nothing bad happened to you," said Ayénat as she helped him with his gabi.

"The real insanity was my leaving home in the hope of tracking down a man that was lost to me for over forty years. The birds were only trying to warn me what may lay ahead, what I may not find. But you are right, it was insane. What's worse I nearly shot myself too, out of desperation. I guess God must have wanted me to hang around for awhile longer because that bullet didn't fire.

"What!! Babaaa!!" cried Asse'ged.

Ayénat held her hand over her mouth and stared at him. The others looked at him with their mouths half open.

"You went to that extreme?!" said Yihoon.

Abraham nodded. "I pointed the muzzle right into my mouth and pulled the trigger—not once, three times. Nothing happened. Zilch. I took out the bullet and reloaded it. Tell me if this is not a divine intervention—the bird that had tormented me all along my journey, the cause of my madness, came and perched right there on this branch above us. I aimed, pulled the trigger and bam; I pulverized the demon with the same bullet I had tried to use on myself."

"Did you feel better afterwards?" said Asse'ged.

"Mighty better. I calmed down and took a nap." He shrugged and stroked his speckled goatee. "I suppose part of my madness was my pride. I won medals for my warfront deeds. Now I couldn't bring down even one little bird in twelve shots.

"This is not you!" cried Yihoon. "You are the one who counsels people, who gets people away from this kind of hot-headed, impulsive behavior."

"I think partly I felt cursed too. Why was I denied my father, first as a youngster, now as an adult. What have I done to deserve this kind of treatment?"

"Nobody knows but the Almighty," said Ayénat. "We're just glad you are well. Let's go home." She picked up the bandolier and the gun and handed them to Damtew. Asse'ged and Yihoon helped Abraham up.

The warrior, stiff and tentative at first, stood erect and walked at his normal gait once they got onto the main road.

FORTY-SIX

After Abraham returned from his aborted trip, he slept every day until noon, avoided contact with outsiders and even his own children who lived outside the home. He ate little and talked little. Occasionally he thought about making another attempt at the journey, although in his current state of depression, the very idea of trying again was exhausting.

If he did decide to make the trip, he would do so without any announcement to the family members. That way if he failed again, nobody would know.

Ayénat was deeply distressed by her husband's condition. She prayed every night and talked to priests who might know a treatment for his woe. Other family members also said prayers for Abraham and brought foods they thought would be of help to him and left them with Ayénat.

Desta was perhaps the saddest of all. Immediately after his father left the first time, he had gone into his daydreaming mode. From the fragments of information his father had shared about his grandfather, he had created the whole person in his mind, complete with a long flowing beard, big eyes, and perfect figure. In his mind, his grandfather was tall and handsome like his father, the only major difference between the two men being their ages. He imagined the old man living in a hut by the church, waiting for his son or grandchildren to come and get him.

From the day his father departed on his journey, Desta had been counting the days until he would meet his grandfather. Now the dream was shattered. He would grow up and get old and die without ever meeting him. This fact depressed him. It was the same feeling he'd had when Hibist was about to get married, after Kooli was shot and after the vervet monkeys left. Those feelings were nothing compared to this. This one was final forever and ever. Now he could never dream of meeting his grandfather—ever. The others, he had known and spent quality time with. Their memories would stay with him for as long as he lived.

It was mid-May now. There had been showers recently and the valley was
once again veiled with a film of green. It was mid-afternoon. A warm but gentle
sun had flooded the valley. A soft breeze was rustling the sholla leaves. The
figs in it were long gone, shared between humans—mostly Desta—and the
birds. He was hungry and wished the sholla still had some figs. There were still
a few hours left before he could go home with the animals and get something to
eat. But these days he wished he didn't have to go home and see his father the
way he had been since that day they had found him in the forest. He closed his
eyes and wished he could do something to help his father out of his sadness and
depression.

It was at this very instant when he heard a voice say, "Maybe you can!" He
opened his eyes and looked around.

There he was! The cloud man! He was as completely visible as when he saw
him the first time by the river with the Deb'tera Tayé—brown with a golden tint
to his cloud-like consistency but with a human form. Desta stood up, terrified
to see him again. This time alone, out in the open. He made a motion to run.

"Don't be afraid. You will not be harmed," said the man. "I am here to solve
your family's problem. You have been chosen as the medium to communicate
what you are about to find out. This should end the agony all of you have been
going through." He spoke softly, his voice like soothing and beautiful music.

Desta became more and more tranquilized by the man's presence and voice.
He wanted to hear what the man had to say.

"Come, follow me," said the cloud man, motioning to him with a hand that
had no flesh or bones, just a form stippled with small dots and tinged with gold.

Desta hesitated.

"Come, come . . . don't you trust me? Have I ever failed you?"

Desta thought about that last question. It was true the man had not failed him
with the prediction he made for Saba.

With hesitant steps he followed the man. All the while, he kept looking
around to see if there was anybody to see where the man was leading him. They
crossed the field, stopping at the exact location where he had found Habté,
Damtew's killed goat.

"This is strange," Desta thought, his mind flooded by the memory of the
goat and the nightmare he had gone through its death. When the man began to
walk, he remained behind, near the spot where he had found the goat.

"What's the matter? Are you not coming?" said the man, glancing back.

"I don't know where you are taking me," mumbled Desta.

"I know what has triggered this sudden fear. For your information, that goat was not killed by an animal. He was sacrificed. But it was all for good."

Desta stood his ground. This additional piece of information was something he didn't understand and didn't want to understand.

"Do follow me. What I will share with you will bring an end to your father's problem and will explain the reason for Saba and her family's move. Do know that you and only you are the privileged to hear this information. It's important you come with me. I assure you the animals will be safe in your absence." The man gazed at Desta with the gentlest of countenances.

Desta stared back at him, unable to move. Was he really the Saytan, as his mother had once said? Was this how he seduced people, by being kind and sweet and luring them to follow him, only to trap them in his hole and kill them? But he had never heard of Saytans killing people. They possessed them and made them do all kinds of crazy things, but they didn't kill them. Was that what would happen to him? Was this man going to possess him and make him act crazy? These thoughts caused his knees to tremble.

The man smiled sweetly, as if trying to give Desta every reason not to fear him. "I will be blunt, Desta. I am here to introduce you to your grandfather."

This information sent a shockwave through Desta's body. The hair on the back of his neck prickled up like porcupine needles and his spine tingled. His palms and forehead turned hot and sweaty, his heart pounded like a hammer. *Was this man saying he could make Desta's grandfather, who was supposed to be living in Lalibela, turn up here, in their back woods?* This suggestion made him doubly suspicious. Now he was using his grandfather to lure him away, knowing how much he has wanted to see him.

Desta stared at the ground, but he felt the man's eyes still on him, waiting.

"This is very, very important, Desta. I command you to come."

If his grandfather indeed was here, he needed to find that out—at any cost. He needed to locate his grandfather and bring the good news home promptly. His father would be so happy and he would recover from his depression immediately, and everybody else would be thrilled. Desta, of course, would be in the ninth heaven. Not only would he meet his grandfather, he would be the one to find him for his father.

As these thoughts played out in his mind, his fear of the man dissipated. He moved forward indicating he was now willing to accept the man's invitation.

"Why have you kept him from us all this time?"

"I didn't keep him," said the man. "Circumstance did."

They walked along an animal track, crossed the southern creek and ended up at the bottom of Saba's old property. The park-like place was dotted with acacia trees. Desta remembered it well. This was where Saba's family had kept their cattle. Back then the grass had been low from continuous grazing but now, untouched, it had grown tall, almost knee high. He had roamed the area with Astair and remembered how they used to get thorns in their feet. He picked his way carefully now through the tall dry grass. If he were to step on a thorn today he would have no way of removing it since he had given his safety pin to his father as a gift for his grandfather.

"I know exactly what is going on in your head," said the man, looking back. "Don't be afraid, I will lead you through the parts of the earth where there are no thorns."

Desta was amazed. *How in the world did he know what was going on my head, just now,* he wondered.

As they strode, Desta grew anxious. Everything was happening so quickly he didn't know what he would say when he met his grandfather or how he would tell if it was really him. He wished his father were there to make everything more comfortable.

He was sure that his grandfather would be much happier to see his own son than his grandson.

It felt like a long walk just to cross the field. The place was peaceful. The shadows from the acacia tress stretched eastward, sharply silhouetted against the seared gold grass.

Ahead of him, the man moved like a cloud. The brown dots stayed in place as if they were glued to an invisible body. He still had a faded golden glow around him. He seemed to glide more than walk, his feet barely touching the earth.

To Desta it felt like a dream. But this was not a dream. He was not sleeping. Nobody was going to wake him, and the scene wasn't going to suddenly change.

At first he thought they were going to cross the entire stretch of field, but once they got to the center of it, near a beautiful canopying acacia tree, the man turned due east and walked toward the place where the creek met another stream that came from the southern side of the property.

He stopped and turned to Desta, saying, "We are here. Your grandfather is behind the tall grass and cattail bushes, down in the ravine. You cannot meet him just yet."

Desta looked to the place the man had indicated, baffled. *Why would his grandfather be hiding all those years behind that grass and those bushes? The rain, the sun, the cold, food, water . . . how did he manage? Or did he recently bring him from Lalibela?*

"I want you to fix in your mind the location of this spot: this very spot! Here on my right is a dead gottem tree. On my left are these kaga bushes. This place is directly opposite from the center of the field by that acacia tree. Here in the east, directly across from where we stand, is the big warka tree on the bank of Davola where we first met.

Desta remembered the tree. There it was.

"You'll not forget it when you come back with your family, will you?" asked the man speaking once again in his kind voice.

Desta looked around at all the landmarks and said that he wouldn't forget.

"If you do, we can be here to give you some assistance but we want this to be completely your own natural way of handling things. I know you want to meet your grandfather, but we prefer you meet him together with all your family. It's better that way."

Desta tried hard not to show his disappointment. How was he going to convince the whole family to come here to meet their grandfather, who according to the cloud man, was hiding in the bushes? It was a crazy notion. As everyone knew their grandfather had vanished some forty years ago from a place one hundred miles from here and he was now supposed to be in Lalibela. *Why would they believe he had suddenly turned up right in their backyard?!*

The man remained at the rim of the ravine staring at Desta as if allowing him time to process his thoughts. At length he said, "Now let's go back to the tree where you were."

Desta followed.

"This time I want to show you a safer route for the group. We will go along the perimeter of the property and cross the creek. This will be a less complicated and thorn-free path," he said as they walked.

Desta was still uncertain about the whole idea. How could he persuade his brothers and the rest of the family to come back here with him without any tangible proof?

By the time they reached the sholla tree, the sun had declined in the west and the shadow of the mountain had begun to form at the bottom of the cattle grazing field. To Desta's amazement, the animals were exactly where he had left them.

At the suggestion of the cloud man, Desta perched on his stone slab under the tree. The man sat on the ground next to him, now appearing like a pile of cloud with his head poking out from the center, just the way he first saw him by the river. The man's feet and hands vanished in his amorphous mass. "I will tell you the full story about your grandfather and other important things in a few minutes," he began to say. "I want you to listen carefully and share this exact information, as much of it as you can recall, at different times if you have to. Give an abbreviated version when your family gathers at the site I just took you to."

As the man spoke, Desta could only see his physiognomy and the outline of his facial features. His mouth moved, his eyelashes flapped and his brows slid up and down with the twitch of his forehead, as he had a habit of doing when he talked. His eyes didn't have the white but just a small black dot in the middle that projected out—eyeballs transmuted into cones.

Desta looked at the man intensely, his heart racing. His whole attention, his whole being, was concentrated on the information he was about to receive.

"First, I must caution you," said the man, glancing at Desta. "I am going to tell you some things you are not going to like. Since we have come this far, you need to know the whole story and the rest of your family needs to know it as well. You are very young but you have the mental capacity and maturity to handle what I am going to share with you."

Desta pulled his feet together and hugged his knees, anxiously looking at the man. The waiting was killing him.

"Are you ready?"

"Yes, I am," said Desta after a deep sigh.

"Bad people did bad things to your grandfather. He is no longer alive."

Desta gasped and covered his mouth.

"The bad people were his wife's relatives—cousins. They had stolen a very, very important item from him, something that belongs to the family line, that had come down through hundreds of generations, something that has the power to bring great fortune to the one who possesses it and help him become a better person. As your father will remember, from stories he has heard, this item is one of two proofs that the skeletal remains your family will find are indeed your grandfather's." Desta looked away, dazed and saddened.

"Is the item the gold coin?" asked the boy, sharply turning and uncovering his mouth.

"Yes. Did your father tell you?"

"He used to talk about it. . . . But he still has the old coin box."

"So to give the background, as your grandfather prepared to pass the coin on to the next generation—to your father on his seventh birthday—he discovered that the family treasure was missing from its box. Then your father's oldest sister, Zere, having heard an excited account about a coin from the daughter of her mother's cousin, told him who might have it. The girl had no idea where it had come from but told Zere how beautiful and unique it was and how carefully her father guarded it.

"Your grandparents had always known that this man, Adamu, was a jealous and greedy man. He had always struggled to accumulate wealth but none came to him. He saw how easily wealth and good fortune came to your grandparents and was very envious. He had heard about the reason for their success—the gold coin. So he came to your grandparents' home under the pretext of working for them. While he stayed at their home, somehow he managed to find the special box, take out the coin and abscond with it.

Desta kept his gaze on the man, hanging onto every word he uttered.

"When your grandfather learned of the location of the coin," he continued. "He secretly bribed the thief's daughter to help him retrieve the family treasure. To keep his mission completely secret, he didn't even tell his wife that he was going after it. Five days before your father's birthday, your grandfather made the day's journey from Kuakura to Avinevra. When he left home, he told everyone he was going to the town of Dangila to get something very special for the birthday boy.

"As soon as your grandfather arrived at Adamu's home, he traded a silver necklace, the bribe, for the precious family item. They had hoped to do this before Adamu came home from work but as luck would have it, he walked in on them shortly after they exchanged. Surprised to see your grandfather at his home without invitation, Adamu became nervous and uneasy. This made your grandfather nervous and uneasy too. After a brief visit with Adamu and his wife, your grandfather insisted that he had to leave and could not be persuaded to spend the night. This made Adamu suspicious, and he went to check on the presence of the coin. Finding it was missing, he immediately recruited

the assistance of his younger brother, Kindé and went in hot pursuit of your
grandfather.

Desta held his breath, as if to ensure that he didn't miss a single word or
fragment of the unfolding story.

"When your grandfather realized he was being pursued, he began to run.
Adamu and Kindé ran too. If they caught him, it was going to be a two-against-
one battle and your grandfather was sure to lose. The best he could do was to
try to elude them. Instead of using the main thoroughfare, he took a smaller
path, which turned out to be a cattle track. Unfortunately, his pursuers saw
him and followed. He had crossed the Davola and kept running south along
the river. When he saw they were right behind him, he turned into the woods.
They caught up with him there. He knew he had no chance of keeping the coin
in his possession. Out of desperation, he placed it in his mouth and swallowed
it, nearly choking to death by the act. The enemies, in horror, saw what he did.
Your grandfather mounted a big defense. He punched, kicked and bloodied his
enemies but he was finally overwhelmed by their relentless attacks and he died.
After they killed him, they ran into a logistical problem. They had no sharp
object to cut open his stomach. Besides, it was dark in the woods by now, and
the operation was going to be a messy one. They threw him into the ravine I
just showed you and left him there until daybreak when they could return with
a knife.

The boy exhaled. Thoughtful and crestfallen, eyes gazing at the man, he
shook his head slowly. He couldn't believe those men could commit such cruel
acts on his grandfather. That he now could never dream of meeting his father's
dad was heart-wrenching. He held back his emotions.

"I know," said the cloud man, noticing the boy's forlorn countenance.
"To continue with the story," he went on. "Although your grandfather was
organically dead, spiritually he was still alive. His spirit then had to wait
around, not only until the body could be buried, but also in this case, until that
coin was safely returned to the family.

"The next day the killers came back with their knives, looking for the body.
They searched and searched, yet they couldn't find it. The body had completely
disappeared without a trace. They couldn't see the trampled grass and foliage
where they had fought and there was no blood or any other telltale mark of
the macabre act they had committed the night before. You see, the spirit had
disoriented them and had masked the body and the place where the fight

occurred.

"Later, when Adamu and Kindé learned that your grandfather's family was distraught, they went to Kuakura and joined the search team. Your grandfather had not told the family where he was going, or why, so there was no way they could be implicated."

Desta felt as if his head was about to collapse under the weight of the sad story. He brought his folded legs together and propped his chin on his knees. And he continued listening attentively to the cloud man's revelations.

"The irony of it was," the man continued, "that your grandmother fled from the good country of Kuakura, trying to distance herself and her family from the people she believed had caused her husband's disappearance. But the harm was actually done by her cousins, here in this valley, where she and her children came to live."

The cloud man stopped, after noticing Desta's cheerless face. "I am sorry to be the bearer of sad news," he said, his eyes holding Desta. "Only you have been chosen as recipient of it, for reasons I don't know."

"I am just sorry for Baba. Now he will never get to see his father, and I will never meet my grandfather."

"It all has to do with destiny, son. Destiny . . . Both you and your father have to be strong enough to accept things as they unfold.

"Let me continue. As for the spirit of your grandfather, it hung around the valley protecting the remains and the gold coin. It had to wait until the time was right and the right child was born to your family before it devised a method by which to reveal itself and to try to replace the treasure in their hands."

Desta stared at the cloud man questioningly, mystified by this new disclosure.

"That is right. The spirit felt that the previous children of your family didn't possess the strength of character, persistence and tenacity to survive the challenges and hardships that may lie ahead for the chosen individual. There is a predetermined mission to be accomplished involving the coin. It had to be placed in the right hands.

"The coin I have been referring to will be revealed when the family is gathered together. It is roughly two thousand eight hundred years old and is one of two identical coins, the only two of their kind in the world.

"The sister coin is located very far away, in a completely different world. For the first time since their creation, they will meet in the lifetimes of the individuals possessing them. When they come together and rest side by side, it will be a very thrilling time for the two individuals because they will witness an event that has never happened in the lives of humans. Did you follow all that?"

"Yes, most of it."

"I know there are a lot of details to remember but they will come to you as you share the information with your family," said the cloud man kindly. "Now do you have any questions for me?"

Desta had not thought there would be an opportunity to ask questions. "I know you told me when we first met; you knew my problems, one of which was finding someone who would take me to the top of the mountain so I can touch the sky. Can you help me?"

"You just have to be a little more patient. In time, it will happen."

"Do you think I could ever meet the spirit of my grandfather?" Desta asked in a low voice, looking at the man squarely.

"Well, well, I think we can arrange that," said the man grinning widely. His teeth were merely outlines, as were his lips and the rest his physique. He paused and looked around, grinning at Desta again. "You might have not heard me clearly earlier, but to speak in plain language, I must say that I am happy to meet my grandson finally, in person!"

Desta was confused at first. Then he reprocessed the words and blurted out, "You are my grandfather!"

"Yes. I feel honored and privileged to meet my grandson openly."

"Wow, I am so happy to meet you too! I can't wait to tell Baba. Can you come home with me so Baba and the rest of the family can meet you too?"

"No, I can't be in human dimension anymore. My body is long lost. I revealed myself to the person of my choice as a messenger of the information I just shared with you: I want my remains gathered and buried and the coin retrieved and placed in the family's possession once again. Then, I can go to my permanent home in heaven."

"Baba has waited so long to see you. He has suffered so much. He kept you in his memory by getting a dog he named Kooli. What an incredible gift it would be for him to see you, even just for a brief moment."

"No, son, he will just have to continue keeping me in his memory. I cannot be revealed to anyone else, but to the chosen one. As for your father, he will be happy once the remains are retrieved and buried, I can guarantee you."

"You know he nearly killed himself a few days ago when his attempt to go and look for you was foiled by the birds."

"I know. That was very foolish, I must say. I was there, watched his behavior. The birds were my messengers. I jammed the gun when he turned it on himself and placed the bird in front of him later to give him his small victory. Like I said, everything will be all right by him once he has closure."

Desta was disappointed. At the same time, he felt a sudden urge to flee. He wanted to go home and tell his father what had happened.

"Are we done? I just can't wait to go and tell Baba I met his father," said Desta, his face glowing with excitement.

"Yes, he and the rest of the family need to know about everything I shared with you. We don't want to burden their hearts with pain any longer."

"One more thing. You need to meet me back here seven days from tomorrow—Sunday—at the same time. Bring the coin box—the one with all those illustrations on it; and fourteen-inch square hard paper, ink, a pen and a narrow and straight horn cup. I have something very important to share with you. The paper has to be hard and durable for longevity. Regular paper won't do. Take it as a challenge. You'll figure it out. You need not discuss this piece of information or any other information you and I discuss in our next meeting. Not necessary. It'll complicate matters. This story is just for you."

Desta touched his lips with his index finger, keeping his eyes planted on the ground. He was puzzled by this request and uncertain where he would get paper harder than the paper his father used. The ink and the writing pen wouldn't be a problem. He could borrow them from Awoke or make them himself. But hard paper? Even regular paper was a luxury.

"Are you okay with this?" asked the man, studying Desta's face.

"I guess . . . I just don't know where I can find something harder than normal paper."

"As I said, you'll figure it out," said the man. "With this I bid you farewell, unless you have any more questions for me."

"No, I have no more questions. I am just so happy to meet my grandpa, finally!" Desta said, trying not to worry about the additional challenge he would be facing.

"I am pleased as well, Desta. I look forward to our next meeting."

FORTY-SEVEN

Desta didn't remember walking when he arrived home after that lengthy private session with the man he first met by the river. His grandfather! It was later in the afternoon and the sun was going home, already just inches from the top of the mountain.

Desta's father, looking disconsolate as usual these days, was lying on the grass a few yards from the house, his great brown eyes downcast and listless. He was a bit better than when he first returned from his ill-fated trip in search of his father, but he still was far from well.

"Baba! Baba! I met your father!" blurted Desta, giddy with excitement.

Abraham gazed at his son incredulously.

"Yes, yes, I did, I did . . . there is proof, too," said Desta, desperately.

"Calm down, calm down . . . What did you just say?"

"I said I just met your father." Desta restrained his excitement.

"Tell me," said Abraham, sitting up. "Did he come flying from Lalibela or was he descended from heaven?"

Ayénat, who was busy gathering dried barley several feet away, had caught a whiff of Desta's bizarre report and had seen his frenzied antics. She dropped what she was doing and walked up to eavesdrop.

"How in heaven did you meet my father?" said Abraham, gazing at his son in disbelief.

"He came to where I was sitting under the sholla tree and took me where the remains of his body are located. Then we came back and he told me a lot of crazy stuff. Wait till you hear it!"

Ayénat drew closer, as a metal to a magnet. She stood behind Desta and listened. "How can you tell me you met my father while at the same time you tell me you have seen where his remains are?" said Abraham, shaking his head.

"Are you possessed by the Saytan again?" asked Ayénat, coming around to look at his face.

"Oh Ma, not Saytan again," said Desta nearly whining. His excitement subsided. Now he felt like he was climbing a mountain. How could he tell his story if she was going to immediately associate him with the Saytan?

"Ma, can you go on with your business? I am talking to Baba."

"I just wanted to know what you were talking about," she said apologetically.

"Go on, Desta. Tell me again what you saw," said Abraham.

"I am not saying anything unless Mama leaves us alone."

"Could you please go?" said the father, motioning Ayénat away with his hand. "I'll tell you the details later."

Ayénat left.

"Do you remember that man, the one I met by the river?" said Desta. "Yes, what about him?"

"He is your father."

Abraham stared at him, shaking his head. "Now I too worry about you."

"No, please, believe me . . . trust me . . . there is convincing proof. You will find out for yourself."

Abraham still looked skeptical. "So the man who appeared to you by the river and again later is the spirit of my father and his body is elsewhere?"

"Exactly! That was your father's spirit we met!"

"How did he come all the way here from Kuakura or wherever else he was last living? Or are you saying he was here when he died?" Abraham's tongue got tangled as an eddy of emotion swirled through him. The remote chance of meeting his father alive was now gone, assuming he could believe his son's fantastic story.

"I'll tell you all about that later. It's a long story. Here is what he told me to tell you. You need to gather all the immediate family so I can take you to where the remains of his body are."

"You have brought me news so hard to believe that I am not sure what the proper way of handling this is. Can you and I go there alone first to see what's what before we get the rest of the family involved? They are all disappointed already with my failed attempt. I don't want them to have another emotional letdown."

"Believe me. There will not be another letdown. You and I cannot go alone. He said the whole family had to see everything at one time. He promised you will see proof that will indisputably show that your father has been here this whole time."

Abraham could not overcome Desta's passionate appeal with any logical analysis of his own. He was completely confounded.

"Let me ask you this," said Desta.

"Yes?"

"Do you think Saba's new baby was an accident or was the man somehow involved in it?"

"I have no reason to say it was an accident, nor have I basis to say the man was not involved, especially when the outcome was so consistent with what he told us would happen."

"Then trust him. Weren't you the one who told me to have faith in him when I had that dreadful dream, the one where Saba was in labor all day and night and everybody was praying, and Asse'ged and Damtew had grabbed me and demanded to know where was my man who had predicted a normal delivery? That had scared me so much. When I told you about it, you said he was trying to test my fidelity."

Abraham smiled. "You have made your points well, son. I'll give you the benefit of my doubts. When can we make the trip to this place?"

"As soon as everybody can come at the same time."

"We'll let everybody know. We can plan it for next Saturday."

"I want Hibist and Enat included also," said Desta.

"We'll do our best," said Abraham, stroking his beard. "Let me ask you something else."

Desta nodded, his mind preoccupied with his father's indefinite answer about Hibist.

"Did that man—I mean my father's spirit—say he will meet with you again?"

"Yes, next Sunday afternoon, but only he and I will meet."

"As you know, I have been waiting very long to meet my father. Can you arrange for me to meet him too?" asked Abraham in a tentative voice.

"That was one of the questions I asked him, but he had said, "No." He said he was only revealed to me for an important reason," said Desta, sadly.

"Maybe you can plead with him when you see him again," said Abraham.

"I'll do my best. I would love for you two to meet."

FORTY-EIGHT

Saturday, six days after the identity of the cloud man was revealed, was chosen as the day when all the immediate family members were to gather and go on a discovery mission of their grandfather's remains. Abraham was anxious and excited. His depression had gradually lifted and he was nearly his former self. Whether it was real bones or an apparition, meeting his long lost father was suddenly within his grasp. Only a week ago he'd had his hopes dashed and had nearly killed himself afterwards, plunging into an emotional downward spiral. Now he even managed to crack a smile once in awhile.

He sent Asse'ged to Hibist and Damtew to Enat to summon them for an emergency family visit. They were to be told something vague about the discovery of their grandfather's remains and an exhumation event.

For the next four days, Desta rehearsed his speech, recollecting as many details as he could. As his grandfather's spirit had said, he needed to make it brief but still cover all the essential points. In his mind, he arranged the order of the main points, then took them apart and reorganized them again and again. He needed to be confident and forceful so nobody would question the authenticity of the information.

THE APPOINTED SATURDAY ARRIVED at last. Hibist arrived with her husband and Enat with hers, after the sun had cleared the eastern mountains. The only sibling who was missing was Tamirat. A message had been sent to him, but nobody knew if he had received it. Desta was very happy to see Hibist and Enat but wished Tamirat were there also. Having trained as a priest, he could have blessed the area before they uncovered their grandfather's remains.

It was early May, about a month before the rainy season would arrive in full force, but sporadic showers had turned the valley moss green and the trees that had shed their leaves during the dry season had sprouted new ones. There was a sense of rejuvenation and revival everywhere.

Slowly the crowd swelled outside Desta's home: Saba with her baby and
husband and two daughters, Teferra, Asse'ged and Damtew with their wives,
Enat and Hibist with their husbands, along with Abraham, Ayénat and Desta.
They were 17 total, anxiously assembled outside to march off to meet their
grandfather's remains.

The sons and their wives were dressed in better than their everyday clothes
but not their white holiday apparel. Abraham wore his brown breeches and
charcoal gray safari jacket, over which he had donned the gabi he ordinarily
wore to church. Ayénat too put on her Sunday clothes, a flowing gown with a
plain neck opening, an older girdle and her older shemma. Desta wore his long
cream-colored shirt with slits in its sides. It was now speckled with dirt. Over it
he wore his gabi. He held his shepherding stick.

Knowing that Desta had met the spirit of their grandfather, some of them
believed they might meet the spirit too. With that in mind, they wanted to look
their best but at the same time show their grief.

This mission was supposed to be strictly for immediate family members and
nobody else was supposed to know about it, so Desta was beside himself when
he saw a man with a white turban walk up to the fence. This was Aba Yacob,
the man who had tried to exorcise the Saytan out of him a couple of years back.
It was the same man who had given him the communion and the mekleft so he
could break the fast afterwards. "Who invited him?" said Desta. It was not hard
to guess. Probably Ayénat, but why? He wished someone would tie the man to a
post and leave him behind.

As he came around the bend of the fence, Ayénat stepped forward and
explained his presence. She wanted him to bless the place where the skeletal
remains were found before anyone tampered with the bones, to drive off any
bad spirits that might be lurking there.

Some of the people nodded their approval; others shook their heads. Desta
vehemently opposed the idea initially, but later when he realized he couldn't do
anything about it, changed his mind. He would feel vindicated when the rash
priest learned the identity of the cloud man he had tried to drive off. Today, he
thought, the priest's ignorance would be put on public display.

ONCE EVERYBODY WAS PRESENT, Abraham stepped forward.

We invited you all here today because, as you know, there appears to
be an important development involving your grandfather—my father, who

was lost to me some forty-plus years ago. It's a strange twist of fate, an incredible turn of events, if indeed what we are about to explore together is true. Despite our understanding of past circumstances regarding his disappearance and subsequent whereabouts, it will be a shock to you, as it has been for me, to learn that your grandfather has been here with us, literally in our backwoods, for those past forty-plus years. This is assuming, I want to qualify this statement again, that what we are about to learn can be linked unequivocally to his identity.

As most of you know by now from past hearsay accounts, he was supposed to have been sighted in Lalibela within two or so years of his vanishing—a very long time ago. Unfortunately, no one made the effort to journey there to verify the claim. I was not yet ten and Baba had no brothers or any other able and close enough relatives who could make the trip.

The reason for his disappearance was believed to be the work of green-eyed neighbors, who were resentful of his wealth and success in life. It was alleged that the perpetrators gave him medicines that caused him to go mad and flee from his own home.

Terrified by the incident, shortly after we lost him, Mother gathered up her cattle, belongings and us children—the oldest wasn't even ten at that time—and came here to settle in this isolated valley.

As I grew up, thoughts of my father never left me. In fact, my sorrow and yearning for him deepened over time. It was right before my seventh birthday when he disappeared and I was just getting to spend time with him, father-son time, when he suddenly vanished. Since there were no other boys of my age around—we lived on a large, secluded estate—he was, before his disappearance, essentially my only companion.

Abraham clenched his teeth and tightened his lips to rein in the emotion that threatened to well up from within him.

I bottled up the loss of my father for many years, at first in obedience to my mother who considered it disgraceful for people to know that our father had abandoned us. Later, when I got married and had children, I thought it pointless to discuss a man I had long lost. But privately I kept my connection with him through tokens that had once linked us together. I named every dog we got "Kooli," because the first dog we had in the house while Father was with us was called Kooli. I tried to do everything in sevens, because my Baba always was superstitious about the number

seven. I have kept his beautiful silk scarf, green gabardine jacket and
all his horse-riding gear, things like that. Most of you don't even know
some of these things because I have kept them hidden away, but my older
sisters and I remember what our father was like.

Saba's baby began to cry. Abraham stopped until the baby was quiet. Saba
began nursing him and tapped him on his back.

When I grew older and became physically and mentally able to make
the journey, the circumstances of his disappearance, the conflicting
stories we heard about his whereabouts, and the idea of leaving Mother
alone deterred me from making the journey. Yet, as the days added to
days, months to months and years to years, my hankering for finding
him increased until it became my passion, my quest, not to finish my life
without finding what really happened to him.

To give you a feel as to the kind of person he was, from the few
things I remember and the accounts given by family and friends, he
was a remarkable personality, a loving, kind and generous man, who
never said "no" to a person in need—whether financially, personally or
otherwise. My older sisters, who remember him better than I do, have
great stories to tell about Baba. Besides his humane qualities, he was
an accomplished artist, horseman, winning many races at annual church
holiday competitions, a great field hockey player during his youth; he was
a successful businessman, and a man of unparalleled honesty, integrity
and civic responsibility.

It's often said you think of your parents when you have your own
children. Over the years, I have also thought how wonderful it would be
for you all to have met him and for him to know his grandchildren, and
even Saba's baby, his great grandson. I must admit, Desta has been a
major factor for bringing out those feelings, and it looks as if he may be
the key for our potential discovery of him today."

Abraham paused for a few seconds and looked down on Desta, who
presently was standing with Hibist in front of him. The father continued.

It was for these and other personal reasons that I finally made the
decision to make the long-deferred journey to that holy land—to find out
whether he was there or ever lived in the area. I figured even if I didn't
find him, at least making the journey—no matter the outcome—would
once and for all, settle the question I have had for years. This I believed

would bring peace and consolation to my heart.

As most of you know, I made two attempts to go to Lalibela, but as fate would have it, each time I was batted down by, of all things, birds—my often self-appointed travel counselors. Although I disobeyed and fought them, even with my own gun, they still had the upper hand. I saw their victory as an evidence of a curse I could never overcome. This realization sent me over the edge. Out of sheer madness, I even attempted to kill myself with my own gun.

Enat and Hibist's hands flew to their chests. They gasped and gazed at their father vigorously. They had not heard the full account of Abraham's failed trip to search for his father. Their husbands shook their heads and stared at the speaker in disbelief.

Thanks to Providence, I walked away unscathed, but when I finally made it home my spirit was broken. Now it appears from recent discoveries, it was for good reason those birds prohibited me from making the arduous journey, proving once again their God-given abilities to know what we ordinary humans don't.

However, here I come to what I earlier denoted as a strange and incredible turn of events. All of you know that Saba was finally helped by Deb'tera Tayé, Desta and this other individual we have commonly been referring to as "The Man." Desta preferred to call him "The Cloud Man." You know the story; I don't need to repeat it. It turns out that the same man who has been actively involved in solving Saba's mysterious miscarriages was none other than your own grandfather—his spirit, which apparently has been residing in this corner of the valley with us. His body—rather the remains of his body—rest at the bottom of Saba's old property. These revelations were made to Desta by my Baba's spirit last Saturday.

Abraham paused after seeing the surprise in the people's faces. Some placed hands over their mouths and gazed at the boy. Others kept their eyes on their father trying to make sense of what they had just heard. Immediately a low chatter ensued but stopped when Abraham began to talk.

Just like you, I initially found the whole notion of Desta's cloud man farfetched and totally beyond logic and I dismissed it as ludicrous. But Saba now has a healthy, beautiful baby who we see here in front of us and considering her past troubles, this is a miracle. With Desta's involvement, the mystery of Saba's problems was finally solved. And so it is that we are here today with Desta poised before us to unravel another mystery. In light of his tangible fruitful record, I gave in to his pleadings and invited all of you to make this trip together.

Desta felt uneasy by the multitude of eyes that were now on him. He looked away to the mountains.

Baba's spirit has requested that we all go at the same time to the location of his remains. Please ask no questions because I don't know anything other than the few bare facts given to me by Desta, the chosen.

What I'd like to add is that if what we are about to discover is true, it's akin to one of those incredible biblical stories our priests share with us at Sunday church services. How I would love for my sisters to have been here and more importantly my mother, who suffered the most, silently. She will never know what really happened to her beloved husband. My sisters will hear the details of the story in time.

Thank you for coming. Now let's follow Desta.

Upon Abraham's order, Desta turned and walked south along the fence. When he looked back, he noticed that all the people, muted and thoughtful, were shuffling behind in single file. When they reached the open field, the crowd spread into rows of two or three. The men were debating the likelihood of their grandfather coming all the way from Kuakura to die in this remote place when he was supposed to have been sighted in Lalibela, not only once but three times. The women whispered similar sentiments among themselves.

Abraham, erect, dignified and thoughtful, walked along, occasionally twirling his goatee, with his eyes fixed on the earth ahead of him. He didn't engage in conversation with anyone. Ayénat, accompanied on either side by Hibist and Enat, followed behind Abraham apprehensively. The priest Aba Yacob walked behind Ayénat.

Saba carried her baby on her back with a fire-red leather sling. Damtew stayed behind Melkam and Mulu. He walked meditatively, with his dark, glum face down-turned. Melkam was more talkative, whispering to Mulu from time to time. Asse'ged and Teferra walked side by side with their wives.

The mood was solemn and tense.

As they walked down the field along the outside of the grove of acacia trees, Desta felt strange to be followed by so many adults, but he also felt a new sense of importance. For the first time in his life, now he was someone to be listened to, to be respected. To his surprise, not only did they respect him, some of them even seemed to fear him. That he had communication power with the spirit of the underworld meant he was different from them. He no longer was the little Desta they knew.

At the bottom of the field, Desta hesitated, trying to remember which way the man said was the safest way to avoid thorns on the other side of the creek. He recognized a gray rock from the bank of the creek, the rock he had grabbed as he climbed the bank with the cloud man. With this reference point, he quickly found the animal track that went across the creek. Everyone followed him.

After they traversed the stream, they went through a thicket of trees and emerged on the northern-most border of Saba's old property. Desta instructed everyone to walk in single file to minimize the danger of stepping on hidden thorns in the open field. He led the crowd along the eastern edge of the field bordering on a row of tall trees along with blackberry and kaga bushes. Once they reached the dead acacia tree, he stopped.

"This is it!" he said, turning around.

Everybody looked around, trying to see what "it" was. Most of them were still in a long single file. They couldn't see what or where "it" was.

Desta pointed out the ravine below to his father. Abraham had the advantage of height to see clear down the ravine, past a tuft of grass, cattails and dried weeds in front of them. He closed his eyes and then opened them to confirm what he was seeing.

At the head of the line, Desta could see quite a bit of what his father saw. When he came here with the spirit, the area was all covered with grass, but now, looking closely, he could see that there were bones in the grass.

Desta didn't know what to think. His thoughts of his grandfather, about someday meeting him and telling him his dreams about touching the sky, were gone. All he was seeing was something that looked like a pile of sun-bleached wood. It had no meaning to him.

His father motioned the family to come forward. Some of them were already standing at the edge of the ravine. The women gasped. Some teared up, shaking their heads. Hibist and Enat openly cried. The men just looked on, showing no emotion.

"How do we know these are not wild boar bones?" Damtew said to Asse'ged, loud enough for most of the others to hear. "There used to be lots of them around here."

"Wild boar bones don't look like human remains," said Teferra without turning his face from the bottom of the ravine. "That looks like a human skeleton to me."

Abraham called Aba Yacob. He wanted him to bless the site before anyone descended into the gulch.

The priest came forward and said his prayers, cutting the air in front of him four ways with his silver cross. Turning to Abraham, he said, "That looks like a human skeleton, but what proof do you have it is not somebody else?"

"There is supposed to be some proof," said Abraham. "Desta, come. Tell us the details."

The crowd took on a crescent shape, and Desta took his place in the center with Abraham and Aba Yacob.

Summoning all his courage, Desta said:

Last Sunday, I saw the cloud man again. It was a hot afternoon. I was sitting under the shade of the sholla tree, keeping an eye on the animals and thinking about Baba's failed trip to look for Grandpa and his sadness and depression because of it. I had been sad and depressed myself, not only because it meant I couldn't meet Grandpa but also to see Baba that way. I was praying to God to help Baba get out of his depression and find him a way to go to Lalibela to look for Grandpa so he could bring him home to meet the family.

Then, out of the thin air, the man who helped solve Saba's problems showed up. He appeared suddenly, right in front of me, and I stood up in fear. He reassured me that nothing bad would happen and asked if I would like to meet my grandfather. I said yes, but I could not go to Lalibela by myself. I asked if he wouldn't mind taking Baba instead.

He said Grandpa was not in Lalibela, that he was near here, and he would take me to meet him if I wanted. I thought he was talking nonsense because we all knew that Grandpa, if he was still alive, must have lived very far away. Then, knowing the power he had, I thought maybe he had brought Grandpa from Lalibela and had hidden him in the woods some place—to surprise Baba and the rest of us. With this thought in mind, I said, 'Yes, I'd like to meet him.'

He brought me to this place, this exact spot and said, 'This is where your Grandpa is but I want all the children to come and meet him at the same time here.' He told me to tell Baba to arrange it. Afterwards, we went back to the sholla tree and we sat there together. He told me about Grandpa and that it was actually his bones that were here, and not his living body. He gave me the full story of why he came here from Kuakura and how, why and by whom he was killed. It's a long story and I can't repeat everything here. But to give you a summary of it, Grandpa had traveled the long journey from Kuakura here to retrieve our family coin that was stolen by a man named Adamu, Grandma Hirute's cousin. He had collected the coin after bribing Adamu's daughter, who knew where it was hidden.

Unfortunately, Adamu had arrived before Grandpa left. When he departed refusing to stay, Adamu became suspicious and went to check if the coin was still where he had hidden it. Finding it was missing, he and his younger brother, Kindé went after Grandpa. Grandpa ran this way, but they caught up to him.

Desta proceeded to tell them how his grandpa, trying to protect the coin from his pursuers, swallowed it, and how they killed him and disposed of his body in the ravine, planning to return the next day to retrieve the precious item. He told them how the attackers, when they returned could not find the body because his grandfather's spirit had masked everything and the spirit had waited around the same place protecting the coin and his remains for the next forty-two years.

Desta then explained that the person he had met two years before during the session with Deb'tera Taye was the spirit of his grandfather and that the coin and one other undisclosed item were to be proof that the remains were his own and nobody else's.

As he talked, all people's eyes were concentrated on him. A wave of chatter ensued when he finished. The older children and their parents found it hard to believe that Adamu and Kindé were capable of carrying out such a heinous act. They knew them well. Both were long dead. Abraham stopped the noise by reminding them they were not there to discuss the killers, but rather to confirm the identity of the man whose bones were strewn at the bottom of the ravine.

The priest recommended that Abraham descend to the bottom of the chasm to search for the clues Desta had talked about.

With a heavy stick Asse'ged and Damtew beat the shrubs and vines away from the ledge of the ravine so Abraham could descend safely. He climbed down carefully, followed by Asse'ged, who had a pick with him.

The bones were covered with dirt, weeds and debris that had washed down

from higher ground and been deposited on and around the skeleton. The
skull reposed against a dirt-speckled stone next to a tuft of tall grass. The eye
sockets, packed with dust and sand, stared blankly up at the sky. The ribcage
was partially obscured by heavy debris and weeds. The extremities were
loosely strewn about.

Abraham began collecting the bones one by one and handing them to
Asse'ged, who in turn put them on a pile. During this gruesome and laborious
process, Abraham found a bone that piqued his interest. It was a hand. He
remembered it when it had been covered with flesh and supplied with blood.
The image floated to him like a dream. It was the hand with a hole in the
middle of the palm. Abraham's childhood memories came rushing back. This
hand was one of the things he had always remembered about his father. As a
boy, whenever he sat near his father or on his lap, he'd had fun sending his
fingers or other small round objects through the hole.

"This must be one of the two clues," he said, raising it to the crowd that now
stood like wall at the rim of the ravine. "I remember this hole in my father's
hand like it was yesterday," he said as he turned it one way and then the other,
inspecting it.

He tentatively dug around the ribcage with the pick, dislodged it from the
mass of material that held it in place. He shook the dirt off and handed it to
Asse'ged, who gingerly laid it by the side of the piled bones.

Slowly but surely the pile of bones grew into a small mound that looked
more like the makings of a bonfire than the remnants of a once living and
walking human being. Although Abraham was satisfied as to the identity of the
man whose bones they had gathered, he still needed to find the second clue.

Carefully he knocked away the dried dirt with the pick and broke it up with
a stone. He did this for a long time, but nothing turned up. Asse'ged sifted
through the mass of material as his father handed it over, brushing off the
remaining grit in a futile search for something meaningful.

Then, suddenly, Desta cried out from the edge of the ravine, yelling and
pointing. "There is something shiny! There is something shiny! Look! Do you
see it?"

Abraham sifted through the broken lumps of dirt in front of him, but he
couldn't find anything shiny. Desta threw a string of pebbles until one landed
near the object. Abraham cradled the metallic article and began breaking off
the dirt from it. Once he had removed the dirt, he rubbed it with the hem of his

gabi. Then he spat on it and rubbed some more. "Oh my Lord," he exclaimed, "I know what this is! It's our coin of magic and fortune!" He studied one side and then the other, hands shaking. "This is our coin of fortune! This was . . . Oh my God! My God . . . This is the most precious thing in our family! Here it is!!"

A crowd of eyes were now on the small object, from which small flakes of light flew as the father turned it over and back again, inspecting its faces.

"This object is as authentic as the hole in my father's hand. I have no doubt these remains are of my father." He continued examining the coin, shaking his head. Tears gathered in his eye and flowed down his cheeks as the memory of his father engulfed him. Recollections of the coin filtered through his mind as well, as he remembered his mother's words so long ago. He wiped the tears away with the back of his hand, placed the coin in his pocket, and said, "I'll tell you more about this coin, but let me finish gathering the bones."

As he dug and cleared debris, he found the bones of his father's feet. "Look at the arches on these bones. They are exactly like mine; they are my father's as I remember them." Mixed in the dirt were also bits of shredded, mud-caked cotton cloth that crumbled into dust at Abraham's touch.

Having gathered every bit of bone he could find, and having passed them carefully to Asse'ged, Abraham climbed back up out of the gulch with the help of Teferra and Asse'ged.

He stood at the ledge and looked down at the pit. He studied the chasm that had held his father for forty-two years. "Let's go home for now. We can bring out the bones for burial tomorrow," he said to the crowd.

They formed a single line and went back the way they had come. Abraham, Desta and Hibist were at the end of the line. Hibist held her father's hand with one hand and Desta's with the other.

The mood was solemn. Abraham thought about the killers, imagining the struggle by the pit. He still couldn't quite believe those two men were capable of such a horrid act. He had grown up calling them uncle. They were the people he and his mother and sisters had come to live with. He had such fond memories of them. How could he hate and accuse them as his father's killers? Besides, what tangible proof did he have to bring them to justice? The only account he had was that of his father's spirit, and even that a secondary one, told to Desta. In a court it would be treated as mere hearsay.

As they returned home, the men did most of the talking—those who knew

the killers—coming to their defense. Others had their doubts but believed they
were capable of murder, particularly if it involved a great fortune. Some of the
women whispered to each other, but most were quiet and subdued.

They gathered outside the home on the grass and discussed funeral
arrangements and the question of what to say to the valley folk when someone
went to the top of the mountain to broadcast the funeral.

After a lengthy discussion, it was decided that instead of mentioning the
death of Abraham's father, it was better to say, "We have had a death in
Abraham's family and would like the community's support and participation
at the funeral." That way, people would respond quickly and would be less
confused, since everybody believed Abraham's father was long dead.

Asse'ged and Yihoon were given responsibility for the broadcasting. Each
was to go to the top of the western and eastern mountains and alternately blow
the horn three times, broadcasting in a loud voice that there had been a death in
Abraham's home.

The funeral was to take place a week and a half later, on Wednesday May
21st. In the meantime, the family would send notices and messengers to distant
relatives, particularly to Abraham's sisters and their children and other close
relatives and friends, and see to the funeral preparations. In their stunned state,
it seemed an overwhelming task.

FORTY-NINE

On the appointed Sunday, Desta sat on his rock slab under the sholla tree, waiting for his grandfather's spirit to arrive. Chin resting on folded knees, eyes fixed on the dead grass, he thought about the prospective reunion with the spirit and the writing tools and the coin box he had told him to bring.

Because his own writing equipment had been destroyed by Damtew over a year ago, Desta borrowed ink and a pen from his cousin, Awoke. The horn cup, wooden board and hard paper—hopefully the right kind—he had found at home.

Of all the items the cloud man wanted him to bring, the hard paper had been the most challenging. From the combination of subtle hints the cloud man had provided and his own past observations, he concluded that a goatskin must be the solution to the spirit's "I am sure you'll figure it out" riddle. Deb'tera Tayé's scroll was a goatskin with the hair side shaved off and smoothed. Desta had also seen Tamirat shave a newly stretched and dried goatskin to make a scroll. Both of these were hard and durable. As luck would have it, there was a goatskin—from the goat killed for Hibist's Wedding Return party—in the house, rolled up and stored between the granary and the living room bamboo partition. It had been forgotten there, it seemed to Desta, and had been collecting dust and cobwebs.

Desta cut out roughly fourteen inches by seven inches of goatskin and brought it with him, along with the contents of the leather pouch. He had no way of shaving the hair off the skin so he hoped that for the spirit's purpose one side would suffice.

Anxious and a little nervous, Desta periodically scanned the landscape. The cattle and horses were scattered about the field, grazing, and the goats were foraging by the acacia trees on the south side of the field, along the creek that bordered Saba's old farm.

It was midday when the tall cloud spirit of his grandfather materialized in front of him. Startled, Desta jumped up, but managed to restrain himself from backing away.

"You still are not comfortable with me?" said the cloud man with a smile in his usual soft voice. To Desta, the voice always seemed to come from somewhere far behind him. The spirit's mouth moved almost mechanically but no direct sound came from it.

"I had expected to see you come from a distance, but you just appeared right before me. I am not used to people coming at me like that."

"I'm sorry. You can come in many different ways when you occupy the dimension I'm in," said the cloud man with a grin.

Desta looked at the man, not knowing how to reply.

"Did you get everything I asked you to bring?"

"Yes I did. They are all in here," said Desta, pointing to his collection.

"Good! I know they have retrieved my remains and found the coin. Did you get to see it?"

"Just briefly. It still had a lot of dirt on it. Father said I'll get to see it more after the funeral."

"You've seen it before. You just don't remember it, perhaps."

Desta was puzzled. As he was about to ask where and how he had seen it previously, the man continued. "Before we begin, would you like to take a walk?"

Desta stared at the man, unsure whether he should ask him where they would go. "Will it be far?" he asked instead.

"No, just a leisurely walk here in the field. I always wanted to do this with my grandchildren. This is my only opportunity to do so."

Desta was touched. "Sure, I will go with you," he said, happily.

From the sholla tree they turned south and walked side by side. To Desta's surprise, his grandfather's spirit walked like his father, his gait rhythmic, graceful and calculated. His father never walked just to walk but rather to make a statement in space, to enjoy the language he expressed with his body—the erect posture, the stately bearing and relaxed yet focused facial expression.

Although the spirit's legs were long and could cover longer distances, he appeared to consciously take one stride to Desta's two or three strides. His face was thoughtful, as if thinking and weighing the things he was about to share with Desta.

Beneath their feet, the seared golden grass was momentarily aglow from a sun that had seeped through a thin, fluffy layer of the clouds. There was a church-like serenity around the valley, broken only by the sporadic din of shepherds' whips in the distant hills and a game the wind seemed to be playing with the small waterfall high up on the Davola River. Intermittently, the breeze appeared to restrain the water from its freefall, holding it up for a few seconds, then easing it down.

"May I have your permission to rest my hand on your shoulders, the way I always wanted to do with one of my grandchildren?" asked the spirit.

This request was a bit too close for comfort for Desta. He tightened his lips and gave a sideways glance at his companion. The cloud man appeared kind and gentle with a warm enveloping presence, not the sort one would fear having physical contact with. "I don't mind," said Desta, finally.

When the cloud man placed his hand on Desta's shoulders, he didn't feel the touch but he did feel the comforting weight of its presence there.

"I want to share a story with you," he began. "It is about a man and a woman, our ancestors and how the coin is connected to them. I didn't know this story when my soul was still a part of my flesh. It was revealed to me during the last forty-two years while I was roaming this valley.

"The woman was called Tashere and the man was King Solomon. He was from a place called Israel and she from a land called Egypt. Very beautiful, Tashere was the daughter of a king called Shoshenq. Solomon, the son of David, was wealthy and wise. He wrote a lot about things and built the first Temple, which was both a church for God and a place where an important document called The Ark of the Covenant was kept.

"Tashere and Solomon met, fell in love and got married. They produced two children, Basemath and Taphath, both girls."

Desta, who had been watching the animals as they strolled, stopped. "The cows seem agitated. They keep looking at us. I wonder if they are afraid of you," Desta said.

"I wonder why," said the man, smiling.

They kept walking but cautiously. Some of the smaller animals ran away. The bulls stayed put but fixed their eyes on the man, watching his every movement.

"These animals really are afraid of you, just like the horses were at our house two years ago. How come?" asked Desta.

"That is for my protection. If they were not afraid of me, I would have long since been eaten by a hyena or leopard, considering how long I've lived in the forest," the man said with a grin.

"Yeah, right," laughed Desta, trying to imagine a hyena or leopard eating a cloud.

"I know what you are thinking. . .," said the man. "Jokes aside, the animals have a different level of perception than humans do. That is why I am seen by them and not by the latter.

"To return to the story, King Solomon was very famous. People came from far and wide to meet him, to visit his famed temple and to hear his words. One of those people was a woman by the name of *Nigest* Saba, also called Queen Sheba."

"Is Saba named after her?" asked Desta, intrigued by the association.

"Yes, your clever father gave your sister that name because she, like Negist— queen—Saba, was a first born daughter. Unlike your sister, Nigest Saba was born to a poor farmer but she nevertheless became the first queen of our country. You remember her story from your father's account, don't you?" said the spirit, turning to Desta.

Desta nodded.

"When Nigest Saba arrived in Jerusalem and met the King, he instantly fell in love with her because she was very beautiful and had the dark olive skin he preferred. When Tashere saw Solomon's reaction to the guest, she became extremely jealous.

"So, when Nigest Saba left for home, she brought with her many gifts from Solomon including his baby in her womb. When the baby, a boy she named Menilk, turned twelve years old, she sent him to Israel so he could meet his father. King Solomon received and entertained his son happily. When the boy was to finally come home, Solomon asked his friends and the officials in his kingdom to send their first born sons with him. One of those young people was the son of the head priest at Solomon's temple. Not wishing to leave his country without the Ark of the Covenant, this young man broke into the temple at night and stole the Ark. He brought it with him when they left the next morning in a caravan of chariots, arranged by Solomon.

"Solomon was unhappy when he discovered what had happened to the Ark of the Covenant, but not so unhappy as to send an army to get it back. It had gone to a country where his son was expected to be king, so he let Menilk keep it."

The cloud man fell silent when they reached the acacia grove where the goats were busy at their endless feeding. A few of the goats came toward them as they approached, which surprised Desta because this had never happened when he was alone, nor had it happened with the bigger animals earlier. He was intrigued.

"It seems these animals don't fear you," said Desta with a smile.

"But they should," said the cloud man with a chuckle. "They are my victims."
Desta glanced toward his companion and narrowed his eyes, mystified.

"Let's walk south a little more. I'd like to see for one last time the place where my remains rested for so long."

As they headed down the field toward the familiar row of bushes and rocks, Desta saw something that astonished him. "Who planted that eucalyptus tree?" he asked. It was the only tree of its kind, supported on either side by two stout sticks. The top of its slender trunk swayed and its dusty white leaves rustled in the wind. Desta gazed at the young tree intensely. "Why here and why just one? Father never said he was planting one of those trees over here! He planted most of them around our house."

The cloud man was gazing in the direction of the former home of his remains. He waited until his grandson finished his thoughts. "That was planted by Damtew in memory of Habté," he said at last. "This is the exact spot where his beloved goat was killed—sacrificed."

"Damtew? Really?" Desta was incredulous.

"You see, in his mind, he saw life as a cycle. When one life is finished, another must take its place and perpetuate that succession, although the form of the new life may be different."

"Wow! I never thought Damtew was that thoughtful . . . or smart!"

"No, he is thoughtful and intelligent. He just lacks the ability to express himself . . . and he has that dark side to him."

"So unlike Father who wished to perpetuate your memory by naming his dogs Kooli, Damtew planted something more permanent and carefree." Desta gazed at the tree.

"I am surprised this is the first time you've seen it. It has been here since the last rainy season."

"There are bad memories associated with this place. I have avoided coming here."

"I understand. Now let's get back to your favorite place and to the project I have in mind."

"Okay," said Desta somewhat hesitantly. They walked quietly for a few minutes, giving him time to think about the man's story of King Solomon and to connect it to the feelings he was experiencing within himself. The story was fascinating to him. He wondered where that place, Israel was. What he had known before about God and Israel had made him believe it must be in the sky, not any place on earth. When his father prayed during heavy storms, he often gazed to the sky, seeking help from the God of Israel, whom Desta assumed must live somewhere beyond the blue dome above.

Desta was very happy being with the spirit of his grandfather. Without saying much, the man seemed to infuse in him so much love. Just his presence, the sound of his voice, the way he told his stories, the way his hand laid softly on Desta's shoulders. He wished his grandfather had always been in his life. He wished he could wrap his arms around him, as he had never been able to do with his father or mother, who were always too busy or too distant. Now he understood why he, like his father, had been longing to see his grandfather all these years and why he had grieved along with his father after the failed trip to Lalibela. He longed to spend moments like these with someone who loved and cared for him.

Desta thought his grandfather too must have wanted love all these years, to give and receive it. Now for the first time, he understood the meaning of love, the way Hibist once described it to him. 'Love is when someone really, really adores you,' she had said. Today, Desta felt the full meaning of those words.

Once they sat under the sholla tree, the cloud man continued. "To come back to my story," the man said, "Tashere was furious at Solomon for treating Menilk in such a grand manner during his visit, for arranging such a huge entourage to go home with him, and for not making an effort to retrieve the Ark of the Covenant, the symbol of his people's heritage.

"The Pharaoh Princess was not to be outdone, however. She demanded Solomon do something for her own two children, Basemath and Taphath, who were eight and ten years old by this time. When he asked her what she wanted, she said something more lasting, something of him that could be passed down to their descendants. Solomon scratched his head and said, "They have me in them already. They are my children, and yours. What can I give them more lasting than what they have already been given?" said the wise man.

"Tashere, of course, was not surprised by this clever and veritable answer. Nor was she satisfied. 'I didn't mean it in that way,' she said. 'I mean your wisdom, your ability to acquire wealth, to create things, to write, your ability to communicate with animals, your gift with magic—all those things that make you who you are.'

"Ahh, well, to bequeath such things we must devise a method where I can transfer not only what I know or as you say, what makes me who I am, but also precise suggestions that can help the recipients lead a good, productive, balanced and happy life.

"Tashere wanted to record those things that would be valuable to her children and descendents on clay tablets because that was the only material used like paper at that time. She and Solomon selected a total of 21 things—three sets of seven—

that could be practiced or recited each day of the week. Two sets of seven words were to be represented by the channels on the opposite sides of the same object. The additional seven words were to be written in the spaces between the channels on one side of the same object, while the interspaces on the other side were to have a general greeting for their descendants, all in ancient Hebrew tongue."

The man paused and stared at Desta when he noticed the latter turned and looked away. "Is all this too much for you?" he asked.

"No, I was just wondering what that ancient Hebrew writing was like," said Desta turning back his head.

"You will get to see it on the coin but let me continue with the rest of the story. The couple had a seven-sided clay disk made, the channels determining the edges, with seven tracks etched on both sides, representing the things that would be useful to their descendents. The messages were to be accompanied by a separate document, a small rectangular clay tablet that explained what each channel meant and how it was to be applied.

"Solomon prayed for three weeks, one week for each set of seven, asking God to bless the clay disks and the messages they carried. Along with his prayers, he encoded his own wishes in each of the messages attached to the channels. Those who would properly use the channels and routinely recite the attributes would receive greater rewards from the disk and the messages it contained."

"Tashere gave these objects to her children on their thirteenth birthdays. But when Tashere's father, Shoshenq, learned about the disks and the auxiliary tablets were made of clay, he arranged to have them sent to Egypt so they could be transferred onto something more permanent. He ordered the same man that made the pharaoh's gold bracelets to make him two discs and two rectangular gold tablets and transfer all the lines and words from the clay objects onto the gold pieces. Shoshenq, with the permission of Tashere and King Solomon changed the discs from rectangular edges into uniformly circular edges, giving them movement like his chariots wheels, and mimicking the sun. The pharaoh also had two elaborately illustrated sandalwood boxes made to house the coins. The pharaoh then had the gleaming disks and tablets shipped back to their owners.

"When they came of age, Basemath married a young man named Ahimaaz and Haptaph married a gentleman called Abinadab. Both men worked for Solomon as governors. Haptaph and Abinadab named their first son Joshua. When the boy turned thirteen, Tashere asked the couple if they would mind sending Joshua, her first grandson to her father's home in Egypt. She hoped her father would make him the pharaoh or leader of that country, just as, she learned, Menilk had become a leader of his own country.

"When Joshua came to live with his great-grandfather in Egypt, waiting for the opportunity his grandmother had planned for him, he met a beautiful Ethiopian girl, named Bisrat. Her father, a master craftsman and architect, was in Egypt to design buildings and statues for the pharaoh. He came from a line of masons and architects who had built the obelisks and Queen Sheba's palace and other structures in a place called Axum in Ethiopia. When Joshua came of age, he married the Ethiopian girl. He never became a ruler of Egypt but was content with his station in life, being with the woman he loved.

Later, Tashere had one more request for Taphath and Abinadab to fulfill: to pass the gold disk and tablet to Joshua. She had hoped the messages, wisdom and magic her husband had placed on the metal disk and tablet would be useful to her grandson who was now far away from home. The couple did so as requested. The same request was also made of Basemath.

"The coin found with my remains is the same coin that had come down through hundreds of generations in accordance with Solomon's and Tashere's wishes. Unfortunately, the tablet was lost along the way. There is a fascinating story behind this coin box too, but I'll tell you next time."

The cloud man paused once again, noticing that Desta, as interested as he was in the information, was overwhelmed. The boy, for his part, was thoroughly confused, but for now just being with his grandfather's spirit was enough.

"Don't worry, in time all this will make sense to you," said the spirit. "I just wanted to leave you with this valuable information that nobody has had for a long, long time."

When they reached the sholla tree, they found the writing things Desta had brought with him. To the spirit, Desta looked tired, and he thought it was a good idea to end this visit. The afternoon sun had advanced and was descending on the blue roof above them. Desta, hungry and thirsty, welcomed the idea.

"Let's meet tomorrow at the same time. I have important details to share with you. Bring your writing tools once more," said the man as he dissolved into thin air.

That evening when Desta got home, the preparations his family was making for the funeral were a blur. His mind was reeling from the spirit's incredible, baffling story. And, he couldn't get over the tree Damtew had planted in memory of Habté or the love he had for the animal even after he was dead.

FIFTY

The following day, Desta's grandfather's spirit arrived in his usual way at the same time, a little before noon. This time, Desta was patiently waiting on the granite slab without scanning the field or looking into the distance. By now he was used to his grandfather's sudden appearance in front of him. The things the cloud man told him to bring were by his side on the slab under the sholla tree.

After a bow, a smile and a cheerful greeting, the spirit, in a more business-like manner, ordered Desta to take out the ancient wooden box and his writing things. Desta quickly obeyed and kneeled next to the slab anxious to see what his companion had in mind. The cloud man sat next to him and instructed him to place the board on the slab and the goatskin with the hair side down on top of it.

"First," said the spirit, "We will draw concentric circles using the horn cup." With his companion's guidance, Desta placed the horn cup with the top side down on the upper section of the skin and traced a circle with his bamboo pen. He then turned the cup right side up and traced another, smaller circle inside the first. At the spirit's instruction he then drew an identical set of concentric circles in the lower section of the skin.

Carefully following the spirit's directions, Desta sketched channels in each set of circles, beginning from the outer edge of the inner circles to the border of the bigger circles, the channels expanding in volume as they ran to the outer ring. Two straight channels that aligned with each other were also drawn in.

What Desta drew was very rough and crooked, but to his amazement the spirit, with just a touch of his index finger smoothed the lines and curves. Next, the cloud man told him to draw two images in the inner circles, the first of a man's face and the second of a horse, configured in a fetal curl, its power and exuberance constrained but discernable. Desta didn't know how to draw such images and told his companion so.

To Desta's relief, the man took the pen and drew these objects with remarkable speed and accuracy. From the family accounts Desta knew that his grandpa was not only educated but also an accomplished artist and a great horseman. He watched the man with avid interest.

Subsequently, with a beautiful hand his grandfather wrote in the attributes of each channel around the outer circle. "These assignments used to be on a separate document when originally created, but that document was lost a long time ago," he explained. "Generations and generations of recipients of the coin didn't know what these channels stood for. They were revealed to me during the last forty-two years, one every seven years, except for the two along the straight channels, which were only recently disclosed to me. The fanning of these conduits was to indicate that more will come to the recipient of the coin in due time."

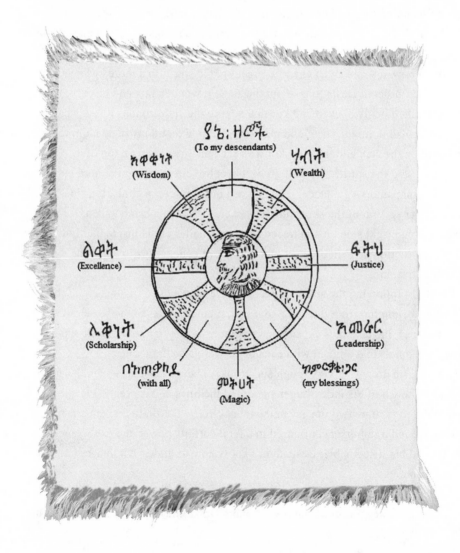

Finally, he inscribed the legend in the interspaces of the channels on the coin face and more words in the same spaces on the tail. "These you'll see in the coin itself, although some of them may be rubbed down and faded. In the actual coin, they are written in ancient Hebrew but I have translated them into Amharic for you."

As the cloud man worked, he intermittently glanced at his grandson, who was dazzled by his manual skill and knowledge. Having long since learned not to ask too many questions, Desta watched and listened in silence.

This activity done, the man studied his work looking at it from different angles, now and then filling in or modifying some details.

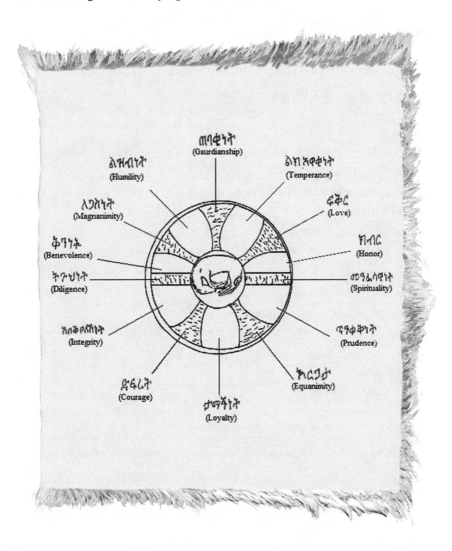

"When the original clay version was designed, Solomon wished to have an image of his temple placed in the center of the coins, but Tashere didn't like the idea. For the children and their descendants she thought an image of him would be more appropriate and meaningful and he complied. Nobody, of course, knew if this was an accurate depiction of Solomon's face or just the artist's creation."

The man studied the coin's face again, made minor corrections and was satisfied. He then stared at the drawing of the other side of the coin. "The horse was a special animal for Solomon," he said. "He had a great number of horses—12,000 of them, despite the fact that it was against his religious order. Symbolically, the horse represented intelligence, courage, speed, power, virility, generosity and grace, which is why he wanted to have it on the coin. He hoped his descendants would have a great appreciation for the animal and all that it represented." The man gazed at the image of the horse for a long time. "I wonder if that was why I loved horses and became a fierce horse racing competitor," he said thoughtfully.

"Can you guess why Solomon ordered the horse to be drawn in a curl?" he asked.

Desta shook his head.

"Because he wanted his descendants to realize that every child born to them has the power to achieve all those things inscribed and encoded in the coin."

Desta gazed at and studied the drawing of the horse in the center of the coin.

Finally, the man lifted the goatskin and held it up and farther away from Desta, first one side, then the other. "Do you like it?" he asked.

"Yes, I do, very much. The images look very familiar to me, but I don't know where I've seen them. It's strange but I swear I have seen them before," Desta said as he studied the final drawings. "I didn't get a good look at the excavated coin, so my recollection can't be from that."

"Good memory, son. You received this coin as a birthday gift the night you turned seven. You also saw it on the dabo your mother baked for your rite-of-passage ceremony."

Desta studied the drawings for a few minutes more. "Yes, that is it. Now I remember the dream and also the dabo my mother made. Who arranged these things?"

"Knowing that your family would not celebrate your birthday and give you gifts, it was arranged that you be given the coin," said the man with a faint smile. "So was the dabo—to signify your event and to give your father a symbolic present. I remember he was particularly wistful of the coin and me that day."

"I remember that the coin I saw in my dream was beautiful but it was gone when I woke. I was so disappointed."

"In due time you'll receive the real thing, but I want you to remember that these words here on the outside are not on the coin itself," said the man, pointing to the outer drawings. "You need to keep this skin with the coin at all times. It will serve as a reference."

To Desta, the fact that this goatskin, which came from a goat killed for Hibist's Wedding Return, would now accompany the coin and be his permanent possession was an incredible and happy coincidence. This piece of skin would serve as an enduring reminder of his beloved sister.

"The recipients of the coin are supposed to apply these messages in their daily lives and share them with their immediate family members," explained the cloud man. "To manifest their blessings, you must run your fingers over the channels. You must do this right before you go to bed and concentrate all your thoughts and energy on the ideas or things you wish to be manifested. After awhile even the mere act of thinking about something you seriously desire will be actualized for you. And, of course, you also need to work hard at whatever it is you are wishing for.

"Of all the channels, the one about magic is most versatile and, if used properly, the most capable of creating opportunity for the recipient. Many unexpected and unnatural things can be made to happen with this channel. Many wishes can be fulfilled. A person can be connected to things and situations they desire just through the air, can communicate with animals, can read people's minds and perceive their actions without actually being there . . . and many, many more," said the man.

With his elbow planted on the slab and his head propped on his hand, Desta watched the cloud man attentively. He wished he'd had the coin a long time ago, so he could have communicated with the animals he befriended and known in advance what was going on in the heads and hearts of his family, particularly Damtew.

"Let's take a break for now," said the cloud man, placing the pen by the side of the goatskin. "I've some important information to share with you when we return to the skin." He turned and spread his amorphous body into a blob. Only his neck and his head were out. His hands now disappeared into the puffy pale mass. Desta turned around and gazed toward the eastern mountains as his companion was doing.

"It looks as if it will be raining later today," said the cloud man, pointing to the dark gray clouds above the mountains.

"Baba will be happy. He wants Damtew and Asse'ged to till the potato field. The rain will make it easier for them," said Desta.

"Your father's wish may just be fulfilled . . . You know what, Desta?" the cloud man said, turning to the boy.

Desta turned and looked at the cloud man.

"There are things in life that you cannot go back and do over again. One of those things is life itself."

Desta's eyes narrowed, puzzled.

"I noticed you were hurt by Damtew's devotion to his goat. I watched your forlorn face as you studied that eucalyptus tree your brother planted in memory of Habté. Were you wondering why he had so much love for his goat but none for you?"

Desta nodded, pursing his lips.

"I don't think your brother intentionally withheld his love from you. It's just that he didn't have it in him to give away. You see, nobody gave him much love when he was growing up. Your father didn't have a good example because I was taken from him when he was seven. He was saddled with his anger after that—still struggles with it today. This has not only affected Damtew, but also the rest of your brothers, and you for that matter. That is why I believe they are distant and un-brotherly toward you.

"The kind of love Damtew showed to his goat was instinctive. It stemmed from deep within his heart. With Habté he experienced this kind of unconditional love for the first time. This also explains his devastation when his goat was killed. Afterward he wanted to perpetuate that feeling of love through the tree he planted. I hope this explanation will help your heart to feel better about your brother and the rest of your family."

Desta was listening dreamily but attentively.

"Did you follow what I said?" asked the man, staring at Desta.

"I did, but nothing you said will change how I feel about my brother."

"I hope you will in time, now that you understand him better. But let's get back to our goatskin. I have some more things to share with you before we part." The cloud man turned to the slab and picked up the pen. "I had planned to give you a detailed explanation of the different words attached to the channels, but that would take a long time. In the years to come, you should not only recite the words and massage the attributed channels but also research and study them. Start with love and the channel attributed to it. I want to add a few more words of my own that can be of help to you." He began jotting the words down on the lower margin, while at the same time called out their definitions.

"Obedience – Happily obey your parents or anybody who plays a role of one or authorities. This is also to say that respect your parents and others without compromising your own self-respect or dignity.

Kindness – be helpful and well meaning to your family and others.

Gratitude – be thankful and show appreciation for favors and kindness extended to you.

Impartiality – always be fair and honest in all your dealings.

Responsibility – be accountable for all your actions.

Trustworthiness – always be reliable and trustworthy, a good base for a relationship.

Patience – have it in you to withstand delays, hardship and pain. In connection with this word, don't ever show anger or disappointment at any time. Anger is for animals because they have no words to express how they feel. We humans have language so we can calmly express how we feel inside without bursting into anger." The man picked up the goatskin and studied the layout of the words and illustrations.

Desta too was studying the layout; his head raised and near the man. "May I have your permission to ask a question?"

"Please do."

"Why are there seven channels?"

The cloud man had watched Desta's dreamy face as he studied the drawings and was expecting this question. "The number seven must have had special significance for Solomon. It took him seven years to build his temple. This may be one reason. There are seven days to the week. God created the earth, mankind and the animals in six days and he rested on the seventh. There are seven heavens and seven angels. There are seven notes to musical harmony. There are seven visible colors in the rainbow. It's for these reasons, son, why seven is the symbol of perfection. Even the brown earth color is gotten from combining the pigments of the seven natural colors. I confirmed this fact in my days as an artist.

"There have been seven times one hundred twenty-three attempts—to steal or destroy the family treasure. Each time the robbery was either foiled or the treasure was retrieved from the thieves' bosoms. This is so because the coins are vested with powers that always cause them to be returned to the family."

"In our family, seven or a multiple of seven has often signified a lucky outcome. I think this is so because of the connection we have to the seven channels in the coin. You were born just after seven months in the womb. You're the seventh child in the family. By one form of calendar, you were born on January 7, 1949. Forty-nine is seven added seven times. This figure is the highest number to which seven could ever duplicate itself—the ultimate perfect state. By our calendar, you were born December 29th in 1941. However while the other calendar stays the same (1949), our calendar become 1942 after our new year in September. Forty-two is seven added six times.

I think these combinations of events make you an unusual child with an unusual future—all favorable, of course.

"In fact, if we look closely, everything that has happened to me, your father and you—the whole family for that matter—seemed to be connected to the number seven.

"For your information, your inability to hear and say things cleared up on your first birthday. This was on Saturday—the seventh day of the week and on the seventh day of the month in January 1950. Your seventh birthday, in 1956, fell on the seventh day of the week and of the month. It was early in the morning on this day you received the coin—in your dream. I was revealed to you on the fourteenth, exactly a week later. When your birthday coincides with seventh day of the week, expect great outcomes. Watch out for these events!

"To give you some more details, it was 2,800 years ago when Solomon had the clay discs created. This number is seven added four hundred times. Your father was seven years old when I was killed at 28 years of age. This number is seven added four times. I was made to wait 33 years until you were born and seven more years until you became seven and could receive the coin, albeit in a dream.

"My forty years of wondering through the forest before I was revealed to my family is itself of some significance. I had to wait while you went through the preparation—were tested through hardship and challenges—for two more years, bringing my total stay here to 42 years, which is a multiple of seven. During this time, seven lives were sacrificed in the name of the coin—my own life and the lives of six goats, including Habté, every seven years since my murder. My remains will be buried and I'll be leaving here on May 21st." the cloud man was saying when he noticed Desta's wide eyes.

"You mean to say that Habté was not killed by an animal?"

"No, he was sacrificed exactly two months before the anniversary of my murder," said the spirit.

"Why did you do that? Did you know how I would suffer as a result of the goat's death?" Desta was upset. How could his beloved grandfather allow that to happen to him?

"Yes, I did. I have this feeling that everything that has happened to us—three generations of men—was set in motion from the moment the coin was stolen from me by Adamu. The events that unfolded may even have been one of those encoded messages in the coin from the very beginning. The string of events that took place was too perfect to be written off as mere coincidence.

"How can we explain the fact that I was murdered by my wife's cousins and then, assuming that I had been poisoned by jealous neighbors and had abandoned my family, she forsook her home and came to this mountainous place to start anew—the very place where I was murdered by the relatives she came to live with. What followed was equally remarkable.

"Later, after your father grew up and married, he moved across the Davola River, settling his family and animals near the place where my bones were strewn. Later still, Saba and her family abandoned their former residence and came to inhabit a piece of land very close to my remains. They had not been uncomfortable where they lived before, but for the story to be unraveled, they had to be included as one more link in the chain.

"Although some of the beatings and verbal abuses you received may not be uncommon here in the valley, yours were compounded by the fact that you were a gifted child and your family didn't know what to do with you—with your inquisitiveness and the challenges you posed. You are the critical link that has brought the family saga to conclusion, to free me from my obligations and responsibility to the coin, to finally extricate me from this confining and foreboding place. It seems to me that all these things were dictated by a force beyond our understanding, by something in the coin, perhaps."

Desta shook his head, unable to fully comprehend what the cloud man was saying. "That tree Damtew planted in memory of Habté, I still can't get over it. He had so much love in him, but none for me."

"Yes, by planting a tree for Habté, he was immortalizing the love he had for the goat, the same brotherly love he denied you. Unfortunately, the love you had for him—for most of your family—was memorialized by the physical and emotional scars left behind. I am afraid these scars may have consequences later in your life, but just as you have risen above your previous difficulties, you have it in you to overcome any further hardships you may face as a result.

"You asked me earlier why I had Damtew's goat sacrificed knowing what Damtew would do to you. Not only did I know what would occur in that particular incident, I have known, as you may have surmised by now, all the things that happened to you since you were born. You see, just as one would watch a lion, without interfering, chase and kill an antelope for its meal, I did the same, knowing that it is the nature of things that for one to survive, another must be sacrificed. Looking at it in the reverse order, for you to survive the many hardships and challenges that await you in your life ahead, you had to be put through the adversities you faced with your family as a boy. The difficulties and tests you have undergone will become the bedrock of your future strength. With everything that has happened to you here, if and when you leave this place, you will have little desire to return home no matter what struggles you may face as you pursue the mission of the coin and your own destiny."

Desta was perplexed. He still didn't understand why the cloud man purposely got beautiful Habté sacrificed, knowing what Damtew would do to him. Then all these other things: his future struggles, the challenges and hardships, and his going out in the world. He was doubly baffled. He wanted to ask him to explain these things, but his mind was already bursting at the seams with information. He just stared away and tried to make sense of what he already heard.

"Let me clarify. You were robbed of your childhood by a family that never understood you, that saw you as an aberration among them. Fearing you were possessed by a Saytan, your mother had you put through that horrid water treatment to drive the bad spirits out of your body. Your father beat you, hoping to make you more diligent at your duties. Your brothers wanted to revenge for losing that land to Saba and Yihoon. I believe all these things happened to you for a reason. It is the nature of things. You must accept things as they come with serenity and move on.

"Magnanimity is one of the attributes of the coin. It means having nobility of spirit, being able to forgive those who have done you wrong. This is a good one for you to work with—after love. In order to move forward with your life, you must purge your mind of bad memories. That way you will have a clean, uncluttered space in your head for the new things that will come to fill it. You must forgive the people who have hurt you—it's for your own good, not theirs—but never forget what happened, as it can be a lesson for the future. Mistakes and problems of prior times, if forgotten, are bound to be repeated."

Desta nodded firmly, as if to concur with what the cloud man was saying.

Momentarily, the man gazed at his grandson with a smile and said, "You may want to share this information with your father. He needs to learn how to forgive too."

To Desta, the idea of forgiving Damtew and all those others who had mistreated him sounded like the absolute worst thing he could do to himself. How could he forgive?

He stared at his grandfather's spirit, thinking he would never forgive himself if he pardoned his brother.

"Just think about it. You don't have to make the decision now," said the cloud man after seeing Desta's thoughtful face. Then he turned and looked at the shadow of the mountain draping the eastern foothills. He contemplated what he was about to say to Desta. Then he said it.

"I am sorry to notice that the day is getting on quietly and quickly. There is yet this important box I have not yet told you about. This coin box has an even more fascinating story about you than the coin.

"Let's meet tomorrow one more time," said the spirit man turning toward Desta. The boy was surprised by the sudden announcement.

"Okay," said Desta. "Do I need to bring the rest of the writing things?" "No, just the goatskin, maybe," said the man as he rose.

Desta watched his fluid-like body rise. Within seconds, the cloud man dissolved into the air.

FIFTY-ONE

With his goatskin spread out before him and the coin box next to it, Desta waited for the cloud man to appear one more time. It was high noon and just as he was telling himself not to be startled again when his companion appeared, the cloud man suddenly revealed himself. Desta still was startled, causing the man to grin.

From his bosom, the cloud man produced a leathery bark with a gooey, amber resin on it and placed it next to the goatskin. Then came two bundles of three and four agam thorns, each bound with a string that the man also placed on the rock slab. "Do you have any questions before I share the story of the coin box with you?" the cloud man asked.

Desta hesitated, distracted by the man's things, then blurted, "I still have not gone to the mountaintop to touch the sky. Can you help me?"

"You just have to be a little more patient, son. You're destined to make the trip up there when the time comes. If it were my choice, I wouldn't want you to have to go," said the cloud man, looking away.

Desta was surprised by the answer and the cheerless note in the cloud man's voice. "Why wouldn't you want me to go up there?"

"Your trip to the mountaintop will be the beginning of the end for the coin as part of our family. We will be separated from it forever."

"Separated from it forever—why?" asked Desta, his eyes going wide.

"Because the information contained on this coin as well as the second coin is needed for all humanity. It was predetermined since ancient times that *you* and the other person will be the *last* bearers of the coins from the two family lines.

After noticing Desta's crestfallen face, the cloud man added, "I was surprised and saddened myself, son, when I first learned about this. Not only had it been in our line for nearly three thousand years, but many possessors, including myself, sacrificed their lives trying to protect and keep it within the family. The reason for my forty-two years by the side of the coin was to ensure that it was safely returned to our fold. Now it seems to me I was just one cog in the giant wheel of a prophecy set in motion from the time the coins were first struck. But it's for the greater good. It's this recognition that helped me overcome my initial shock. Don't preoccupy yourself."

Desta shook his head, eyes fixed on the goatskin to the left of the coin chest. "I was just thinking about my father too. Now, not only will he not meet you, but he also won't be able to keep the coin. He had yearned for you both for so long."

"It's neither his fault nor my doing he wouldn't realize his wishes. It's beyond our power—like the chain of events that happened to us—or understanding, like this coin box or this meeting between us. Nobody would believe that someone like myself, in this state, would have lingered this long here on earth, let alone reveal himself and engage in a conversation with his grandson."

"I know, even father needed to be convinced before he could accept what I told him about you."

"No doubt," said the cloud man. "Before we part, I need to share with you a few more important things. Some of them may not make sense to you. Don't worry. I just want to place these things in your head so they will serve as future references for you."

Desta sat back, folded and crossed his legs, did the same with his hands on his chest. He wanted to give his complete and undivided attention to the information he was about to receive.

The cloud man picked up the coin box, placed it on one palm and said, "Shoshenq had two chests made—one for each of his granddaughters—to house the gold versions of Solomon's clay disks and tablets. He thought that not only would the boxes keep the coins and tablets together, but they would also protect them from damage." The cloud man's eyes flickered from the box to Desta as he talked.

Desta was staring at the box, which, to him, with the man's pale and unsubstantial hand supporting it, appeared to be merely suspended in the air.

"Afterwards," continued the cloud man, "Shoshenq presumably sent the chests to their owners along with their contents.

"Although Taphath received her three items, Basemath never got her box. She received only the gold disk and tablet. This mysterious incident, along with Shoshenq's oversight in bequeathing nothing for Basemath before his death, while leaving a number of things to Taphath and her children, led to animosity and bad kismet between the two sisters. They said this inequity by her grandfather had upset Basemath so much that she went around with a dour face and sour taste in her mouth until she died. Unfortunately, this original sin still lives on, and you are destined to be affected by it."

Desta crinkled his brow and narrowed his eyes, baffled.

The man glanced at the boy briefly and continued. "Although the box was made to keep the two precious items safe," said he holding Desta's eyes. "It seems it was also designed to describe one of the pharaoh's descendants—You!"

The Ancient Sandalwood Coin Box

Desta jerked his head as if awakened from a slumber.

"Me?" he retorted.

"Yes, you! Here is what I mean," the cloud man said, dropping his eyes and pointing. "There are 3s, 4s, 5s, 7s, 9s, 12s, 42, and 49 in this box."

Desta pushed his head back and brought his face close and looked into the box. He saw nothing inside. He gazed at the man the way a child would look at a magician, in awe and wonder.

The cloud man shifted his puffy cotton-like form slightly toward the boy and said, "What I mean, son, is the box is 4 digits or fingers wide, 5 digits long and 3 digits high. The various combinations of these numbers relate to your birth date and year. The period from your conception to birth and your standing among your siblings is also here. Some of these numbers even define your person and the things that interest you."

Desta shook his head, baffled, his eyes fixed on the mysterious box.

"Let me explain," said the cloud man, holding Desta's eyes again. "Four plus three is seven, and you know what that stands for, right?"

The boy nodded. "My birthday, my ranking in my family and also the number of months I stayed inside mother."

"Also the symbol of perfection, harmony and light," added the cloud man.

"Furthermore, if we add the two independent total lengths of the box opening and height with the bottom perimeter and height, we get 42 digits. Add to this number 7 digits, the vertical and horizontal lengths of the cross on the lid, and we get 49 digits. You know what these two big numbers stand for, right?

"Yes. They are my birth years in different calendars."

"Very good. Let's go on. The sum of just the length, width and height of the box is 12. This number, you'll find it interesting to note," said the man smiling, "is how many months it takes for the sun to travel in one year from the bottom of the gap up to the side of the eastern mountains and back to the bottom. You're the only one in this valley who discovered this path after keeping track of the sun's movements along the horizon for a year."

Desta placed his fingers on his mouth, tightened his lips, amazed by his relationship to things the man continued to point out.

"Let me tell you something else that would further relate you to the box," said the cloud man with a quizzical grin, after registering the boy's reaction.

"Do you see this carving?" said the man, pointing to a relief of a cross with a circle above the horizontal line.

Desta nodded.

"In the old times, in our ancestral country, Egypt, this cross used to represent life and eternity. It also had another purpose. It represented the rising sun and the path it travels during the day."

"What do you mean?" asked the boy, dropping his hand from his mouth.

"Well, the circle above the horizontal line represents the sun. The horizontal line of the cross itself symbolizes the horizon. The vertical portion, below the circle, denotes the path the sun travels on," said the cloud man, with a knowing smile.

"Was that why I always loved to watch the sunrise, and I gazed at it as it traveled across the sky?" asked Desta.

"I believe so. In fact your interest in the sun is an atavistic one. The sun played a prominent role in the lives of our ancestors. You are the first out of many generations to have such an avid interest in the sun."

Desta shook his head again, stunned.

"To illustrate my point," said the cloud man after picking up the lid and holding it before Desta. "Let's look at the place where the sun rises," he said, turning his head like a top without moving his body. Desta turned but twisted his body from the waist up.

When they turned around and studied the position of the circle, the wavy lines on the crossbar and the dip in the middle, they determined that what they observed on the cross was an exact representation of the mountains and the sun's relative position, the same mountains Desta had gazed at for so many years.

At that moment the boy felt as if his life had not been his own. He was living to fulfill somebody's grand design. He could never have believed that his interest in the sun had something to do with a coin and that strange cross on the mystical box. He sighed, frightened. *What else will be happening to me?* he asked himself under his breath.

"There are a lot of strange things here, son. That's why I likened our roles with the coin as mere cogs in some mystical wheel of prophecy that was set in motion nearly 3,000 years ago—maybe even much earlier than that," said the cloud man as if he were reading the boy's mind. "What else is in here—only the coin and this box know."

Desta shook his head slowly with his eyes still on the wooden case. The late afternoon light was filtering through the sholla tree, dappling the grass where they sat and seeming to add butterflies to the plethora of animal images that were already on the box. He wished the cloud man could tell him more about the illustrations on the exterior wall of the box. He had been dying to find out what they all meant.

"I can spend the whole day telling you about the meaning and purpose of all these objects on the box," said the cloud man, picking up on Desta's thoughts.

"In the interest of time, I'll just give brief details about the illustrations."

"Many of the animals are here because of their protective power, as our ancestors had believed," said the man, glancing at his grandson. "The others were thought to induce our women's ability to produce children. Others still were thought to enhance and perpetuate certain natural events."

"For example, the lion is the protector of the sun as it rises and sets at the horizon. The coin represents the sun and therefore the lion is here to protect it. So are the vulture and the falcon. Incidentally," said the cloud man, changing his thoughts. "Your father may remember this. The evening of the day I left to get him something for his birthday, he saw a man being murdered at the horizon. He didn't know at that time, but he was symbolically witnessing my own murder. The sun the man swallowed represented the coin I actually swallowed. Similarly, the two vultures that flew west were symbolically meant to protect my body and the coin, not eat them."

"But father never talked about a man that ate the sun," said Desta shaking his head. He stared at the box amazed by all the strange things it was associated with.

"There are many more hidden pieces of information in this chest that relate to you. In time, you will come to discover them yourself. Before we part, however, I want to leave you with a few reminders, advice and clues I have been given where you may find the other coin," said the cloud man with a serious but meditative voice.

Desta placed his hand on his mouth, bit his nail and gazed at his companion.

The cloud man studied Desta's face for a few seconds and said, "Someday you will go past these mountains and the sky to pursue your dream, the dream that had been cut short by your brother, Damtew. Just as Kooli served as the impetus for your discovering the existence of other worlds beyond here, your climbing of this mountain will be the springboard to your future life. You are destined to travel far, but the path to your dreams will be strewn with obstacles, hardships and even suffering. The key is, no matter how difficult the process, never give up."

Desta's imagination had its wheel turning when the cloud man mentioned to him his traveling beyond the sky and the mountains. *What would the world beyond the mountains and sky look like?* he wondered.

"And as the last bearer of the coin and this box," went on the cloud man, "Your responsibility will be to protect these items and make the finding of the companion coin, and ultimately their uniting, your life goal. In the meantime, the chest and the coin will serve as your secret companions, open doors to the supernatural and function as your navigators while the sun will function as your compass. Just as Kooli and Hibist were your trusted friends in this world of yours, the two items will assume that role in the next world."

Desta unclenched his nails from his teeth and dropped his hands onto his lap. "Just like Kooli and Hibist?" he asked, happily. Yet he couldn't imagine how a piece of metal and a wooden box would replace his two beloved individuals.

"Yes, son. In some way even more than them. And don't forget number seven," reminded the cloud man, as if wishing to change the subject. "Your destiny is intertwined with this number. There will be seven levels of goals or challenges you have to meet. The only way you know you have overcome each challenge is when you realize the dream you have set for each."

The cloud man pushed the box aside with his fuzzy, pale hand and stared at the coin drawings on the goatskin. "You can use the seven channels to keep track of the seven challenges you will face," he said. He pointed his index finger to the horizontal channel on the left of the bottom illustration and said, "Not counting what you had gone through before your birth, once you get to the mountaintop, you'll have met your first goal. So let's say that this channel is for the first challenge you have overcome. You will have six more to go . . . After you achieve your next goal, go right on the circular panel, and you will have reached the second channel. With the accomplishment of your third goal, you'll have reached the third channel and so on, until you've reached this last channel," said the cloud man, planting his finger on it.

Desta stared at the man. He wanted to ask questions, but he didn't know where to begin. The information given to him was too much. All he could do at that moment was listen.

"In the end," said the cloud man, turning to his grandson, "Just as seven added to itself seven times ultimately reaches forty-nine, beyond which it can go no more, you, with the coin and box, would have traveled as far as you could go and will have come to a place beyond which you can go no more. It's here where you will find the bearer of the other coin—your cousin, the ancestral grandchild of Basemath, this person having come just as far and realizing he or she could go no more."

"Where is this place?" asked Desta, surprised by the cryptic information.

"I'll give you some clues," said the cloud man after a pause. "The place is a valley like this one, but the mountains are not as tall, the basin not as rugged, nor is the space as narrow and enclosing. The valley doesn't have many creeks that course the mountainsides and there is no river that slices its floor like we have here. Some of the hills, valleys and canyons are mantled with verdure, but there are no vervets or colobus monkeys or a plethora of birds in the trees." The cloud man stopped and looked away for a few seconds.

Desta was trying to visualize the place when the cloud man turned to him and said, "When you have reached this land, you will know your journey has ended because there will be things that would remind you of home: the reddish brown color of the soil, the gentle warmth of the sun, the layout of the terrain and the clear blue skies. The evening there will mimic the morning here because the sun appears to set in the part of the sky from which you were accustomed to seeing it rise.

"No cattle, horses, goats or sheep roam the land, nor are there any farms.

"You know you have come to the end of your journey when you find that the sky, the object of your dreams, no longer touches the mountaintop or distant lands but has tumbled down into a restless, vast blue sea, its clouds rumpled, wetted and smudged. Don't be heartbroken or disappointed if the sky continues to elude you; instead be thankful for the opportunity it gave you to go the distance in life, just as Kooli had done for you."

Desta's face and eyes brightened at the mention of his deceased dog.

"You'll know you have come to the end of your journey when you find that it's not a reclining man or a distant, hazy earth that swallows the sun, but the same restless deep blue sea.

"The last rays of the sun will still flicker on the cusp of the eastern mountains just like here, making you wonder once again, if you had not come home after traveling a full circle. This realization is but one more manifestation of what had been encoded in the ancient coins: the cyclicity of things."

"Cyclicity of things—what do you mean?" asked Desta, narrowing his eyes.
"Here is what I mean:

> Of life: birth-death-rebirth or renewal.
> Of time: morning-evening-morning.
> Of seasons: spring-summer-autumn-winter-spring,
> Of the coins: creation-journey-reunion-recreation or rebirth.
> Of you: Departure-adventure-feelings of coming home." The cloud
man paused and glanced at his grandson.

Desta brought his hands together into a steeple and rested them against his lips, thinking about what his companion just described.

"It's in this valley where you should concentrate your search for the second coin. Look in the streets, churches, recreational places, places of work, in the marketplace—in short, wherever people gather, for someone whose name means sweet and sour. This person shares the same birthday with you and would have also come from very far away and settled in this valley, realizing they too had come to the end of their journey.

"Shares the same birthday with me? Why is this person called sweet and sour?" asked Desta, dropping his hands on his lap.

"Yes, this person was born exactly on the same day—January seventh. Sweet and sour is not their name, but the meaning of it—just like happiness is the meaning of Desta."

The cloud man continued. "Just as forty-nine is the end of seven's trip and, at the same time the beginning of life, your birth year, our coin will end its journey here. There will be a reunion party for innumerable guests, but there will neither be food nor drinks. There will be plenty of music unlike any you have heard before. It will be the happiest event for all who come. It will be at this event when the coins officially unite—and become one. The now single coin will be blessed to benefit not just the two lines of Tashere and King Solomon's descendants, but all of humanity.

"After the all-night party is over and the guests have left, go outside before dawn and wait for the sunrise. Once the golden orb has cleared the cleft in the eastern mountains, bow in its direction and give your gratitude for providing guidance to the place of your ultimate destination. Then stand straight up, close your eyes and give thanks to Solomon for his wisdom and for the messages he encoded in the original clay disk, to Tashere, for her insight to have Solomon draw the channels and encode his knowledge into something lasting and transferable, and to Shoshenq, for his acumen for moving the original information onto metal and for rounding the edges of the new disk, thereby giving it life and motion. Then remember everybody that played a part in the success of your journey—Kooli, who sacrificed his life for you, topping the list.

"This should be the day when you realize it was worth all the sufferings, the struggle, your losses, your trials and tribulations, and all that you endured was worthwhile. You may have not achieved the goal you had set for yourself, but you will have achieved things much grander and far-reaching, not to mention all the great adventure and revelations you will have had with the coin and the box.

"For your father, you'll have made up for all the disappointments and heartaches he had with his older children. For me, it will make all the years I spent in this hole until you were born and came of age to receive the coin meaningful.

"It's a big responsibility that awaits you, but it is because of the strength of spirit you bear, you were chosen for this task," said the cloud man as he placed the lid back onto the box.

Desta was overwhelmed by what he heard. Both were silent staring at each other. The boy then closed his lips tight and gazed away.

"As you heard," said the cloud man, "Don't stress yourself over this. You will get to know all this in time as more is revealed to you."

Desta put his head down and stared at the grass thoughtfully. Much of what the cloud man told him didn't make sense at all, but the idea of him going to another world brought threads of happy thoughts.

"I'll do something with you and give you one more piece of advice, though, before we part," said the cloud man glancing at Desta.

The boy looked up at his companion wondering what else he had in mind.

"I am going to put a talisman on you . . . something that will protect you from harm," the cloud man said, picking up the three-thorn bundle.

"What would that be?" Desta said, staring at the needle-like thorns, puzzled. The talisman, he knew, was a document written on a parchment in red ink, folded several times until it was small enough to be bound in a leather pouch and hung on a cord around someone's neck.

"I am going to tattoo on you the coin, emphasizing the magic portion of it. This coin image will be readily accessible to you. The actual coin may not always be."

Desta felt his hair stand on end, his skin tighten and his nerves on his face tingle. *I am constantly guarding my feet from ordinary thorns when I walk around the field, now this spirit man thinks I would allow him to poke me with those horrific barbs?* He was contemplating how he should decline the suggestion when he suddenly heard himself say "Where?"

"It will be on the left side of your chest, above your heart," said the cloud man. "And you won't feel a thing. . . . I'll make sure it's so."

Those last words gave Desta courage. And he believed the man.

"Lean against the rock and pull down your gabi," commanded the man. Hesitant and nervous the boy did as told.

"Close your eyes and keep them shut until I am done,"

Before he complied with the order, Desta saw his companion dip the three-thorn bundle into the viscous resin. Eyes closed, lips locked, nerves tense, the boy waited for the first painful piercing on his skin. But then shortly after, he started to feel drowsy as if he were medicated. He fell asleep. Half an hour later he woke with a slight soreness on his left chest. He looked down on it. To his surprise above his nipple he saw the exact replica of the coin that he drew on the goatskin a few days earlier. The channel above the horizontal line, the one dedicated to magic, was heavily colored. The rest were mere outlines.

"That image is your protector, including your things and those around you," said the cloud man observing Desta's gaze on the darkened channel. "You are to touch it at any moment that you feel you might be in danger."

Desta liked having the coin on his chest. He was particularly pleased that it didn't hurt when it was being tattooed.

"Will it be there all the time?" asked Desta, remembering how quickly the charcoal paint he and Hibist put on had disappeared from their faces.

"It will be for you to see but not for others," said the cloud man. "The colors will soon fade but the image will still be there. You'll see it whenever you focus your gaze down on it."

Desta was puzzled and disappointed by this report. He would have liked to have shown it to Hibist and anybody else who would like to see it.

"That the color fades is to hide the coin's identity and to protect you from having to answer curious minds every time they see it."

"Why did you need so many of those long thorns? Their sight and purpose had terrified me."

"I have to comply with the power of seven, son—our family's magic number," said the cloud man with a grin. "I used the bundle with three thorns to tattoo the channel lines and those with four to concentrate the ink at the channel dedicated to magic." Desta was excited about and anxious to try out this unique channel.

"Remember, though, that there are other great benefits to that channel. You'll discover many of its attributes in due time," said the cloud man, seeing the boy's smiling face.

Desta was happy to hear this, especially if this meant that this channel could

enable him to read people's minds and communicate with animals on their
level, one thing he wished he could have been able to do with Kooli.

"One more thing," said the spirit man studying the boy's happy countenance.
Desta looked up at the spirit man.

"Have you ever seen your face in a *mestawit*—mirror?"

Desta thought about this unexpected question for a bit and said, "No, not for
a long time, Why?"

"You will find the answer when you get a chance to look at yourself in a
mestwit again."

Mystified by the man's response, Desta kept his eyes on him hoping he
would tell him what exactly he was seeing on his face.

"I need to go but let me share with you the advice I had in mind before I
leave," said the cloud man, as if wishing to change the subject. "Don't always
trust your eyes or your ears, but always follow your instincts. This is one
universal wisdom all creatures share, from the smallest to the largest. Instinct
was the medium that connected you and Kooli and the vervet monkeys. And
most importantly, don't ever question any messages you receive through the
coin, that image of it on your chest or this box!" said the spirit man, glancing
down on the wooden holder.

Then he rose and said, "I hope to see you one more time," and vanished.

SOON AFTER THE CLOUD man left, Desta ran toward the Davola River,
hoping to find some pooled water in which he could see his face. While on en
route, he remembered the part of the river where the local boys and men came
to swim, which always had dammed water even in the dry season.

Winded and breathless, he arrived at the riverbank. He felt a sudden
queasiness in his stomach as he looked down on the pooled water. This was the
very place where his brother, Damtew, once tried to drown him under the guise
of teaching him how to swim. Desta shuddered.

He shook his head, trying to chase the memory away and took a deep sigh. He
doubled over and searched for his face in the water below. He could see only a
distorted and blurred reflection of himself in it. The water was calm but he was too
high up from the surface to see the details of his face. To get closer to the water, he
must first cross the river and approach it from the opposite shore.

He walked around the curving bank and entered the river where its course
was accessible. The water chilled his feet when he first stepped into it but the

exposed, sun-basked rocks he landed on as he hopped across sent waves of pleasant sensations to his feet.

Desta stood near the water and stared at it, once again struggling to hold back the emotion that surged through him. Thankfully, the sound of the waterfall upstream drowned out his thoughts and calmed his nerves. Near his feet, he could see white pebbles and his silhouette underwater. Realizing he needed to be in the deeper part of the river to see his face clearly, Desta waded farther, watching waves of gray circles ripple away and startled water bugs skid across the table-like surface.

He stopped at a place where the water level was knee high. He bent over and peered into the liquid and was pleased to see a face he had not seen for a long time staring back at him.

The mid-afternoon sunlight on his face had made his countenance bright, allowing him to see the details on it. He studied his tapering nose, his big brown eyes and his ashen skin and the chapped lips and unkempt hair. He saw nothing on all these areas that would warrant his consulting a mirror. He nonetheless kept gazing at his reflection, wondering if per chance he missed some subtle details.

Seeing nothing, he was about to stand straight and walk out of the water, when he saw tiny hairs trace a line from the left corner of his right brow, down to the base of his nose, up the other side and reconnect to the right corner of his second brow.

Then suddenly a dot of light appeared and rose along the interior wall of the cup, getting brighter as it ascended. Desta's eyes flickered, stunned. Knowing that the Saytan lives in pooled waters like the one he was in, he wondered if it were He who was playing tricks on him. His spine prickled and his heart raced. Baffled by the strange occurrences, Desta quickly waded out of the water and crossed the river to run back to his animals, while at the same time turning and looking to see if something or someone was following him. He sat in the field and inspected his surroundings. Everything was as normal but what he saw on his face in the water was still a mystery, if he could believe his eyes.

THAT EVENING, shortly after Desta fell asleep, he saw the cloud man once again in his dream. Desta was sitting on the grass in the open field, enjoying the gentle afternoon sun while looking after the animals.

"I came to explain the cup-shaped image you saw on your face when you looked into the river water this afternoon," said the cloud man, shortly after he arrived. Desta had not expected him, yet he was not startled or surprised by the spirit's sudden appearance.

"That image is no ordinary matter. It represents the half-full cup you saw at your coming-of-age ceremony, and is similar to the chalice from which you once drank God's blood when you went to receive your communion to cure you of the supposed dog disease. The same object is also a miniature imitation of the gap in the eastern mountains. The rising light in it corresponds to the sun that rises through the mountain gap everyday." The man stopped and gazed at Desta.

"I cannot make sense of what you are telling me or why you are telling me all this," Desta said, bewildered.

"You will come to realize the purpose of all this information but let me share with you a few more things. The figure I have been referring to is a part of a very important and powerful ancient symbol called Ankh, which incidentally is also on your face. This will be apparent to you as you grow older.

"The cup-shaped form is similar to the first letter of our alphabet, which is identical to the 21st letter of a language called English. Interestingly, the various combinations of the numbers corresponding to these letters generate numbers that are identical to those found on the coin box, the most important being your birth year, in the two different calendars. Some day you will figure out how these two letters and their corresponding numbers contain information which represents you.

"As you must remember, twenty-one refers to the number of messages encoded on the coin.

"Just as the chain of events that happened prior to the discovery of the coin and my remains are not mere coincidences, everything has to do with the cup-shaped objects, and the letters, numbers and symbols it corresponds with are not mere coincidence. I think your birth at this place and all that happened to you was probably predetermined not only by the coin and coin box but also by the gap in those mountains, at the time of its formation. The ancient people who created the orders of their alphabets—ours and the English—may have thought of you when they organized the letters in their alphabets. Desta looked at the man quizzically.

"Who knows, you know? How else can we explain the cup-like letter called "U" in the English language is the 21st letter of their alphabet?

"Lastly, when the cup-like hair grows between your brows, don't ever shave it off, as people are apt to tell you to do. . . . Any questions?"

"When are you coming again?" Desta asked abruptly, unable to say anything else.

"Not in the immediate future, but we will probably see each other briefly after the burial of my remains. Down the road, in your dreams, we could see each other perhaps. And much later, if you have not forgotten me by then and care to invite me to the coin's reunion party," said the cloud man with a smile.

Desta shook his head, frowning. "I am sorry this is the last of our meetings. I have a lot more questions."

"I am sorry too, but I need to go," said the cloud man as he rose and straightened his fluid-like body.

Desta rose too and gazed at his companion pensively.

"Before we part," said the cloud man, his eyes holding Desta's endearingly, "I want to say that although you and I had not met prior to that first encounter by the river and I waited forty-two years on your behalf with the coin, I am very pleased with the moments we have spent together. I am proud of our relationship and proud of the way you managed everything you have been put through. You are only a small boy but you handled all that happened to you like a man. For me, it was worth the many years of wandering in the woods waiting until you came of age so I could transfer our precious family heirloom and relay all the information about it to you. I feel blessed to have been chosen to have you as my grandson. I hope the love I have for you will heal your consciousness and soothe your soul.

"From here on, I trust that the coin and the box will serve as your family, friend, counsel, protector and guide as you navigate through life. Remember to keep the skin with the coin at all times. Practice until you're properly able to read, live and breathe the virtues and ideals inscribed in the coin. Recite the words and visualize the outcome you desire. Study and understand all the powers and benefits of the illustrations on the box. And finally, learn to forgive. That way, you will grow to be a happy, healthy, successful man. May God bless you!"

The cloud man extended his arms as if to hug Desta, and Desta did the same. He felt the presence of the spirit's arms and body but he couldn't feel the touch. His own extended arms hung in the air, anticipating the embrace. He felt the spirit's enveloping love, warmth and kindness.

"This is the last of our private meetings. I'll see you at the funeral," the spirit man said and once again dissembled into thin air.

FIFTY-TWO

The skeletal remains of the grandfather were brought and placed in a simple wooden casket that had been made from a bored-out tree trunk. The family then had to decide the funeral arrangements. Did they want to keep it simple, involving only immediate family members and close friends, or would they include distant relatives and parishioners as well?

The discussion quickly became heated, with Asse'ged and Teferra facing off against each other as the leading spokesmen for the opposing sides. The others were split equally, largely along gender lines. Those who followed Teferra—Tamirat, Damtew, Yihoon and Ayénat—wanted a small gathering of just the immediate family. They argued that not only would messengers have to be found to contact the many who lived far away, but it was unfair to obligate them to attend a funeral service for someone who had died so long ago and one whom many of them didn't know or had long forgotten.

Asse'ged's group included Saba, Enat and Hibist. They wanted a big funeral including their three aunts and their children as well as any other friends and relatives who wanted to come. They argued that the funeral service was not just for their grandfather but also for their father and his sisters who had grieved for so long. Sharing their sorrow and memories in a grand way could help bring closure for them, they maintained.

The priest recommended the inclusion of the parishioners, enabling them by participating to express their appreciation to Abraham for his many years of selfless service to the community.

No one asked Desta's opinion, but he thought he would go along with whichever option his father supported.

Abraham listened closely to the pros and cons of the two proposals. Having a speedy ending to his grief and sharing it with a greater crowd was not important to him. On the other hand, acknowledging his father in a big way would be some consolation for the sacrifices the man had made on his behalf.

He knew his father would not have lost his life if he had not gone after the coin he wanted to give Abraham for his birthday.

Although his sisters had not shared their feelings about their father in the recent past, Abraham was sure they would want to be included in the funeral service. Attending it would bring closure for them as well, he thought. In the end, he sided with Asse'ged, and a decision was made to invite relatives and friends both near and far and all of the parishioners who could make it.

The funeral date was set for Wednesday, May 21, 1958—seventeen days from the day they retrieved the grandfather's remains. Fortunately, it was the time of the year when many of the farmers were still in their hiatus from work, making it possible for them to attend the event.

They moved forward quickly with the logistics. Asse'ged was to go to Kuakura, where his eldest paternal aunt, Zere, and her four children lived. Zere was old and her vision was bad, but Abraham wanted to include her. If making the day-long journey would be too hard for her, her children might be able to attend.

Tamirat was sent to Bosena, Abraham's immediate older sister who lived in Talia. Bosena lived with one son and she had long been battling a lip cancer. It was thought that she too might not make it but her son and daughter might. Desta remembered how terrified he was when he last saw Aunt Bosena six months ago. Her lips were disfigured, enormous, and crusted with wounds. She used a straw to take her food and drink, always covering her mouth with the hem of her shemma, and she could hardly talk. He thought she probably wouldn't come, as she had stayed in the house and avoided people the last time they came to visit.

Damtew was to go to Aunt Welella. The youngest of the aunts, Welella lived in Lij Ambera with her tall, strapping husband, De'goo. She was healthy, wealthy and beautiful.

It was decided that Ayenat's relatives should be invited as well. All her half brothers and father lived in a place called Gumbla, which was close to where Enat and Tenaw resided. Tenaw was to stop by on his way home to extend the invitation to them. Word was also sent through market-goers to any other relatives and friends they could think of.

Many of the parishioners were informed through word of mouth. The day before the funeral, Yihoon and Tenaw were to go high in the mountains, one on each side of the valley, to publicize the funeral by blowing a horn three times at the top of their lungs.

Having learned that the spirit of the father of their loyal parishioner and community arbiter had been roaming the valley for forty-two years, waiting for his remains to be formally buried, the priests suggested an all night prayer and Bible-reading service.

Not wanting to burden the grieving family, they ordered the congregation to prepare food and drinks and bring them for the funeral attendees to Abraham's home.

For their part, the priests brought their canvas tent and set it up outside the home. Abraham's household supplied a selection of skins for the clerics' comfort.

Impressed by the kindness and compassion extended to him and his family, Abraham decided to return the favor by killing a bull and feeding all those who took part in the services. It was the least he could do, he thought, to honor a man who had sacrificed his life on his behalf, trying to retrieve the family treasure. He also thought that capping off his forty-two years of personal sorrow in such a manner could be a good way to finish with his past as he prepared to usher in a new chapter in his life.

Teferra was assigned the job of killing the bull with help from a few able-bodied men and making the meat available to the women who would be preparing the dinner.

Two days before the funeral the aunts and many of their children began arriving. Aunt Bosena kept her face mostly covered, her cancerous lip protruding underneath her shemma as if she were holding some grotesque object in her mouth. Aunt Zere, weak and nearly blind, also managed to attend but had to rest before she joined the rest of the family for the evening meal. Aunt Welella came with her husband and five children. She looked as beautiful and youthful as ever.

Monday and Tuesday, people came in great numbers from both far and near. Some of them had heard the story of Beshaw Mekonen's death and discovery and were curious to find out the details. Others came to show support for the grieving family. The home and grounds were packed with people. The local women brought three to five gallon-jars of tella, drinking cups and baskets of injera. Ayénat was touched and grateful for the support and generosity of the women.

On Tuesday afternoon, a dozen priests arrived with their kettle drums,

Bibles, prayer staffs, and centrums and took residence in the tent. They stood on the goatskins and plush cowhides and prayed and chanted from right after dinner—around 8 pm—until midnight. After sleeping briefly, they rose again at four in the morning and continued praying and chanting to the beat of their mournful drums. Beshaw Mekonen's casket was left at the priests' tent outside.

The bull was killed Tuesday evening and many of the guests were fed raw meat with hot sauce and injera. The women worked through the night cooking the meat and making injera and big pots of sauce to be served for the mourners and guests when they returned after the funeral the following day.

On Wednesday morning, the casket was carried by Desta's four oldest brothers, led by a mule fitted out with an embroidered cloth and a saddle and reins around which cascaded straps of leather decorated with red, green and gold yarns.

Because Abraham's father had been an accomplished horseman, Dama was fixed up beautifully and walked alongside the mule, making her appear diminutive against his massive physique. The horse was draped with a white cotton cloth and his reins were adorned with colorful yarn. The grandfather's silk scarf and his green gabardine jacket hung from the saddle.

The priests walked immediately behind the casket, dressed in brocades of emerald, blue, red and gold. They were followed by Abraham and Ayénat, Enat, Hibist and Desta, followed by the three aunts and their children. Desta noticed that his father was somber and thoughtful. He walked slowly and meditatively, in tempo with the priests and the pallbearers.

The casket was placed under the sholla tree at the north end of the cow field, where Desta often took shelter from the rain or the sun. The priests began chanting, praying and singing, accompanied by the somber thump of their kettle drum and the brass rattles and the swinging movement of their prayer sticks.

The rest of the crowd, which had grown throughout the morning, gathered in the open field. After the casket was placed under the tree and the mule and horse were tethered, the family joined the crowd. The assembly gathered around them as they walked in a circle, weeping and sniffling. Qualified persons took turns singing melancholic songs, some composed in advance, others improvised just then. The crowd harmonized. The songs were deeply personal and touching, and the family, with the exception of Abraham, cried silently as they listened to the powerful words and the melancholic voices.

After an hour of singing, they picked up the casket and proceeded toward the church. Along the way more people joined in the procession. At the head priest's instruction, the pallbearers rested the casket under another big tree, a warka, and once again there was a display of mourning and singing. The mourners moved in circles, symbolic of the cycle of life, sang the funeral songs and softly wept for half an hour before moving on.

When they finally arrived at the church grounds, the priests and close family members went through the eastern entrance of the stone wall with the casket, circled the church three times, sang and mourned for another half an hour, then took the casket out through the western gate. A grave had been dug near Abraham's mother's tomb on the eastern side of the church, near two lofty juniper trees, thirty feet from the stone wall. The crowd marched somberly to the benches where Abraham held court on Sundays.

Desta, who had been with Hibist the entire time, took her by the hand and they walked to the periphery of the crowd to watch as the casket was lowered into the grave.

Desta and his sister looked on as the four brothers brought the casket to the burial ground. The boy could see the hole was dug lengthwise running east-west. The priests chanted and read from the Bible. The head priest, Aba Yacob, blessed the grave by passing his cross in a criss-cross manner. The brothers lowered the casket with the head pointing west and the feet east and threw dirt in afterwards. The women, who stood far from the grave, gasped a low cry as they started throwing the dirt. Abraham looked on gravely, sad and thoughtful but not tearful.

As soon as the grave was completely filled with dirt, a remarkable event took place. The cloud man he met by the river, the same man who led him to the discovery of the coin and his grandfather's remains, who finally revealed himself as his grandfather, appeared before him and tapped him on the shoulder. He whispered, "Be good, my boy. God bless you. Good luck with your adventure. I will be on the lookout for you." Then he rose into the air, gave Desta a wink and a smile and floated gracefully toward the blue heaven. Desta capped his eyes and gazed. Seeing him, others craned their necks in the same direction but saw nothing.

"What did you see? Why are you crying? What happened?" said Hibist, pulling on Desta's arm.

"The man, the man, the man . . . my grandpa just . . . flew off," said Desta pointing to the sky.

"Ssheee, don't let others hear you," said Hibist, covering his mouth with her hand. "He left, he left. I'll probably never see him again," he said tearfully.

After the funeral, the head priest gave a speech. Now that the remains were laid to rest, he said, the children and grandchildren would carry on as the living representatives of the deceased. Grieving brings no dead persons back, he told them. Therefore, you shouldn't torture your spirits by endlessly thinking about him. You should move on with your lives, happy to bear the torch and pass it on to the generations that follow.

As the crowd dispersed, many people shared their condolences with Abraham and the other family members. There seemed to be an endless number of people that came, sharing their feelings and thoughts with the family.

The immediate family, along with all the priests and some of the deacons that provided the service went back to Abraham's home. The parishioners and all the others who attended the funeral were invited, and those who didn't have to travel great distances came to share the farewell dinner.

The food brought by the parishioners and the food prepared at home the night before was kept warm by Melkam and Mulu. Ayénat had asked them to stay behind to have the food ready when the others returned from the funeral service.

People ate and drank abundantly into the early evening. Close to one hundred people attended the dinner, but with the many hands involved in preparing and serving, the work was hardly noticeable to Ayénat and her helpers.

After dinner, Abraham stood in front of the group and shared as much of the story of his childhood as he remembered. Aunt Zere talked tearfully about her days with her father—how he carried her on his shoulders and walked the countryside looking for flowers in the spring season, how proud he was of her as he introduced her to everyone that came to visit them. Her face was half covered to protect her eyes from the direct light of the beeswax candles.

At midnight the parishioners and priests left in the moonlight. The priests were invited to spend the night in the tent but preferred to go as they needed to rise early for Sunday Mass.

On Sunday, after brunch, many of the immediate family members gathered in the tent to hear the full account and how they had come to discover the grandfather's remains. Abraham told them as much as he knew, and Desta filled them in on more of the details.

Many likened the story to a miracle. "After forty-two years, for the ghost of my father to be revealed to this boy and to give such an account of what had happened to him is unbelievable. The story behind that coin and box is nothing but a miracle of biblical proportion," said Zere.

Everybody nodded.

Abraham asked his oldest sister what she remembered about the coin.

"I was just about to tell," began Aunt Zere. "I'll share with you something incredible."

Everybody's eyes turned toward her.

"As the first born child, I was supposed to receive that coin. My father had told me this on many occasions. He used to bring out the box from where he hid it, take out the coin, show and tell me the stories behind it—what each of the channels meant, for example. I can't tell you what they all meant now—I was only seven or eight years old—but I think I remember those about happiness, love, being rich of the mind and finance . . . and I remember the ones on prosperity, happiness and love. . . . Am I repeating myself? Anyway, things like that."

"Do you remember how Adamu stole it?" asked Abraham.

"Yes. He was supposedly sick. He came to receive the holy-water treatment at Ba'tha Mariam and he stayed with us for a week. After he felt better, he wanted to help our father with a farm project he had—what it was I don't remember now. During that time, he told me he had heard about our family's coin and how it was the cause of our wealth. He wanted to see it and begged me to show it to him.

"I was so naïve. One day when father and mother were out, I fetched the coin from the small wooden box where my father kept it and showed it to him. He kept asking me if he could touch it so he could be rich too. I said no and ran back to the bedroom and put it back in the box. He was so anxious and excited about the idea of touching it, but I don't remember him following me and seeing where I put it away."

"How did you come to learn it was Adamu who stole the coin?" asked Welella.

"That was an interesting story in itself," said Zere, pulling her shemma down over her face to protect her eyes from the late morning glare.

"His daughter, Misrak, who was my age, had come for a holy-water treatment herself from some childhood disease. She also stayed with us. One afternoon shortly after her father left, we were out in the field playing when she said out of nowhere, 'Someday we'll be as rich as your parents!'

"When I asked her how they were going to be rich, she told me about this old brass coin someone had given her father. It was supposed to make people who owned it very rich. Then she described the coin with an amazing detail, except that ours was gold and not brass. Still it sounded like our coin and we were supposed to be the only ones in the whole country who had a coin like that. I remember being disappointed with my father for telling me something that was not true. Now the daughter of my mother's cousin was telling me they had one too.

"I ran home, flew really, anxious to tell him about the second coin. The girl thought I was suddenly possessed by the Saytan and she kept calling after me to wait. Luckily, I found Father outside carving furniture and I told him what Misrak had said. He looked at me as if I were out of my mind. Then he stopped what he was doing and went into dream-like state. It seemed he was not even looking at us, but through us. Misrak was standing next to me by this time. He told us to wait there and went inside. Shortly after, he returned with a face I had never seen before, bloodless and pale, yet very controlled.

"He sat us down and rather casually began asking Misrak about the coin. She told him everything she told me and more. She said her father sometimes brought the coin out and rubbed it between his hands saying, "Make me rich, bring me wealth like Beshaw Mekonen. At other times he would rub his body, neck and face with it, saying the same things. Misrak had not told this before. As I said, I nearly laughed, imagining her father worshipping the coin like that. After she finished her story, Father just said, 'Thank you . . . that is interesting,' and resumed his woodwork. Afterwards though, he spent more time with Misrak, privately talking. When she left he gave her something that made her really happy. Neither she nor he would tell me what it was. And that is what I remember of the coin and its disappearance. The irony of it was when I told mother this story right after she discovered it was missing, she didn't believe me. I think later she also had asked Adamu about it but he had completely denied having anything to do with our missing coin. At that time mother's primary suspects were our old neighbors and she didn't think of him as the culprit. And he was so close to us."

The family listened attentively as Zere narrated. A few times Bosena looked as if she wanted to add something to Zere's account. She moved her jaw and fat lips under the cover of her shemma, which now was all the way to the bridge of her nose, but no words came out. Her thoughts started and died in her eyes. Welella gave a light movement to her head, pressed her lips together and fought her tears mightily when she saw her sister struggle to speak. Others just looked away after seeing what Bosena tried to do.

For a short duration the place went silent, then the silence was broken by Kifle, Zere's oldest son. "Mama, did you think that the coin would have been yours if Grandpa had brought it back safely?"

"Well, that was what he told me. As his first born, I was entitled to it. He didn't call me Zere, his seed—for no reason. I was supposed to be one of the important propagators of his descendants. But he also put a condition on it. He said he would pass it on to me after seeing what kind of husband I was going to marry—as if I'd have any say in the matter. Knowing how my marriage ended up, I wonder if he would have given it to me," said Zere, a ghost of a grin crossing her wizened brown countenance."

"Baba was not a bad man," said Almaw, Zere's youngest son. "I bet you he would have allowed you to have it."

"It doesn't matter now. The sad thing is I am sorry he had to lose his life over it. It's a shame we grew up without him and mother had to fend for us on her own. All these years, I had not given up hope because there was a side of me that didn't want to bury him without solid proof. I am glad this boy was chosen as the intermediary between his ghost and us to find his remains, to allow us to finally bury him physically and in our consciousness. This should bring an end to all our long silent sufferings."

Everyone nodded.

"As to the coin," said Aunt Zere in a low voice, turning to Abraham as if she were talking to him privately. "If Father later changed his mind and decided to give it to Abraham, that was his decision. I remember when he left, it was four days before Abraham's seventh birthday. He told us he was going to get something special for him from the market. Now it's Abraham's decision about whom to pass it to." She smiled at him. "You'll know whom to give it to in time. There are family angels that make the decisions. We only act upon their suggestions."

"It's a big responsibility, I didn't want it to land on my lap like this," said Abraham looking away. "But as you said, I don't have to make the agonizing decision whom to pass it to, although in this case, it wouldn't be difficult."

Everybody looked at Desta. Damtew gazed at him with disdain.

"We need to get going," said Welella as she rose. "Thank you for inviting us. It was a long wait but it's good to have an end to it. Now, when we draw our last breaths, we won't be wondering what really happened to father."

Her five children got up and began gathering their personal belongings. Bosena asked for water to fill her nickel canteen for the trip. Of the three sisters, she had the shortest to go. Zere and her children also gathered up their belongings and prepared to leave.

Abraham suggested to Ayénat that she bring the dabo kolo from his aborted trip and distribute it among the travelers. As Ayénat scooped out the dried rolled breads and transferred them to the opened corners of the travelers' gabis or netelas, Abraham told the story behind the dabo kolo and his failed trip to Lalibela.

"This dabo kolo was meant to be in one's person's belly but now it's going to be entering so many different bellies," said Welella. "Thank you for giving it to us. It will be a handy snack."

All the others thanked him also. Some of them tossed a kolo or two into their mouths and chewed them with smiles on their faces. They all said how wonderful it tasted.

The guests hugged, kissed and held hands before they parted.

Abraham stood outside the tent and watched thoughtfully as his sisters with their children shuffled off in different directions.

FIFTY-THREE

Shortly after the guests left, Melkam and Ayénat removed all the furniture and food items from the tent. Abraham, with the help of Asse'ged and Damtew, took down the canvas covering, folded it, and put it aside to be returned to the Avinevra church. Following this activity, the two brothers left and Abraham decided to take a walk.

It was the first time in three weeks he had been alone or without pressing things to plan or arrange. It was also the first time he felt he had his full senses back. In the three weeks since Desta's bombshell, he had been too confused and shocked to think clearly.

He walked on the path that led to the southern creek, his mind swimming in all the things that unfolded in recent weeks. *What can I do with this information now?* Abraham asked himself, every time he thought of his father's murderers. His beloved cousins, who were now long dead, were being put on trial in absentia before the jury and judge—himself. Adamu and Kindé meant a lot to him, his mother and his sisters.

Now he had learned that these same men were his father's killers, and that they were the reasons they abandoned their former estate, the reason he and his sisters grew up without a father, with their mother struggling to raise them on her own. And there was the missed opportunity to benefit from owning the coin. *Should he throw himself into a rage at these men for what they had done to him and his family? Should he now hate them, despite all the happy memories he had of them?*

Having reached the creek, Abraham stood and gazed at his reflection in the dammed stream where the family fetched their drinking water. For a long time he stared at his fatigued features and sleep-deprived eyes, as if the answer to his questions might be found there.

He crossed the creek and continued on the path to Saba's old homestead. It was the first time he had ventured to this part of their property since the family moved two years ago.

He shuddered when he thought of the plans he'd had as he grew up to avenge his father's disappearance and reclaim the coin. After he heard suspicions from the adults that it was their old neighbors in Kuakura who stole the coin and caused his father to disappear and his mother to abandon their home and land, Abraham had planned to return there one day with a gun.

He had vowed never to forget their old neighbors' deeds. This was one of the reasons he kept a dog called Kooli, to remind him of his missing father and the coin, and thereby the wrongdoers.

To his disappointment, by the time he was old enough to acquire a gun, he had learned that the two alleged culprits had died, denying him the opportunity to exact his revenge. Later, the resentment and anger he had toward them began to haunt him. He often couldn't sleep and when he did, he slept fitfully, walking or talking in his sleep. The problem even began to affect his relationship with his wife and children, and he often lost his temper with them when they misbehaved.

Now, looking back he understood what a costly mistake it would have been to go after those old neighbors. Not only would he have gone to prison, he also could have started a cycle of violence between the two families. How ironic it would have been for his mother to discover it was her own cousins who had committed the crime and not the old neighbors she had run away from.

Still deep in thought, Abraham reached the site of Saba's old homestead, now covered with knee-high dry weeds. He stopped and let his eyes wander over the cursed land. It all seemed a mockery to him now.

This land, which they had once perceived as the harbinger of miscarriages, disease and destruction, had also been the deliverer of the family coin, his father's remains and spirit and in the process, liberating him and his sisters from their long, silent suffering. In a strange way, the whole place seemed liberated now. It felt more serene and enveloping than he had ever remembered it.

He gazed toward the place where they dug up his father's remains. On the other end of the property, across the Davola River, the top of the warka tree, under which Deb'tera Taye had done his spirit work with Desta and Astair, rose like a mushroom. Abraham was happy to see it. It was there, under that spreading tree, that the journey to his family's liberation had started. He was grateful that Providence had led him to the big tree.

At that moment, Abraham wished he would be overtaken by his emotions, to feel happiness at the outcome of his family's saga and to release the anger inside him. He waited and waited for the tears, but none came. Giving up, he slowly walked home.

That night he tossed and turned, thoughts of his father and his killers churning in his head. He needed to bury them once and for all, or they would haunt him for forever.

The following day, he rose before daybreak. He put on his work shorts and shirt and wrapped himself in his gabi. He pulled a pick and a shovel from the loft above the horses' stall and went outside.

The air was cool and the ground was damp from a drizzle that had fallen during the night. He felt the chill on his feet and hands. Much of the eastern half of the sky was veiled with soft gray clouds, making the valley appear shadowy, hushed and brooding. Abraham walked down the footpath that went to the field below his home. He left the trail and strolled across the southern border of the field, went halfway down and stopped. He dropped the shovel and pick where he stood. There was still time before dawn, so Abraham decided to walk in the open field before heading to his destination.

His six-foot-three frame was slightly stooped, as if he were weighed down by the thoughts that were percolating in his brain. He walked from one end of the field to the other. By the time he had completed his third round the sun had broken free, diffusing light throughout the valley. He lifted up his pick and threw it over his shoulder, grabbed the shovel and followed the animal path along which Desta had led the family to his father's remains. At the creek he gathered seven white round pebbles and put them in his pocket.

Once he got to the old gravesite, he beat down the tall grass near the ledge, then dropped the pick and shovel by his side and sat. For a long time he stared at the dug up soil, the tussled bushes and the strewn rocks in the ravine, left from the time they unearthed his father's remains. Images of events that had occurred over forty years ago began to filter through his brain.

In his mind's eye he saw two events take place, one where he sat, the other a hundred miles away, at his childhood home in Kuakura. From Desta's account, Abraham visualized the attacks on his father by his mother's cousins near where he sat, while at the same time he saw his own image as a boy running in and out of the house, waiting for his father to arrive with his birthday present.

His eyes flickered as he continued to watch the images rolling in his mind.

He tossed his head a little, as if to chase away sleep or stem his emotions.

The next batch of images showed his father covered in flies and ants, mouth gaping, eyes closed and sunken, his face wilted from the sun. Back in Kuakura, he saw his mother's worried face and her anxious, sleepless eyes. He and his sisters were running to the gate, gazing at the long twisted path that came around a grove of trees. His eyes brimmed with tears.

On an image of the third day, Abraham saw his father's decomposing body. In his mind, he smelled the overwhelming stench; it was so bad that vultures refused to come near it and hyenas ran away. Only flies found it delectable, covering it like bees in a hive. When he switched to his childhood home, he saw his mother sitting on a bench with her arms around Zere and Bosena. They were all crying. Welella, his four-year-old younger sister sat beside them, crying too. Abraham was there also, sad but hopeful his father might still come with his birthday present.

Back in his old home, on the fourth day, Abraham viewed a gathering of friends and relatives arranging for a search team. He was hoisted onto his uncle's shoulders and urged to call after his father in hopes that he would come back if he heard his son's voice. The family had believed he could be somewhere in the area in a stupor from the medicine they believed the jealous neighbors had given him. They told Abraham that since his father loved him, if he heard his voice, he might come back. Abraham bent his neck to let the tears fall on the ground, but instead they ran down his eagle-beak nose and dropped onto his chest. He shook his head and brought his mind back to focus. The next series of images saddened him deeply.

He saw white russet-tipped worms, crawling and somersaulting out of the corpse and slithering away as if they too wished to distance themselves from the reeking body.

Abraham blinked. Tears streamed down his cheeks and soaked into his gabi. The alternating images continued to stream through his memory in tandem with his tears.

Once he had finished viewing all the images and purged himself of the many painful memories, he felt better. He thanked his father's spirit for protecting the coin and for solving Saba's problems and giving him his first grandson.

Then Abraham had to think about his father's murderers—Adamu and Kindé. He couldn't bring criminal charges against them. They were long gone. There was so much he didn't understand, so much mystery wrapped up in the

coin. He would have to try to remember them for their good deeds. He needed
to forgive them. He also needed to forgive the spirit of his grandfather for
refusing a meeting with him. And he needed to forgive himself for wrongly
blaming the neighbors at their former home in Kuakura.

He rose. He threw the pick and shovel to the bottom of the ravine; he walked
around to a less steep part of the ledge and rappelled down, anchoring himself
on a branch of a bush. He gathered the shovel and pick, took them to the center
of the ravine, to the exact place where his father's body had once rested, and
began to dig. He dug and shoveled until he had created a trench three feet deep
by seven feet long.

He stood outside it, thought of all the bad things that had happened to him
and his family, including the murder of his father by his mother's cousins and
the anger that had been festering inside him all these years. He took the pebbles
from his pocket and dropped them one by one at equal distances from one end
of the trench to the other. They were to represent all the bad things that had
happened to his family, the pain he had suffered and the anger and grudges he
had held against people. Then he pushed the soil back into the hole, fast and
furiously. Once the hole was completely filled, he said his prayers, threw his
pick and shovel onto the embankment of the ravine and scrambled up the way
he had descended.

After his private funeral rite, Abraham felt that all the painful things of the last
forty-two years associated with his father were now buried, just like his father's
remains were formally buried at the church yard. Now he could go on with his
own life. He would take Damtew's lead and plant eucalyptus trees—seven of
them—around the perimeter of the ravine to memorialize the site of his father's
murder and to immortalize his deeds on the account of the coin. He wanted
future generations to know that this was the place where Abraham had buried the
trials and tribulations of his life on account of his father and the once-lost family
heirloom.

As he walked home later that morning, Abraham felt a great sense of relief
and contentment—closure, at long last. Only one unanswered question still
nagged at him. The Italian soldier's gold watch. What had happened to it?

That night a great sense of peace came to Abraham as he covered his face
with his gabi and closed his eyes. "Now I can go on living," he said with a long
sigh.

"The moment he fell into a slumber, he began to snore, deep and long rattles," Ayénat said a few days later. "I didn't dare to disturb him. It seemed as though he needed that rest as much as the air he had struggled to breathe."

THE FOLLOWING DAY, Abraham woke with a smile. Desta counted seven flashes of his father's chipped tooth, and that was not even counting the ones he bestowed upon the mookit goats as he patted and bid them farewell for the day. Abraham was not talking with anyone nor was anything funny around the house, but he kept beaming, as though there was something hilariously amusing going on—or he was in some sort of internal bliss.

When his father smiled, the chipped tooth always drew Desta's attention. It was not an unattractive feature, really. It was more like a dimple in a chin or a small mole. But because it was slightly shorter than the others and interrupted the perfect flow of his otherwise even, white teeth, it always stood out when he smiled.

There was something odd about the continuous smiles. He was doing this on the fourth day after he buried the remains of his father, when he should have been mourning, not smiling. Other family members noticed and said they hoped nobody outside the clan saw him beaming like this. Desta too couldn't understand why his father was so happy. He had always wanted to find his father alive, but now instead of being sad like everybody else, he seemed happy to have buried him.

"I hope nobody else sees you smiling like this," said Ayénat when she saw her husband grinning from ear to ear.

"You don't know what it's like to be free," said Abraham. "It's as if someone has removed a shackle I have been fettered with all these years. I am not sure how to handle this freedom . . . because of it I have this great internal sense of joy."

"It was only four days ago we buried your father—the father you long grieved over and now you are happy? It would look bad if outsiders saw you," said Ayénat.

"Firstly, there are no outsiders here. Secondly, I am entitled to express my feelings however they come to me. I just didn't realize how emotionally bound I was to my father all these years. I believed since I was seven years old that he would someday come to us and that someday we would meet him again and introduce him to his grandchildren. Now, from just the simple knowledge that none of these things will happen and he is gone out of my life for eternity, I feel freed from forty-two years of bondage.

"It doesn't mean he will be dead to my memory, of course, but I will no longer dream of seeing him again. My children and my sisters' children will live and die without ever knowing their grandfather—that still saddens me—but as far as my connection with him, I am free at last!"

"It also means you no longer have to have another dog named Kooli anymore," said Desta, glancing toward his father, with a half grin on his face.

"Yes. The Kooli we have now will be the last of the Koolies, the end of an era for Koolies," said his father, flashing his chipped tooth.

"It has been a long wait. It's sad that it ended this way," said Ayénat, looking away.

"I know, but any end is better than no end at this point. I just wished it had been sooner. I wish Desta . . . uhhm . . . Desta," stuttered Abraham. He was looking at his son when his wife interrupted.

"It was not meant to be."

Desta looked at his father expecting him to finish his sentence.

"I just wish Desta had been born sooner, so that we could have dealt with the problem sooner."

"We've no control over God's will," said Ayénat, smiling a little.

"It could have happened with any of the first four children. If that were the case, we could have been freed years ago."

"They were not in the scheme of things, apparently," said Ayénat.

"I need to bring this closure to the children as well," said Abraham. "They too are now freed from thoughts of their grandfather, and so is that land now free—to be walked on, to be grazed on, to be inhabited."

"How true that is," said Ayénat. "We have been terrified to look at it, let alone step foot on it there since Saba and her family left. Now perhaps Damtew, Asse'ged and others can split it. It's time for Damtew and his wife to have a home of their own."

Desta recalled that he had visited the land after Saba left, the night when Damtew's baby goat was lost. He had not been struck down or fallen ill from spending the night in Yihoon's shed on Saba's old property.

"That was what I was thinking too," said Abraham. "I know Damtew will soon start bugging me to give him a share of that land. We need to be a step ahead, to divide it up among the deserving children."

FIFTY-FOUR

July

It was grandpa's Teskar, the fortieth day after he was buried. Ayénat had been preparing for weeks. During the last few days, she brewed tella, prepared the spices for making sauce and made a great quantity of dough for injera. The preparations were similar to those for her children's weddings two years ago, but this time no guests were invited.

To Desta's prying questions, Ayénat explained that the food and drink she prepared was going to be taken to church for the priests who were going to provide the prayer services for his grandfather and for the poor and the aged of the valley who were invited to come for the event. They were doing these things on Grandpa's behalf so that God would have mercy on his soul and send it to heaven.

They had had prayer services for Grandpa on the third, seventh, twelfth and thirtieth days of his funeral. On each of those days they prepared food and drink, not so extensively as for the Teskar, with one jar of tella, and some forty injeras with a good quantity of sauce to feed the priests and some of the immediate family members who came for the services. "Why all this trouble?" asked Asse'ged when he saw all the food. "Grandpa's soul suffered enough here on earth. Being trapped in this valley for forty-two years is hell enough. I am sure God has already given him enough credit to enter His Kingdom."

"We cannot know how God decides these matters. We need to do these routine things just in case," said Ayénat as she brought one more basket of injera and placed it outside for the men to carry to church.

Everybody in the family—Yihoon and Saba, Teferra, Asse'ged, Tamirat and Damtew with their wives and Abraham and Ayénat—went to church, all except Desta, who stayed behind to look after the animals.

He watched the line of family members leave along the path, men carrying baskets of injera on their shoulders and women carrying jars of tella on their backs. The only ones who had not come for Grandpa's Teskar were Hibist and Enat and their husbands. When Desta asked his mother why not, she explained that the service was not a celebration but rather to give provisions to the priests and the poor, the aged and disabled so that God would look at Grandpa's soul favorably.

ABRAHAM AND AYENAT wanted to take advantage of the Teskar to apportion Saba's old property and to announce who was to receive the ancient coin. Abraham thought it would be a good idea to disclose the future bearer of the item at this important milestone since the coin was one of the reasons his father's soul had stayed on earth for forty-two years.

It was late afternoon when everyone who had gone to church returned carrying empty baskets in their hands and clay pots on their backs. Desta was driving the animals home when his father approached and told him to make sure that the animals were put away early so he could be ready when dinner was served.

Three mossebs were set—two for the adults and one for the children. The two parents sat at one mosseb with Yihoon and Saba and Teferra and his wife. The other three adult brothers sat at another with their wives. Desta, Astair and Zena were seated in a corner of the living room near the central, roof-bearing pole.

Before they removed the tops from the mossebs, Melkam brought a pitcher of water and a wooden bowl so the dinner guests could wash their hands prior to eating. She placed the bowl under the hands of each person and poured the water as that person rubbed their hands together. Then the adults prayed quietly for the grandfather's soul. Desta and the other children put their heads down and listened to the adults' muffled words. The covers were removed from the mossebs and everybody began to eat.

There were two separately cooked sauces, shiro wat and potato and dried beef wat, which were poured on top of the layers of injera. The adults ate their meals with their tella, chatting about the service, the appreciation expressed by the priests and the poor and disabled who came for the event and the simple eightieth day and one-year anniversary services yet to come.

After dinner, Melkam brought the pitcher of water with a bowl, and everyone washed their hands.

"We want to take this opportunity to discuss some important family affairs.

It was part of the reason we wanted you to come and have dinner with us," said Abraham after the dinner guests had washed their hands.

Everyone looked at him wondering what he was referring to. They had experienced surprises after big family dinners.

"Now that Baba's spirit has left the area, we need to bring Saba and Yihoon's old property into our possession. We have decided, as a replacement for the new property given to them, Asse'ged and Damtew should receive Saba's old property and share it equally—how they divide it can be decided between themselves."

Everyone's eyes turned to the two brothers. Asse'ged smiled openly, showing all his teeth. Damtew grinned with his mouth closed as if he was afraid to show his perfect teeth, but the cloud of gloom that always seemed to occupy his shadowy countenance was suddenly raised to show another layer of his personality. No words came from his mouth, nor were his beautiful teeth ever revealed, but the look on his face spoke volumes for him.

Teferra and Tamirat looked at each other and then their father. They couldn't wait to hear what was in store for them.

Abraham drew a mouthful of tella from his tumbler, spat out a few colloidal granules and resumed. "Teferra, since you live on my mother's old property, you can keep that property for yourself. To make things even, we have purchased a sewing machine and paid for your lessons. If you decide to give up farming, you can give us back the property and continue with the tailoring business.

"Tamirat, since we were not certain if you will return home from your in-laws and live here permanently, we did not consider a piece of land for you, but you can have a portion of the new property we have cleared two creeks to the south of here. Yihoon and Saba, you have your new place. We are happy that you have now your new child and your animals are doing well."

"Thank you, Baba. Everything is going well for us. We couldn't have asked for more," said Yihoon.

The brothers and their wives smiled happily, chatting among themselves, sharing their excitement. Saba stole glances at Desta. The brothers didn't seem to consider his existence or the possibility that he might also receive a share.

Abraham let the chatter die down before he made his next announcement. When all was quiet he continued.

"The last—but not least—piece of property will go to Desta," said Abraham.

Everyone looked at each other wondering what that would be. "Do you have a piece of land we don't know about, Baba?" asked Asse'ged.

"No, I meant the coin."

"Ohhh that . . . that metal object. You confused us when you referred to it as property," said Asse'ged, glancing at his father.

"It is property—valuable property, from what your grandpa said. I never had the good fortune to receive it as a boy, as my father had intended, so I don't know what it really does. But I feel obligated to pass it on to Desta because he was Baba's choice. And there obviously was good reason for him to have guarded it for forty-two years."

"It seems like it's a dangerous object for one to possess," said Teferra.

"There is a great deal of responsibility that goes with owning it and not everyone is capable of handling that," said Abraham.

"It sounds like a joke to me," said Asse'ged. "How can Desta ever defend and protect it? From the accounts we have heard, you have to be physically big and strong to guard it in the event someone tries to steal it."

"Firstly, Desta will grow to be big and strong. Secondly, it's not sheer physical size that is important, it's intelligence. Desta has the latter and I am sure he will have the former in due time."

"For whatever reason, Grandpa chose Desta to have it, and it's he who should have it," said Saba, frowning at her younger brothers.

"I don't think Asse'ged was saying Desta shouldn't have the coin," said Teferra, glancing at Saba. "It's just that if it needs to be protected, it should be placed in hands of someone who would be physically capable of handling such a job."

"You mean somebody like Damtew or Asse'ged?" said Ayénat.

"Or Tamirat and me. Are you prepared to lose this ancient family treasure again?" said Teferra, turning to his father.

"You all seem to want this curious metal piece," said Tamirat, turning to Teferra. "Leave me out of it. I'm not interested."

"Have you all spoken your minds?" said Abraham, looking at his adult children. They heard and saw the seriousness of his voice and his face.

"Then I will answer my own question. Desta, and *only* Desta, will have the coin. You can stay here and argue until dawn, but my decision will not change."

Under the shadow of the earthen ledge that circled the roof-bearing pole, a few feet above the ground, where a beeswax candle burnt brightly, Desta listened and watched as his brothers battled their father. They sickened him.

WHEN DESTA LAY in bed that night, he thought about the coin. His brothers
might actually be correct with regards to the safekeeping and protecting it.
He did not feel physically able—now or in the future—nor did he want such
a responsibility. More importantly, the coin had little value to him—less than
the safety pin he used to remove thorns from his feet. It was not like a shilling
or *cantim* he could buy things with. Why on earth had his grandfather gotten
himself killed over it? And why had his soul guarded it for forty-two years? It
was beyond his human understanding. *All for a mottled metal disk that one
would toss into the garden like a broken piece of clay!*

When he thought about what his grandfather had said—how old the coin was
and how many bearers had lost their lives trying to protect it—it scared him.
Terrified him, actually. As much as he appreciated Grandpa revealing himself to
him and making it work out so he could be the recipient of it, he wished he had
passed it on to one of his brothers instead, like Damtew. Let him die over it.

Desta searched his mind for a situation in which he could imagine spilling
his own blood for something or someone. It would have to be someone or
something he truly loved. For example, he could see himself dying for Hibist.
Or if someone got in the way of his desire to go to the top of the mountain. And
maybe even for Kooli and the vervet monkeys—perhaps more for Kooli than
the monkeys. But the coin; he had no connection to it whatsoever. No feeling of
passion came to him when he saw it and touched it. He didn't even particularly
like the way it looked. *How can I give up my life trying to protect the coin as
Grandpa did?*

Then he remembered another thing grandpa had said. "There is a sister coin
somewhere in the world. The two coins will unite within the lifetime of the
bearers. When they do, an event that has never happened before or will ever
happen again will take place. *What did that mean?* He thought of the images
of the coin that he and Grandpa had drawn. There were all those channels and
their attributes that he needed to recite every morning or evening, rubbing the
coin between his palms to have his wishes fulfilled. All these things were too
complicated to comprehend.

Desta thought about the stories his grandfather shared and illustrated on
the goatskin, trying to piece together the details. How would all the things his
grandfather told him come together when he finally possessed the coin? What

did he need to do to prepare himself?

A message to his grandfather:

Dear Grandpa, as I am now going to be the bearer of the coin please give me the mental and physical strength to protect it. And please make me love it. Only then can I sacrifice my life for it. You never told me where exactly that sister coin is so that I can look for it. I hope somehow in my dreams or in person you will advise me what I am supposed to do with this coin. I am sorry if I insulted you by complaining and doubting the merits of your wisdom. I don't mean to dishonor the privilege you have given me. I am just voicing my fears. I'll leave it up to you. Good night, wherever you are!

FIFTY-FIVE

The morning following Desta's acknowledgement as the recipient of the coin, he went to the back of the house with a knife. Under the eaves, he had buried a clay cup containing the Italian gold watch and two Maria Theresa silver dollars. Knowing how much his father would have liked to have the family's gold coin, Desta thought he might be able to convert the gold watch into a gold coin if he left it stowed away with the other coins. That had been four years ago, when he was five. The idea had taken root one day when he asked Hibist how one could change one object into another. "Only God can do that," Hibist had told him.

Desta had removed two silver dollars from Abraham's collection in a jar, placed the watch between them and dropped them together into the cup. He had sealed the cup with mud, dug a hole in the ground and buried it with the three items inside. He thought if he prayed to God often, the watch would transform into a gold coin. Then, once it happened, he would give it to his father as a gift. He had planned to leave it buried for seven years, as this number had magical power in his family.

Now all that had changed. The family coin had been retrieved and he was to be the owner of it. It was time to check on the watch. He dug up his treasure and opened the container. To his disappointment, the watch was still there, though now covered with a film of whitish mold. The silver coins were tarnished black.

He polished them with a cloth and brought them home.

"Baba!" said Desta when he saw his father sitting on his stool waiting for breakfast. The bright morning light was streaming through the open front door, lighting up the house.

"Yes, Desta!" said his father cheerfully.

"You gave everybody something last night but nobody gave you anything. I have a gift you might like," said Desta, smiling.

"What have you got for me, son?"

"Something to take the place of the coin you always wanted but never had," said Desta with a broad grin.

"Hmmm," said Abraham. "I was not meant to have the coin, but you were. I am happy for you. The grandson you helped give me is gift enough for me." He looked at Desta thoughtfully, stroking his goatee.

"I didn't do anything. I just repeated what grandpa's spirit told me."

"No matter. You were still the agent for our success."

"Close your eyes and open your hand," instructed Desta.

Abraham did as he was told.

"Era!" said Abraham, gazing down at the familiar object. "Where did you find this?!" He suppressed the impulse to scold the boy for having said nothing when he was looking for the watch two years ago.

"I buried it in the ground between two silver dollars, hoping it would become the gold coin one day and I could give it to you as a gift," said Desta, smiling.

"That is very nice of you, son," said Abraham. "A watch won't turn into a coin no matter how long it's buried with other coins, but thanks for your thoughts."

"You can still think of it like having the family coin as you used to years ago."

"No, but we have to find a way to return it to the family of the dead soldier from whom I took it."

"Why?" asked Desta, saddened.

"This watch may be their family heirloom," said Abraham.

"Where would you find them?"

"Well, we need to start with the sincere desire to return it. God will take care of the rest."

Desta was confused and disappointed.

"I'll do my best to track down the family of the soldier and return it to them," said Abraham. "If I can't do it in my lifetime, will you promise to do it on my behalf?" asked Abraham.

"How can I find them?" asked Desta, puzzled.

"Don't worry about that. Just have the sincere intention to do it, and God will help. That is one of the cardinal rules of the coin we own."

"Yes, I promise," said Desta with a smile.

"Thank you," said Abraham. He embraced his son with tears in his eyes.

FIFTY-SIX

September

Desta paced the green grass between his home and the open apiary, waiting for Saba to come. It was approaching noon on a Saturday and nearly everybody had gone either to the market or to visit families or friends across the river. Patches of clouds spread across the azure dome above, others hung over the mountains. The bright sun brought the yellow, blue, red, pink and violet flowers into full exuberance.

As he paced, Desta watched the bees hover in and around the bamboo hives, buzzing about a bit and floating off. Some landed gracefully on the yellow daisies that grew plentifully inside the fence of the potato and collard green garden, others hummed and skittered on the white potato petals, but the purple, cup-like petals of the sweet pea vines that wrapped the fence posts didn't attract them. If his mind had not been so preoccupied by his impending, long-awaited trip to the top of the mountain, Desta would have enjoyed watching the industrious creatures shuttling in and out of their home. For now though, his mind was elsewhere.

Nearly three weeks earlier, when Saba came for the New Year celebration, she told Desta that shortly after the Maskel holiday, she would fulfill her promise of taking him to the top of the mountain. In the nights and days following this discussion, Desta had thought about nothing but his anticipated trip. He had prepared and stowed away everything he thought he would need: a long slender bamboo, one end of which was stuffed with a ball of cotton cloth, which he planned to use both as a writing device and an extension of his own hand in the event he was not tall enough to reach the sky; a leather sack in which he would gather and stow as much of the clouds as he could; a small gourd filled with red dye dissolved in warm water, which he would use to write his name and draw a banner on the sky; and an old *ankasay*, the pointed metal tip of which he hoped to use to widen the rain holes in the sky so he could see

God, Israel and the God of Israel. All these items Desta had hidden in an empty, barrel-like hive in the bees' shed.

The night before, Saba had sent Astair to remind him she would come near midday. By her instructions, Desta had driven all the animals to the field so that Yihoon's nephew could attend to them while he was away.

Desta kept watching on the path that was going to bring Saba to their meeting place. The serpentine path disappeared into the bushes so he wouldn't know if she was coming until she had cleared them.

She appeared suddenly while he was momentarily pulling out the things he had put away in the hive, anticipating her impending arrival. "Ready?" Saba asked, startling him.

"Very much so," said Desta, happy to see her.

"What are all these things for?" Saba asked.

"These are the things I need to use when we get to the top of the mountain." Desta told his sister about the items and how he planned to use them.

Saba's eyes grew bigger and her lips tightened almost into a grimace as she watched her brother's excited show-and-tell presentation.

"What's wrong?" asked Desta, perturbed.

"Nothing . . . just that . . . just . . . I think this is too much to bring. This mountain is unforgiving, nearly impossible to scale even for those who have had plenty of experience in climbing."

"These are very important to me," said Desta. "Without them, we might as well forget the trip."

Saba looked away for a long time. "Can you promise me something?" she said, turning back to her brother.

Desta looked at her puzzled. "What?"

"At some places the mountain is too high to be reached easily. Of course we'll do our best to be as near to the top as we can, but if it happens that we don't make it all the way, you won't be too disappointed, will you?"

"No . . . no I won't," said Desta, not sure if he was telling the truth. "That is why I have this long pole," he clarified.

"Even then," said Saba, averting her eyes.

"To me, just getting as close as I can is very exciting," said Desta, trying to reassure his sister.

"Good, then let's go before it gets too late and too hot."

Desta gathered his things. He closed the ink-containing gourd tightly and placed it in the leather sack. The thought that it might spill and stain the leather—and the cloud he planned to put inside—concerned him. He took it out, tightened the wooden lid once more and tilted the container to see if the ink would spill. It was good. He dropped it back into the sack and closed it.

Saba had her own problems. She carried a large freshly baked dabo in a cloth sack on her back. The warm bread was making her sweat, causing her dress to stick to her back. While Desta was getting ready, she removed the sack and aired out her back by reaching over her shoulders, pinching her dress and shaking it. She also carried a nickel canteen filled with water.

Seeing that Desta was not big enough to carry his leather sack and all its contents, Saba swapped her canteen for his luggage and threw it on her back, slipping the cords around her shoulders. Desta tied the leather handle of the canteen to his pole and carried it over his shoulder.

Having all their items in order, the pair started up the mountain, passing Teferra's newly-constructed but still vacant home. Outside, Saba noticed several pieces of wood that could be used as walking sticks. She picked a stout straight stick for herself and a shorter one for Desta.

The upper end of Teferra's property bordered the forest that stretched midway to the mountain. Desta was familiar with this forest, as he had watched the morning sun trace its journey down the valley over the blanket of green, but he had never gone up the footpath. The trail went straight up, splitting Teferra's property in half.

As they approached the forest, on either side of the footpath Desta saw the three kaga bushes and a strawberry vine that draped a gottem tree. A flood of memories came to him. Hibist and he used to come and raid those bushes and vines when their berries were ripe. Desta wished Hibist were with them now. He heard his sister's voice in his head: "Some day you and I will go to the top of the mountain and touch the sky together." Desta was sorry this dream had never come true. How much fun it would have been if she were with him that day!

Saba was preoccupied with her own reflections. Knowing what she knew about the untouchable nature of the sky, she thought it was cruel to make Desta travel such an arduous journey only to learn in the end that the sky was not within his reach.

Twice she thought about telling him the truth and aborting the trip altogether, but each time she thought it would be doubly cruel to tell him now, after he had spent weeks preparing for this journey. Climbing the mountain would be rewarding in and of itself, but she also wanted to mentally prepare him.

"Do you want to hear a story?" she asked Desta as they entered the forest. He was springing up the inclined path in front of her, his eyes scanning the forest floor and trees as if he were looking for something.

"Yeah," he said, turning to his sister.

Saba cleared her throat and quickly gathered the details of the story from her memory.

"Once upon a time there was this fox who came across red-hot figs high in the branches when he was strolling along in the forest. They looked succulent and beautiful and he badly wanted to eat them. He jumped as high as he could, but he couldn't reach the figs. He tried again, this time walking back and coming at a running speed. He nearly touched them but still couldn't grab them. He tried a third time, again with no luck. Finally he walked away, gracefully just the same, saying, I will come and try again when I am better prepared. These figs might be sour anyway."

"That is too bad for the fox," said Desta.

"But do you know why I told the story?"

Desta shook his head.

"To remind you that if for some reason we are not near enough to reach the sky, you have to be as strong and carefree as the fox, to walk away with equanimity and grace. If you can't reach it this time, you shouldn't be too disappointed. You can always come back and try again."

She might as well have put those words to someone with deaf ears. Desta didn't want to think about not reaching the sky. He was determined to do it, now or in the future. He said nothing.

Birds chirped in the forest, rustled in the leaves and darted in front them. The floor was mottled with yellow light and the air felt cool and invigorating.

Desta kept looking for vervet or colobus monkeys, the familiar animals he had once befriended. He saw none. He asked Saba where they might have gone.

"Probably by the creek, where they usually hang around," she said.

The rain-washed path was dotted with brown rocks of different shapes and sizes. Desta and Saba avoided them by walking along the side of the trail. The ground off the rocky beaten path was strewn with dead leaves, dead twigs and fallen moss-covered trees. Weeds grew through and around the twigs and the tree trunks. The path was straight in the flatter areas but twisted and turned as the terrain rose sharply.

Saba had told Desta that it wouldn't take them long to clear the forest, but by the time they emerged at the other end, it felt like a long time had passed for Desta. Along the steep portion of the path, their conversation stopped and they breathed deeply. Saba huffed and puffed as she tried to keep up with Desta, but every time he turned around, he noticed his sister had fallen farther behind. When he stopped and she caught up to him, Desta saw perspiration on her cheeks and forehead. Some trickled down and nestled on her chest. She wiped her face with her sleeve.

"You want to rest, Saba?" said Desta, smiling.

"Good idea. I need to drink some water also," said Saba as she nearly staggered to sit down on the grass, winded. "I'm out of shape. I haven't done much walking after the baby was born. We have treated him like some precious object. Yihoon doesn't want me to do anything but attend to his boy. Now look how rusty I am. I used to walk these mountains without a bit of exhaustion."

Desta gave her the canteen and watched her guzzle a long swig.

"How about a snack?" she said, pulling the dabo out from her cloth bag.

"Yeah, I am hungry more than thirsty," said Desta. "I didn't eat much this morning as I was excited about the trip."

Saba broke off a wedge of bread for each of them.

As they ate, they looked down at the valley. Desta noticed that their homes appeared tiny and squashed flat to the ground.

The panoramic view, with the dense forest below and the patches of farmland mantled with crops at different stages of ripening, the uncultivated fields veiled with green pasture and the flaming wild flowers that adorned the hills and mountains, was breathtaking. The cattle looked like mere ants and the goats and sheep blurred into the bushes.

The sky above was sapphire blue, the way Desta always dreamt it would be when he came to feel it with his hands. Puffy clouds hung idly above the eastern mountains, and there were spreading gauze-likes ones on the north side of the valley but there was no blemish of any kind above the mountain Desta and Saba were climbing.

"Shall we continue?" asked Desta, rising to his feet.

Saba nodded, rose and gathered her things.

As they climbed, Desta occasionally put down his things and waited for Saba to catch up.

"You are amazing, Desta. You don't even have a drop of sweat," said Saba when she drew near him.

"I've been dreaming about this trip for a long time. All my thoughts have been so focused on reaching the top that I don't have time to feel how tired I am."

"Well, we are a little over halfway there," said Saba.

"I don't see any clouds. Do you think we will find them when we get there?" asked Desta.

"Maybe they will come when we arrive."

"I really want to gather a sack full of them for Hibist. They will be proof that I have finally reached my dreams," said Desta, beaming.

"You don't need proof. Just tell her about your experience and she will believe you."

"Yeah, but I really want to see how she reacts when she opens the sack, when the cloud shrouds her face and blankets the room. I'm going to make sure I give it to her while she is inside the house."

Saba suppressed a laugh. "Let's keep going. The sun is rapidly descending and we need to return before it gets dark."

Desta quickly gathered his things and began walking. The path split into two, one went to the right, the other climbed straight up, winding and turning.

"Take the one on the left," said Saba preemptively. "It's a shorter way to the top." Desta followed Saba's suggestion.

With every few feet of climbing, he began to feel more anxious. His heart raced and the blood pulsed in his temples. He wondered what it would feel like when he first touched the sky. Would it be cold, warm, rough like a rock or smooth like his mother's clay baking pan? Would it make an echoing sound when knocked upon, like a clay pot, or would it be solid, giving rise to only a dull thud?

When he wrote his name, would it be like paper or so smooth that nothing stuck to its surfaces? How far down could one see his name when he wrote it on the sky? How clear and visible would his banner be? The more questions he asked himself, the more nervous he got.

"Have you ever touched the sky?" he said, turning to Saba.

He had left her too far behind. She didn't hear him. When she caught up to him, he asked her again.

"No, I never have. Never tried to. But it sure would be fun," she said, stopping to catch her breath.

"Why didn't you?"

"Nobody could take me to the top of the mountain when I was a child. Then again, I never had a great desire like you have. Later, I was too busy with work."

"You can touch it with me today," said Desta, turning to press on.

"I am looking forward to it."

"You can use my stick at places where we can't reach it with our bare hands. But you need to give it back to me when I am ready to sign my name and paint the banner," said Desta looking back.

"I am at your service," said Saba, smiling a little.

Happy with his sister's answer, Desta trotted up the mountain, sometimes following the zigzag course of the path, other times walking straight up, bypassing the trail.

The higher he climbed, the farther ahead he got. Whenever his sister fell behind, he stopped and waited for her and then continued. As they neared the top, Desta became even more anxious and nervous, chaotic thoughts racing through his head. All the while he kept looking up to see if they were getting nearer to the sky.

As they approached the top of the mountain, the land became flatter but the sky was still high and they couldn't see where it was joined with the earth. Heart racing, Desta became increasingly bewildered and terrified by what he was observing. When they cleared the steep side of the mountain, he saw the earth curving and more land stretching beyond that. At the very top, they found a pea farm. The stalks crept on the ground, some bearing ribbon-blue blossoms.

The path ran along the outside of the pea farm. Desta perched on a large boulder and waited for Saba. He was baffled and wanted to ask her a question. Beyond the flatter part of the mountain, another hill rose abruptly. He couldn't see anything beyond it. To the right of the mountain the land sloped gently, revealing more earth.

"What is going on?" he said, when Saba finally arrive. "I thought the sky joined with the earth here but it looks like it's still as high as it was when I saw it from below."

"Well, that was what I was telling you," said Saba looking at Desta's bewildered face. His eyes were brimming. "Some places it's like this. At other places it might be different. This route is as new to me as it is to you. Let's see if the sky is any closer when we climb this next hill."

"But it seems to me there is more land beyond these mountains. Can you see the tips of those mountains?" said Desta, squinting toward the distant hills in the west.

"Yes, of course. There is always more land. You thought where we lived was all there was to the earth?"

"Yes, I thought there was nothing beyond these mountains," said Desta, fighting back tears.

"Let's move on and see if the sky is touchable when we climb this next one," said Saba, encouraging Desta on with a light push on his back.

Desta was lost in thought. He walked meditatively, measuring his steps, trying to make sense of it all.

"Saba," he said, looking back as they began climbing the massive incline ahead of them.

"Yes?"

"Are there things you have withheld from me about this sky and earth business? Where is it? I had hoped to see and touch it once we cleared the top of the mountain. Now I don't know. I am really confused."

"I can't answer those questions, Desta. I know it has been your dream for many years to come to the top of these mountains and touch this blue thing above us. My job is to chaperone you in your mission of discovery. I thought you knew there was more land beyond the mountains because you have heard Baba talk about Kuakura, which is far away. As far as touching the sky, I have wondered about it for many years myself and we are just about to find it out— you and I. Let's finish climbing this peak. Be prepared. If we cannot reach it with our hands, we can at least try to do so with your stick," said Saba, trying earnestly.

Saba had shared a lot of information. Desta needed time to process it. He said nothing. For now he hurried, anxious to reach the final plateau and discover everything for himself. He quickened his pace. His heart was beating like a hammer. Everything looked like a dream to him.

He looked around for clouds; the only real, tangible things he thought remained of his dreams. He scanned the sky, looking east, the section of the sky where the clouds always hung. Sure enough, there was an expanding charcoal gray cloud back there. To his amazement, through the passes and gaps of the eastern ridges, he also could see waves of mountains shrouded in blue-gray haze. The sky was not connected to those ridges either. His long held theory was crumbling right before his eyes. He began to feel empty inside.

He trotted faster and faster, frightened, to get to the top. He slowed when a new thought hit him, then he picked up speed again as the desire to reach the top impelled him onward.

As he neared the top, Desta slowed to a molasses speed, taking cautious, measured steps as if he were stalking a prey. When he finally reached the peak, the sky was as far away as it had always been when he looked up from his home. Unfolding before him was more land—far and wide—some hilly, corrugated and jagged, some flat as a tabletop. The line where the sky met with the earth was a mere mirage, buried far away in the smoky mist. The tears that he long fought finally came. He had no power over them anymore. They flowed like water. Saba held him close to her bosom and let him cry as long as he wanted.

"Let's make sense of this," said Saba when Desta's cries subsided to sniffles. She wiped his tears with the hem of her netela, brushed off the remaining streaks with her fingers. She held him by the hand and led him to the highest spot of the peak where they could see their homes at the bottom of the valley as well as all the distance lands beyond the peak.

They perched on a flat moss-fringed rock and looked. All around them, the plateau was rocky with the scrubby grass and wind-beaten shrubs clinging fast to the soil.

"If I go by the amount of tears you shed, it is obvious you are very disappointed by your discovery," said Saba, caressing Desta's wooly hair. "Perhaps we could have told you the sky is not near enough to be touched by a human hand, but I myself often wondered if there might be a mountain so tall one could lay a hand on the firmament..

"I had hoped we could do it up here and looked forward to the joy of that experience with you today. But it was not meant to be. We found what we found. Still, you must admit that all this land is exciting, not to mention the pleasure you had had all these years dreaming about one day touching this blue dome."

"Yes, but I can't believe you all let me go on all those years believing something that didn't exist," said Desta in a sad tone, his eyes probing the deep hazy horizon below the sun.

"Of all the children in our home and probably from the homes of the entire valley, you are the only one who came up with this bizarre idea of touching the sky. Baba told everyone not to interfere with your fertile imagination. It was better you found out for yourself than to kill your dreams. As I said, since I first heard your dream, I have often wondered if somewhere in the world exists a tall enough mountain where one could reach the sky. I was thrilled to have the privilege to join you in your quest." Saba glowed with renewed excitement.

"Had I known the truth, I wouldn't have wracked my brain all these years," said Desta, his eyes still fixed on the hazy western sky.

"Had you known, you wouldn't have had the pleasure of thinking about all the possibilities. And you wouldn't have discovered all this land at such an early age. Most boys and girls do not leave the valley until they get married or are old enough to carry things to the market or run messages for relatives who live outside the valley."

When Desta said nothing, Saba continued in a perky voice. "Speaking of discovery, let me tell you what is what and who lives where in those distant lands." She pointed to an outlying valley. "There in the northeast beyond Lehwani is called Jemma. That is where that man lives who took Baba's sheep to breed—his name escapes me."

"Melaku," said Desta,

"Yes, him. That is where he comes from." The land in the east, where you see snatches of hills through the pass, is called Lij Ambera. Aunt Welella lives there with her family. The road to Lij Ambera is very rocky—hard on the soles of your feet—the terrain is very rugged. Here in the south, beyond Afer Masha, is Talia. Aunt Bosena lives there with her son. It is hot in the dry season and they grow a lot of corn and fruit. Over there to the southwest is Gumbla, where your Grandpa Farris lives, and not far from him to the right is where Enat and Tenaw live. Beyond them, on that plateau is the town of Yeedib, where we go to market every Saturday."

"You mean you walk all the way over there, after climbing this mountain?" said Desta, squinting and trying to assess the distance. His voice was grave.

"Yes, but rarely do we come straight up the mountain as we just did. We usually take the road that goes along the side of the mountain, past our former farm, until we get to the main caravan route which is less steep and easier to walk on.

"Let's see, there in the north is the town of Fagita. This was where Teferra took his lessons to become a tailor. Past Fagita, in the thick haze is Kuakura. Aunt Zere lives there with her three children. As you know, that was where Father was born. Way beyond Kuakura, near the blurred horizon is . . ." She stopped as if she'd had a lapse of memory.

Desta turned to her to see what had happened. She was staring off into the remote, invisible land, her eyes glazed.

"That place is the town of Dangila, where I went to see that woman with milk-white skin and yellow hair," she continued in a halting voice.

Desta saw that something bad had suddenly come over Saba. Her eyes had filled with tears, and her face looked forlorn.

"She said she didn't know the answer to my problem and gave me a few useless round white things to take . . ." Tears streamed down her cheeks as she spoke. "All those trying years before her, with the herbs and roots, the trips to places near and far, the holy water and nothing worked." Desta wrapped his arms around his sister and let her cry, as she had done with him a few minutes earlier.

"I was not expecting this," said Saba, trying to laugh off her sudden display of emotion. "After all those years, my answer came in the form of my little brother, Desta . . ." She began to cry again. This time she wrapped her arms around him.

Desta wriggled his hands out of her grasp and wrapped them around her neck.

"A million thanks, Desta," said Saba, resting her head on his little shoulder.

"A million thanks to you too for bringing me here to see all this land and for helping me realize my dreams, no matter the outcome," said Desta, attempting to smile.

"You know about this crying thing, I feel so much better, as if a dark cloud has been lifted. I had bottled it up for so long. This was a great relief, a farewell to my difficult past. You know, Father had his private catharsis after the funeral. Remember the smiles and his happy disposition just a few days after we buried Grandpa's remains?"

Desta nodded, smiling. "Yes, I counted seven flashes of his chipped tooth."

"Well, I had not had the opportunity to do that until now. This trip is going to be good for me in more ways than one. Thank you for helping me find my freedom."

"The feeling is mutual."

As the sun angled west, the clouds it passed through glowed white. There was less blue to the sky over their valley than there had been earlier as more clouds had pushed over the eastern ridges and gathered over their home. The sky in the west was partially clear with discrete, sheet-like clouds floating high above them. The sun was in and out of these clouds as it descended, brightening the haze and the uneven landscape before them. They could see several homes scattered in clusters of three or four and domestic animals grazing on the open fields and the bushes that sheltered the creeks below.

A quarter of a mile from where they sat a road went north to south along the ridge of the mountain. Saba said this was the caravan route for the people going to the market. They could see people and animals on this road, donkeys loaded with cargo, mules carrying men, pedestrians hurrying to get home,all carrying something on their backs or shoulders.

Plumes of smoke seeped out of the thatched roofs from several of the homes. To Saba the smoke was an indication that the women were probably cooking dinner, something she should be doing soon, too.

But Desta still had one more task to accomplish: stuffing his leather bag with clouds. He had taken a gamble in bringing the sack, as there were fewer clouds as the spring season advanced. To his luck, there was a cloud hanging a few hundred yards from the side of the mountain on which they sat, and was approaching the plateau at a low enough height that he thought he could touch it.

He ran to the edge and held his sack open waiting as the cloud came in low and thick. Saba stayed on the rock, laughing as she watched Desta excitedly holding his bag open, waiting for the cloud. He called for her to come and help him stuff the clouds into the sack while he held it open. She ran to him laughing uncontrollably.

Although Saba clawed, pushed and blew the cloud into the sack, not much collected. They could see the cloud in the sack, particularly after she blew on it, but nothing stayed. It all slipped out immediately. Desta handed the sack to Saba and told her to hold it open while he scrambled with his hands and gabi to retain the white thing. To his disappointment once again, nothing stayed. He wanted to cry, but when he turned and watched as the white mass floated away, he saw something that moved him to the depth of his soul.

The sun had painted the western sky a brilliant marigold. The clouds above and below the celestial orb glowed as if they were about to catch on fire. Desta had never seen anything like it. He dropped the empty cloud bag and took a few paces forward, transfixed by what was unfolding before his eyes.

Saba matched his steps and stood next to him. She knew they had to go home soon but didn't want to distract him. Desta trotted to the round flat-topped rock and perched there. What he was seeing was going to take time. He needed to watch it undisturbed. Saba had followed him, this time to tell him to gather his things so they could go home. To Desta, the sun was the only believable and credible object left in the sky. He had to wait and see the amazing conflagration to its conclusion.

When the sun broke free from the clouds, Desta noticed something else that puzzled him. It looked much bigger than he was accustomed to seeing it, something like a gigantic coin painted in gold and tinged with blood. He was captivated by the palette of colors forming and constantly changing as the sun tumbled down in the red sky.

Saba pulled on Desta's gabi and urged him to get up and gather his things so they could go home. With his eyes fixed on the setting sun, Desta sat unmoved.

"It's getting too late. We'll lose our way back if we don't leave now," pleaded Saba.

"I don't want to go home . . . I am not going home."

"You will have to go home, darling."

The fire-red embers around the sun became fiercer and brighter, like the red ink he had hoped to use to paint the sky. The sun was doing his job for him and on a much grander scale, but it didn't sign his name.

"Is this what happens every day when the sun goes home?" he asked Saba, tears filling his eyes.

"Yes, every so often . . . We can come and watch it again. For now we need to go home, okay? Your brother-in-law was kind enough to let me come with you but now he will wonder what happened to us. I need to prepare dinner for him and the children."

Desta was contemplating Saba's request, when she added, "Look, our valley is already in the shadows while there is plenty of sun here."

Looking over the lower peak, Desta saw the dark gray shadow that had fallen over much of the valley. The only light he could see was a pale band that stretched across the top portion of the eastern mountains.

He turned back to the setting sun. It looked about to touch land in the deep, dusty, crimson, dazzling haze far away, past the ménage of hills, patches of flat, inky gray earth. To Desta the sun seemed to slice the earth, leaving behind it hues of orange, cadmium red and pink. With its farther descent, the colors began to fade with a halo of red and other softer shades around the sun. In the end, all the colors coalesced into a mute charcoal gray.

To Desta, this was his consolation prize. He had discovered a phenomenon that would remain in him the rest of his life—a sun that goes home with such amazing display of variegated colors. What a beautiful sight it was to behold!

"If we don't leave right now, darkness will fall and we will become meals for the hyenas," snapped Saba.

Grudgingly, Desta hopped down from his perch and gathered his things. He wanted to throw the bamboo stick and the gourd of ink away but Saba discouraged him from doing so. He might need the stick on their descent down the mountain, and his mother could still use the ink to color the straws for the baskets she weaves.

They ran on the flatter ground and scurried along the downhill path. As they began the steep path of their descent, they were pleased to see a full moon rise over the eastern mountains. It was not going to be as pitch black as Saba had thought. They could take their time on the arduous route so they wouldn't risk falling and breaking a leg or an arm. They spiraled down the path, avoiding rocks and other obstacles. *They could even engage in a conversation now,* Desta thought.

"Saba, do you think you could take me to the market sometime?" he asked.

"I would be happy to," replied Saba. "You can come with me one Saturday. Yihoon's nephew will be with us helping with the harvest for a few more months and I'm sure we can get him to attend to the cattle again."

"Great! I would love to come with you the next time you go."

"I'll let you know, for sure. For you, I will do anything you wish," said Saba sincerely.

Once they reached the lower part of the mountain, where the side road met with the main trail, it occurred to Saba that the forest they were about to traverse would be nearly pitch black. The thought of blundering into the darkness terrified her. Desta too felt uneasy entering the forest. The idea of taking the main road back up to the villages they saw from top of the mountain and seeking shelter for the night crossed Saba's mind.

While they were debating what to do, they saw someone coming up the road with a flashlight. Both felt a sudden surge of relief and excitement. Saba guessed right. It was Yihoon, who had come to look for them.

"What took you so long?" he asked as he reached them.

"Desta and I were so caught up with everything that was unfolding before us, we ended up returning later than we wanted to," said Saba.

"What was unfolding that made you forget to come home?"

"The sunset had such a captivating hold on Desta that he couldn't leave without seeing its complete disappearance."

"Is that so, Desta?"

"Yes. It was incredible. I am sorry I have lived all my life without seeing such a thing. I wish we lived up there so I could see it every day."

"Well, anything you see for the first time is always a novelty and exciting. I am sure you would get bored with it after a while," said Yihoon.

"I don't think I would ever get bored with it. I always thought the sun came out from a hole in the ground, but now I saw what really happens. It seems to slide down the other side of a land. I wish I could follow the sun and find out where it goes to."

"It's a mystery to all of us, Desta. Nobody really knows. God has arranged everything for us, and we can't question his work. Just accept it and be happy with what you have," said Yihoon.

This almost fatalistic view disturbed Desta. If he listened to Yihoon, he might as well stop dreaming, thinking and asking questions—just accept everything as God's mysterious handiwork.

"Let's talk about your mission. Were you able to touch the sky?" asked Yihoon, with lightness to his voice.

"Not even close. I wish you all had told me before so I wouldn't have wasted all those years thinking about touching it."

"Certain things are better untold. It was a wish of your father's and a wise one. It is better you found it on your own. It will be a good learning experience for you."

"Desta, do you not consider our trip worthwhile?" asked Saba.

"No, I do. I saw so many things that were worthwhile," said Desta apologetically.

They didn't talk much once they entered the forest, instead concentrated on where their feet landed on the ground, following the moon of the flashlight that glided along before them, itself shaky and tentative as if it were afraid of the dark or the rocky path.

They stumbled, staggered, fell, got knocked up by rocks until their feet bled, but they managed finally to emerged from the forest.

"What happened?" What happened?" asked Ayénat, when Desta arrived home.

"I discovered the sky is not real . . . the cloud was not real . . . but the sun is. It painted the sky red, yellow and gold. I also saw a world full of mountains, plateaus and valleys."

"I am happy you finally made this long awaited journey," said Ayénat. "Now you no longer have to torture yourself. You can concentrate on the animals."

Desta didn't want to continue any more dialogue with his mother. He wanted to be by himself and in his mind, to revisit the mountaintop, to see the land he discovered and the spectacular sunset, to think about the clouds he couldn't collect and the sky he could not reach. What had happened during his visit at the mountaintop was moving, exciting and disappointing all at the same time.

He went to bed right after dinner. He covered himself with his gabi and began to recreate the visual and emotional experiences he had had at the top of the mountain that day. In his mind's eye, he saw the craggy, wave-like mountains that rippled away to the east close to where the sky met the earth through the dark gray haze, the mist-shrouded lowlands in the south, the plateaus, valleys and the multicolored crop fields of the west and the olive green expanse of earth in the north that was veiled with hoary miasma.

As Desta recreated these images in his head, he was elated and exuberant all over again. He had felt a wonderful sense of freedom when he observed them earlier, and now he felt it again.

He also thought about his heart-wrenching disappointment when he discovered that the sky was neither touchable nor the clouds collectable. Now in his thoughts, he realized that the larger world he had found and the spectacular sunset he had witnessed were more rewarding than the mere touching of the sky and gathering of the clouds. These were exhilarating.

AS HE TOSSED AND TURNED thinking about these things, he also thought about some strange and mysterious coincidences. Just as his father had not been able to meet his father after all his years of yearning, Desta, when he eventually made his grand trip, had not been able to touch the sky.

He thought about how the clouds were involved in solving some of their family problems. It was the cloud-like spirit of his grandfather that solved Saba's miscarriages, allowed Abraham to discover the remains of his father, brought closure to his yearnings and freed him from his past. The clouds were one of the two beckoning calls that drew Desta to go to the mountaintop; causing him to realize the non-existence of the things he yearned for, but at the same time allowing him to discover new places and events. The clouds now also had given him the hope of freeing himself from the mountains that had walled him in all his life.

Moved both spiritually and emotionally, Desta was thrilled in a way he had never been before. He couldn't wait to get out of the valley again.

FIFTY-SEVEN

September

The day when Saba had promised to take Desta to the market finally arrived. Desta rose way before the sun, released the animals and drove them to the field for Yihoon's nephew to look after in his absence. After breakfast Desta leaned against the fence outside his home, waiting for his sister to arrive.

"We need to climb the mountain before the sun gets too strong," she had told him the day before when she came to inform him of their trip.

For Desta, it was not just the going to the market that he anxiously awaited, it was also the opportunity the trip would give him to see all that land outside his realm once again. Since he returned from his trip to the top of the mountain, he had spent many a sleepless night thinking about the distant land, the names of places where his relatives lived, and the glorious sunset he had witnessed. With this trip, he planned to closely study how wide the earth was and what the landscape really looked like. God willing, he also hoped to see another sunset.

The sun had barely reached the bottom of the valley when Saba appeared driving a stout gray donkey laden with a big sack of teff. The animal walked past Desta as if he were carrying a pack of feathers. He sniffed, snorted and blew through his nostrils, sending up a cloud of dust.

"Have you been waiting for me long?" asked Saba.

"Since before dawn. I have been dying to get out of this valley again. After that trip to the top of the mountain, I have developed this enormous desire to travel," said Desta, grinning. He wore his gabi over a soiled white shirt and carried a hockey stick.

"You are too young to develop a taste for traveling. But I am glad you liked what you saw on our first trip enough that you want to see it again."

"I wish we were living on other side of these mountains."

"I know . . . Let's hurry up," said Saba anxiously. "It's going to be hot climbing the mountain. You lead the donkey."

Up the hill they went. They ran into Teferra, who was preparing to go to the market with an assortment of clothes he had made. This was his first trip to the market with his clothes and he was excited. He smiled and greeted Saba happily, but said nothing to Desta. When Saba told him they were going to the market, he glared at his little brother. "What's he going to do there?" he demanded.

"He wanted to see the market place and I am fulfilling his wishes," said Saba, smiling. "It's a small token for the great favor he did for me."

"He won't be buying or selling anything, and I am sure he won't be of any use to you. It seems a waste of his useful time to take the boy that far and put him through the difficulty of climbing this mountain."

"There is no point in discussing this," snapped Saba, motioning to Desta. "We are here and we are going. We'll see you at the market."

As they walked away, she turned back to Teferra. "You all refer to him as a boy. The fact is, Desta has a maturity and intellectual capacity that exceeds many adults in this valley, including guess who?"

Desta thought Teferra sounded more and more like Asse'ged and Damtew, who fortunately had stopped bothering him when they got their land.

They cleared the forest above Teferra's home in no time. At the point where the road split, Saba thought it would be easier to go north following the contour of the mountain. This route would take them longer, but it was less arduous. At the top of the plateau, the road linked with the main caravan route, where they turned south.

They joined a number of market-goers who were driving donkeys or riding on horses and mules, leaving a cloud of dust behind them along the road. Saba's donkey seemed pleased to find companions and he needed no urging to keep up. Saba met people she knew and chattered her way along the meandering ridge behind three women who marched hurriedly side by side. There were many people behind and ahead of them, leading laden animals, riding them, or walking with loads on their shoulders or backs.

Desta was happy being left to his own devices. He could let his eyes and mind wander.

He stared deep into the distant haze and wondered if that was where the earth ended and the sky began. Twice he wanted to ask Saba where exactly the woman with the yellow hair and milk-white skin lived. Each time he changed his mind. He didn't want her to cry again in front of the other women.

He brought his eyes back to Saba's bare heels, watching them pound the dusty earth, stirring the powdered soil to life. With his eyes on her feet, he

wondered if the sky existed at all, and if it did, where in this world it touched
the earth. If somebody told him where that place was he thought he would
go there, no matter how far or hard to reach. He hated to think he might die
without ever laying his hands on the blue thing that had looked down on him
for as long as he could remember.

The west side of the ridge sloped gently before it fell into a creek basin that
ran along the foothills. After a point, the ridge itself descended slightly to a
flat area, before it rose sharply into a pommel-like mass. Their caravan route
met up with another that came around the east side of the peak, bringing more
marketgoers.

"That is Wendegez," said Saba, turning around and pointing to the ascending
knobby landmass before them. Scattered bushes covered the mountain face but
the vegetation on top was scanty.

Desta looked up toward the mountain, remembering the story of the Italian
soldier his father killed and from whom he collected the gold pocket watch. He
wanted to ask Saba exactly where that had happened, but she was still talking
with her friends. Then Desta saw a great number of people and pack animals
coming from the other caravan road and merging with the one they were on,
interrupting his thoughts of the soldier's story and causing him to study the
newly added travelers.

People scurried in groups of four or five, driving their animals along the stony
route, which, soon after they left the saddle-seat like terrain, curved around the
west side of Wendegez before it dropped down the steep side of the mountain.

The travelers with laden donkeys stopped to secure their cargo as the descent
could easily cause the animals to slip and drop their packs. One of the women
helped Saba adjust the sack and fasten the strap on her donkey.

The road on the slope was rocky and twisted. Its sides had long been washed
out by floods, making it hard to follow. In some places new, easier to step-
on paths had been created. Some of the women complained about their knees
buckling as they descended. Occasionally they rested at the bottom of the hill,
visually estimating the distance they had yet to cover. Saba steadily walked,
keeping an eye on her donkey.

Desta enjoyed the view of the long, wide treeless valley beyond the foothills.
"That is where we are headed," said Saba, pointing to a plateau covered with a
thicket of trees. "We have to travel this wide land before we get there, but it's
all flat and easy to walk," she assured Desta.

"How long before we get there?"

"Probably a little over as long as it took us so far, but you need to be prepared for that hill," she said, pointing to the vertical side of the plateau.

Desta didn't pay attention. He was anxious to get to the market.

In the company of the people they had already met and some more who had joined later, the walk across the wide flat terrain went pretty quickly. They traversed small creeks and rivers and passed several villages and two churches. Desta wanted to ask what all those places were and who lived in them, but once again he didn't want to interrupt his sister's conversation.

Saba was right. Climbing the steep slope up to Yeedib was very hard. Everyone sweated, huffed and puffed and stopped frequently to rest. The animals grunted and faltered as they strained under the weight of their burdens.

As they came to the top of the hill Desta was hit by a familiar aroma. He had smelled it before when he had gone with his father to the nursery by the river. The fragrance of eucalyptus trees was overpowering. As they drew nearer to the town, he noticed another familiar odor from the bushes at home where they went to the bathroom. Then came a medley of other smells: a little bit of tella, a little bit of animal dung and body odor, buttered hair and oil-stained clothes. The scent of the eucalyptus trees was drowned out by the new odors.

When they neared the outskirts of the town, Desta was impressed by the tall, dense grove of trees that surrounded it. "Those are the same trees Baba is trying to grow," said Saba, seeing Desta crane his neck.

"If this is how tall they get, Baba's have a long way to go."

"They grow very fast."

As they entered the market, the din was deafening. Desta watched people scurrying about, walloping their animals to get them to advance through the maze of humans. Everybody seemed to be talking at the same time. The clamor reminded Desta of birds feeding on ripened figs in a sholla tree. People were moving about every which way, with seemingly no order or purpose to their movements. More people poured through the entrance behind them, driving goats, sheep, and donkeys loaded with sacks or carrying chickens with their feet tied, hanging upside down from their shoulders or the sides of the donkeys' packs.

Saba told Desta to go on the outer edge of the crowd, where it would be easier and faster to get to the row where they sold teff. When Desta lingered to look at the people, she went ahead with the donkey, spurring him on with Desta's hockey stick, steering him through the crowd.

While Saba was navigating her way, a woman stopped her. "Is that teff?" she asked, stabbing the air with a bird's beak of a hand, pointing to the sack.

Saba acknowledged that it was.

"How much?"

Saba looked at her sack and then the woman. "I am not sure. I have not seen how the market is doing today."

"There is a glut of it. Harvest time," said the woman.

Saba's face crinkled. "We'll find out," she said, glancing at the woman indifferently.

The donkey sniffed the ground and snorted. Saba was about to spur the animal on with her stick when the woman said, "I bet your animal is anxious to be relieved of his burden. I can do that quickly if we come to terms on your price." She smiled, her eyes still holding Saba.

Desta studied the woman. She had clean, fair skin that glistened a little in the sun as if she might have dabbed it with oil. Her soft dark hair shone in the strong midday sun also. She had even teeth, big eyes, a pretty nose and soft tapering fingers. She wore a pleated navy blue dress that hugged her waist. Desta had never seen a dress like that. All the women he knew wore long, wide cotton gowns that they kept off the floor with wide, multi-colored cotton girdles. Around her shoulders she had wrapped a white, spotless netela with a wide purple border. She wore shiny leather things on her feet.

"I wouldn't know what the price is without seeing how much others are getting for the equivalent sack of teff," said Saba firmly.

Desta saw a tall man glance toward the woman intermittently as he talked to two men in the crowd a few feet away. He wore a dark green, thick, fuzzy shirt, long pants and heavy leather shoes. On his head, he wore a puffy round hat, similar to his shirt and pants in color and texture that hung to the left. He had a silver star in the middle of the hat and on his shirt above his pocket. These items, too, were new to Desta.

The man said something to the men, then broke off and came straight toward them. "How much does she want?" he asked the woman.

"She wouldn't tell me."

Saba's face suddenly had become tense and bloodless.

"Give her fifteen birr," said the man authoritatively.

With this bold offer, Saba's face relaxed.

The woman produced from a small leather pouch two crinkled papers, one pale red and one faded orange, and extended them to Saba.

Saba didn't take the money. "I can sell it to you for fifteen birr but not for that kind of birr," she said nervously.

"You people never get it, do you?" said the man angrily. "The other birr is banned. It's no longer in circulation. It's not our money. It was brought into our country by the ferengies. Do you hear me, that money doesn't have the picture of our *Negus*: Do you understand?"

Saba said nothing, her face taut and pale.

"You take that money or I will arrest you and put you in jail!" barked the man. He snatched one of the dollars from the woman. He held the ends of the paper with both hands and shouted, "Look here! This is our Negus. He is called Haile Sellassie. This money is our currency, issued by our Negus." He shouted stabbing the picture several times with his index finger.

"Give it to me," said Saba, nearly in tears. She took the bills, pulled open the neck of her dress and stuffed them in.

"Come with me," said the woman to Saba. "We need to transfer the grain into my sack at home."

The man said something in a hushed voice to the woman and disappeared into the crowd.

Saba followed the woman with the loaded donkey. Desta whacked the animal when he hesitated. They walked around the crowd and cut north when they came to a hard, grassless expanse. The woman led them along its border then turned onto a straight wide pathway bordered by tall eucalyptus trees with a mixed row of tin and grass roof houses on both sides. Some of the houses were closed; others were open, with people drinking tea or coffee. At one particular house, a boisterous group of men sat on a bench, drinking tella and honey wine from glass tumblers. As they pushed farther from the market, most of the houses were closed. Beyond fence enclosures, women washed clothes or played with their babies.

Desta kept looking for boys of his age. There were none. He wondered if young boys and girls lived in towns.

The woman's house was at the end of an alley. She pushed open a rickety corrugated tin door and Saba followed her inside. Getting the loaded donkey to pass through the opening was tricky. The two women managed by moving the sack askew while it was still on the donkey's back. Inside, a girl brought a thick canvas sack. With the help of the girl, Saba and the woman transferred the teff.

Before they left, the woman offered Saba tella and Desta water. She said she was sorry she didn't have injera, which she would have offered to them. Saba thanked her just the same as they were not hungry. They quickly downed their drinks and left.

"If you bring teff or any other grain next time, bring it here first. I will pay you top dollar. You don't have to wait around baking in the sun, trying to sell it," said the woman, smiling.

"Thank you. We will," said Saba mechanically.

As they walked back to the market with the donkey, Saba wondered who would accept the kind of money she had just received. Although she had seen the money before, she had never used it to purchase anything or accepted it from anyone. "It's paper, just paper!" she shouted.

To Desta, Saba sounded as if she had been robbed.

"I will see if . . ." The rest of the words never made it to her lips.

A long line of smartly dressed boys and girls appeared before them. At the head of the line one of the boys was hoisting a green, yellow and red striped cloth above his head. They came chanting and singing from a side street, turned right and headed toward the market.

The trio waited until all of the boys and girls had filed out into the main street, then followed them at a distance. Two men walked behind the singing children, one of them was tall and dark, the other short and slender with a fair complexion. He wore glasses attached to metal frames that hooked to his ears. A uniformed man like the one whose wife had given Saba the paper money walked in front and told the crowd to stay clear. As the boys and girls marched through the market, the onlookers parted, letting them pass.

Desta trotted near his sister and asked her who they were.

"They are *asquala temareewech*. I have seen them once before," she told him. When he looked puzzled by her answer, she elaborated that they were modern school students, different from those who attended church school where they lived, like their brother Tamirat.

After the last of the students passed, the crowed mingled again, blocking Desta's views of the students. Saba wanted to go to find Teferra in the men's clothes row, then tour the rest of the market with Desta. He begged her to follow the students, but she refused, saying it was a waste of their precious time.

Desta followed his sister and the donkey to where their brother was sitting, then slipped away, weaving his way through the crowd in search of the students. He found them near the north end of the market. They were circling the market, chanting and singing. As they passed, the crowd parted, lining up to watch the marching boys and girls. Desta followed them, snaking around the crowd. After they had made the complete circle of the marketplace, they marched back out the same way they had come in. Desta stood at the periphery of the market and watched them till they disappeared into the trees.

He was startled when the same policeman who had threatened to jail Saba earlier appeared behind him and wrapped his big hand around his arm. "Is this the boy?" he said, turning to a woman who was crying. Terrified, Desta craned his neck around the policeman's big frame to see who he was talking to.

"That is him!" shouted Saba.

"Here take him," said the man as he pushed Desta toward his sister.

Saba wiped her tears and yelled at Desta for disappearing, threatening never to take him anywhere ever again.

They went back to Teferra's stand. "Don't you dare move from here," said Saba waving her index finger at Desta and walked off. Teferra dressed Desta down with his eyes.

Various people were picking out trousers and jackets from his pile and trying them, putting them down, picking up others, examining them, holding them up against themselves imagining how they would look.

Sitting by his brother, Desta recalled the marching students: how clean they looked, their hair, clothes and feet, even those who didn't wear shoes. And then he realized what impressed him: all of them wore shorts or long trousers. Then the beautiful multicolored cloth that danced in the wind high up in the air. How Desta would have liked to have touched that cloth to examine its colors, textures and patterns. He remembered seeing a cat-like drawing right in the middle of the cloth and wondered what that cat was doing there.

Saba returned. She apologized for being angry with him. She forgave him because she understood how curious he always was, but she thought it would have been safer if he had asked her to accompany him instead of going off on his own. She seemed to have forgotten that he did ask, but she had declined.

"Let's go and see things," she said grabbing Desta by the hand.

First, they walked down the aisle where Teferra was, the men's clothing row. Men on either side of the aisle stood or sat behind their piles of newly made clothes, proudly displaying their merchandise. Farther along, the aisle changed into rows of other goods. Under grass sheds, men and women displayed a medley of merchandise: soaps, perfumes, assorted colored yarns, buttons, safety pins, needles, sugar cubes, coffee beans, and hundreds of other objects. There was a pile of blue glass ring beads in a bowl, like the ones taken from Desta when he was robbed by those boys when he had run away.

Next, Saba took Desta to the teff row. As she walked down the row talking to the people, Saba learned that a sack of teff was selling from six to seven silver birr, depending on whether it was white or brown. Saba had undersold her white teff by two silver birr, but there was nothing she could do about it now. It had been the police who had purchased it, so she had to take the paper money given her. She explained to Desta that three bills of paper money would exchange for one silver birr. What the woman had given her was equivalent to five silver birr.

Continuing around the market, they saw barley, potatoes, spices, poppy red pots and pans, black drinking cups, incense burners and candle holders but none of these held Desta's interest. He merely followed his sister, listening to her engage with the merchants and farmers or rattle away about various things she was showing him.

When they completed their tour, Desta was thirsty and hungry and wanted to know where they could get water. Saba took him to a little hut at the periphery of the market where drinking glasses were laid out on a rickety long bench-like table. There were men all around the table. Saba went to the door and told the young woman she would like to buy bread and water. The woman invited them in and brought them tella for Saba and water and a small round dabo. They ate and drank quickly and left.

Saba wanted to leave before it got late, as they had a long way to go. It was midafternoon, so they gathered the donkey, loaded him with the empty sacks and a few things Saba had bought and made their way out of the market.

Overwhelmed by the crowd, the smell and the noise, Desta was happy when Saba suggested heading home. Questions were reeling in his head, and he was anxious to be alone with Saba so he could ask them.

Only a spattering of people were leaving the market when Saba and Desta got on the main road home. With hardly anything on his back, the donkey trotted happily downhill behind Desta. Saba walked alongside. A few folks were behind them. Others were ahead of them scattered along the road from the outskirts of Yeedib to the river at the bottom of the mountain.

"Can I ask you a question?" said Desta.

"Go ahead."

"What is a police?"

"They are persons who put people in jail for doing bad things like stealing, hitting or killing someone, getting into fights or breaking the king's law. A jail is a place where people who do those things are locked up. They are only allowed to come out for food, to go to the bathroom or for limited exercise."

Impressed by Saba's knowledge, Desta thought about what she said for a long time, trying to make sense of it. "Why did that man say he would put you to jail if you don't accept his wife's money?"

"Because we are not supposed to use the silver dollar anymore. It's not our money, he said. I always thought it was. We have been using it for such a long time. Anyway, that is what he said."

Saba needed to relieve herself. She walked away a few yards, hid behind the bushes for a few minutes and returned.

"There are three parts of this trip to the market that I dread," she said, "climbing and descending this mountain, the one at the other end of the valley and the one above our home." She measured with her eyes the distance to the bottom of the mountain. "I have another question," said Desta. "What is Negus?"

"The leader of our country, like Baba is to our community informally."

"Where does he live?"

"In Addis Ababa."

"Is that far?"

"I think so. I have never been there and I don't think Baba, as much as he travels, has ever been there either."

"I would like to go there someday," said Desta.

Saba laughed.

"What's funny?"

"One, it's too far, and two, what good would it do you to go there?"

"I don't know. It would be fun, particularly if that is where the sun goes every day after it leaves here."

"That I don't know. Is the sun your new fixation now?"

"It seems more real to me than the clouds or the sky. It comes and goes without missing a day. The sky is very elusive."

"I am sorry you're still disappointed, but you shouldn't be so quick to judge. I am sure there must be places where the sky is touchable. I just don't know where."

It was Desta's turn to relieve himself. He scampered along the side of the mountain and squatted behind a big boulder. Saba stood with the donkey and waited.

Shortly after, Desta rejoined them. He noticed that the donkey tried to graze on the dry grass, but the dust and the grass blew into his face every time he put his head down. He finally gave up. Three men and a woman passed them. Watching these travelers move so quickly spurred Saba to hurry up. They needed to get home in daylight.

At the bottom of the mountain, the river ran silently. The water bugs skidded on the flat part. The donkey bent its neck and drank water for a long time.

"Poor thing. He must have been very thirsty. Had he been able to talk, he would have begged us for water a long time ago," said Saba.

Desta chuckled, imagining the donkey talking.

The land beyond the river was flat as his mother's baking pan. The grass was shadowy green. The ground was soft and springy, and the air cool and vitalizing. Desta and Saba found this part of their journey to be a pleasant change from the mountain, where they had to step carefully to dodge potholes, sharp rocks and loose stones.

Saba said the flat, circular land with the spongy turf was called Godir. The caravan road split it in half. On the northwest side of the road, near the foothills, stood a church enveloped by a grove of juniper trees. At the church's annual celebration, a break-neck speed horse race took place on the field outside the church, and people came from all over to watch.

Desta thought he would like to bring the cloud horse formations and ride them in the races to make his father proud. But they were only clouds . . . just as illusory as the sky.

He was holding the donkey's lead as they walked but Saba told him to let the animal free to munch on the green grass. The donkey gratefully dove into the tufts of grass along the roadside.

"I hope you won't get tired of me but I have some more questions," said Desta, glancing at Saba.

"Go ahead. Nothing is a bother if I can be of help to you, Desta. You know that."

"Do you think Baba would let me go to asquala temareebet?"

"That is a hard one. Frankly, I don't know. But I can also give you my own overall view on that subject. I hope this won't disappoint you. Maybe you're inured to disappointment by now. I think it is only fair for you to know the facts. If something else happens, you can count your blessings."

"Tell me."

"First let me say that I feel fortunate and I think the rest of the family should feel fortunate that, despite your age, we can talk to you like an adult. You have matured beyond your age of now, what, nine?"

Desta nodded.

"The good Lord has obviously blessed you. The spirit of our grandfather chose you and you have become the bearer of our family's treasure. As Baba said, this in itself is a big responsibility. God and our grandfather's spirit didn't choose anybody else but you. They obviously believe in your ability to handle circumstances that may come involving the coin. Just as Grandpa sacrificed his life for it . . ."

Desta wished Saba would get to her point.

"Therefore, what I am going to say to you is something I'd not share with any other young adult, let alone a boy, but you have been through a lot and you can handle what I am about to say. To get to my point, I think Baba is disappointed by what has become of his older children. He sent Tamirat to church school for 12 years to become a respectable priest. And what did he end up doing? Abandoning it. What a waste! Had Baba known, he would put him to farm work at an early age.

"He had hoped Asse'ged would take up horse riding and make him proud by winning at some of these annual church holiday races. But Asse'ged, though athletic and strapping, has not a whit of interest in horses. As Baba has often said, he can't even ride a donkey. He is a brilliant farmer a devoted son, but he never achieved the kinds of things Baba had hoped for him.

"Teferra is now a tailor, thanks to Baba. Since he is the only one in the valley with this skill, everybody flocks to him for all kinds of jobs. He is doing very well financially, but even he has not gone out on his own and done something that distinguishes him from the common folks.

"Good fate has not come to the girls that married either. One married a young man with fat feet, another married a man who was supposed to be of high breeding but was not. I blame Baba and your mother for the girls' circumstances. They should have checked the husbands' backgrounds before they married them off.

"Anyway, coming to your wish, with these sour experiences with the older

children, I am not sure Baba would be disposed to make another gamble. I
know he always said that he wished all his children could go to school, but that
is next to impossible now for any of them, including you.

"You are the last of the boys left unmarried. Your mother and Baba are going to
need someone who will do the farm work after Damtew and his wife move out.

"Baba doesn't know how to farm. He is a great businessman but not a
farmer. He has always depended on help. In their old age, they will need
someone to support them, farm for them. That lot will now fall on you." She
looked at Desta and smiled sadly. "That is what I think."

Desta's heart sank. His stomach tightened and lurched as if Saba had
punched it. What she said was all true and it hurt. He felt as if he were in a
jail, locked in by the mountains that surrounded him, stunting his personal and
intellectual growth, locked in by circumstances he had nothing to do with. He
wanted to cry but he had cried enough in his life. This time he kept his tears
inside. He needed to find a strategy to break free.

Then and there Desta made up his mind not to let his family or the
mountains be the ultimate decision-makers on his life. He had gone through so
much already. He was stronger and wiser now, ready to make his own decisions
about the things that were important to him.

Saba's donkey chased after a female donkey that had passed them by awhile
back. They ran to catch up, calling out to the female donkey's owners, who
grabbed Saba's donkey by his lead and detained him for them.

Talking very little after that, they crossed two low, humpy fields with thin
brown grass. Saba hummed a tune. Desta kept thinking about what she had said
about his fate. It all seemed dismal. He really did not want to remain a farmer
like everyone else. He had to find a way somehow to leave and attend school,
even if he had to dig a tunnel through the mountain to do it.

After passing the church of Gumbla on their right, they began climbing
the steep mountain behind the shoulder of Wendegez. Tired and thirsty, they
concentrated on their climb. Desta ran to the trickling creek on their right and
gulped as much water as he could, scooping it with his cupped hands. Saba
hesitated at first, but joined him once she saw how much he was enjoying the
cold water. Afterward they were able to finish climbing the mountain with
renewed vigor.

As they marched comfortably on the easy terrain of the wave-like ridge,
Desta thought of a new tack.

"I have an idea," he said.

"Tell me," said Saba, cocking her ears. The sweat on her brown forehead glistened in the setting sun.

"Do you think you could talk to Baba on my behalf?"

"Meee? Nooo way. I have no favor with him and I really don't have the persuasive skills. You should ask him yourself."

"You already told me how he feels about his children. How can I reason with him? What can I say? 'Send me to school. Find a new herd boy and farmer'. Father won't agree to it. My mother would be floored."

"You know who would be good? Teferra's wife. Baba has a very high opinion of her. She has already scored many points with him. I think she should be the person to broach the idea."

"Can you talk to her?"

Saba nodded.

"That I can. In fact, I am seeing her tomorrow. I will do my best. The rest is up to God and your good fortune."

As they walked along the crest of the mountain, Desta kept his eyes on the sun. He watched the progressive morphing of colors on the western sky as the lurid orb inched its way to the portal that would bring it to the other world. As the orange transitioned into red, just before the sun nestled into the fiery haze, they reached the junction of the main caravan route and the road that would take them home.

"Not tonight. Not now. No," said Saba when she saw Desta turn to gaze at the fireworks unfolding in the western sky.

It was hard for Desta, but he reined in his impulse and complied with his sister's wishes.

As they descended the mountain above their home, there was white light on the mountains in the east, as Desta had observed before at this time of the day. It was one more phenomenon of nature he could not understand. Why did a red sun cast white light? Why was the sun not red just before it dipped behind the mountain above their home? Was the sun mocking him too, as the clouds and the sky had done before? When would he see the red ember of the setting sun again? When would he be able to sit and watch it undisturbed until the end of the show, until the curtain of darkness fell?

"Thanks for everything," said Desta as he entered his home.

"You are very welcome."

"Don't forget what we talked about."

FIFTY-EIGHT

The trip to the market was another eye-opener for Desta. It was in this trip, along with his first journey to the mountaintop, when Desta discovered the existence of other worlds—worlds that were bigger and wider than the walled valley in which his father's family, seeking peace of mind and safety, had long isolated themselves. It was these findings that started him imagining a different kind of life for himself. He saw for the first time that he might have options, that there might be an opportunity for him to break out of his imprisonment. At the very least, the discovery of other lands left open the possibility of a mountain tall enough for him to try again to touch the sky.

For now he was happy to pursue his newfound dream of going away to school to watch the sunset every day and to dream of traveling to other lands, meeting people and making friends. But how could he fulfill these dreams? As Saba had wisely pointed out, given the circumstances it would be a heroic task to win his freedom from the obligations placed upon him by his family.

Both Desta and Saba realized that the main person they had to convince was their father, the ultimate decision-maker. Desta thought it would be best to have a dual-pronged attack to the problem, to recruit all those who might be able to influence his father and to plead his own case subtly and tactfully. There were already a number of things that would strengthen his case not the least of which was the current absence of anyone who could read his father's court documents and letters. Since Tamirat had left, Abraham had been taking most of his papers to church for one of the priests to read, but some of the documents were very private and sensitive. For these he used Desta's cousin, Awoke.

He was always in need of someone to whom he could dictate his court cases. The priests were too far away and not readily available. Lately they had been charging him 25 cents a document, which he thought was very expensive.

Abraham had always wanted a son who would make him proud. Desta recently had heard his father talk glowingly about a beautiful umbrella and a raincoat the judge in town had been given by his son who taught in a distant town called Gonder. Desta could promise to do those kinds of things for his father if he put him through modern school.

He would promise to do so well in school that his father's head would grow bigger than ever before. He remembered his father telling a guest how he felt his head grown bigger when Tamirat's teacher told him about his son's brilliance. Desta could make his father's head grow twice as big if he sent him to school.

Abraham also talked about all the court clerks and the judges who took bribes, how he wished there was an honest judge who decided on cases on their merits, and how he wished he had a relative who worked inside the courts to process his papers more quickly. That possibility could exist if he gave Desta a proper education.

Desta thought there were more arguments he could come up with, but for now these were enough. He shared his ideas with Saba and she advised him to bring them up at the right moment, when their father was relaxed and in a good mood. From his past observances, Saturday, when his father was ready to go to town, and Sunday, when he wanted things read by the priests, would be the best times to approach him.

It was only a week later when Desta saw an opportunity to try out his first strategy. It was a Wednesday morning. Abraham was crouching by the entrance, in a spot flooded with sunlight. He had brought out the oval, Damtew's fat-bellied straw box where he kept his important papers.

When he walked in, Desta noticed his father had emptied the contents of the box and spread them on a cloth. The papers, folded multiple times into small squares, gleamed in the morning light, some of the newer ones throwing off a strange dull reflection on the smoke-stained ceiling above. Abraham moved the papers around, spreading them over the cloth, without opening any of them. He would lift one of the papers, look at one side and then the other and then put it down. He did this to a number of the folded papers.

Desta was intrigued. "Baba, how do you know which is which without opening them?" he asked.

"Some of them I know by the way I folded them and some by their age, or the kind of paper," said his father without looking at him. His fingers continued to sift through the pile.

"Wouldn't it be better if you opened them and looked?"

"That would confuse me. You know I can't read."

"Have you considered studying the alphabet and learning to read?"

"I am too old for that. . . ."

"Awoke can teach you. He taught me."

"I forgot. That is right! You did tinker with reading a little, didn't you?"

"That was nearly two years ago. My brothers thought it was a waste and I stopped."

A tear ran down his father's long nose and hung glittering in the light. Desta was about to tell him that the drop would fall and wet his papers, when Abraham brushed it off. Without a cause, Desta had once in awhile seen a similar pearly, stray tear well up and collect in his father's right eye and then roll down his cheek.

He looked at Desta. "Can you try reading some of these?"

"I doubt I remember it all but I'll try."

Abraham opened one of the four folded letters he set aside and passed it to Desta. "You're halfway there, Baba. At least you know how to hold the pages right," said Desta, smiling.

"I am not blind," said Abraham defensively. "I can see where the firma is located, my fingerprint, and where the dates and the address lines are. I didn't start dealing with written documents yesterday, you know."

Desta was surprised by his father's sensitivity about such matters.

"Okay, that is pretty good. Let's see what you've got," said the son as he scanned the letter. For the life of him, he could not make sense out of the lines of text. He identified some of the letters but couldn't read the words. "Who wrote this?"

"I think your brother."

"Is this how badly he writes?"

"Now don't criticize his writing. Others have told me he writes rather well. You just don't have the knowledge to read it. Give it back."

Desta's ego was bruised, but he handed his father the paper. "I just wish I had continued with my learning," he said.

"I think the document I'm looking for is in one of these four or five papers. I'll have to take them all with me and let someone from the courtyard determine it for me," said Abraham as he gathered the papers into a pile.

"If what you are looking for is not in one of them, then what? Come back and try again?"

"If I have to, yes, but I am sure it's one of these."

"Why don't you take the whole box?"

Abraham beamed. "That would confuse the reader to hell. No, I won't do that. Besides, I don't want to scandalize Damtew by taking this box publicly."

"Something just occurred to me," said Desta. "Would you consider putting one more of your children through school?"

Abraham looked at Desta through his top eyelashes.

"I mean it."

Abraham said nothing.

"Could you?" said Desta, holding his father's eye.

"Like who?"

"You are looking at him."

"Yeah, right."

"I mean that. If you put me through school, I could save you trips to people's homes or church whenever you need someone to read your papers."

"I am through with that game. I have given up. I won't be fooled three times. You will be a better service to me and yourself if you concentrate on the animals you tend now and prepare yourself to become a good farmer when your time comes."

The finality of his words and tone of voice depressed Desta. His heart dropped and his mind blanked for a second as the ray of light he had been clinging to was suddenly taken away from him.

His father quickly grabbed the paper from Desta, folded it, gathered the other three and put them in his breast pocket. He then gathered the rest and put them back in the box. He dropped the box in the middle granary, grabbed his walking stick and left.

A FEW DAYS LATER, Desta ran into Saba. She told him she had talked to Teferra's wife but was not sure if she had broached the idea with their father.

A WEEK LATER Desta and Abraham were sitting alone by the fire.

"Baba—"

"Yes, Desta"

"Don't you want a son who finally makes you proud?"

"Who?"

"Me."

"Ahh, what is it you have for me this evening?"

"I want you to put me through school, Asquala Temaree Bet, not church school."

"You have not given up on that idea. It seems that you have agents working for you too now. Laqechi pleaded with me the other day, and Saba has had her share of opinions about you going to school. All these people seemed to want to manage my life and yours—instead of worrying about their own."

"Really, I promise to be the best student I can be. I can someday buy you things, like a beautiful umbrella and a raincoat like the judge's son bought for him. I can work in the court so you don't have to bribe the judges and clerks. I can do many, many things for you. Have you already forgotten that even grandpa's spirit chose me? He said I have been given the ability to do many great things, including caring for the coin."

Abraham quietly listened as Desta rattled off his great ambitions. "I think you are very correct in your last statement," he said thoughtfully, caressing his goatee. "I wish we could afford to let you go, but you are the only help we have around the house—for now and in the future."

"Teferra said that I would only be gone in the dry season. I would come back in the winter, the crucial time for help."

"Have you gotten any dinner? I need to go to bed soon," said Abraham glancing at Ayénat, who had just come from the back room.

"Soon."

"We'll talk another time," he said to Desta.

Desta's heart leaped. He sensed a possibility, a shred, a sliver of chance.

TWO WEEKS LATER, Ayénat sent Desta to Teferra's house to retrieve a sieve Teferra's wife had borrowed. Teferra and Laqechi, Abraham, Yihoon and Saba were there, drinking coffee and chatting.

Saba and Laqechi were pleased to see Desta. They ordered him to sit down. Desta sensed something, from the attention everybody gave him.

A minute later, Abraham said, "Are you still interested in going to school?" Desta held his breath. "Very much."

"You have been pestering me, by yourself and through your agents." He looked at Saba and Laqechi, grinning. "We have decided to give you a chance. I won't be surprised or disappointed if you come running home after a week or two, but like everyone here has been telling me, I will give you the benefit of the doubt."

Desta stared at his father, stunned.

"Thank you! Thank you very much, Baba!"

"Aren't you going to kiss his knees?" said Saba.

Desta rose and lunged toward his father and kissed both knees.

"One would have been enough," said Abraham, chuckling. "I am glad to see you are enthusiastic. Like all of us here agreed, you can try it. If you don't like it, you can come back. No questions will be asked. The timing is convenient enough. The sheep are long gone. There are no more baby goats. The cows can roam. We'll find someone to bring them home in the evening."

Desta had not yet recovered from his shock. In his mind he was seeing wide open lands, distant hazy horizons, brilliant sunsets. He saw himself dressed in smart clothes, marching with boys and girls at the Saturday market, his family coming to watch him with pride.

"Aren't you going to kiss the rest of them?" asked Abraham. "They did the work. I only agreed to their united wishes."

As if awakened from a dream, Desta staggered toward Laqechi and kissed her twice on the cheeks. She kissed him back three times. Next he did the same to Teferra, although his brother never retuned his kisses. Yihoon kissed him three times and Desta returned his. The last and the best Desta saved for Saba. He wrapped his arms around her and kissed her tightly on her cheeks, crying silently with his arms locked around her neck. She didn't get a chance to kiss him back. She too was overtaken by emotion and began to cry.

"Go ahead. We are not jealous. She was the lead campaigner and did most of the leg work," said Laqechi, chuckling. The others chuckled too.

"I will make you a pair of shorts and a jacket," said Teferra.

"We'll take you next Wednesday morning," said Abraham. "I have a business trip to make and we'll drop you off with your Uncle Mekuria. He has always offered to do something like this. He will be thrilled to have you."

The first opportunity he had, Desta flew home. Night had fallen and it was pitch black. He fell twice and bruised his arms and legs. He couldn't wait to tell his mother the news.

"I am going to school! I am going to asquala temaree bet!" he said the moment he arrived.

"Whose idea was that?"

"Mine, but it was Baba's decision."

"He decided to put you to the Saytan's school? What about our church school, if he wants you to waste your time like that? Wouldn't it be good enough for you, for your soul and good Christian life? Yeferenge—white people's—education is Saytan's work.

Desta froze. He had not expected his mother to react like this. He stared at her as she ranted.

"No Mama, no . . . I want to go to asquala temaree bet, modern school."

His mother went on, complaining about the house help, how wanton and irresponsible it was of Abraham to want to send him to modern school, how the community and the family would be better served if he took his lessons with the mergeta at their church and became a priest, how her husband wanted to waste a productive life of one more child.

Desta ignored her.

FIFTY-NINE

March 1959

Two days before Desta's scheduled trip to register for school, Teferra sent Laqechi to bring Desta for measurements for the clothes he was going to make for him. Desta excitedly went to have his measurements taken. The next day he went to try on his new clothes. He was ecstatic to see the jacket and shorts his brother had made for him. They were dark brown—chosen to withstand dirt as they were the only outfit he would be wearing every day. He kissed Teferra's knee and thanked him profusely.

The day Desta was to be taken to Yeedib to start modern school, he got up early and found his father preparing a sack of honey and a bale of cotton he was going to take to town. Desta watched as his father washed his hands and transferred honey from large clay pots into a brand new leather sack that stank. He wondered why on earth his Baba would put the beautiful, sweet honey into something that released such a horrid odor and why people would buy honey that was stored in such a stinking leather sack. The inside of the sack looked velvety clean, but the smell was sickening. When Desta asked his father about the smell, he said it was because of the way the tanners processed the skin and that the odor would go away after a while.

Teferra came and had breakfast with their father. Desta was given his own on a separate tray. He was so excited that he could hardly eat. He just wolfed down what he could and pushed the rest aside.

"It's a strange thing to see a ten-year-old boy get so excited about leaving his family and living in a strange place," said Ayénat to Teferra.

"Everything is new to him," said Teferra. "Don't worry. He will come running home when he is hungry. They don't have the abundance of food in town, like we have here."

"I will prove them wrong,'" said Desta to himself. With such a pessimistic prediction from his brother, he became even more determined not to give up, no matter what happened.

"I can't wait to see that," said Ayénat. "If he is still excited about learning, we can put him in our good Christian school."

Abraham and Teferra loaded two horses with the cotton and honey and left.

THE TRIP TO TOWN was blurred in Desta's memory. After they arrived, they went to a large corrugated-tin roofed building that had nothing but sacks of things, piles of them. In front, a short stocky man in a greasy jacket and long, baggy pants stood by a large rectangular metal bed with metal columns and something that slid. Abraham placed the sack of honey on the metal bed. The man pushed a metal load along a bar one way and then the other, until the bar came to rest evenly. He went through the same exercise for the bale of cotton. The man and Abraham haggled a bit about the price. The man counted shillings from a cloth sack and handed them to Abraham

At the end, Abraham asked the man if it was okay to leave the horses tied to one of the posts in his compound. The man said it was fine and offered to have someone feed them some grass while they were gone. Abraham thanked him for his kindness and they left.

They followed an alleyway through a grove of eucalyptus trees that were thick, shady and dark. At the end of the path was a grassless courtyard strewn with dead eucalyptus leaves. Beyond the courtyard stood a thatched-roof, circular house, not much different from their own in the country. The door was open and a man came out. He was short and brown skinned with soft features and thick bushy hair. He smiled at the guests and greeted them graciously. Desta vaguely remembered him and thought he must be his mother's half brother, Uncle Mekuria.

The adults kissed. Mekuria put his arms around Desta and kissed him.

They went inside. Mekuria's wife, Tru, who must have been about half his age, about 22 years old, greeted and kissed the guests after hesitating a little. They all sat on the raised and built-in, lunar-shaped earthen structure that lined the living room wall. Tru brought three glasses of tella from a back room and a glass of water for Desta.

They chatted for 20 minutes, then the three men and Desta went to register him at the school. The school, a solitary building of wood and mud with a corrugated tin roof, stood at the foot of a gently falling, wind-swept slope on the west side of the town. It was mid-afternoon and the classes were in session.

Mekuria knocked on the corrugated-tin and wood-frame door. A tall, dark, gray-haired man with a stubby beard and tired eyes opened the door and asked why they were there. Mekuria explained they had brought a student to register in the school. The man glanced at something shiny and metallic on his wrist and told the visitors to wait for a few minutes for the afternoon break.

While the three men stood in the open and chatted, Desta let his eyes and mind wander freely on the landscape. First there was a tall wooden pole, a few yards from the school. The same multi-colored cloth he saw carried by a student at the end of a stick when he came to the market with Saba was hoisted on top of the pole. Desta craned his neck up and watched the enchanting fabric for a while as it danced in the wind. Then he brought his eyes down to earth. He noticed that the land beyond the school grounds was rocky and dotted with thorny bushes, but farther ahead the earth sloped into a flat green field bisected by a sleepy river that came down in a sweeping curve from somewhere in southwest of the green. On the north side of the field were clusters of homes bordered by groves of eucalyptus trees and fenced brown lots. On this side, the land was a quilt of stubble and tilled farm lots. To the south and directly west from Desta's line of sight, there were no trees or farms, just cattle and sheep that grazed peacefully on the green, rolling hills.

"That is Gish Abayi, the source of the Blue Nile," said Teferra, pointing to a copse of tall juniper trees at the end of the green field and rolling hills. Beyond the field and hills, the land turned upwards to a dry and rocky heap, on the other side of which appeared to be a precipitous escarpment. The name rang a bell in Desta's head but not in connection with a river. He was about to ask Teferra what else Gish Abayi was famous for, when a light went off his head. Gish Abayi was supposed to be one of the holiest of places, where holy water that cured lepers, the deaf, blind and dumb and all manners of other ailments, gushed out from the ground. There was supposed to be a church in that mound of juniper trees. When Desta was going through his dog bite treatment, Ayénat had threatened to take him to Gish Abayi. He was pleased to know he was going to live close to such a holy place and to be able to see open land that stretched for miles in many directions.

The door of the school opened again. A horde of children—mostly boys— spilled out. The boys were wrapped in their gabis but also wore jackets and shorts beneath the white-turned-brown cotton clothes. The girls wore colorful dresses that hugged their waists. Desta was shocked to see that they wore their dresses half way up their legs. *Mother would have a heart attack if she saw one of her daughters in those skimpy clothes,* he thought. His sisters' dresses were never allowed to be more than one finger width higher than their heels.

Moments after the students came out, the same man stepped out of the door and motioned the visitors to come in. He introduced himself as Brook.

With Desta trailing behind, the three men followed Brook to a back corner room where they found a short, thin, fair-skinned man with glasses and intense eyes sitting behind a rickety rectangular table. The man rose as the visitors and Brook entered the room and introduced himself as Yitbarek. Mekuria greeted him familiarly and introduced Abraham and Teferra.

"We came to register this boy, my nephew, as a beginner. His name is Desta," said Mekuria, glancing at the new student-to-be and then at Yitbarek.

"Good," said the man, as he sat down. From underneath a pile of papers and books, he pulled out a dark blue tome with crimson strips on its borders and opened it. He then picked up a long wooden pen with a brass tip, dipped it in the blue inkwell before him and poised the hand over the page.

"What did you say is his name?" asked Yitbarek, looking up to Mekuria.

Abraham motioned Desta to step forward. "Desta Abraham," he said, his hands on Desta's shoulders.

"Date of birth?"

"January 7, 1949—A Christmas baby," said Abraham, smiling.

"That makes him ten years old," said the little man.

"Slightly over ten," corrected Abraham.

"I take it you're not from this area as you came with Ato Mekuria."

"No, we are not from here. We are from a place called Jomer," said Abraham. "It's about a half day's journey from here," said Mekuria. "And it's a terribly treacherous and mountainous place."

"That is wonderful . . . I mean not wonderful that you live in such a place, but that from such a place there can be such a far-thinking individual who would bring his son to a modern school. We couldn't get the farmers who live next door to us bring their children. Here we have a person like you, sir, who has a thirst for knowledge for his son. . . ."

"Thank you, we have always tried to provide our children with opportunities to help them advance in life. It doesn't always work the way we hope, of course, but this boy, the credit goes to him. It's he who pushed us to bring him here. Because this school is far for us, we generally would have preferred the local church schools for our children."

The man looked at Desta through the top of his gold-rimmed glasses. "Well, that is even better. It means we won't have to push him to study hard and do well in his lessons."

"Let's hope so," said Abraham, glancing down at Desta.

"You are the local contact then?" said Yitbarek, turning to Mekuria.

"Yes. He will be living with us."

The men shook hands with Yitbarek, bowed and stepped out.

On their way out, Brook gave them a tour of the school. Desta took notice of things. It appeared to him that the whole school was one rectangular building divided into four sections by two crossing interior walls.

In the first room, there were three rows of flat stone seats on the bare, dirt floor and a fourth row in the back with a crooked wooden bench that could seat four to five students. In the corner was a small open window. Its shutter, made from the omnipresent corrugated tin and wood, was cockeyed and sagging. To the left, on a bamboo partition, hung a blackboard and a large, square, cream-colored cloth with the Amharic alphabet printed in giant letters along with the numbers and other characters Desta didn't remember seeing in Awoke's Fidel.

A long thin reed leaned against the wall to the right of the hanging cloth. Brook said this room was for the beginners, like Desta.

The visitors followed Brook to the next room, on the other side of the bamboo partition. It had a two-feet square window and one long wooden bench that ran along the back wall. In the middle of the bamboo partition hung a flat black square board, with a ledge containing two round white sticks. Brook said this room was for the first and second graders. The third room, which adjoined the registrar, was like the last but had an extra bench. The third and fourth grade students took their lessons together in this room.

Grand tour completed, they stepped out into the daylight where a group of boisterous boys and girls were still on their afternoon break. Some were standing in clusters, talking and giggling. Others were chasing and kicking a round cloth ball.

"I will be right back," said Mekuria. He sauntered over to one of the groups and returned with two boys, one tall and thin with a narrow face, named Sayfu, and the other short and stocky with a big round face, named Fenta. Both were fair-skinned with dark curly hair. Mekuria introduced the boys. They were his neighbor's nephews. He told them that Desta was a new student and asked them to bring him home after the school was over. With this arrangement, the three men left.

As soon as his relatives left, Desta found himself surrounded by a half-dozen boys. Remembering the time he was robbed of his beads on his way to Hibist's house, he was suddenly possessed by fear. Instinctively, he reached for his neck, as if to guard his long-lost beads. But the boys didn't threaten him and after a moment he began to relax. Some of the boys asked him questions, but he didn't have time to answer them. The bell rang. It was time to get back to their lessons.

After all filed in, Brook led Desta to the back of the first room and sat him on the wooden bench. He told him to repeat the letters of the alphabet along with the other children, following a lead boy who would be reciting them. About a dozen boys sat in front of him on the individual rocks. Another four sat with him on the bench. A small boy got up with the thin long reed. He pointed to the Amharic alphabet on the large cloth on the wall and he began to call them out: "Hä Hoo He Hä Hã Hi Ho". The class repeated after him. Desta quietly mouthed the letters, proud that he had studied on his own and knew them all.

Brook came and whispered to Desta that he should shout out the letters like the other kids. He could learn them faster that way. Desta complied.

At the end of the Amharic alphabet were letters in a single line. The boy started reciting these: A, B, C, D . . . Desta followed but he had no idea what the letters were or why they were learning them. At the end of the strange characters were two sets of numbers, the Amharic version he was familiar with and another foreign version which he didn't remember seeing in Awoke's fidel.

After the boy was finished, another boy took a turn. He went through the recital of the Amharic letters and the strange characters and numbers at the bottom part of the hanging cloth. Then a third boy took a turn. The rote recitals went on till the end of the day.

At five o'clock the students were released. The two boys, Sayfu and Fenta, came from the back room and fetched Desta to go with them. The boys walked on either side of Desta asking him a string of questions.

When he noticed that other uninvited boys followed them, Desta started to feel uneasy again. The eavesdroppers kept glancing at him, his new clothes, and his unwashed feet. Desta became confused and scared. *Was there something different about him? Was he going to be surrounded like this every day?*

When Sayfu and Fenta sensed Desta's uneasiness, they chased off the other boys. Up on the hill, right before they entered town, Desta turned around to

look at the setting sun. It had begun to color, just a little. The boys stopped too
and looked at the sun but didn't see anything unusual.

"Let's move on," said Sayfu.

"Can we remain here for a while? I like to watch the sunset."

"Why? Have you not seen a sunset before?" chortled Sayfu.

"Not really."

"What?!" said Fenta, with a side glance.

"Did you live in a cave or something?" jeered Sayfu.

The two boys laughed at the very idea.

The other boys who had been chased off ran back to find out the source of
Sayfu and Fenta's hilarity. Sayfu chased them off again.

"It was sort of like a cave," said Desta, gazing at the descending sun. "All I
saw when growing up were shadows—shadows in the morning, shadows in the
evening—no actual sunrise or sunset. The shadows were our timepieces too.
That is how we would know whether it was still morning or afternoon. In the
afternoon, the longer and thinner the shadows were, the later in the day it was."

"Where is this place?" asked Fenta.

"Far from here, where the mountains stand like walls."

"Here you can watch all the sunsets in the world, until you get tired of it,
until you are so tired of it you cover your mouth and retch."

"Till then, can we stay here until the sun goes home?"

"Our uncle would wonder where we are. You can find your way back. It's
easy. Once you have finished watching the red sun, go up this street . . . it comes
to an open space . . . Gashé Mekuria's house is in the bunch of eucalyptus trees on
the left, in the middle," said Sayfu.

"I remember," said Desta, relieved they were going to leave him alone.

Alone and unhurried, he watched the unfolding drama in the pencil-gray
haze. Lemony orange colors magically transmuted into gold. Soon this dazzling
metal turned to poppy red, then to rose pink, to magenta, to red earth, to burnt
sienna, to nutmeg, to dark brown and finally to black. How the ordinary sun
could assume these many faces, teasing the world with its chameleon looks,
Desta couldn't fathom. *Where did it go after this dazzling firework?* He wanted
to know.

It was getting dark now. He had just gotten up to head to his uncle's home
when he saw Mekuria coming toward him down the footpath.

"What kept you here this long? This is your first time; you don't yet know the place. . . . We were worried. . . . Thank God, Fenta told us where you were. Why such preoccupation with a sunset?"

"I had only seen it twice before, and each time I didn't get to watch it to the very end without being hurried. Today I couldn't resist taking advantage of the privilege I got."

"You came here to learn, not watch the sunset. This is no good for you to do this from the start. Will you promise you won't do this again?"

Desta nodded and followed his uncle home, happy to finally have had the opportunity to watch the sun's dazzling journey from beginning to the end, until the last glow of the smoldering orb was engulfed by the brooding blackness.

SIXTY

Mekuria's wife, Tru, had prepared a nice meal—injera with sweet-tasting pea sauce and beef-jerky sauce. After dinner, she spread a goatskin at one corner of the high earthen seat and laid out a green and sky-blue checkered wool blanket and a small cotton stuffed pillow.

After Mekuria and Tru disappeared through the door-less opening of their bedroom, Desta took his new clothes off and carefully folded them. As his first shorts and jacket, they were precious to him. When he was in bed, Tru blew out the kerosene lamp in their bedroom and darkness enveloped the house.

Desta lay on his back with his bent knees poking the blanket like a tent pole. He rested his head on the pillow and stared into the darkness. The brooding night was intimidating. This was the first time he had seen the night so black and quiet. At home there was always light in one of the fireplaces and someone still up puttering around when he fell asleep.

Everything felt like a dream. Just a day before, he had been pacing the field below his home in the scorching March sun, tending the animals. Now he was in a place he had visited only once before, living with two people he barely knew. Yet, he was neither afraid of the future nor stirred with emotions for the family he had left behind.

He was looking forward to getting up in the morning and going to school. He had no idea what going to school meant or what he would become once he finished school. His brother Tamirat nearly became a priest after going to church school. What did one who studied in modern school become? A court clerk, a teacher or what? For now, he wouldn't bother himself too much about the future. He was just happy to be out of his confining valley, away from his brothers and the animals. From here on, he would be spending his days with boys and girls his own age. His uncle had introduced him to Sayfu and Fenta already.

He thought about the kids who had surrounded him after school and his reaction to them. He had been nervous and fearful when they were all curiously looking at him, unable to suppress the memories of the boys who had robbed him of his beads. It would probably take him time to adjust to being around by so many of them. After all, he was not used to being with other kids. The only friends he'd had growing up were Hibist, Kooli and the vervet monkeys.

Desta's feet hurt and his partially covered legs were chilly. The room seemed to be getting colder. He stretched his legs, crossed one over the other and tucked the blanket under them.

Before he could win friends among his schoolmates, he needed to be worthy of them, Desta thought. He remembered the words of his grandfather's spirit: Before you can let new people into your heart and mind, you need to purge out any bad ones that may already reside there.

Desta needed to mentally and emotionally part with people and animals that had caused him pain and suffering in the past. *Like Grandpa said, I must start with a clean mind*, said Desta to himself. This I must do tonight before I fall asleep. That way I will be free and happy when I rise tomorrow morning to go to school.

Forgiveness, his grandpa had told him, is the first step to healing. Although he had never thought he would forgive Damtew for all the horrible things he had done to him, he knew he had to force himself to forgive him. This was important not only to follow his grandpa's advice, but also to apply one of the cardinal rules of the coin—magnanimity, showing nobility of spirit toward people that have hurt him.

To make it easier to get started, Desta thought he would begin with the animals. Briefly he acknowledged and forgave Lomee the bull for being the cause of his beatings by his father and Damtew on two separate incidents. He forgave the goats for having caused him so much anguish and frustration from fear that they might lose their kids to wild animals when they buried themselves into the thorn bushes. He absolved the sheep for the time they disappeared for two nights causing problems for his family and great worry and distress in Desta.

He then moved on to the harder part: the people. He forgave his father for beating him after the animals had destroyed Gizaw's crops and for not punishing Damtew for beating him. He exonerated his mother for always siding with Damtew and for putting him through that horrific water treatment, believing he was possessed by the Saytan. Asse'ged he forgave for being Damtew's accomplice in his dreams and for the last beating incident. Teferra, he pardoned for being cold and unfriendly towards him.

Desta was exhausted by thinking about all the people who had done him wrong. At times he found himself angry and hateful but he tried to rein in his emotions.

He rolled over and put his face down on the pillow. It smelled old, smoky, musty and greasy. He pulled a part of his gabi up and covered as much of the pillow as he could. Unable to shield himself from the odor, he turned over once again and lay on his back.

Damtew was next. He closed his eyes and thought. Then opened them and deeply sighed.

"Damtew," he whispered. "For nearly three years, you put me through so much. I lived in fear under your constant threats. You wanted me to recant my story of the cloud man about Saba and Yihoon's move. At every opportunity you had, you bullied and browbeat me. You thought your sheer physical presence and menacing glare would cause me to shrivel like a leaf, but it didn't work. You and Asse'ged terrorized me in my dreams. You attempted to make a water sport out of my body as you dropped me in and out of the river at the end of a rope. Thank God, Mogus was there to stop the torture. That last time you chased me across the back of our property into Saba's new land; you kicked, whipped and terrorized me. Trying to rob me of my dream of learning how to read and write, you shredded my exercise papers and books. You poured the ink over me, crushed my pen and hurled away my inkwell. You tried everything but you could never undermine my will or take away my dream. Here I am in a modern school, pursuing my education one more time. You saw only my size but never knew my passion or determination. Now, in obedience with grandpa's wishes and in compliance to the family's blessed treasure, I forgive you for all the things you have done to me. May you and your family have a happy life at Saba's old property."

Tears. They came and came and came.

Finally they stopped. He blew his nose and wiped off his tears.

He lifted his head and cocked his ears, listening to the battle going on outside. The wind, it seemed to Desta, was waging war against the tall eucalyptus trees around the house, making it sound as if they would come crashing down on the thatched roof. They clashed, whined and gusted. Now he knew why they called Yeedib the windy town.

He rose, pulled out his tear-drenched gabi from underneath him, flipped the pillow onto the other side and lay down again. His mind was fuzzy but he felt wonderfully calm inside. By degree his anger and resentment were giving way to happiness, serenity and freedom. He felt physically free from the confining, jail-like place where he was born and raised and liberated from the emotional bondage of his family.

Desta closed his eyes once more and listened to nothing but his own joyous feelings and thoughts. As he relished the moment, he also considered the meaning and consequences of his newly found freedom. He realized he would be alone in this new world in which he came to live. This recognition effected a string of questions in his mind. Would the adults in town and the students in school treat him like an outcast, the way his family used to do? Would there be boys here like those who robbed and beat him when he was en route to Hibist's home? Whom could he talk to about any problems?

Desta felt uneasy and fearful knowing there were no answers to any of his questions. He struggled, trying to suppress his concerns and calm his nerves. Just then, without command from his brain, his right hand moved over his left chest and rested on the area where his grandfather's spirit had tattooed the image of his family's ancient coin. He felt a stirring and then a slight pulsating under his skin. Not long after, peace and serenity descended upon the boy.

The things the spirit had shared at their different meetings floated back to him: The coin would be his protector and family in this new world. He had to be strong and learn how to live with strangers. There were many reasons for his leaving home, one of them being to fulfill an ancient prophecy of finding his ancestral family's twin sister coin and uniting it with the one he owned. The reunion of the coins had been predicted to be a momentous event that would benefit all humanity.

Desta opened his eyes, moved his hand from his chest and shook his head wondering how a metal piece or the tattooed image of it could replace someone like Hibist or Saba. Why was he fated to become the bearer of it? How or where could he find the other coin, and how was their union going to benefit people? Knowing he had no answer to these questions, Desta pushed his fears to the back of his mind. For now he would rather focus on his gratitude and earlier happier thoughts.

He remembered what Ayénat had once said: When good things happen to you, you should be thankful to God. Desta wanted to thank not only God but also the people and animals who meant a lot to him here on earth.

He sighed and thought. "The vervets," he began to say. "I want to thank you for being my friends. I probably laughed more when I was with you than with any of my siblings, excepting Hibist. You taught me social skills: how to influence and win the hearts of strangers. Those eight months I spent trying to win your friendship and learning how to interact with you will be useful to me with all the people I will be meeting in this new world. For this and for your friendship I thank you."

"Kooli, you were one fine dog. You sacrificed your life for me and in doing so you started me on my journey to freedom. As though through a window, the first time I discovered the existence of the outside world was that time when I went to church with mother for my communion to treat me from the disease they thought you had passed on to me, and for which, sadly you were killed. You did something for me I can never repay. All I can say now is thanks! Thanks for being my companion and playmate all those years and for starting the course to my liberty.

"Hibist, I don't know what my life would have been like without you. For those years we were together, you were my parent, companion, confidant and protector. You taught me a lot about life and about the meaning of love. I will forever be grateful to you. I am certain that thoughts of you will always filter back when I sit idly or I pick up that goatskin that came from a goat killed for your Wedding Return and which now is a very important document that will accompany the coin."

Next, Desta thanked his grandpa's spirit for solving all the family's problems, for sacrificing his life and guarding the coin for so long and for the sweet and intimate times they spent together.

Desta thanked his father for granting him permission to start modern school and Laqechi for actively soliciting his father on his behalf. He was immensely grateful to Saba for fulfilling his lifelong dream of going to the mountaintop, for taking him to the market and for being the means to his freedom.

He was excited about his future once more. He was looking forward to watching his first sunrise. He had already seen three glorious sunsets but never a sunrise. He couldn't wait to see if the sun painted the sky red and gold when it rose as it did when it set. He was looking forward to going to school and spending all day learning and reciting the alphabet and making new companions with his schoolmates.

Desta straightened himself in his bed and placed his right hand over his left chest once again and closed his eyes for the last time. The gentle pulsating of the coin beneath his skin lulled him into the cradle of another world, the beginning of a new journey.

Acknowledgments

My first gratitude goes to my wife, Rosario, who has given me support, encouragement and allowed me to have the quiet and secluded place I needed to write this novel. There have been many times when she had more hope for *Desta* than I did and for this I am thankful. Her kindness and equanimity are unparalleled. I am forever grateful to my father whose many wonderful personal traits have lent material for the Abraham character in *Desta;* and to my mother who taught me I can do anything I want, including writing a book.

Lori Schyler took a personal interest in *Desta,* and I am grateful for her gentle and masterful editorial work. Her advice, suggestions and encouragement were valuable to me as well the wonderful working relationship we had. I thank Caroline Leavitt who reviewed the content and plot of the story and gave me suggestions for its improvement.

I am indebted to Monika Rose, who not only read the whole manuscript and gave me editorial comments, but also for sharing this novel with her students at Lodi High School in California. Her young readers' enthusiasm for the story inspired me to not only make this first book the best I could make it, but also gave me encouragement for the future series.

Dr. Victor Gold, Professor of Old Testament at Pacific Lutheran Theological Seminary, was very helpful to me with his suggestions about how I may be able to incorporate some of the ancient historical facts that appear in this novel. R. Kramish generously translated the English words and legends I had on the coin faces into ancient or paleo-Hebrew. Janet Langton masterfully drew the coin box based on the ideas and suggestion I gave her. I am thankful for their contributions and efforts.

I extend my appreciation to my friends from Writers Unlimited—Dave Self, Glenn Wasson, Janet Langton, Joy Roberts, Linda Field, Jackie Richmond, Stephen Holmes, Ted Laskin and Sunny Lockwood for their comments, support and encouragement with the book. I also extend my thanks to all those students who offered their insightful comments on the manuscript.

I must thank my online friends for their comments and suggestions. These include Norma Alvarez, Chris Conrad, Margaret Murray, Laura Novak, Ron Repp, Terry Greenwell, Mark Wilson.

I must thank my friend, Jin Chenault, my web designer and graphic illustrator, for all the great work she has done for me and—most importantly—for putting up with my sometimes obsessive perfectionism. Jin has been wonderful not only in her willingness to do any design work for me but also in her encouragement and moral support from the start and to the completion of the book.

I also thank my nephew Tadesse Alemayehu Ambaw who refreshed my memory on many of the cultural details and sent me material I needed for the book. I thank Fasil Yitbark for his scholarly translation of English words that appear around the coin images into their Amharic equivalents.

I wish to express my gratitude to my friend Leila Hanson, with whom I first shared the Desta manuscript to test whether the American reader would like it. Her phone response, "I really did, I really did," in a whisper as if she wanted to confide a secret to me, was encouragement enough to share my book with complete strangers.

Lastly, I am grateful to the Creator who gave me healthy faculties so I could record what I saw, read, heard and experienced to use as material for this novel.

DESTA's Characters

Humans

Abraham – Desta's father

Aba Yacob – The head priest at the local church

Abinadab – Husband to Haptaph

Adamu, Kindè – Abraham's mother's cousins

Ahimaaz – Husband to Basemath

Almaw – Aunt Zere's youngest son

Amsale – Tamirat's bride

Asse'ged – The second oldest son

Astair – Desta's niece, Yihoon and Saba's older daughter

Awoke – Desta's second-generation cousin, Yisehak and Maray's son

Ayènat –Desta's mother

Azal, Grandma – Saba's mother

Basemath – Daughter of Solomon

Beshaw, Abraham – Father

Birhan – Husband of Kiwin

Biserat – Wife to Joshua

Bogay – Tamirat's second wife

Bosena – Abraham's immediate older sister

Damtew – Desta's fourth oldest brother

Dawit – One of the best men at the wedding

Deb'tera Tayè – The sorcerer

Degay – Abraham's distant relative

Enat – Desta's older sibling (the fifth youngest)

Fenta – One of the two students Desta's uncle introduced to him

Genet – Cousin to Desta

Hibist – Desta's favorite sister

Joshua – Solomon's grandson

Kindè – Adamu's younger brother

Kiwin – Abraham's niece and wife of Birhan

Koomay –Mawa's son

Laqechi – Teferra's wife

Maray – Yisehak's wife

Marta – Zeru's mother

Mawa – Neighboring woman

Mekuria – Desta's uncle, his mother's half-brother

Melaku – Abraham's sheep breeder

Melkam – Damtew's bride

Mekonen – Abraham's grandfather

Menilek –Sheba's son by Solomon who became the first Emperor of Ethiopia

Misrak – Daughter of Adamu

Mogus – Distant relative

Mulu – Asse'ged's wife

Nega – Hibist's father-in-law

Saba – Abraham's daughter from his first marriage

Sayfu – Second student Desta's uncle introduced to him

Sheba – Menilek's mother, the first queen of Ethiopia

Solomon – King of Israel, builder of the first temple

Tamirat – The third oldest brother who was studying to become a priest

Tapath – Daughter of Solomon

Tashere – The pharaoh princes, King Solomon's first wife

Taye, the Debtra – The middle-aged witchdoctor who invoked the cloud man

Teferra – The oldest son

Tenaw – Husband to Enat

Tilahun – A shepherd boy

Tru – Mekuria's wife

Welella – Abraham's youngest sister

Yihoon – Saba's spouse

Yisehak – Abraham's uncle who lived across the river

Yitbarek – The head teacher and administrator at the elementary school where Dests registered

Zegeye Farris – Desta's maternal grandfather

Zena – Desta's niece, Yihoon and Saba's daughter

Zeru – Hibist's husband

Zere – Abraham's oldest sister
Zeru Belay – Parent to Bogay

Animals
Begiziew – The young bull who was the rising crop destroyer
Dama – Abrahams beloved horse
Colobus Monkeys – The black and white haired, docile, aloof, tree-bound watchers
Goats, sheep, cows and horses – animals Desta is learning to look after
Habte – The kid goat, Damtew's dream of wealth and comfort
Kooli – Desta's beloved dog and best friend
Lomee – A dangerous crop-raiding bull
Mandefroshi (Mandy) – The family cat
Salle-Ayiset – The notorious crop destroyer cow
Tizitaw – Welella's dog, renamed Kooli by Abraham
Vervet Monkeys – The silver-haired, notorious crop raiders, Desta's friends

Spirits
The cloud man – the ghost-like creature invoked by Deb'tra Tayé and revealed to Desta
Saytan – Satan
Zars – are perceived to be spindly, fair-skinned creatures with frizzy golden hair

Cultural terms and their definitions

Aba – Father, a generic term of respect applied to most elderly men.

Abalo – A type of bush whose leaves are fuzzy and soft.

Abo – A luxuriant plant with large and shiny leaves that are often used to wrap dough and bake in a fire pit.

Abugeeda – A term assigned to a passage containing specially arranged Amharic letters, designed to facilitate the student's ability to read.

Agam – A thorny bush whose needles are long and strong.

Affin – A creature nobody seems to have seen but which kills lambs and kids by cutting their air supply. This could apply to any of the predators.

Anir – Leopard

Ankasay – A rounded pointed metal tip (similar to the spear) with a long barrel for inserting into a wooden rod, used largely for hunting game animals.

Areqey – A double or single distilled home-made whiskey.

Asquala Temareebet – Modern school. "Asquala" is derived from the Italian or Spanish word with similar name "esquela". Temareebet literally means house of learning.

Ato – The Amharic equivalent of Mister.

Bahar Zaf – Eucalyptus tree, first brought to Ethiopia from Australia in the late 1800s by Emperor Menilk. Widely grown in small and large groves around towns and cities as well as in the countryside.

Beredo – Hail

Besmam wold woaman fis kidus – A prayer- or blessing- opening phrase involving the Trinity.

Budas – In Ethiopian folklore, Budas are a class of people considered to have evil eyes. Budas haunt gravesites looking for newly buried bodies to dig out and bring home to eat. Budas supposedly use the hyenas as their draft animals to carry the corpse home.

Cantim – A cent.

Cheebo – Dried, bundled twigs used as a torch.

Dabo Kollo – In the countryside, this is an apricot-size dried bread travelers bring with them as a snack. In cities, dab kilo comes in different sizes and is served as a snack anytime.

Dabo – Loaf

Diba - Rings of blue glass beads.

Dik-dik – A type of diminutive antelope.

Dulet – Liver

Era – An expression of surprise, not really a word.

Eskista (Skista) – A form of Ethiopian dance involving the body above the waist, performed by see-sawing the shoulders or vibrating them into a frenzy.

Ferenge – A term used to refer to all white people, similar to the Mexican's Gabacho or Gringo.

Fidel – The Ethiopian alphabet.

Gabi – A double ply heavy cotton cloth, roughly 7 feet by 6 feet, worn for warmth over the shoulders like a blanket.

Gashé – A term of respect used to address an older male, usually as prefix to the first name. Example: Gashé John, Gashé George, Gahé Tom, etc.

Gessa – A rain protective covering made from dried kettema, woven into a mat, folded and sown together on one side while the other side is left open so one can slide the head in and let it hang down.

Gomen-zer – An oil rich gomen (Ethiopian collard green) seed often burned on a brand new clay baking pan to cure it.

Goosa – An old monk who lives in a forest who often is invisible to ordinarily folks.

Goozgoozo – Two layers of injeras, topped with cheese and red pepper paste and garnished with spiced, liquefied butter.

Gottem – A round tree whose branches grow packed together with small dark green shiny leaves.

Injera – A spongy, flat bread made from fermented dough of teff, barely or wheat

Insocila – A root, the size and shape of a cassava or sweet potato that is often cooked and used to henna hands and feet. In some part of Ethiopia, insocila is used to color these same body parts of brides. In Northern provinces, one can often see even married women with hennaed hands and feet.

Irsas – Pencil

Kaga – A thorny bush that produces berries nearly the same in size, shape and color of cherry tomatoes. The skin of kaga berries is thicker but when ripe it becomes soft and delectable.

Kettema – A tall pulpy grass, often sprinkled on the living room floor during a holiday.

Kirkaha – Bamboo

Koma – A sparsely branched willowy tree which grows to 20 to 30 feet. Its pliable branches are often used for making walking-sticks or canes.

Konjo – Beautiful

Kosso – One of the rare trees in Ethiopia that can grow to a height of sixty to eighty feet and about twenty to thirty feet wide. Its bark is fuzzy and so are its wonderfully soft leaves. It is used largely for making furniture and home construction.

Kusha – A type of plant whose broad leaves and hollow stalk are covered with prickly fuzz and whose fibrous skin is peeled and used to make ropes.

Lemlem – A verdant, beautiful place. In Ethiopia, the New Year is the beginning of the spring season. At this time, much of the countryside is mantled with green grass and wild flowers. So the term lemlem may have to do with the land itself. Lemlem is also a feminine proper name. **Note: To my Ethiopian readers:** I have modified the English version of our classic song to make it sensible to an English-speaking person's ear. The apparent variation is not an error.

Maskel – The finding of the True Cross, celebrated in Ethiopia on the 27th of September.

Medehaneet – Medicine

Mergeta – Teacher

Mekleft – The bread (injera) the church goers break their fast with.

Mookit – Applies generally to a male goat or bull whose testicles have been pounded to a pulp of tissue so that it won't waste its energy chasing she-goats or cows. This goat or bull becomes fat and big, fetching top price when taken to the market.

Mosseb – An often colorful basket with a round skirt-shape bottom and a lipped circular top used to serve food. It comes with a cone-shaped and colorful top.

Netela – A single-ply fabric, worn mostly by women as a shawl or to drape the shoulders with.

Quagmé – The last or the 13th month of the year. (Ethiopia has 12—30-day months.The remaining 5 or 6 days are grouped together as a month, giving the

Ethiopian Tourist Organization, its slogan of "The Land of Thirteen Months of Sunshine.")

She'etto – Perfume

Shifta – An outlaw or a bandit.

Sholla – Related to the warka tree but less rugged. It produces a great number of green figs which turn edible and fire red upon ripening.

Tabot – A square wooden plaque upon which the Ten Commandments are inscribed. It is kept in the inner sanctuary of the church, wrapped in a colorful cloth. On church holidays, the Tabot is carried by a selected priest and taken on a procession out of doors accompanied by dancing and harmonizing priests.

Teff – The smallest grain in the world which comes as either brown or white variety, and is the staple food of Ethiopians.

Tej—Honey Wine

Tella – A black or brown home-made beer made from hops and barley.

Timket – Epiphany celebration – where priests carry on mass by a lake or river and sprinkle the congregation with blessed river or lake water. Timket is a big holiday in Ethiopia. People wear their best clothes on this day.

Timtem – A white turban worn mostly by priests.

Tsed – A variety of juniper tree with an aromatic bark and wood

Tottas – Vervet Monkeys

Warka – A spreading, large-trunked tree with broad, thick, leathery leaves and long, hefty branches. Perhaps related to the sycamore tree.

Map of Africa

What Student Readers are saying...

Monika Rose's Advanced Placement English Classes
Lodi, California

Brea Richmond

A heart-warming, intriguing and unique story that captivates the reader . . . I have never read a book like this and I really enjoyed it . . . very educational. It allowed insight into another culture and their ways of life . . . The story gives readers hope for their own dreams and aspirations.

Rochelle Lippert

I loved Desta's dreams of touching the sky . . . Desta gives people hope and ambition to reach for their dreams . . . makes you want to go for your desires and feel like anything is possible, even touching the sky . . . very inspiring. I think students my age would find this story enjoyable and educational because it has very creative imagery, and because it makes you think about and enjoy another world.

Kayla Hieb

A touching and extremely inspiring story. I had a real attachment to Desta's character and when sad things happened to him I felt bad. It's also very entertaining and educational. I learned a lot from this novel.

Justin Kah

An amazing novel! . . . Very different from anything I have read. There are a few books I can read continuously without getting tired of them. This book is one of them. I loved the characters and the setting . . . It taught me many valuable lessons as well as kept me entertained . . . reminded me about the importance of following one's dream no matter how hard it may be.

Guicela Marissa Sandoval

Desta really touched my heart! I thought the story was magical, hopeful, mysterious and adventurous . . . A real treat to read! I completely think that people my age will find this book to be very interesting. Desta's story is one of inspirations. Who wouldn't like it?

Marissa Nall

The setting of the novel was a very vivid and beautiful place. It was full of many opportunities for imagination and exploration. Desta's story was very interesting and detailed with unexpected twists and turns. The work seemed very well researched and provided a glimpse into an intricate and fascinating culture . . . There are magical, touching and gripping places throughout the book.

K. Carter.

Really enjoyed reading this book. Very different from all the books I have read. Every time I went to read it, I felt like I was temporarily entering a whole new world. Very touching . . . Sent a message to always go after your dreams, no matter how far they may seem or how challenging your circumstances maybe . . . Allowed me to look at life from different perspective. I think many students my age would love this book.

Harbir Dhillon

I loved the story and simply couldn't put it down . . . I loved the characters, especially Desta . . . I loved his determination and his motives and the love in his heart. A very inspiring, heart-warming and educational story.

About the Author

Getty Ambau is a graduate of Yale University. Although educated both in the natural and social sciences and has run his own businesses over the years, writing has always been his inner calling. He has written books on health and nutrition which have sold internationally. *Desta* is his first in a series of novels. He lives in the San Francisco Bay Area with his wife, Rosario and a devoted terrier called Scruffy—perhaps not as devoted or self-sacrificing as Desta's pet and friend, Kooli.